CROWCHANGER
A CHANGERS OF CHANDRIS NOVEL

A·C·SMYTH

Crowchanger :A Changers of Chandris Novel
Copyright © 2013 by AC Smyth. All rights reserved.
First Print Edition: January 2014
Published by Chandris Publishing

ISBN 13: 978-0-9927196-2-3
ISBN 10: 0-9927196-2-3

Editor: Karen Conlin
Cover and Formatting: Streetlight Graphics

DEDICATIONS

With thanks to Barbara, Charmaine, Elizabeth,
Jackie, Joanne, Lisa, Monika and Penny,
for encouragement and friendship, and for
endless rereads of subtly different material.

To my husband and daughter, for putting up with
me tapping away on the keys hour after hour.

To my editor Karen, who is probably twitching
at all these ungrammatical phrases.

To the folks at Streetlight Graphics
for the cover and formatting.

And to Jo and Merilyn: it's ALL YOUR FAULT.

CHAPTER 1

L ET IT BE TODAY.

  Sylas glanced at the sun, already well above the horizon. By rights, the ritual of thanks for a new day should be performed at dawn, but he didn't think the Lady would mind his lateness. So many Chesammos had forgotten the old ways; at least he remembered.

 Let it be today.

 Sitting cross-legged, he pressed his palms to the ground. There was good soil here, not the ash and dust of the desert. Grass and wild flowers grew in abundance around the buildings of the changer city: lush greenery, instead of the barrenness of his old home. The mountain breeze carried the scent of woodsmoke, the pungency of herbs, the promise of rain. Even after a year, it worried him to venture outside with nose and mouth uncovered, but the Aerie, unlike the ash desert, was rarely troubled by the caustic breath of the volcano.

 She was Eurna, sacred to the Chesammos and giver of life.

 The Lady.

 Sylas pressed fingers and thumbs together in the peaked shape of the mountain that dominated the skyline to the south, and touched fingertips to his lips. He sent up a silent prayer.

Let it be today that I fly, if the Lady wills it. Maisaiea-yelai.

Master Olendis didn't expect him to fly today. If he did, Sylas's transformation lesson would be outside, rather than in Olendis's study. Sylas often watched the lessons on the field, wishing he could be out there. One novice after another achieved first flight; they swooped and soared over the Aerie with the changer master in close attendance. One day, Sylas told himself; one day that will be me. Even after so many disappointments, the hair still stood up on the back of his neck at the thought. But he saw his peers fly and be apprenticed to masters and move on, and still he remained: the changer who could not change.

Master Olendis watched for Sylas's arrival from his study door. "Come on then, if you are coming. Don't dawdle like a lazy servant. I don't have all day." Master Olendis gave Sylas a withering look which conveyed both irritation and a firm belief that shape changing was utterly beyond his current pupil.

The study verged on austere. Sylas's other masters had personalised their rooms with tapestries and paintings, vases of flowers, the occasional trinket. Master Olendis was one of the younger masters, only recently elevated and not yet under consideration for the changer council. Maybe he had not yet acquired decorations he considered suitable for a master's study. Or maybe he preferred to keep his room simple.

Sylas eased himself into one of the large wooden

chairs. Most masters replaced these uncomfortable things with padded armchairs, sometimes even upholstered settles suitable for lounging. No such comforts in this room. New masters were either overly friendly, remembering their own novice days, or overly strict, to win the respect of those they taught. Olendis tended to the latter extreme.

The master leaned on the table, steepling his fingers in a gesture uncomfortably like the Lady's sign. Sylas tried to ignore the unintended blasphemy. "So, how long since you last marked?"

Between novices' teaching days, marking with blood elder suppressed their changing. As an additional precaution, Olendis used a muted training pipe which only carried the length of the Aerie. This reduced the risk of a novice changing as a result of a call intended for another. Sylas suspected he could hear a full call from a master's pipe without trouble. Unfortunately.

"Two weeks, Master, as you suggested." A week longer than usual, to see if he was unusually susceptible to marking.

Olendis grunted. "It should have worn off by now. Have you heard calls these past few days?"

"Four times yesterday. Three the day before." Sylas frowned as he cast his mind back. "Once the day before that, I think. Maybe twice."

"No trouble resisting it, I suppose?"

When Master Olendis blew the training pipe for the other novices, Sylas heard the call, but it never came close to forcing the change upon him. He could hear the kye—the bird spirits that enabled the change from human to bird form. Each call

7

over the past few days had caused a flurry of kye in his head—but he had never heard one over the others. His own kye remained as much a mystery to him now as at his first lesson.

"No, Master." He remembered the first time he had told Master Olendis that he heard more than one kye. That he was sorry, but he could not make out which voice to listen to.

"What sort of lie is that?" Olendis had bellowed. "The untalented hear one kye. One only until such time as we can link with a higher kye to take on a second form, and even that is beyond some. No one hears many kye, boy. No one, do you hear me? Not Cowin—the youngest master in over a century. Not Elyta—the most talented changer in decades. If you have to come up with an excuse for your failure, Sylas, at least make it plausible. Understand?"

He understood. And held his tongue. When he remembered.

"Even if the blood elder affects you more than others, it should have left your body by now. If you weren't running out of options I'd not have chanced it. But the risk of you changing by accident was minimal." It would have been nice, Sylas thought, if Olendis could have kept the sneer from his voice.

After so long as a novice, Sylas had a rash of the red marks left by piercing his skin with a tokai needle dipped in blood elder tincture. All changers had a few—relics of their training days—but Sylas's chest looked like he had been switched with a nettle. The marks were less livid on his golden-brown skin than on a fair Irmos, but still noticeable. On Casian's Irenthi skin they were like a drop of blood in a pan of milk, bright red on white. Casian's skin bore three pinprick marks. He was not only the first Irenthi changer in generations, but had taken naturally to changing. If Sylas did not love him so much, he would resent him bitterly.

"Well then," said Olendis. "Shall we begin?"

Sylas closed his eyes, his muscles tensing even as he attempted to relax. This constant cycle of trying and failing had become something of an ordeal, making this part harder for him each time. Still, he would not have utterly failed until he gave up, and that he would never do unless the council sent him away.

He let his mind float, as he had been taught, extending his consciousness in all directions. He felt the aiea-bar—the energy the changers drew upon to make their change—as a pressure across his ribs. It came from the island, the Irenthi said. But Sylas believed, as did all the desert Chesammos, that the power came directly from the Lady herself. She depended on the changers, and the changers on her. Without that relationship, the island would die. He drew the aiea deeply into himself, like taking a deep breath of air before putting his face into water, and waited.

Master Olendis took the pale green linandra pipe from a pouch at his belt. Sylas noticed, as he prepared himself, that Olendis checked he was ready before putting it to his lips and giving one long, steady blow. The note that tumbled out rang clear as spring water. It rushed through the room like a summer's breeze, and the aiea-bar responded.

And so did the kye. He tried in vain to separate

one voice from the others, but they yammered like the noise in the great hall when all the Aerie came together for feast days: hundreds of conversations piling one on top of the other, incomprehensible. His hands twitched with the impulse to cover his ears, but it would do no good. The voices were inside his head; they spoke in his mind. Covering his ears would shut them in, trapping the insanity inside his skull.

"Sylas?" Master Olendis prompted.

"I... I feel them," Sylas said, stumbling over the words. "They call to me, but I cannot understand what they say."

Olendis sighed, dropped the pipe back into his pouch, and pulled the drawstring tight.

"That will do. We can try tomorrow, but I shall be speaking to Master Jesely and Master Donmar." He waved Sylas away, like shooing a fly. "Go. I have told you before what I think of this nonsense."

Idiot. Stupid, stupid idiot. He knew not to tell Master Olendis what he heard, but once again he had forgotten.

The air didn't smell as sweet going back across the courtyard. His heart felt like a weight in his chest. The unused aiea lay heavy across his ribs, crushing them. He couldn't face anyone. His friends knew when his lessons with Olendis were, but they rarely asked him how they went any more. Not one of them had been novices when he arrived—those youngsters had all moved on—but each new intake so far had accepted him. He dreaded the day when they did not.

He hardly noticed Benno charging up the gravel

to meet him, arms flailing in excitement. If he had to meet anyone, Benno would be his first choice. The child's cheerfulness might lift his mood.

"Hey, Sylas." The lad galloped along with the awkwardness of a child whose legs have grown and who hasn't yet got them back under control. He grinned, showing a front tooth missing. "Where've you been? I've been looking for you."

"With Master Olendis. And before you ask, no, I can't wrestle right now. I'm not in the mood."

"Transformation class, huh? Hope I'm a changer when I'm older. I've watched them change on the field. It doesn't scare me. Will you wrestle later?"

"Maybe." He enjoyed teaching Benno to wrestle. At least he was good at something. "Why were you looking for me?"

"You asked me to keep watch for Casian, so I've been watching."

Sylas's heart leapt. He could cope with Master Olendis's displeasure—even being reported to Master Jesely or Master Donmar—if Casian were back at the Aerie.

"He's here?"

"Uh huh. Arrived a few minutes ago. I tried your room and the refectory, and one of the others said they'd seen you come this way."

Sylas ran for the main Aerie building, Benno's voice following him. "So when's my wrestling lesson? Sylas? Can I see you later?"

But Sylas did not look round. Casian was back.

Casian lay stretched out on his bed, hands behind

his head. His visits to his mother were pleasant enough, but it was good to be home. The Aerie was home, after five years. The students' quarters were not as opulent as his mother's house, where the rooms dripped luxury as if to compensate for being on the edge of the ash desert, but he added personal items to soften the basic decoration. His mother had been delighted to see him, as ever. The servants had fallen over themselves to meet their young lord's needs. Here he was just another journeyman changer. His talent gave him status, but no one at the Aerie cared that he was heir to the holding of Lucranne.

He had come straight from the field when he landed. Stripping off the tunic he had been given to cover himself, he fell into the half-doze that often restored him enough after a night flight. His kye took the form of a white owl with black-streaked wings. It preferred to fly by night, so the Creator knew he needed sleep, but he had important news for the visitor who would come.

The sound of the door roused him. The soft clunk of the handle; the pause while the person on the other side listened to see if the noise had wakened him; the grate of hinges as the door swung open. Back in Lucranne, he would have been wide awake in an instant, reaching for the dagger he kept beneath his pillow, nerves alert against possible assassins. No assassins here. He opened his eyes a crack to see Sylas's familiar form just inside his room.

"I won't stay," Sylas said softly. "I needed to see you for a moment."

Casian sat up, patted the edge of the bed, and shifted to allow him enough room to sit.

"Something's bothering you." He surprised himself with his ability to read Sylas. On the surface, they could hardly have been more different, the Irenthi nobleman and the desert-dweller, but they shared a bond he could not explain. Casian reached to stroke a dark curl from Sylas's face, as always amazed at the contrast between the white of his own skin and the golden-brown of the Chesammos.

Sylas smiled. "I've missed you."

"I've missed you too. What's wrong?"

Sylas sagged like a puppet with its strings cut. "I need to go and see Master Jesely. Things didn't go well today."

"A lesson? Olendis or Gwysias?"

"Master Olendis. I said 'they' again, and he says he's going to report me. If Master Jesely won't put in a word for me, I think I'm finished here." His friend's voice was empty. Becoming a changer meant the world to Sylas.

Casian squeezed Sylas's thigh and Sylas leaned into him. Funny how natural that felt. Casian could sense his friend's pain, but this could make his own decision a lot easier. Mismatched couple they might be, but Creator help him, he cared for the man as much as he had ever cared for anyone, besides himself.

"I told my mother about you."

Sylas raised his head, gave Casian a confused look. "You told her? By the Lady, Casian, what were you thinking? You are the heir of a great house.

Your mother will have you sent home."

"She wants to meet you. She says I seem happier. That you must be 'good for me,'" he raised the pitch of his voice a little, trying to mimic the tone of his mother's voice. He wanted Sylas to smile. The attempt fell flat.

"You're joking. I couldn't meet your mother. Not the lady of Lucranne." A flutter of panic laced Sylas's voice.

On the face of it, it did seem improbable. When Jesely had told Casian he was to take care of a Chesammos boy, new to the Aerie and struggling to find his feet, Casian had returned to his room, slammed the door, and sworn profusely in a way he would not have dared do to the master changer's face.

Casian had always thought of Chesammos as little better than savages—near-slave labour to dig the precious linandra stones in the south, and work the farms in the north. He resented being given a lowly Chesammos to watch over, and Sylas had been raised to be suspicious of the Irenthi rulers. But dislike had turned to tolerance on both sides, and then friendship, and more. Casian found himself won over by Sylas's good nature. Sylas was confused to discover that he could like one of the hated Irenthi, and then somewhat awestruck to find himself liked in return.

But there was a difference between being friends with a Chesammos and telling his mother he had taken one as a lover. Casian had made that step. Now he needed Sylas to go along with his plans.

"Why shouldn't you meet her? She knows things

are different here—that being a changer levels our status. You'd be equal to the king himself here, if he were a changer."

Sylas peeled himself away from Casian's side and stood to go. "But not outside, Casian. We'll never be equals beyond the Aerie walls. However broad-minded your mother thinks she's being, it will all change once you go back to being your father's heir." He sighed. "I'd better go see if I can find Master Jesely. Maybe if I can get to him before Master Olendis does I can offset some of the damage."

"Want me to come?" Jesely had set Casian to help and protect Sylas, after all. He could hardly object if Casian did just that.

Sylas stooped to kiss Casian's cheek. "Master Jesely disapproves of our friendship even inside the Aerie. I'll be better off alone. Sleep. You look exhausted." And he left.

Casian lay back once more. He had gone to his mother in part to ensure Sylas had somewhere to go if the council threw him out. Casian had heard Sylas's stories about his father, and being destined for the linandra pits. Better Lady Boreana recruited a new Chesammos servant than Sylas be sent to mine linandra. And if that servant attended on Casian whenever he visited, so much the better. Casian might be inclined to visit his mother often, if that happened. Very, very often.

CHAPTER 2

JESELY RECOGNISED THE SUBMISSIVE LOOK of a creature that knows it is prey from his flights in hawk form: the shoulders-hunched, head-drawn-in posture of a creature resigned to its fate. Coneys and desert dhevas and sand squirrels—they all looked that way, caught in the open beneath the hawk's shadow.

Sylas sat across the table with that same look. The lad's eyes spoke of resentment, wariness: a youngster accustomed to taking a beating and getting back on his feet before the next blow landed. Jesely wished he would not look like that with him. The Lady knew, he had the boy's best interests at heart.

The trouble was, no master would take Sylas on until he showed signs of achieving control of his changing, yet Jesely had a nagging feeling that being accepted as apprentice would be just the boost the Chesammos boy needed. And he *was* a boy yet, though he would soon wear the linandra bead on a twisted wire through his ear. He would hardly have time to draw breath, Jesely thought, before the lad's father had him married and producing children.

For all Jesely was Chesammos himself, he didn't hold with this practice of marrying youngsters off before they were grown, however much their race had declined. Sylas needed his mother more than a wife and family.

"You want to talk about something?" Jesely had come to his room to find Sylas waiting on the bench outside. At Jesely's invitation, the boy had followed him into his study and taken a seat. Jesely had made his study into a cosy retreat, and the chair into which Sylas settled was well-worn leather, scuffed and marked but comfortable. The tapestries behind him, at which so many young changers had stared over the years hoping to find the answer to a particularly tricky question, conveyed scenes of Chesammos myth and legend. A framed charcoal portrait of a young Chesammos girl took pride of place on his desk.

The lad shuffled his feet and Jesely repressed an impatient sigh. Jesely, as an empath, often mentored students; yet these days he struggled to read Sylas. He kept up his guard, rarely if ever letting his defences drop enough for Jesely to get even an inkling of what he was feeling. When others complained of him, Jesely maintained that all youngsters of Sylas's age were much the same—defensive and truculent—but it did little good. Some of the masters had written Sylas off, and that made Jesely all the more determined to help.

"You go home soon." Jesely had approved Sylas's visit home for his manhood ceremony and his sister's wedding. Combining events had become more usual in Chesammos villages, now that times were hard. The lavish feasts of Jesely's parents' and grandparents' days were now a memory, yet weddings and piercings were still reasons to celebrate.

"Two days, Master." That at least brought a flicker of pleasure to Sylas's face. "Later than many boys, but at least it will be done."

Jesely's hand drifted to the linandra bead at his own left ear. His had been pierced later still. Aerie-born and raised, his parents had left the decision to him whether to wear the traditional Chesammos coming-of-age symbol. It had taken the death of his mother's father, when Jesely was twenty-one, to show how much his heritage meant to him. His grandfather had told the young Jesely many of the traditional stories. The earring was in his memory.

"Will you be allowed zacorro at your ceremony? At mine I poured myself a full wine goblet—drank it all, too. I think I begged my mother to kill me for three days after. I had been warned, of course, but I thought I knew better."

Sylas laughed. Zacorro was a Chesammos spirit so potent only those with the strongest heads and stomachs drank more than a thimbleful.

"I will bear that in mind, Master. If my father does not provide it, someone will. It is not often the village sees a piercing and a wedding on the same day."

He fell silent. When he forgot himself, Sylas could be a charming young man, intelligent and well-spoken. Jesely wondered what had changed. Was it mixing with Casian that had the lad so withdrawn? Or that he knew Jesely did not approve of the direction their relationship had taken?

Two men together did not bother the master changer. Far from it. In an environment where changers left their bird state naked, and often chose to enter it that way too, a relaxed attitude to sexual attractions was almost inevitable. Relationships were fluid, although many married, and liaisons between members of the same sex rarely caused so much as a raised eyebrow. So if, in Chesammos terms, Sylas wore his krastos blade sheathed to the back, it was none of Jesely's business. But Casian, now, he *was* Jesely's business, and for more reason than the young lord being Jesely's journeyman. The Irenthi was devious and manipulative, and Jesely had yet to establish what exactly he hoped to gain from a relationship with the Chesammos.

"So will we lose you to a wife soon?"

Jesely took care to keep his tone light. He didn't want the boy to think he was trying to send him away. The Lady knew the lad was touchy enough about his changing problems without suggesting he would be dismissed from the Aerie as a result. Even so, Sylas's face clouded.

"My father wants that."

"And you?"

Sylas shifted uneasily in his seat, and Jesely regretted putting him on the spot. He remembered the discussion with Craie when he first brought Sylas to the Aerie. Jesely mentioned to the ash brick maker that his son could remain at the Aerie, if he felt suited to that life.

"He will be a linandra digger," Craie had said. "He has been tested and he has the sensitivity. He will go in the dig team, drawn in the ballot or not."

The ability to sense the linandra stones deep under the ground was both a gift and a curse. A gift because the villagers received food and clothing, and cut stones to raise their children to adulthood in return for the linandra. A curse because the diggers rarely lived long, their health destroyed by the ash they inhaled and the fumes that rotted their lungs.

When Jesely asked what say Sylas had in his future, Craie had snorted.

"He is Chesammos. He does what he must. You have never lived among us, changer. You do not know what it is like."

That was the crux of it. Jesely was Chesammos by birth, with all the stigmas and prejudices that entailed, but had been raised in the Aerie among shape changers. He had never lived among the Chesammos and that, to them, made him an outsider. He understood well enough the need for the villages to hold onto their young people. But Sylas was valuable to the Aerie. Changers were not so plentiful that Jesely would relish seeing this one lost to the linandra pits.

"Master Jesely, has Master Olendis spoken to you today?"

"Master Olendis? No. Why?"

Sylas's fingers twined, and he picked uneasily at his thumbnail. He swallowed hard, then glanced up at Jesely from under generous eyebrows. "I made him mad with me today. The way you were talking—well, it made me wonder if he had complained to you. If he doesn't come to you, I think he will go to Master Donmar."

For Olendis to go directly to Master Donmar, head of the changer council, Sylas must indeed have upset him. Jesely leaned on his desk and waited for Sylas to explain. The lad dropped his gaze back to his lap, resuming his fidgeting.

"I want to stay, Master Jesely. My father wants me home, I know, and the masters... Well, maybe I'm not as quick to pick things up as they might like." He paused, and Jesely knew exactly which masters' faces were in the boy's mind. "But I am trying hard, Master. I want to be a changer more than anything."

The quaver in his voice told Jesely he spoke the brutal truth. If Sylas returned to his village he had little future: a forced marriage; digging the uncut linandra gems out of the pits with krastos knife and fingernails; and an early death, his lungs dissolved from the inside by poisonous fumes from the volcanic vents.

"I know, lad. I see how hard you try."

All the reports from Sylas's tutors—with two notable exceptions—said the same thing. He studied hard, applying himself diligently, yet what came naturally to other boys his age seemed beyond him.

Sylas met his gaze, and a flash of hope lit his eyes. "Maybe if you were to speak with Master Olendis? With my father? They might listen to you."

"I spoke with your father when you first came here. He was determined that you should not stay with us. The longer you take to control your changing, the more impatient he will become, I fear. As it is, he sees his son apparently learning nothing from us when he could be more useful at home."

Sylas gave a long sigh and his shoulders fell once more. "Then it is decided."

Damn it. Jesely would not lose a young changer without a fight. He tapped the flat of his hand on the table to get Sylas's attention. "Maybe not. The changing, now. Tell me what you feel when you try to change."

"I relax, send my mind floating as if I were going to sleep. I can do that. I can feel the aiea here."

Sylas laid a hand across his ribs. Many felt the energies there. Jesely himself felt it higher, up across his chest. A few experienced it as a weight across their backs. It made no difference. The aiea took no form and added no weight to the body. It took up no space. What was important was that the changer could sense it, could feel his reserves of it, and could draw upon it when needed. At least the boy could get that far.

A changer had to cast his mind out as if stretching to the farthest reaches of the island, then let it go farther, into the lands beyond. There the kye—the bird spirits with whom the changers had a partnership of sorts—waited to link with the changer and help him take on his bird form. Then came the part that was impossible to explain to one who had not experienced it: the pulling, the twisting, when the bird form and the human form exchanged places. Then the person's consciousness entered the bird form and flew, fully aware of what he or she did, and changed back to human form at the end of the journey.

"And then?"

Sylas frowned. "This is what annoyed Master Olendis. Then I hear voices in my head. They scold me and beg me and chatter at me until I..." This time he *did* hold his hands to his ears.

Jesely knew that covering his ears would not shut them out. Jesely could hear three voices. The first was the kye for his lower bird form, the one he had learned when he was a novice like Sylas. The second was his higher form, a hawk in Jesely's case, learned shortly before he achieved mastery. The bird forms all used the lower energy—the aiea-bar—and most, but not all, changers could take a higher form with a little effort. The last was his talent kye. Sometimes manifesting before the lower bird form, this kye gave its partner an ability of some sort. This kye used the aiea-dera, which only about a third of changers could access.

Sylas had no talent, and he fell far short of being a master. At this stage he should only be aware of one voice: that of his lower kye. That kye should be helping him to change into his bird form. But according to Sylas, he could not hear his own kye for chatter from others he should not be hearing.

Jesely believed him. Even without using his empath talent, the master detected no hint of falsehood in Sylas's voice and posture. Yet only one changer in Jesely's experience had ever heard more than three kye: Shamella, the girl in the portrait.

"Can you help me, Master? I know I need to hear one voice, but I do not know which one I need to hear out of so many, and I don't think I could shut the others out if I did know."

Jesely sighed. "I'm sorry, Sylas, I can't. But now that I understand the problem I can investigate. I know of one other changer who heard more kye than normal. I shall see what I can discover."

Sylas perked up. "What happened to him?"

"Leave me to investigate. It was a long time ago and I don't remember it clearly." The bell struck three times, and Jesely rose to go.

"I have a class now. Do you have somewhere you need to be?"

"Yes, Master. I have a lesson with Master Gwysias."

"Very well. I doubt I shall have any news for you before you leave for home, but maybe when you return I shall have an idea how to proceed, if the Lady wills it."

"Maisaiea-yelai," Sylas echoed him in the Chesammos tongue, pressing his thumbs and fingertips together in the Lady's sign. As he made the gesture, Jesely caught sight of the boy's palms and drew a breath in through his teeth. Few of the masters took a switch to their pupils, much less on their hands, but Gwysias the master of the scriptorium did, from time to time. Gwysias was convinced that Sylas's failure was due to laziness or downright stupidity.

Jesely did not walk as briskly as usual on his way to his class, but turned what Sylas had said over and over in his mind. The lad was a puzzle, that was certain. In all his years dealing with failing novices—the slow learners and the dull-witted—he had never encountered one like Sylas. The boy was bright enough. His mother had, against his father's wishes, taught him the rudiments of reading and writing. But kye voices calling in his head? Was the bird kye refusing to make itself known to the boy? Or were so many kye trying to claim him that he was becoming confused, unable to hear the one to which he should be bound?

The council and Sylas's father alike were demanding results, if for different reasons, and if he was to help Sylas, Jesely was going to have to dig into old history. He would have to turn up parts of the past that he would rather leave forgotten. For he had loved Shamella, and she had died when she was scarcely older than Sylas was now. If the kye had killed her, he owed it to Sylas to save him, if he could.

Sylas sat hunched over a long wooden table in the library, flanked by bookcases holding tomes bound in leather or linen. The smell of parchment and dust and old ink hung in the air, and settled on his skin. The room whispered of generations of changers before him who had studied here, but none, he would wager, had ruined more work or spilt more ink on their fingers. He was so absorbed that he did not notice Casian until he spoke.

"Very nice. I like the way you have drawn the veins on the leaves. What is it?"

"Medelerinn. That's what we call it, anyway. It grows in the cracks in the rocks near our village. Not much grows there—the rain kills most plants before they can even take root—but medelerinn can grow pretty much anywhere. My mother steeps the leaves into a tea that cures headaches. I saw some outside this morning and it made me think of home."

He turned in his seat to look up at the silver-blond Irenthi man. Casian, freshly washed and dressed in clothes befitting a lord's heir, looked fully recovered from his flight. Sylas's mouth dried at the sight of him, as it always did, his breath taken away by Casian's pale skin and high cheekbones. The haughty air of one who has grown up in wealth and status and come to expect it as his right only added to his glamour, in Sylas's opinion.

"And this one?" Casian pointed to the sketch below.

"Esteia. Another desert plant. That flower forms seed pods about so big." He showed Casian the length of the first joint of his index finger. "The seeds look like nuts—tempting if you're out in the desert and short of food—but they're deadly poison. Eat one of them, or just lick your fingers after picking one, and at first it looks like you've got a fever. Then you get bruises all over your skin. Eight or nine hours later, you're dead. It dissolves important parts of you from the inside."

"Nasty. Any antidote for it?"

"Yes. There's another plant often grows nearby. Boil the leaves up and use it as a tisane. Works, if you catch it in time."

"You lived in the desert where next to nothing grows. So how come you know so much about plants all of a sudden?"

Sylas chuckled. "I'd only seen five or six types of plant before I came here, so I found out more about them. And see what section of the library Master Gwysias always seats me in?"

Casian turned to check. Sure enough, they were in the section with all the botanicals and herbals—row upon row of leather-bound books about plants and their uses. Realisation crossed Casian's face, followed by accusation. "You're meant to be working."

"I was. But look at my writing. Everyone else seems to use their right hand, and I don't. When I learn to make the letter shapes with charcoal, he gives me this stupid thing," Sylas glared at the brush in his hand as if it offended him. "Why do changers write with brushes? Just because quills are made of bird feathers doesn't make them wrong, ashini?"

"I love it when you do that." Casian grinned at him.

"Do what?" Sylas didn't know whether to grin back or be affronted that Casian wasn't more sympathetic. Easy for him. From the time he could hold a stick, he'd been tutored to make shapes in a sand tray.

"Use Chesammos words when you get upset or excited. *Ashini*. That's 'you understand' or something, isn't it?"

"More or less."

"So how come you can draw with the brush, but not write?"

Sylas tossed the brush to the desk in disgust. "If I knew that I could write better. Different part of my mind doing it? I don't know. I concentrate so hard to write and it looks a mess, but I switch my mind off and a drawing comes out."

Casian nodded towards the parchment. "Master Gwysias must think you are coming on, though. He wouldn't have given you parchment to work on if he didn't think you were making progress."

Sylas turned it over to display a piece of work marred with an ugly ink blot.

"The library copyist ruined this piece, so Master Gwysias said I may as well have a try with parchment and ink. But the ink soaks into the page and makes splotches." He sighed. If a person knew the marks he had made on the paper were letters they could decipher his writing, he supposed. With prior knowledge of the text. And a copy of the original before them.

"And does Master Gwysias know that you've been drawing flowers all over your transcription work?"

Sylas's eyes widened. "Omena's wings!" His exclamation shattered the quiet.

Casian laughed. "Another Chesammos saying? What's that one about?"

"Now is not the time or place to tell you the story of Omena Stormweaver. Remind me when I'm less likely to be murdered by a librarian." Sylas licked a finger and tried to rub out a part of the leaf, knowing as he did that it was hopeless. The edge of the leaf smudged and ran into the damp parchment, and the evidence of his crime stayed firmly on the page.

"That's never going to work."

"Omena's wings," Sylas muttered it this time, staring at the parchment and clasping both hands to his forehead in despair. "I'm doomed."

Bad enough that his writing looked like it was trying to crawl off the page, but to draw on his work as well...

"What were you copying?" Casian leaned closer. "An obscure and learned treatise on the nature of kye, by the looks of it. Your version looks like chicken scratches. I'm sure Master Gwysias can only consider it improved by the addition of a weed that can cure headaches."

Sylas grasped handfuls of his dark hair. "I promised Master Jesely that I would work hard and now this. How could I be so stupid?" He stopped, staring at Casian. "What's the matter with you? It's me that's going to take a switching."

"Jesely?"

"Yes, I told you I was going to see him."

"So you did. I forgot. What did he say?"

"He asked about my lessons with Master Olendis and I told him about hearing lots of kye. He said he'd heard of something like that a few years ago and he'd look into it for me—see if he could find out what happened to the other changer. If he never learned to control it, at least I'd be forewarned."

Casian's temper showed signs of fraying.

"So he's still spending time on you. Time he could be using helping me find my higher-level kye. Time that I'm wasting trying to rise to the rank of master while Elyta presses on ahead of me. She will get the next council space and I'll still be a bloody journeyman!"

"But you can't be a councillor until you are a master."

"I know that. But Jesely is far more interested

in you. I'm the only Irenthi changer they have—the only one! Don't you think it would benefit them to have me on the council? And he wastes his time with you. You can't write neatly but you can draw perfect bloody daisies!"

Casian pulled the parchment from Sylas's hands and ripped it from top to bottom.

Sylas stared numbly at his ruined work. The harsh words—they meant nothing and would soon be forgotten on both sides. Casian had a short temper sometimes, and maybe what he said was right. Maybe Jesely *should* be concentrating his time and efforts on Casian. But Sylas did so want to be a changer.

"Why are you disturbing my student, Casian Owlchanger?" They both whirled round at the voice behind them. Neither had noticed Master Gwysias's approach. Sylas licked his lips, reaching for the parchment, intending to hide it beneath the book from which he copied. Casian knocked his hand away and grasped both pieces.

"I was reprimanding him." Casian held out the parchment. "He has been drawing on his work."

"I see," Master Gwysias came closer. A short man, with straggly hair turning to grey, he held the two pieces together and peered down his nose at the writing. "Shocking. Quite shocking." And then he glanced at the drawings.

"Do you think parchment is in such plentiful supply that you can draw pictures on it, heh?"

"No, Master," said Sylas, hanging his head and knowing what was coming.

"I don't see what else I can do for you. I have

been teaching you for nearly a year and I can see little improvement. Most novices come to me already able to write better than this. Hold out your hand, boy."

Sylas turned his hand palm up and waited, anticipating the blow. The length of plaited blade grass, all too similar (albeit narrower, with a sharper bite) to his father's belt woven from the same, whistled through the air and cut into his skin, leaving a reddened welt across the soft gold of his palm. Sylas could feel his colour rise. It was bad enough to be switched like a child without Casian witnessing it.

"Shows we shouldn't waste time trying to educate Chesammos, eh, Master Gwysias?" Casian said. "Master Jesely and Master Cowin excepted, of course. For the rest of them, the right place is in the desert, doing what they know."

Casian left in Gwysias's company with never a backward glance for Sylas, continuing his pretence of the lofty nobleman. Except it wasn't a pretence. He *was* a nobleman. Even after all this time, Sylas could never be entirely sure that Casian didn't believe what he said.

Sylas clenched his stinging palm, aware from bitter experience that the hand would be stiff in the morning. The welt was matched by the blow to his pride, and the sudden pain in his chest was the price he paid for loving above his station. This was the cost of loving an Irenthi.

CHAPTER 3

YESTRO CLAWED HIS WAY OUT of the vent and dragged the mask off his face. On the surface, in what passed for fresh air in the ash desert, he could at last stand upright. That had been one of the tightest vents yet. His back muscles shrieked in agony.

He counted his men out of the pit. Each in turn did as he had, discarding the masks that kept the worst of the rock dust and fumes from their lungs. They reknotted their caigani smallclothes, then brushed away the dust that clung to sweat-streaked golden skin and matted dark hair. Another day over—the last of this dig. The last day and all his team alive, thank the Lady.

The pits deserved their brutal reputation. Even wearing masks the diggers took in lungfuls of dust, and when the Lady breathed her poison into the air, their eyes and throats and noses burned. Outsiders said they could tell linandra diggers by the raw, weeping sores where their skin had cracked and peeled away, and by the hoarseness of their voices. Truth was, by the time they got to that stage, they were already marked for death.

But now he and his men had some time. Time to go back to their wives and families. Time to forget the backbreaking work and the pain. Time to live for a while, instead of simply not dying.

They had all lost in life's lottery, having been selected for the dig teams when they were no older than Pietrig there—the bead fresh in his ear and no more hair on his chin than on his mother's backside. The Chesammos dug linandra or starved, and Yestro had been chosen. He never complained. What would be the point? But he hoped the Lady understood when his prayers were often filled with resentment.

He licked parched lips, tasting ash. A pile of empty water skins lay some distance from the opening. His last skin now held only a few mouthfuls. They would have no more water till they reached home. A swanflower plant's watery pulp would keep a man alive for a time, but it was bitter—worse even than the acrid tang of the water in their skins—and often caused pain in the guts. Better to conserve what water they could than resort to swanflowers.

"You thought any more about what I said?"

The speaker was Ilend, Yestro's second, one of the younger men on the dig party. Yestro took his time retying his caigani and pulled on a loose tunic. He had known this conversation was coming. He scratched at his chin, at the beard caked with ash and sweat. The young men now went clean-shaven on a dig, against tradition. Maybe he should do the same himself.

Yestro picked his words with care. Ilend was fiery and Yestro preferred to avoid confrontation. "I don't know. We could bring trouble on the whole village. Namopaia isn't equipped for rebellion."

Around him, men brushed the ash away as best they could before dressing for the return journey. All the faces surrounding him were drawn. A stint in the desert took it out of a man, however hardy, but despite their weariness they were listening. Whose side would they take, Yestro wondered. Were they preparing for rebellion like Ilend, or like Yestro did they hope for peace?

"That's nonsense. Namopaia will be more isolated if we don't join. We're one of the smallest villages, and the Cellondorans don't take us seriously as it is. I was nearly refused entry to the wrestling at Cellondora last trip home. They said if we would not stand with them, they wouldn't fight us in the circle."

One or two men behind Ilend muttered their agreement. Wrestling was serious business to Chesammos, and a village never turned away any competitor who brought his entry price.

"Their diggers have been hiding linandra for months," said another man. "They have a bag as big as a man's fist hidden away. Can you imagine what a stash that size is worth? Enough to arm a village. A small fortune, ashini?"

Ashini? Yes, Yestro understood well enough the value of linandra. The island's whole economy depended on it. That was why they were out here, digging precious stones to line the pockets of the Irenthi rulers. He tried another argument.

"We don't have a linandra singer, and trying to sell unsung stones is the quickest path to awkward questions." This talk of rebellion was foolishness. They were Chesammos. Chesammos used no weapons but the slings that put a coney or a dheva or a sand squirrel into the cookpot from time to time and the knives to skin and gut them. What business did they have, talking of weapons and uprisings?

"Craie's wife was a singer once, they say. That's where she got that necklace of hers," said Ilend. "And the boy's a sensitive. He'll be out here, maisaiea-yelai, once the Aerie bring his changing under control. I've heard he prefers men. Maybe she'd sing them for us if we promise to go easy on him."

One or two of the men chuckled at that. Damn it! As if Yestro didn't have enough to worry about without nursemaiding a boy.

"I don't know," Yestro said. "It's my neck, ashini? The Aerie won't help us if we're caught stealing linandra, and if the Aerie doesn't help us our children go hungry. No, Ilend. Cellondora can play at rebellions, but I'll not get Namopaia into something like that, not without the say-so of better than you."

He thumbed open the spout of his water skin and raised it to his lips. The tepid water tasted sulphurous, but he needed it. He restricted himself to a few sips.

"Shame," said Ilend, tossing a few small, greenish stones on his palm. "That's what we've put aside this time out. You've not spotted the scales coming up short and neither will the Irenthi. We've been careful. We won't get caught, maisaiea-yelai."

"I said no, Ilend." Yestro wiped his mouth with

the back of his fist and held out his hand. "Without the stones the village is not fed and clothed. And if we don't get the quota then we don't get the stone Craie needs to put his boy on the way to manhood, and then we don't get him, changer or not. A sensitive left in the village because we reckon him a child would be a waste, whoever keeps his bed warm."

"That necklace of Zynoa's holds enough beads to name men for the next year or more. If Craie doesn't get one from the elder he can use one of his wife's. We need swords and bows. If it takes a few empty bellies to get them, that's what we'll do."

"You'll get us all killed, is what you'll do. We'll not defeat the king's army by putting swords in the hands of untrained men." Yestro turned away. As far as he was concerned the conversation was over. He would go to Skarai when they returned—get the elder to make them hand over the stones. "I will not sanction this. Do you hear me?"

"You have no choice," said Ilend. He pulled out the short krastos blade with which the diggers prised the linandra from the vent walls, and slashed it across the leader's neck.

Yestro put his fingers to his throat and they came away bloody. He fell, his blood soaking into the ash.

"So now I lead," said Ilend. "We'll hide the stones and Craie's boy will find us plenty more. He's a pretty lad too, eh, Pietrig? I hope you'll not keep him to yourself. Need to get him to share his favours."

The young man trying to make himself invisible

at the back of the group cast anxious glances at the body at Ilend's feet. He had received the bead nearly two years before, but he still didn't shave more than once a week. His golden-brown skin had not yet been touched by the desert, but was smooth and unblemished, if a little green at his first sight of a death by violence. "I—I said I'd talk to him, and I will. But I can't make any promises. I'd not trade, in his place."

Pietrig's eyes flickered and he swallowed reflexively when Ilend levelled the bloody blade at his throat.

"I suggest you find a way to be very persuasive," said Ilend quietly. "I'm sure Skarai is using his influence to have you taken off the team, but I'm also sure he can get me Craie's boy in exchange. I need a sensitive to find the good deposits. The boy does us no good at the Aerie. We need to make sure he comes home, ashini? And soon."

Ilend pushed Yestro's body into the vent and with a few scuffs of his foot covered the blood-stained ash with fresh. The wind was rising. By the time the lord holder of Lucranne's guards came to collect the stones, the hole would be covered. They would not see that the vent had become a grave.

He scanned the men's faces, seeing resolve, fear, sadness. "The lord holder's guardsmen accused us of stealing linandra and killed poor Yestro despite his denials. Rather than carry his body back, we made a pyre here and gave his ashes back to the Lady like good Chesammos. Ashini?"

He glared at the faces around him, and poked his finger towards them like a dagger stabbing a throat. "Ashini?"

They understood. It was time to stand against their oppressors, and when they had enough linandra to buy weapons the Irenthi had best watch their backs. The Chesammos were a peaceful people, but when you take away what a man has to live for, you give him a reason to die.

Sylas had yearned to fly home. In his mind he pictured himself swooping towards the beehive-shaped houses of Namopaia. His mother would have been overjoyed; he might even have gained the grudging admiration of his father and sister. Stranger things had happened. Instead he found himself bumping along in one of the supply wagons, sent by the Aerie to supplement the foodstuffs provided by the Irenthi lord holders. As he perched on the bench seat beside the Irmos wagoner, it struck him that he now took it for granted that the people around him would wash regularly. Maybe he was acquiring the fancy airs his father had accused him of on his last visit.

He smiled to himself. Fancy. Yes, that was why he sat next to a man who spat out of the corner of his mouth to punctuate what little conversation he made and who stank like a midden. And why, apart from the scenery passing to either side, and the children running alongside the wagon in villages they passed through, his view was of the leathery backside of the pair of draught cheen. While horses were more common, cheen were better suited to hauling loads in the desert, Their thick hides lost little moisture, and their plate-like hooves were more stable than horses' on shifting ash.

Sylas edged across the seat to distance himself from the wagoner's aroma and to avoid the flick of the tail of the cheen in front of him. Scaled like a rat's, it swished away flies less effectively than a horse's, but if one struck human skin it stung like a whiplash. He already had a weal the length of one thigh.

The swaying of the wagon and the rhythmic clopping of the cheen's hooves made him sleepy. As he drowsed, he remembered his first trip home from the Aerie.

In those early days, the towers and halls of the changer city were unimaginably elegant. Even the fine weave of the clothing the servants gave him was luxurious. Casian, elegant Irenthi lordling, sniffed at the changers' linen and wool and wished for the silks and supple leathers of his castle home, but to Sylas it was all bewilderingly fine—a far cry from the Chesammos homespuns that scratched his skin. And the food! Sylas had never seen such food. He felt transported to a land of plenty.

On his first return to Namopaia, the dome houses had been a welcome return to normality. His friends had clamoured to hear of his experiences and his mother had been delighted to have him home. His father, however, had wasted little time getting him stripped to his caigani and packing the molds for the ash bricks. In the morning Sylas's muscles had ached and his father had complained that he had already become soft.

"Life is too easy for you now. You wait and

see; you'll get flabby round the middle, and your muscles will get weak, and you'll suffer for it when you come back."

His father had not mentioned the full thumb's width that Sylas had grown in his few weeks at the Aerie, but Sylas had noticed. He would be taller than his father, broader too, especially with good food and clean air. Then Craie had best watch his mouth.

He had wrestled with his little brother, Lynto, though he had compared Lynto's skin and bone frame against the well-nourished youngsters from the Aerie, and had worried for his health. Even his sister, Aithne, had been made tolerable by her excitement over her betrothal to Kael. He had been glad enough to return to the Aerie, but he had not said goodbye without a pang of regret.

Sylas sighed. That had been the last time he had seen Lynto. The lad fell victim to a fever a few months later. By the time news reached him at the Aerie his brother was dust, burned on a pyre in Chesammos fashion with family and friends watching for the spirit to leave his body. He liked to think that Lynto was among the kye. Maybe his voice had joined the many Sylas heard when he reached to the Outlands. Maybe Lynto would link with a changer and fly like a bird.

He would have liked that.

The farther south they travelled, the patchier and scrubbier the vegetation grew until they passed into the desert proper. He and the wagoner both pulled caiona over their faces to block the fumes. It helped with the stink, but it didn't stop the spitting. Instead the man drew up a corner of the cloth before hawking spittle into the dust to either side of the track. Maisaiea-yelai, the Lady would stay calm for their crossing, and they would reach Namopaia without streaming, reddened eyes or flaking skin on their faces. Sylas pulled his sleeves tightly around his hands. Any exposed skin was at risk, when the volcano vented through the desert floor. They drew closer. He scanned the horizon for the insect-bite nubs that marked a Chesammos village.

On his second visit—the one after Lynto's death—his village had seemed smaller and dirtier. And sadder and quieter, without his brother. Everywhere he went, everything had reminded him of Lynto. His father was devastated at the loss of his more promising son, but Craie's face dared Sylas to spot any grief or to show any of his own. A man must be strong, whatever the Lady hurled at him. Sylas's old friends had kept their distance, but whether to avoid intruding in his family's mourning or because they no longer considered him one of them, he didn't know.

His sister had wrinkled her nose at him, saying he sounded different and smelled like an Irenthi— as if she knew what an Irenthi smelled like. He might have sounded different. Weeks of speaking Irenthi instead of Chesammos had led him to adopt some of that language's speech patterns. And he smelled of the fragranced soap used by all the changers. Did it hurt that he was clean, instead of stinking of old sweat?

He had worked for his father again, wishing afterwards that he could soak in warm water to ease the pain in his shoulders and back. But baths, much less warm ones, were an unknown luxury in Namopaia, with every drop having to be drawn from wells so deep it took all morning to haul the buckets to keep the families in water for a day. He had hardly been able to move next day when he tried to rise from his pallet.

"You see," his father had said, "he is too good for us now. The boy can hardly stand after a single day's work. He'll suffer in the linandra pits when they finally decide he's learned enough to come back, or throw him out as a waste of their time. And he'll struggle in the wrestling competition at his piercing, up against the men for the first time. No doubt he'll disgrace us."

Craie's Chesammos tongue had sounded harsh to Sylas's ears. Maybe he *had* become 'fancy' after all. The village had felt too small, the scent of poison gases on the air oppressive. Villagers had felt the fine cloth of his clothes and rolled their eyes. He had returned to the caigani, not because he was more comfortable in it—he felt self-conscious and exposed—but because his shirt drew catcalls and comments about how he thought himself a lord now he had spent a few months with the changers.

They envied him, he told himself: no more than that. He did not put on airs and graces and pretend to be superior. Not at all. They wished they could live at the Aerie, eating well every day, sleeping under warm clean blankets and with the chance of a better life. Namopaia was no longer his home. He had outgrown it—wanted beyond reason to stay at the Aerie. This would be his last trip home in a wagon, he vowed to himself. The next time he came to Namopaia, he would fly.

CHAPTER 4

WHILE SYLAS ENDURED HIS RIDE to Namopaia, the Aerie mourned a changer whose death had touched them all. Young Adwen had only been fourteen years old, yet he had been a controlled changer and a remarkable talent. Not all the people who crossed the Aerie's lake for the dedication of his niche had known him well, but all knew his parents: his late father, Kerwen, and his mother, the healer Ayriene. Many made the crossing for Ayriene's sake, but there were younger faces too: friends of Adwen and his older brother and sister.

Boats crossed back and forth for most of the morning, carrying changers and humans, young and old. There were many more people than places in the boats, and those who could row well were kept busy shuttling the mourners across in parties. Early arrivals wandered the island's paths, visiting niches commemorating friends and family or forming small groups to stand and talk in respectful tones.

The island was small and rocky, and its craggy interior was full of the small alcoves cut into the rock that the Aerie used to remember their dead. In a society where some members were buried, some consigned to the Lady on a funeral pyre, and some returned to their own lands, these niches became their permanent memorials. Nearly all held personal effects—small items of jewellery, portraits, and the like. Most held a feather to show the person remembered had been a changer. Some held a pipe or a piece of parchment to denote a master changer or a scholar.

Ayriene and her surviving children crossed last, with members of the changer council. This would be the final public ordeal for Ayriene, although she knew from losing her husband six years before that there were difficult days to come. Kerwen had died of a wasting disease for which the Aerie's healers had no cure. That had been hard enough, but Adwen had died from a fall: from wounds Ayriene would have been able to heal had she been on Chandris. But the mother and son had been on the mainland, far from the aiea-dera—the island's energy which enabled her gift.

The ceremony went past in a blur. She trusted council leader Donmar to give Adwen a heartfelt oration, and she coped with the ordeal by withdrawing—refusing to hear his kind words and effusive praise of a talent wasted. She linked with her kye, taking herself partway into the Outlands. This should not be happening. She could not lose Adwen. Not her baby.

Her other son, Garyth, said a few words which she hardly heard, and her daughter, Miralee, gave a subtle nudge when the ceremony required her participation. She would face her grief in a time and place of her own choosing, and without others' eyes on her, however sympathetic those eyes might be.

Donmar's voice cut through her detachment. "And now we come to the most symbolic part of the dedication. Ayriene, do you have the feather?"

Ayriene's throat constricted when he spoke. All she had to manage were two small words, but now that it was time she could hardly choke them out.

"I do."

"Would you like to lay it in the niche?"

Donmar spoke softly and Ayriene could hear the concern in his voice. As a newly-raised master, Donmar had taught both Ayriene and her husband, although his duties as head of the changer council had curtailed his teaching by the time her children underwent the change. All three of her children were changers, two of them talents. Adwen, her youngest, had been only the second healer talent, along with Ayriene herself, in several generations.

Miralee's grasp tightened on her forearm. Ayriene knew her daughter was finding this difficult. Miralee always showed her emotions openly, and the taut control of the dedication would be stretching her endurance to its limit. Garyth stood at her other elbow, silent and strong. Her two remaining children, giving her as much support as they were able for the duration of the ceremony. For her sake, repressing their own grief.

Of course she had the feather. Not one of Adwen's actual feathers—he had died in human form, as all changers did—but one she had found on the lake shore that morning. Pure white, she lovingly stroked its vanes back into place until it was perfect. Like her perfect boy.

She stepped forward, Miralee and Garyth shadows on either side, and placed the feather into the niche carved into the rock. Ayriene paused, adjusting it, placing it just so. As if it mattered how the feather lay.

Her son was dead.

Donmar uttered the concluding words and the crowd dispersed, negotiating spaces in the returning boats as soon as they considered themselves far enough away from the family group. Donmar had an embrace for Miralee and Ayriene, a handshake for Garyth—and then he left them. Miralee walked a few paces away along the shore, taking the opportunity to cry, free from the intrusive eyes of the other mourners. Garyth watched after her anxiously, torn between sister and mother, assessing which of them most needed his strength. He compromised by pacing restlessly between the two, transforming his grief into action, as he so often did. Her eldest had always been a bundle of barely-controlled energy, even as a child.

Ayriene sat on a rock opposite Adwen's niche. Her legs, wobbly through the ceremony, finally felt as though they would give out. Garyth handed her a water skin and she drank deeply. Of her children, he was the only one without a talent. He maintained it didn't matter—that as the first child, everyone was only concerned he proved to be a changer. After two changers in the family, he said, all the pressure of expectation had fallen on Adwen. Even with both parents able to feel the kye and transform, no child could be certain of inheriting the gift. Her youngest had more than risen to the challenge.

Adwen's death left Ayriene once more the only healer talent. The thought made her tired. A healer talent, and she still had not been able to save him. Some days the tiredness and guilt almost consumed her.

The three waited, Miralee red-eyed but back in control. Their silence was punctuated by birdsong on the island, the buzz of conversation on the shore, the gentle splosh of oars cutting through water as the rowers went back and forth carrying their passengers. They had no words, but each took comfort from the others' presence.

Ayriene retreated into herself. It was how she had coped when Kerwen died: that and the need to care for three young children. When there were no more mourners to transport, two rowboats set out from the lakeside, a single rower in each. The young men waved to Garyth; they were friends of his.

"We thought you might like a boat to yourselves," called one, getting into the boat with his friend. Thoughtful, like Garyth himself.

They waited for the two young men to set off back to shore before taking their places in the one remaining boat. Garyth took the oars and Ayriene and Miralee shared the bench seat in the middle.

"It's all right to grieve, you know," Miralee said, squeezing Ayriene's hand. "I don't think I'll ever stop missing him. You don't need to hide it with us."

The pit of Ayriene's stomach clenched, twisting

as if she were entering her transformation. It had never occurred to her before how similar the two feelings were: the crushing void of bereavement and the wrenching coldness of leaving part of oneself in the Outlands. She had left part of herself in that niche.

"It was my fault."

Garyth and Miralee exchanged looks—her daughter as golden-haired as she, her son dark like his father and brother. They had been so alike, Garyth and Adwen, but Adwen's face had still been round, smooth, and boyish where Garyth's, four years older, was taking on the more chiseled planes of manhood and had the dark shadow of a beard on its cheeks.

"You can't blame yourself," Garyth said, cutting a path through the water with the oars. "It was an accident. Things happen."

They did not understand. How could they? She was the healer of Chandris and she had let her son down. She concentrated on her breathing, feeling her gut unclench, the aiea rushing in to fill the emptiness.

"I took him off the island. I could have healed him here, but so far from aiea-dera, I was just a hedge herbalist." Hardly that, she admitted to herself. With the Aerie's knowledge and training behind her she was far more accomplished than a common village healer. But that was how she had felt, with her child facing death and she being unable to help.

"We can't all stay on the island for fear of what might happen," Miralee said. "Look what you came back with. All those plants and bushes to grow here. We've used the yellow edmea, did you know that? Jasia's baby threatened to come too early no matter what the midwives did, and the tea has made the baby rest easy. If it roots here, we can send cuttings out to midwives in the towns and villages. Who knows how many babies will be saved?"

"So it is a trade then? Jasia's baby for Adwen? Your brother, and a healer talent, for a servant's child?"

"I didn't mean that." Miralee's face clouded. "You know I'd sooner have Adwen back. But at least some good came of the trip."

"And I didn't mean to imply that one life is worth more than another. But I find it hard to see anything but waste in Adwen's death. Anyone could have fetched the edmea; it didn't have to be me. It didn't have to be us." She focused on the geese strutting on the shore, trying to stop her vision blurring. Cold filled the empty place in her heart, like the lake water rushing back in after the dripping wooden oars had passed.

"What will you do now? You know the infirmary would love to have you here training healers for a time."

Ayriene paused. She knew the reason for Miralee's question. Ayriene coped by carrying on as normal, by forcing the grief to the back of her mind and pressing herself to work. It only suppressed the grief—contained it like water behind a dam—but she held it deep inside, letting it out rarely and only in private. Miralee would sit with Ayriene every chance she got, talking about Adwen and Kerwen, remembering them and crying.

Garyth handled it differently still. He threw himself into physical activity—whatever and wherever he could find it. When his father died, he had helped the gardeners who tended the Aerie's fields and orchards, digging and pruning and carrying loads from sun-up till full dark. He had become a great favourite, and still worked there now. Ayriene felt bad, but sharing Miralee's grief might break her this time. Her daughter would have to carry her own burden.

"I don't know. I thought I might travel. There are so many people out there who need a good healer."

Miralee's face fell. "I hoped you'd stay for a while. You and Adwen had the same talent, so it was natural that you'd spend time together. We see so little of you." Her voice caught in her throat. "I miss you."

Miralee would cope if Ayriene left. She had Garyth to help her, and must have other friends her own age. But her words had pricked Ayriene's conscience. If Miralee felt neglected, Ayriene could not leave her daughter to grieve alone. "Maybe for a while, then."

Ayriene did not need to be an empath to read her daughter's delight. She would stay then, if it meant that much. The infirmarians would need instruction on the correct use of the herbs she and Adwen had found, for one thing. And they were always short-handed; they could use a trained healer. Maybe she could cope with Miralee's reminiscences, if she could immerse herself in her work. As the prow of the boat crunched onto the black sand shore, Ayriene resigned herself to staying in the Aerie. For now.

CHAPTER 5

WHILE HE WOULD HAVE PREFERRED to fly into Namopaia—to see the admiration on the doubters' faces—at least arriving on a wagon had one advantage. Until he could control his changing his father could hardly forbid him to return. As long as Sylas could, in theory at least, respond to a call from a master's pipe, his only option was to mark with blood elder for the rest of his life. Craie would see sense, surely, and allow him to return to the Aerie to complete his training, would he not?

Few villagers greeted him. Most were more concerned with the contents of the wagon than the returning changer. The feast to celebrate Sylas's piercing and Kael and Aithne's wedding depended on the foodstuffs in the barrels and sacks in the back.

He had not expected a rapturous welcome. His old friends had their own concerns, and many were married with families to think about. But the atmosphere in Namopaia bothered him. There should be a buzz of activity before a celebration,—a busy feeling to the village. Instead, people went about their business in near silence, scarcely making eye contact. Something felt wrong.

They called it a feast, but that was an exaggeration. Namopaia had not enjoyed a true feast of the belt-loosening, stomach-bulging, over-indulging sort in Sylas's lifetime: not like those he had attended on occasion at the Aerie. Those he had always gone to with a vague feeling of guilt at celebrating Irenthi feast days,—at least until he saw the spread on offer and decided the Lady would not begrudge him the chance to eat his fill. But after tomorrow's feast the village would go hungry for two days, maybe three, until the next supplies arrived.

His mother made up for the villagers' indifference with her enthusiasm at his return. Her attention made him a little uncomfortable, but he allowed her to fuss. He knew she missed him, especially with Lynto gone, and Aithne would join her husband's family, as was traditional. They had been close, Sylas and his mother. Even now, in the midst of his change from boy to man, she understood him. He could tell her anything, but rarely needed to; she always knew his thoughts as well as he did. Zynoa didn't quiz him on his studies, for which he was grateful. His father would do enough of that when he returned. That he had ridden home after a year told her a lot. His silence on the subject likely told her the rest.

Sylas was enjoying his meal—simple by Aerie standards, but anything prepared by his mother's hands took on an extra flavour for him—when fists pounded on the door.

"Now who could that be, making such a din?" Zynoa went to the door, wiping her hands on a cloth. Outside stood a young man, a year or two older than Sylas, with the linandra bead glittering at his left ear. His beard was coming in, but his shaved cheeks marked him either a linandra digger or a changer, and Pietrig was no changer.

"Your pardon, Zynoa, but is Sylas here? I heard he arrived."

Sylas turned to see who the visitor might be. A warm smile crossed his face at the sight of his old friend and wrestling partner.

"Pietrig," he said, setting aside the bowl and jumping to his feet, then frowning as his mother's face hardened. Pietrig had been like another son to Zynoa since they were children. He and Sylas had been as inseparable as brothers.

"He is eating, Pietrig, and then he needs to sleep. He has had a long journey and must be rested for the ceremony."

In the normal course of events, Zynoa's house would always have been open to Pietrig. Sylas couldn't understand why his friend was not already beside him on the mat with a bowl of soup and talking excitedly about what had happened since they last met. Pietrig had been in the linandra pits the last time Sylas had come home, and Sylas had been looking forward to seeing him.

"I'm not that tired, Mother, really—"

"But we have things to discuss. Things that do not concern your friend here." A slight emphasis on *friend*. Sylas studied his mother's face, hoping for a hint of her thoughts, but Zynoa's face had taken on the mask-like stillness that Sylas knew meant she had made up her mind. What had happened to cause friction between his mother and Pietrig? Zynoa had guessed her son's nature years ago. Did she fear the relationship between them? Sylas loved Pietrig dearly, and he believed Pietrig loved him too, but Pietrig was also popular with the village girls and he returned their affections. Pietrig was the elder's son, required to observe the proprieties. He would marry and have children, and pretend their youthful explorations had never happened.

"We must talk!" she said determinedly and pushed against the door. Pietrig leaned his weight into it—not enough to force his way in, but enough to stop Zynoa closing it on him.

"Don't believe them, Sylas! It's not true, I swear it. Don't believe them, for the love of the Lady."

Zynoa shoved the door to, then turned to lean on it for a moment. She looked tired, Sylas thought. The grey hairs on her head now outnumbered the dark. He sat again, taking up his bowl, then pushed it aside with the soup unfinished. Neither spoke. This was not the homecoming he had anticipated: his mother anxious; his friend not welcome in his house. And the village, so subdued, as if the people were frightened.

"What's happening, Mother? What was Pietrig talking about? What's going on here that I don't know?"

She came to sit beside him, one hand patting his knee. His back tensed. He was not a child, to be fussed over. She drew her hand away as if sensing his unease.

"All is not well in Namopaia, son."

"I can tell. What has changed since my last visit?"

She sighed. "You'll hear sooner or later. Yestro is dead."

"Yestro? The dig team leader?"

"He was murdered."

Sylas sat up straight, staring at her as if she had gone mad. Murder? In a Chesammos village? Impossible. The Lady ordered that each should care for all. Any sort of violence between Chesammos was unheard of, with the exception of the wrestling at weddings and manhood ceremonies and festivals. And that was a way to let the men work off some of their aggression without actual harm befalling anyone, save the occasional strained shoulder or bruised ribs.

"What did—? Who killed him?"

"That's why Aithne and your father aren't here to greet you. She is with Yestro's daughters, helping comfort them. They always were great friends, you know. His family was one of the few that did not look down on her for being one of only three. And your father is with the menfolk. Ilend is the obvious choice for the new leader, but it will take them a full day's arguing before they agree on something the women would settle in a few minutes."

"What has this to do with Pietrig?"

Sylas's mouth went dry. They couldn't think Pietrig had killed him? No, he would not be roaming freely in the village if they thought that. And Pietrig was no killer. A fine wrestler, but he would no sooner kill a man than Sylas would.

"What? Pietrig? This has nothing to do with Pietrig. Lord Garvan's guards killed Yestro. They said some of the dig crews have been coming up short, so the soldiers were sent to make sure all the linandra got handed over. Yestro protested that his crew had never come up short and the soldier struck him with his sword. Ilend said they searched them all and didn't find any more stones than Yestro gave them. There is trouble coming from the Irenthi. Some of the men are talking of arming themselves."

Lord Garvan was Casian's father. In the Aerie, Sylas could forget that one day Casian would rule the area of Chandris in which Namopaia lay, yet here were Casian's father's troops killing one of the village's prominent men. He found he didn't want to give that too much thought.

"Arming?" The Chesammos never used weapons, on each other or anyone else. They were a peaceful folk and even petty crime was rare in a Chesammos village. No one had anything worth stealing, mind. Trouble brewed when someone envied what another had: money, status, husband, wife. Nobody had much to covet here except children and grandchildren. Perhaps that was why status was determined by how many offspring a man sired.

His mother nodded glumly. "There is talk of raids by soldiers on some of the other villages. Houses burned out. People injured. Stay in the Aerie, Sylas. Stay as long as you can. You will be safer there."

"But Pietrig? What did he mean I wasn't to believe what I heard? And why did you send him away?"

His mother slumped next to him and he wondered if she was ill. Her hand strayed to her neck, then drew from inside her dress the linandra necklace that he remembered seeing from childhood. Unknotting the end, she slipped one bead from the thread. She held it out, then laid it on his outstretched palm.

"This is for your piercing."

He had known his bead would come from his mother. Zynoa had quietly provided beads for those families so far down the social order they might wait months, even years, for beads brought by the Irenthi, unable to have their children receive the adulthood rites that were their due as Chesammos. Ironically, his was one of those families. His mother's beads were small, barely more than chips, misshapen and imperfect, but the ones the Irenthi brought were little better. The Chesammos got the ones too small or too flawed to be of value to merchants.

Then she reknotted the thread and held out the necklace.

"I want you to take this," she said. "It would come to you anyway. You can keep it safe in the Aerie. If they come and find me with this—if they think we have stolen these beads—it could go badly for me."

"But it is yours. The only thing you have from your family. If I took it to the Aerie someone might steal it. Some of the boys are not as honest as they might be. This is the only bead I need from you." He held the single bead between his finger and thumb. It glowed faintly, responding to him, showing his sensitivity to the stone that made him valuable to the diggers. "We can bury the necklace somewhere if you are worried. By the hearth, maybe, but I'll not take it. It should go to Aithne. What would I do with a necklace?" He gave her back the stone. She would give it to his father for the ceremony. The thought of Craie piercing his ear made him uncomfortable.

"You may find you need it, someday. You more than Aithne."

"You are talking in riddles, Mother. Tell me simply. What is wrong with Pietrig? What has this to do with your necklace?"

Her eyes flashed, their placid depths roused at last.

"He has betrayed your friendship!" she said. "Pietrig has arranged with Skarai to have you replace him in the linandra digging team and get your father to take him on as brick maker."

Sylas swallowed. He knew he would go to the pits whatever the result of the next ballot; his sensitivity to the precious gem had made that all too likely. But for his father to sanction this exchange was inconceivable. They had never been close, but surely even Craie would not trade his own son, would he? Especially after losing Lynto to the fever.

"But what about me marrying? The family he wants me to have?"

Sylas had known from childhood that he would be expected to father many children. If not, he and his parents would stay low-ranked in the village. His father counted on Sylas and his sister to rear plenty of Chesammos babies and remove some of the stigma that Zynoa bearing only three children had put on the family. Linandra diggers had families, of course, but they tended to be smaller. The diggers spent most of their time in the desert, and then there were the health problems they often suffered.

She covered her face with her hands. "Your father said if you took Pietrig's place on the linandra team, Skarai would betroth you to Fienne."

Fienne was Pietrig's sister, close to Sylas in age and a childhood friend. If he had to marry, Fienne would have been his choice; but, for them to be used as a bargaining tool like this was unthinkable even by Craie's standards.

His throat tightened. *Don't believe what they tell you. I swear...* "And what do we get out of this? What do I get out of it?"

"Your father gets a seat on the village gathering as father to the elder's daughter. You and Fienne get a house provided, as they will provide for Pietrig and his betrothed, when his marriage is settled. Being linked by marriage to Skarai will benefit us."

Poor Fienne. Sylas wondered if she realised the man to whom she was to be betrothed loved her brother better.

"And me? What about me?"

His eyes met hers and he saw she knew the truth—had likely known before he did. He knew of at least two others in the village with a preference for a male bedmate. In fact, he had spent a year trying to deflect the attentions of an older man who liked young boys. Yet in a society where so much emphasis was placed on producing children, it was a lonely path to tread.

"You have someone? At the Aerie?" She had never asked him anything of the sort before. It had remained unspoken between them, only surfacing now they had reached the point at which he had to decide the course of his life.

"Yes."

"You love him?"

He thought of Casian's fair skin and silver hair—the way he tossed it back when he laughed. "Yes."

"Then you must go back to him. Be a changer, my son. Do what it takes to achieve that dream and try not to think about those you leave behind. It has to be, you will see. And I am sorry for what will come of it." She patted his knee once more, and this time he welcomed her touch. He would have thrown his arms around her if he had not been too old for such things.

All his life, she had been the only one who understood him—had known him deep down, as if she knew his thoughts and feelings as well as he did. Her words puzzled him, but comforted him at the same time. She wanted him to go. He knew she would miss him, as he would miss her, but she wanted this for him as much as he did for himself.

He took the bead necklace and put it back around her neck, drawing her hair out from beneath the cord.

"Thank you. But I will not take this from you. It is yours."

And then his father returned.

Alike in looks, yet so different in personality,

father and son locked gazes until Sylas broke the contact, as he always did. Craie blamed Zynoa for letting Sylas become soft and for filling his head with a useless education that would leave him discontented. Sylas had never fully understood the friction between his parents, particularly with regard to their children, yet had been aware of it since he was old enough to notice such things.

The first time Sylas could remember squaring off against Craie he had been no more than four or five—beating helpless little fists on his father's chest. He could not remember what had triggered it. The way his father treated his mother, most likely. That had been the first time he had felt the blade grass on his legs, his mother sobbing that he was too young to be beaten. Much too young. Craie dominated Sylas by strength and fear after that. But he and Craie now stood eye-to-eye. Soon Sylas would have his father's breadth of shoulder and depth of chest. Older than Zynoa, Craie was well past his prime and heading for decline. Sylas knew the days of Craie's dominance over him were coming to an end.

Craie's lips parted in something close to a sneer.

"So you're back. I hear you rode back?"

Sylas nodded. He didn't want to talk to his father. Other boys would get a back slap or a brief hug from their fathers. He got a staring match and a greeting that would never suggest how rarely they saw each other.

"Still not mastered it then, this changing?" The way Craie spoke of it, with a sneer in his voice, it sounded as if changers were the despised people on the island, not the Chesammos.

"Not yet." Sylas heard the strain in his voice—his jaw clenched so tight it almost cracked—and made an effort to relax himself. He unfisted his hands, forced his shoulders lower, finally released the tension in his jaw.

Craie grunted. He had not listened when Sylas explained about the kye and the calling, pronouncing it 'changer nonsense.' Sylas was sure Craie thought he made most of it up. He realised with a sinking heart that his father's only interest was in how soon he could be brought back from the Aerie and set to work digging linandra.

There was no shame in the work—the village ate only if the diggers found linandra—but Sylas had glimpsed a better life. He now knew it was possible to learn, live in freedom, and maybe, just maybe, take his mother there to give her the life she deserved.

"Father, when I have controlled my changing, may I stay at the Aerie? There is so much more I could learn and—"

"You truly think I would allow it?" Craie's roar filled the house and from the corner of his eye Sylas could see his mother quaking. Even now, with Sylas on the brink of manhood, Craie was quick with his blade grass belt, and Sylas held up his hands in a placating gesture. It was on the tip of his tongue to tell Craie that he would do as he pleased and Craie could not stop him, but if he were to be rejected by the Aerie he would have no home here—no place to go. He had heard of others in a similar situation, making their way to

Adamantara, selling their ear bead for the price of a passage to the mainland, never being heard of again. It would destroy his mother if he did that.

"I only thought..."

"What good do you do our people up there on the mountain? Do you breed more Chesammos to help us? Tell me, are there Chesammos changers up there with you?"

There were three Chesammos on the council, Sylas told him. Master Donmar, Master Jesely, and Master Cowin. All highly respected. Beside him, his mother tensed and Sylas glanced at her in reassurance. He would watch what he said—try not to inflame his father's temper.

"And are they married to Chesammos women? Do they make more Chesammos to help us survive?"

Sylas hung his head. "No, Father."

Master Jesely had been married—to an Irenthi, of all people, albeit a low-ranked one. A daughter of one of the minor houses who had died bearing their only child. Their daughter had died with her. When Jesely made any comment about Sylas and Casian, Casian went off on a well-worn rant over his supposed double-standards. Master Cowin had recently married Mistress Elyta, an Irmos so fair anyone would take her for Irenthi until they drew close enough to see her eyes—light hazel, not the blue or green of the true Irenthi.

"Then you will come back. Work the pits. Be a man, not some pampered bird up in your mountain nest."

"And marry Skarai's daughter, so that you may sit on the council?" He regretted the words as soon as they left his mouth.

Craie's eyes flashed past him to Zynoa. "You told him?"

Sylas knew that look. Craie barely held his temper in check.

"It wasn't her fault. Pietrig said something. I pressed her. She would not have told if I had not made her."

Craie's lips drew back, showing teeth.

"I should let both of you feel the cut of the grass for that."

"And have your wife and your son bloodied and beaten for the festivities? That would hardly be auspicious." And would hardly suit a gathering member-to-be, Sylas thought wryly. Luckily the same thought must have crossed his father's mind. He glared at Sylas and stormed off, leaving Zynoa looking as shaken as Sylas felt.

She lowered her eyes.

"That's why I didn't let Pietrig in. I do not believe he means you harm. I know he does not. But he is involved in this scheme whether he likes it or not, and I did not want him raising an ash storm, ashini? I see so little of you and it is your piercing day. I want calm desert and blue skies until you must leave."

He felt guilty that he looked forward to leaving. However much he missed his mother—and he did— he longed to be a changer. Maybe a councillor, maisaiea-yelai, although councillors were nearly always talents, and he was not. When that happened he would fetch his mother to live with him. Away from Namopaia. Away from his father.

CHAPTER 6

SYLAS STOOD MOTIONLESS IN THE centre of the wrestling circle waiting for the needle to pierce his ear. He could feel his father's hands steadying his head, then the sudden, acute pain of the tokai needle and the smooth, velvety flow of blood. Elder Skarai spoke the traditional welcome to adulthood and Craie put the bead on its twisted wire through the newly-made and bleeding hole. By tradition, the boy's father did the actual piercing—or an uncle or other close male relative, if the father were dead—but Sylas would have preferred anyone other than Craie to have done the deed. Anyone else might have given him a reassuring smile before, a hug of congratulation after. But his father turned away, wiping blood from his fingers onto his clothes, forgetful that these would be his wedding clothes later. Sylas wondered what sort of omen that was: a man going to his daughter's wedding wearing the blood of his son on his tunic. He studied Craie's face for any sign of pride, but saw none. Sylas was a disappointment to Craie, who had always favoured Lynto.

He wanted to grab Craie's arm, turn his father to face him, tell him that he would have given himself for Lynto gladly, if that had been possible. But he could see only emptiness in his father's eyes: the knowledge that the only further use Craie had for Sylas was for him to marry Skarai's daughter and raise his own status in the village.

His mother and Aithne came to admire the bead, and Kael, his sister's husband-to-be, slapped him on the back and called him brother. They, too, wore their wedding clothes. At least there were a few hours before the wrestling. The rules forbade targeting the ear wire, but it would still be vulnerable so soon after the piercing. He would not remove it, though. A Chesammos never removed the bead, once inserted. It went with a man's body to his funeral pyre, the flawed beads often shattering in the fire along their fault lines. He wondered what would happen when he transformed. Would the bead be left on the ground with his clothes, or would it transform with him? He would have to ask Master Jesely. He didn't want to risk losing the bead once he finally had the knack of the transformation.

The wedding came next, and Craie showed little more interest in or emotion at that. What good was a daughter to him, when he needed sons? Aithne would be claimed by Kael's family now, and while any grandchildren she might produce would have some small effect on Craie's position, the greater part would go to increase Kael's parents' status, and that of Aithne and Kael on their own account. No, Craie needed Sylas and Fienne married and breeding. Sylas shuddered.

After the simple ceremony ended with a call to the Lady to bless their marriage with many children, Craie spent some time talking to Skarai. Sylas was uncomfortably aware that they would be discussing their plans for Fienne and him. When Fienne brought zacorro for the two men in cups made from hollow cane and little bigger than Sylas's first knuckle joint, Craie eyed her as if assessing a cheen before making an offer to buy it. She brought the tray to Sylas next, and he tried not to meet her eyes when he took a cup and downed the bitter spirit. It burned his throat, nearly choking him, and his eyes watered with the unfamiliar taste.

He scanned the crowd for Pietrig, but with no luck, and wondered if the two families were contriving to keep them apart. He would see him at the wrestling shortly, but he needed to clear up the awkwardness that might arise between them because of his mother's hostility. Then his head spun and he remembered Master Jesely's warning about the zacorro. To be in any fit state to wrestle he would have to recover his senses. Slipping away from the drinkers, he made his way to the well and lowered the bucket down into the water.

Like all wells this far into the desert, it was deep, and it took him some time to haul the water back to the surface. As he heaved the bucket over the low stone wall that surrounded the well shaft, his sister joined him.

"I thought you might have gone looking for Pietrig," she said.

He kept his voice casual. "They seem to want to keep him away from me. Do you know where he is?"

"He's in the elder's house. He came looking for you, so they shut him away."

"Did they at least let him out for the ceremonies?" His stomach twisted at the thought that his friend might not have seen his piercing.

"He saw. I spoke to Fienne. They let him out for that and the wedding. And he will wrestle later." She dipped cupped hands into the cool water and drank deeply. He did the same. "Ah, that's better. Kael is over there being plied with zacorro. I doubt he'll be fit for anything on our wedding night."

Sylas chuckled. "I had one cup. I'd not find my way to the wrestling circle if I had any more than that. Are you happy?"

"Yes. But it will be hard on Mother, having us all gone."

"I might be back soon," he said, although the thought made his heart sink.

"Did Mother speak to you?" When he nodded, she continued, "Then you must do as she says. She will miss you if you stay at the Aerie, but it would hurt her more to see you a linandra digger. She has high hopes for you. Mother says you were meant to be a changer, and I think she's right."

This was the most Aithne had opened up to him since they were children. He didn't know how to take her words. A few years ago he would have thought she was trying to get him to stay away from her, but she sounded sincere. Sad, but sincere. And he didn't think she would urge him to do anything that would hurt their mother unless there was good reason.

Aithne squeezed his arm and turned to go. "It's

nearly time for the wrestling. Remember, whatever happens you must stay at the Aerie. Follow your dream, brother. This village is not a good place to be."

He drank another handful of water, then splashed his face, washing the wound at his earlobe. Squaring his shoulders, he walked to the wrestling circle. For the first time, he would take his place among the men.

The Chesammos loved their wrestling. At any celebration, men from other villages would come to see or participate in the sport, bringing a contribution to the feast to gain entry. Many walked hours, sometimes days. Sylas had not competed since he went to the Aerie—there had been no celebrations during his visits—but he had easily outclassed all the boys apart from Pietrig. The two of them had always been closely matched. Sylas was out of practice (Benno certainly didn't challenge him enough to prepare for bouts at this level), but he desperately wanted to fight Pietrig.

Pietrig was a formidable opponent. They had learned together, practised together, so that Sylas might have been fighting his reflection. He did not need his mother's uncanny understanding to know what the other young man was thinking, what next move he was planning. Although there were others more skilled, he and Pietrig would form the closest contest, and an evenly matched pair were absorbing to watch. However, Sylas had not reckoned on the way the matches would be organised. The entrants were put into four groups, each with an equal number of youths and experienced adult wrestlers. The resulting four winners then faced off for the overall victory. He and Pietrig were in different groups, and they had little chance of more than one fight each, since straight away they would be up against older, heavier, more experienced fighters.

Sure enough, Sylas was defeated in his first bout, ceding to a vicious choke hold from a visiting wrestler. Nearly twice his age, and half as much again in weight, the man had the better of it from the start and Sylas went out of the competition nursing a bruised neck and an even more bruised pride. The look on his father's face showed that he had expected more. Sylas brooded at the back of the crowd. Craie would be angry later.

Pietrig made it through the first round, forcing a submission from a local man a year or two older than he. Sylas had sparred with the man several times and knew him to be a good opponent. That young man sat out the remainder of the competition with a face like sour swanflower fruit. At least Sylas lost with better grace.

In the next round, Pietrig drew a man at least a handspan taller, with tree-trunk legs and thick arms to match. Pietrig submitted quickly, retiring to the crowd amidst words of commiseration, rubbing his shoulder ruefully.

Sylas watched to the end, the sick disappointment in his stomach abating as he appreciated the skills of the fighters. Pietrig and he had learned this way as boys. They had studied the games at weddings and festivals, memorising the moves and practising them until they became second nature. He still had so much to learn.

After the final fight, a Namopaian was pronounced the winner, following a highly tactical bout against an outsider. The locals greeted the win with a roar of approval; home wins were always popular. The noise had hardly died down when the referee—an experienced official from another village—took to his feet and clapped his hands for silence. "A special contest has been requested and approved under the accepted forms."

Sylas perked up. Named matches rarely occurred, and had to meet certain conditions regarding the suitability of the contest. The combatants often had good reason to ask for the match: a grudge; two rivals kept apart in the main contest by the division of the fighters; a hefty wager. They generally resulted in a spirited fight. Sylas was shocked, then, when he heard his name called.

"A fight between Pietrig son of Skarai, the challenger, and Sylas son of Craie."

Sylas sought Pietrig's eyes across the ring. Pietrig did his best to feign nonchalance, but Sylas knew him well. He was tense. Was this Pietrig's father's doing? But no, the announcement had named Pietrig the challenger. If another had asked for the fight his name would have been given and both fighters asked to agree to the match.

Craie glared at Sylas, livid, willing him to decline the fight. Looking across the circle, Sylas could see Skarai looking no less annoyed, pulling on Pietrig's arm and talking to him urgently. There was no shame in turning down a challenge—it happened all the time—but when he looked back at Pietrig he could see something in the other man's eyes. A need for this. A hunger. Sylas understood. His need was no less. In his mind he had fought Pietrig a hundred times in the last week. He would not let the opportunity pass.

Sylas nodded tersely at the official. The man reminded the pair of the rules. It didn't take long; Chesammos fights were more or less anything goes. The winner was the man who forced the other to cede, nothing more complicated than that. The only moves prohibited were biting, gouging of the eyes, ripping of the earring, and deliberate breaking of bones. Beyond that, the fighters had free rein and a lot of scope for inflicting the pain needed to draw a submission from their opponent.

They indicated their readiness to fight, and circled each other warily, bare feet seeking for purchase on the ashy ground. Wrestlers rarely spoke once the fight was called; indeed, most considered it bad sportsmanship. Talking to your opponent could be considered trying to throw him off guard or interrupt his concentration. But as they locked eyes, then arms, each watching for the chance to catch the other a fraction off balance, Pietrig murmured, "I didn't ask for the exchange. You have to believe me."

Sylas stared at him. Was this why he had called him out? To try to convince him that he had not betrayed him? He would never believe that of Pietrig, and for all Zynoa's apparent anger, he didn't think she believed it either.

He let his glance flicker down to Pietrig's feet—

saw the other man's gaze follow his for the fraction of a heartbeat it took Sylas to grab Pietrig by the shoulders and try to force him down. But Pietrig was heavier and had wrestled plenty over the last few months. He managed to stand his ground and hook a foot around the back of Sylas's legs to throw him off balance. These two had traded these opening moves so many times they knew them like the steps of a dance. All that remained was for one to put a foot wrong, make a misstep, and the other would take advantage.

They spun, crashing to the ground. Sylas could taste ash on his lips, feel it grinding into his skin. They jostled for position, first one on top, then the other, limbs entwined more intimately than lovers. The sheen of sweat coated bodies and dampened hair, and skin slid on skin as it became more difficult for either man to get a grip.

Pietrig pinned Sylas, hands grasping both his arms, body pressing against Sylas's chest. As Sylas strained and heaved to shift him, Pietrig bent and hissed in his ear. "They plan rebellion. The linandra teams hide stones from the Irenthi. You must tell the Aerie. They will know what to do."

Sylas ground his teeth, arching his back to throw Pietrig off. Surely this was a ploy to distract him? Chesammos were peaceful. The idea of rebellion was so alien to them that Pietrig had used the Irenthi word, lacking the ability in their own language to convey what he meant. But Yestro had been murdered. That was inescapable truth.

Squirming out from under, Sylas threw his weight to one side, rolling over to reverse their positions. The hum of the onlookers' voices rose to a low buzz at this development. He had his hands on Pietrig's neck. If he could only hold it, a choke on the windpipe was an effective way to achieve a submission. But Pietrig wrapped one leg around Sylas's back, bringing his other foot up into Sylas's midriff, kicking at his stomach, trying to push him off.

Forced to release Pietrig's throat, where a red weal rose on the skin, Sylas rolled and Pietrig once again scrabbled to get free. The two men faced each other on hands and knees, panting for breath.

"Stay in the Aerie if you can," Pietrig gasped. "They mean to use your mother too."

His mother would be no use to rebels. She had that string of linandra, but the beads were small and misshapen, hardly more than chips—the sort the linandra diggers would leave at the pit, knowing them worthless. Why a singer had even bothered to bore holes in them he couldn't understand.

They engaged again, evenly matched. They were dirt-caked now, the dust and ash from the ground clinging to their bodies. Sylas rubbed his eyes, then wished he had not. They stung with sweat and dirt and he was momentarily blinded.

Pietrig pounced.

Catlike he swept Sylas over, landing him on his back with a thump that knocked the wind out of him. Sylas felt his arm twisted unnaturally up and over his head. Before he could retaliate, Pietrig had his legs twisted around Sylas's shoulder, his foot forcing Sylas's head to one side. His other leg wrapped around Sylas's arm, and Pietrig pulled on his foot to draw the limb up farther. He leaned over Sylas's face.

"Meet me behind the kiln later. I promise I tell the truth."

Pietrig heaved on his foot and Sylas could feel his shoulder joint opening as if it would pop. Sylas moaned, sweat beading his face. Pietrig had him. His friend pulled and Sylas cried out. His shoulder would dislocate if he strained much harder—if it was not half way there already.

"Do you cede?" Pietrig's voice held the grim satisfaction of one who remembered every victory over his friend, every loss to his foe. Sylas remembered victories also, but this would not be another one. If he allowed Pietrig to dislocate his shoulder it could be weeks before he could try to fly. Physical injury manifested in the bird form, and no bird could fly with an injured wing.

"I cede."

Pietrig gave one last savage heave on his shoulder. Sylas's vision swam. He thought he might pass out from the pain.

"Do it properly. Let my father see I beat you fair and square."

Sylas's free palm struck the ground. Once. Twice. Three times. Pietrig sprang to his feet, taking the applause from the crowd. Sylas tried to sit up and groaned. His shoulder burned like fire, and it would be a struggle to get to his feet unaided. A shadow loomed over him and he raised his good arm. "Help me up, will you?"

He looked to see who it was and saw Craie, his face as strained as if he had swallowed an ash brick whole. Craie stared down at his son.

"Even at your piercing you manage to shame me," he said in a dangerously low whisper. "A victory would have been something at least, to ease the humiliation of you being beaten in your first fight, but you are bested by the elder's son."

His bare foot kicked ash into Sylas's face and he strode away, leaving Sylas lying on the ground in the wrestling circle. It was not until one of the village youngsters, an old friend of Lynto's, came to help him that he managed to get to his feet and stagger after the wedding party.

Pietrig's words came back to him. Behind the kiln? Very well, he would meet with him and hear him out, but if he persisted in this notion about revolution, well, Sylas would not know what to think of it. Still, he had to talk to Pietrig one last time if this was to be his last night in Namopaia. He would not leave with suspicion between them.

CHAPTER 7

L IKE THEM OR NOT—AND DEYGAN did not—the Chesammos played an essential part in the island's economy, and recent rumours unnerved him. Chesammos raising opposition after several hundred years of domination by the Irenthi was bad enough, but his sources claimed they had stashes of the linandra stones hidden in their villages. He leaned back in his chair, surveyed the ten assembled lord and lady holders, and mentally tallied those most likely to oppose him. Those holdings which used the least Chesammos labour were likely to lend him their vote, but those who relied on Chesammos workers might be more problematic. He would have to take this slowly— ease his ideas in one at a time. Deygan was an able politician; he usually ended up getting his way in the lord holders' assembly, often without the members realising they had been influenced.

Today an additional chair was drawn up to the table. Prince Jaevan, eldest of the king's three surviving children, sat at his father's right hand. Deygan's first wife had failed to give him a healthy child, and by dying had saved him the distress of setting her aside. His second wife produced three sons and a daughter before her death two years previous. The daughter had not long survived her, but the king had a new wife; more children would likely come.

The lord and lady holders sat beneath the vaulted roof of the assembly chamber, its clerestory windows decorated with stained glass, the lower walls hung with the finest tapestries. They met here so frequently that the surroundings no longer impressed them, but Jaevan was newly enough admitted to their counsels that he still regarded the room with something approaching awe, his fingers stroking the table where the windows cast coloured ripples like oil on water. Deygan remembered that feeling. He had attended his father in this chamber as a boy, learning how to rule as he observed his elders wrangling over points of law. And the Chesammos. Always they discussed the Chesammos.

Deygan was proud of his son. At twelve, Jaevan knew two languages besides his native Irenthi, and was an accomplished archer and fencer, although his physique did not yet lend itself to Deygan's preferred broadsword. In an unusual move, masters from the Aerie had tutored Jaevan and his brother, Marklin, for a time. Deygan intended the changers' slant on the history, philosophy, and religion of the island and its inhabitants to give Jaevan valuable insight into the people he would one day rule. The youngest prince, six-year-old Rannon, would join his brothers in their lessons soon.

Deygan noted how Jaevan made careful notes with quill and ink as his elders spoke, the tip of his tongue poking out from one side of his mouth in concentration. He wrote a good hand, and he tucked a stray lock of white hair behind his ear when it flopped across his face as he wrote. Deygan himself wore his hair tied away from his face with a simple leather thong. His head was bare. He rarely wore his circlet any more. Let the other holders wear theirs if they wished; he wore his rank in his posture and demeanour.

"There's more to it than that," Lord Holder Garvan said from his position midway along the table on the opposite side from Deygan. "Linandra production has been falling steadily for the last few months. I have ordered my men to search returning digging parties starting on the next rota."

"The number of Chesammos in the desert has fallen," said Lord Holder Tramalick of Easthill. "Could that be behind it? Or the lack of activity from Eurna recently?"

"The mountain's activity goes in peaks and troughs," Lord Garvan returned. "And the time between the peaks has been getting shorter over the past few generations. The last peak of activity was nineteen or twenty years ago, as I recall, around the time you came to the throne, Sire."

Eurna had been very active then, and Chandris had seemed likely to suffer a king's death, a major eruption, and an enemy invasion in the space of a few weeks.

Deygan nodded. "Indeed so. There are always tremors, of course, and the movement of the desert brings new deposits close enough to the surface for the Chesammos to detect. There should be no shortage of linandra. Does anyone else have any theories?"

Beside him, Deygan could feel Jaevan's attention subtly altering. For whatever reason, the lad had always been fascinated with the Chesammos and the changers, and Deygan wondered if allowing Jesely to tutor him might not have been a mistake. The lad had acquired some unconventional ideas about the Chesammos from that particular master.

To King Deygan, the Chesammos were only important to the island for the work they did— producing the ash bricks to build Irenthi towns and cities, and digging the precious linandra stones on which the wealth of the island itself was built. The few that remained in the uplands laboured in the fields or kept the livestock. If any managed to rise to become changers, or master changers, that elevated them beyond their race and gave them the status that their abilities accorded. For the rest, all Jaevan would need to know was how to keep them in line.

"The Chesammos are becoming more and more idle," said Garvan. "A few raids on their villages should shake them up—remind them of their place."

If Garvan considered using his small but well-trained militia, he must be concerned by recent events. Garvan was a tolerant man, by Deygan's standards. He regarded the Chesammos as irksome, as most of the lord holders did, but largely let them be. Tolerant, but not soft. If he needed to send troops into the desert to sort those blasted savages out, then he'd do it with no half measures.

"Master Jesely said they owned the island once."

Deygan winced at the sound of Jaevan's soft

voice and the holders' heads all turned to his eldest son. Damn that Jesely! Deygan had hoped the boy had enough sense to keep his mouth shut, not spout some of the nonsense the Chesammos master had put into his head.

"He said this was their island and we invaded and took it from them. He said they ruled here, except they didn't have lords as we do. But everyone worked and then the Aerie made sure everyone had all they needed. That's what Master Jesely said, anyway." Jaevan's voice trailed off uncertainly.

Deygan made a disgusted noise in the back of his throat. No one could claim that Jesely had told Jaevan lies, but Deygan didn't like his version of the truth. The island *had* been occupied by the Chesammos alone at one time, but that was hundreds of years ago. The Irenthi had brought trade and roads and cities and, well, civilisation to the island that the Chesammos called Cha'andris in that barbarically twisted tongue of theirs. And things had changed. Opening trade routes brought prosperity, and prosperity brought the constant threat of invasion by states that cast covetous eyes at their linandra.

"That's as may be, Jaevan," Deygan said in a voice soft but laced with warning. "But they need to accept how things are now. We give them food to eat, clothes to cover them, shelter for their people. How else would they survive, out in the desert where there is scarcely any food?"

Jaevan opened his mouth as if to speak, but subsided at Deygan's warning glare. Deygan knew what he had been about to say. That before the

Irenthi invaded the Chesammos had farmed and cultivated the island, that those who worked in the desert were supported by those who did not, and that no man worked more than five years in the desert in his lifetime. How such a system had been made to work escaped Deygan's understanding. There had to be order in the world and that meant lords and commoners, workers and overseers. This way of the Chesammos of making things 'fair' for all—that was nonsense for children and simpletons. No wonder the Irenthi had taken their island from them without a fight.

Sheinna of Aquis, the only woman to head a house in her own right, cleared her throat. "They do not have enough to eat, Sire. Not all of them, and not all the time. Not in the poorer holdings like Aquis. Once food and clothing would come from those in the north of the island to help those in the south. Now the northern Chesammos struggle almost as much or have been displaced to the south. They do not have any to spare, or they simply have lost touch with their southern cousins and are unaware of them and their hardship."

"Hardship, you say? None of the people of Chandris live in hardship." Deygan's green eyes flashed their annoyance. "If they do, it is because they don't work hard enough. The Chesammos have been encouraged to slack on their work by misguided handouts and these family networks of yours."

"With respect, Sire," Garvan said in a quiet voice that made the others take notice, "the handouts, as you call them, are part of the old system.

The way the Chesammos tell it, generations ago all changers were Chesammos. Other than the training of changers, the Aerie's main function was to redistribute goods—a marketplace, as it were, for the Chesammos with different products to exchange what they had for what they had not."

Deygan made an irritated noise. Who did Garvan think he was, to give him a history lesson? Granted, his house should know about changing better than any, with their background. Generations ago, before the ruler of Chandris claimed the title of king, Garvan's forefathers had been high holders of the island, displaced when the two elder sons of the house were found to be changers. They had bred clean of the taint since, but now Garvan's own son was at the Aerie—a changer talent, they said. Deygan had heard talk that Garvan intended Casian to stand down, since he could not set him aside, throwing the succession of Lucranne into doubt.

"I have heard that said, but now that way of doing things is outdated." Deygan raised a hand as Garvan readied himself to protest. "One of the main achievements of my father's reign, and something I pride myself to have continued, was reducing the payments into the Aerie. Our goal must be for the Aerie to pay its own way. It can take money from the wealthy in exchange for tutoring their children, or fees from the sick for the attention of their healers, but they will receive no more help from the holdings. And we must maximise production of the linandra. If that means bringing Chesammos from the north, so be it."

"And how would we manage in Martch and Waymar if you took our field Chesammos and sent them to the desert?" Koranne, regent of the holding of Martch, was a striking woman. She held the region for her son, only seven years old and too young to attend these meetings even as an observer.

"The supply of linandra is more important, Lady Koranne," said Deygan smoothly. "The alternative is to send Irmos to mine linandra. The Chesammos must be sent south. Not all at once, but by degrees the farms of the north must be worked by Irmos alone, and the Chesammos sent to do the jobs for which they are most suited."

"The hardest ones," said Jaevan. "The dirtiest, most dangerous ones."

Deygan indulged his son in many ways, but he would not be challenged by him, especially in full assembly before his holders. A flash of angry heat flushed his skin. Jaevan pushed him too far. Creator, the boy was only twelve. What would the lad be like at eighteen or twenty? He must learn that he was not yet king of Chandris.

"Because they lost," Deygan said through clenched teeth. "They gave up the island without a fight, and with it any right to be treated with respect. If they try to withhold linandra to manipulate us, they will soon learn the error of their ways."

"But—"

"Enough!" Deygan stood abruptly, motioning to his lords and ladies that the meeting was done. "Garvan, send those soldiers to the pits. If Chesammos are stealing linandra, I want them caught. Actually..." He stroked his beard thoughtfully. "Reduce the number of cut stones sent back to the villages. The adulthood ritual is important to them, I believe. Make it clear that as long as production continues to fall, so will the number of their young they can raise. That may make them rethink their stance."

"Of course, Sire," said Garvan, sketching a small bow, and the lords and ladies left the chambers.

Deygan turned to his son, who awaited his father's displeasure with resignation. The king jabbed a finger at Jaevan's chest.

"If you want to pander to the Chesammos when I am gone, that will be up to you. You can give them alms and dress them in silks, and see how far you get. The holders will oppose you. The Chesammos will see any softening as a sign of weakness and exploit you. The Irmos will see that to give better to the Chesammos they have to accept less for themselves, and they will defy you."

Jaevan's face fell and Deygan reminded himself that he was only a boy. Deygan had expressed similar ideas in his younger years. The boy would learn the hard way that realism displaced idealism when one became king. He forced himself to relax his shoulders and unclench his fists before continuing.

"You must rule, Jaevan, not simply wear the crown. That means making harsh decisions when necessary. We cannot afford to support the Chesammos and receive nothing in return, not with threats from those who would invade us from the mainland. There are soldiers to train, weapons to be traded for. If we need to send all the Chesammos to the pits to dig enough linandra to pay for that, then it will be done. Do you understand me?"

"I understand, Father."

Deygan got the impression that his son understood well enough, but did not agree. But he was young yet. He would learn.

Casian hesitated before knocking on the door of Mistress Yinaede's study. This was ridiculous. The conversation he had overheard between Garyth and Miralee in the refectory the night before might have had nothing to do with him. But he had heard his name over the hubbub—had heard it with the clarity with which a person always picks out his own name from a mix of voices. Trying not to be noticed, he wandered within earshot to listen to the rest of the conversation.

"I think you should tell Mistress Yinaede," Garyth said.

His sister pushed her hair away from her face with a restless motion. "What if it's nothing? What if it's not Casian? I said it looked like him, but older. I didn't say it *was* him."

"I'm no seer, but you said all seeings are recorded and kept, in case they become significant later."

"They are, but it wasn't significant. Just people talking."

"They must hold snippets like that too, in case they can piece fragments together later and make a bigger picture. And this is your first proper seeing. She will want to know you're making progress, even if you don't understand what it means."

They had changed the subject shortly after that and Casian drifted away, but it preyed on his mind. Had Miralee really had a seeing about him? If so, he wanted to know what it entailed. He could ask her, but that would reveal that he had eavesdropped, and he didn't know her well enough to strike up a conversation out of the blue. He finally settled on his plan to return to Yinaede's sessions, in the hopes of extracting the answer.

He had been to the study many times in the past. Casian was a talent—they had established that much early on, when Master Jesely observed disturbances of the aiea-dera around him. 'Talent knows talent' as the changers said. He stopped attending Yinaede's lessons after two or three months, after all his attempts at seeing had failed. His talent remained a mystery to the masters, although Casian had worked it out for himself. He had a compulsion talent, the ability rare enough to have been virtually forgotten, and worth keeping hidden. Returning to Yinaede's classes might even confuse the trail a little longer.

Casian rapped on the door and heard Yinaede's voice calling him in. He had not been in Yinaede's study for many months, but little had changed. The study had much the same layout as Jesely's. A few more feminine touches, perhaps: a sprig of blossom in a container; a painting of a landscape on the wall; a stack of books beside a comfortable chair covered with a thick blanket; a child's picture in charcoal and chalk pinned to a board. Essentially, it was the same small office in which all masters received their students.

Miralee was there when he arrived, deep in conversation with Yinaede. The girl flushed when he entered, and he suppressed a smile. She was stunning, a golden-haired Irmos, and the colour in her cheeks suggested she had noticed him too. He wondered if he could conceal an involvement with her from Sylas, or how upset the Chesammos might be if Casian shared his affections. Very, probably. The Chesammos was strangely emotional.

"Come in, Casian," said Yinaede. "It's good to see you back, if a little surprising."

He took one of the wooden chairs near the wall by its back and swung it closer to Miralee. "I am sorry, Mistress. I have still not discovered the nature of my talent, so I thought—" he flashed the smile he knew few women could resist—"maybe I could resume studying with you. This time we might make a breakthrough."

She grunted. "So you are here because you have not found your place anywhere else. Or maybe because a recognised talent would help your bid for mastery. Mistress Ayriene is back at the Aerie. Has it occurred to you to have her check you for the healing talent?"

Not a good start. Mistress Yinaede had never favoured him.

"I have shown no aptitude for healing, and the talent is rare. But maybe Miralee could introduce me to her mother, just in case?"

Her blush deepened. "I'd be pleased to, Lord Casian."

"Not lord in the Aerie. Just plain Casian."

"Miralee seems to have had her first true seeing. Miralee, do you have any objection to telling me with Casian present?"

"I..." Miralee licked her lips, clearly uncomfortable. It *had* been about him, then. If about anyone else, surely she would not be as awkward. "I suppose not. I just saw an image—not even anything that made sense. But it was clear, and not at all like a dream."

"That's more than I've had." Casian tried to appear encouraging. He leaned closer to her, "Do tell us. Give me something to emulate."

Miralee managed a nervous laugh and Casian could swear the girl trembled. Trembled! Whether from his closeness or simple nerves, he could not tell. If because of his proximity, maybe it would be worth risking Sylas's upset. Soft and peachlike, her imagined taste tempted his senses. As if she could read his mind—just his luck if the girl had a touch of empath talent, too—she tucked her skirts tighter round her legs, so that the fabric did not touch him, and clasped her arms to her sides, shutting him out. He could take things slowly— tease her open like a spring bud.

She squirmed on her seat, putting another finger-width or two of space between them.

"I saw a man—an Irenthi. He was in a high room. The ceiling was high, I mean, not that it was high up. Although it may have been that, too. I think it was in a tower." She paused, giving a shrill laugh. "I'm sorry. I'm nervous."

"Take your time," said Yinaede. "It is strange at first."

Miralee took a breath and continued more slowly. "He was in a room—in a tower, I think. The ceiling was high and vaulted, and there were coloured glass windows around the top of the room."

"The assembly chamber at Banunis?" Casian raised an eyebrow. It sounded like the place where he had attended his father at meetings, learning what it meant to be lord holder of Lucranne.

"I don't know. I have never been there. Does it look like that?"

"Very much. Were there tapestries on the walls?"

Her brow furrowed in thought. "I think so, yes. Maybe hunting scenes?"

Casian nodded. "That's the assembly chamber, all right. No surprise that there was an Irenthi there, in that case. Did you see anyone else?"

"Yes. He—the Irenthi—wore a gold circlet with a green stone. A linandra, I think, but a big one. Bigger than any linandra I've ever seen. The metal was inscribed with scrollwork, like vines."

"The crown," said Casian. "You were seeing the king." Casian had only seen Deygan wear his crown once, for a formal event, but the girl had described it exactly.

"But the king is older," she said. "This was a younger man. Late twenties. No more than thirty." And the king was fifty, at least.

"Jaevan?" Yinaede asked.

"I don't know," said Miralee. "I've never seen Prince Jaevan, and he's what—twelve?"

"What else did you see?" said Casian.

"There was a Chesammos talking to the king—a clean-shaven Chesammos."

"A changer?" Casian could not understand why a Chesammos would be in the chamber at Banunis, unless he was a friend of the king. And how many Irenthi had Chesammos as friends?

"Probably. Most Chesammos wear beards, don't they? Except Master Cowin and Master Jesely and Master Donmar—they keep clean-shaven because it's the changer way."

"Even Master Cowin has been known to wear a beard from time to time," said Yinaede. "When he is travelling and doesn't want to call attention to himself, mostly. How old was your Chesammos?"

Miralee narrowed her eyes, staring at the ceiling as if trying to picture the scene. "I'd say the same sort of age as the Irenthi. Maybe a little younger."

Casian's heart lurched. Sylas was three years younger than he. An Irenthi wearing the crown of Chandris, speaking with a Chesammos of similar age, and in the assembly chamber of Banunis? Casian knew that his house had once ruled Chandris. Could he hope—could he dare to hope?—that it could come round again?

"There was a woman there too," said Miralee. "A young woman. My sort of age. Sixteen. Eighteen. Certainly no more than twenty. She was Chesammos too, or very dark Irmos."

So if the men were Casian and Sylas, the girl was a child yet. No more than ten years old. No point puzzling over her identity; that would become clear in time. Casian's head spun at the thought of himself wearing Chandris's crown. If Miralee had seen it, then it had to happen, didn't it? Was he destined to be king?

CHAPTER 8

A LIGHT GLOWED BEHIND CRAIE'S KILN. On the outskirts of the village so that the noise and smells would not cause a nuisance, it was a meeting-place for many of the village's youngsters, who took advantage of the lingering warmth for comfort in the coolness of evening.

Sylas scanned the building, eyes hooded. The rest of the village was still at the feast and he jumped at every noise nearby. His father would skin him if he noticed Sylas had slipped away before the end, but he had to know what was happening. Something had changed in Namopaia since his last visit. Even if nobody said it, Sylas could feel it. He did not need an empath talent to feel in his gut that something was seriously wrong. He wanted to know what danger awaited him if he returned to Namopaia.

A figure stood in the shadows, barely outlined by the flickering of a fire bowl. It raised a hand to beckon him closer, then slid back into the darkness behind the building. Pietrig.

Sylas pushed the door open and went inside, Pietrig following. The fire bowl illuminated the hesitant smile on Pietrig's face and made his dark eyes glitter. He leaned in and placed a gentle kiss on Sylas's lips. The zacorro spirits with which they had toasted Aithne and Kael hung on his breath. Sylas pulled over a rush mat and they sat cross-legged on the sooty floor.

"I hoped you would come. Your mother guards you closely. I don't think she thinks well of me at the moment."

"But I hear my father thinks very highly of you." Bitterness edged his voice like a blade. Everyone knew Craie would sooner have had Pietrig for a son than Sylas. With his looks and status, Pietrig had girls falling over themselves to marry him. Although he had been given the earring years ago, his betrothal had not yet been announced. Skarai negotiated with all the families from Namopaia and beyond eager to offer a daughter for Pietrig, and he drove a hard bargain. With eight children of his own, he could sacrifice the time to make the right connections.

"I have zacorro." Pietrig waved two of the tiny tumblers and a container much smaller than a water or wine skin. "You wear the bead at last. Take a man's drink with me."

Pietrig's cheeks had taken on the flushed look of one who had drunk more than he was accustomed to, and the way he tossed the spirits back in one mouthful suggested a grim determination to get himself utterly, blindly drunk. He coughed and wiped his mouth, then Sylas raised the spirits to his own lips. It tasted like the Lady's breath in liquid form, stinging his tongue, then burning like fire down his throat. Even when he had fully swallowed it he could feel the flames in the pit of his stomach. He spluttered, eyes watering, and laid the beaker on the ground.

"So what's this nonsense about rebellion?" Sylas used the same Irenthi word Pietrig had used earlier.

Pietrig's voice rasped with the effects of the drink. "I will tell you all I know. But I warn you, they mean to involve you in their schemes and not even the Aerie will save you." Pietrig poured himself another beaker and waved the skin questioningly at Sylas. No, he did not want any more; it was not to his taste. Besides, he needed a clear head to understand Pietrig's words.

Pietrig gulped at the drink with an air of desperation, coughing up as much as he swallowed and wiping his mouth with the back of his hand. "The linandra teams from the villages are hoarding stones—keeping them back from what is handed over to the Irenthi. They mean to buy weapons and fight."

'Weapon' was also an alien concept to Chesammos. Pietrig's exact words meant 'tools for the hunt.' Sylas shivered. This hunt would be for men—men like Casian. If this rebellion became more than a few desert dwellers with forbidden swords, his friend would become involved, and what that might mean for their friendship, Sylas didn't like to think about.

"So you said. But how will the village manage on reduced supplies?" The Irenthi were careful never to say the villages bought the supplies with the linandra. No, they came by the grace of the lord holder to reward the hard work of the Chesammos.

To say the Chesammos bought them would imply a value—an ability to negotiate and set a rate of exchange for the stones—and that the Irenthi would never allow.

"The ringleaders say the Aerie will help if we go short. Will they, Sylas? Will the Aerie help us?"

His friend assumed he knew what happened in the changer council, but he was far removed from their deliberations. Officially, the Aerie did not meddle in politics. Unofficially, it helped where help was needed. Recognising the Chesammos as the original source of the changing ability, the Aerie tried to aid them where it could. That was one reason the Irenthi hated having changers among their people. It reminded them that somewhere back in their ancestry, however far distant, they had Chesammos blood. He honestly didn't know what stance the Aerie would take if they were caught between the Chesammos and the Irenthi. He liked to think they would help the indigenous people, but their support might falter beneath political expediency.

"I think they will aid us if they can," he said slowly, "but they have less power now. There are fewer changers, and the Aerie's wealth is lessened since King Deygan reduced the tribute. Lord Garvan is one of the more enlightened lord holders, with his son being a changer, but now that he has killed a digger..."

Pietrig's face twisted. "That wasn't soldiers. Ilend killed Yestro. Yestro would not go along with Ilend's plans and Ilend slit his throat. We were all sworn to silence. You must say nothing, but these are dangerous men—desperate."

Sylas stared at him, the zacorro churning in his stomach. He felt sick. So the hunt had begun already, and with one of their own kind the first victim. For a Chesammos to kill another went against all the Lady's teachings. If the Chesammos abandoned the Lady they abandoned themselves. Omena's wings! What would he be coming home to? The sooner he could get his mother away from this poison the better.

"They are amassing a fortune in linandra," Pietrig continued. "Unsung, of course. They could not take it to a singer on the island—all are loyal to Deygan, or under observation by his men, or both. They plan to take you into a dig team and make your mother sing the crystals for them."

His mother? They had to be mistaken. His mother was no linandra singer.

"My father would not let them threaten her." Or would he? If Zynoa held that sort of power then his father gained power by association, and Craie would sell his soul for status. Sylas swallowed bile. If what Pietrig said was true, his mother could easily find herself involved in these men's plans. He forced himself back to what Pietrig said.

"...if they could get you out in the desert they could..." Pietrig stumbled over the words. "They could... Ah, Omena's wings, they could force you to lie with them. They know you prefer men. They say your mother would do anything to save you. Then they mean to buy weapons and turn against the king and the holders to make them treat us more fairly."

Sylas's head spun with more than the zacorro. "You told them?"

Pietrig shook his head. "They guessed. They say there are ways to tell when a man sheathes the krastos to the back."

They had not guessed about Pietrig. But then Pietrig liked a beautiful girl, would flirt, steal a kiss when he got the chance. He had put up enough of a smokescreen that they had not spotted him. Or his father was powerful enough that they ignored it. Or both.

"Then I must do as they say, and so must my mother."

"No! If you stay at the Aerie you are both safe, don't you see? If you are with the changers they will have no hold on you or Zynoa." Pietrig raised a hand to cup Sylas's cheek. Sylas's skin tingled, as it always did when Pietrig touched him. "Stay away. Keep yourself safe. I would not have you or your family harmed."

"But then you will have to stay with the dig team. You will grow old before your time and cough your lungs up like an old man. I can't let you do that."

Pietrig took Sylas's face in both hands, talking urgently. "I was selected in a fair draw, but my father will get me released. He has the influence. It may take a while, but he will do it. If you came back you would dig linandra until you died."

Sylas leaned to rest his forehead against Pietrig's. Skin against skin, he felt their breathing synchronise, their shoulders rising and falling in unison. He had already decided he would never return to Namopaia, but the reality of his choice hit him.

"If I do not come back, then I never see you again."

The silence hung around them as they both considered that word: never. They had grown up together, more or less, although Pietrig had always taken the lead. Despite the differences between them—Pietrig's father never quite approved of Sylas as a suitable friend for his son—they had stuck together, supported each other. They had never dreamed their ways would be so different. Pietrig, the more advantaged, to the linandra pits and Sylas, lowest of the Chesammos, to the opulence and privilege of the Aerie.

Pietrig spoke softly. "When we were all children together, I hoped that you'd marry my sister. You know that." Simpler times, before the love of friends, of closer-than-brothers had become a physical love. Not forbidden, not exactly, but certainly shunned in a society where refusing marriage and children was a betrayal of their people.

Sylas tried to smile, but he could not ignore the sadness. "And I hoped you would marry Aithne, for all I thought her the most annoying girl in the world. Then we would truly have been brothers."

"I'm not strong enough to stand against them. I have nothing worth making a stand for. But you are. You do. You have a new life at the Aerie. Your mother would want you to stay there, no matter what it took. The Lady knows I'll miss you more than anything, but—" Pietrig's voice cracked. He shook his head and scowled, clearly annoyed at himself for showing such emotion. Some of it was the zacorro, Sylas knew, but his own throat ached with unshed tears. He craved Pietrig's lean wrestler's body next to his own. He held Pietrig tight, and his friend laid his head on Sylas's shoulder. Pietrig gave a short, bitter laugh. "Soon I'll have a wife to keep me warm at nights, imagine that. Maybe she'll even make me forget you."

So, Pietrig thought Sylas was strong. He didn't feel strong. He kissed the top of Pietrig's head and his friend lifted his face to him. The kiss they shared set Sylas's blood aflame. For an instant his thoughts flashed to Casian. How would Casian react if he found out? Casian was not faithful to him, Sylas knew. Each rumour of a new conquest cut him like a blade to his flesh. But his body responded to Pietrig, and the zacorro flowing through his veins made his blood hot with longing.

Pietrig leaned close, spoke softly in his ear. "Fienne has never had her flows. My parents fear she may be barren. No one would take her, if they knew, so they use her to tempt your father. My father knows Craie is desperate for children from your marriage, and he laughs behind his back. How stupid Craie is. How clever they are, marrying Fienne to you. They would kill me if they knew I had told you. Leave here tomorrow and stay away. Please."

Pietrig stroked his cheek. "I will miss you, but I can bear the digging team if I know you are safe and happy and being what you were meant to be. I just need you one last time." He kissed Sylas again, his mouth urgent and demanding. Pietrig slipped a hand up inside Sylas's tunic and Sylas groaned as his need grew unbearable. Pietrig loosened the ties of Sylas's breeches, fumbled with the ties of his own. They shed their tunics, and then, clad only in the caigani, they began their second wrestling bout of the day.

They grappled on the sooty ground and, as it had in the wrestling circle, ash clung to sweat-dampened bodies. There was passion, as there had been earlier, each man struggling to assert himself. But when Sylas found himself pinned by Pietrig for the second time in one day, he was glad enough to cede, and they thought of nothing but each other and their pleasure.

Sylas never understood how the village knew when it was called, but the residents came, drawn by some sort of collective consciousness. As they had the previous day, they gathered at the wrestling circle as the first rays of the sun rose over the desert.

Fienne stood there already, in a long, loose gown with her linandra bead on a thong around her neck, nestling between her breasts. If Pietrig had told the truth, she was not entitled. Only men and women fit to be married should wear the bead. But she was a pawn to be traded, as was Sylas.

Sylas's clothes were fresh off the supply wagon he had ridden to Namopaia. And he was scrubbed, his skin and hair still damp from the bucket of cold water and the rag his father had made him wash with, cleaning away the dust and grime of the night before. His parents had raised eyebrows at his disheveled and filthy appearance, but neither asked. Neither wanted to know, today of all days.

"I'll not marry," Sylas muttered as the chill water ran down his back. "I want to be a changer." And his father scowled and slapped a tunic across his ribs.

"You'll do as you're damn well told, boy. Elder Skarai is bringing his daughter to the circle this morning. You'll be there to take her hand and say the words or I'll take every strip of skin from your back."

Craie stayed icy calm during the preparations. In some ways that was worse than his temper. Craie's cold determination left Sylas more chilled than the water: chilled to his soul. Pretend all was well. Pretend his son would not prefer to lie in the arms of his bride-to-be's brother. Pretend the marriage was all both families had ever desired.

And now Sylas found himself facing Fienne across the circle, his earring glowing in the early sunshine. The Lady's energy flooded into him in joyous waves and the kye hovered on the edge of his consciousness. Their maddening chatter was a muted whisper, but it was the first time he had heard them without the pipe. Maybe he had caught the tail-end of a call from a lesson at the Aerie. The call carried a long way—much farther than the sound itself. Or perhaps he was learning to hear them for himself, his abilities increasing with time.

Fienne smiled shyly. They had been friends from childhood – if forced to marry a girl, he would have chosen her—but the nerves churned his stomach. Did she care that he loved Pietrig, or given her condition did she only think of snaring a husband, no matter what it took?

Sylas scanned the crowd. Pietrig was there; of course he was. He stood with his family, watching Fienne intently. Everything—every look, every gesture—took on a new significance after the revelation of the night before. For a moment Pietrig looked straight at Sylas, but sight of him made Sylas so heartsick that he had to look away. His mother stood with Aithne and Kael, clustered beside Pietrig's family. Catching his mother's gaze and holding it, he tried desperately to know what she was thinking, as she so often read his own thoughts. Why, when he needed to speak to her so badly, did she seem so far away?

Zynoa shook her head slowly and turned to look north. The Aerie mountaintop was barely visible in the morning light, but it was there, surrounded by swirling mists, beautiful and mystical. He belonged there. He would miss his mother, and she him, but his future lay at the Aerie. Zynoa smiled, nodded, and spread her hands, rippling her fingers to mimic the beating wings of a bird.

"Fly away," she seemed to say. "Fly away." Then she raised the linandra necklace to her lips and kissed the beads. Her blessing to him. She wanted him to follow his dream. His throat clenched. To leave her, Pietrig, all he had ever known, for good— it terrified him. When he first went to the Aerie, he believed everything would remain as he had left it—that he could return and be the old Sylas. Each visit home had shown him more clearly how wrong that belief had been. Namopaia was not enough for him anymore. He was changing, and the people he loved were staying the same; that was the tragedy.

Skarai took Fienne's hand and led her across the circle. Craie took Sylas's elbow and made to steer him to meet them in the centre, but Sylas shook his arm away.

"I'll not do it," he muttered. "I won't marry her. I don't belong here."

Craie leaned forward and hissed in his ear. "You bloody well will. You may have had a year at the Aerie but I've had a lifetime here, grubbing around at the bottom of the heap. You'll not take away my chance to rise higher. You'll marry the girl and she'll bear children if I have to father them myself."

Fienne stood opposite him now, her lips tight and narrow. From the corner of his eye he could see Pietrig, standing beside his mother and siblings. Sylas could not see the expression on his friend's face, but imagined it was much like his own: horror. Revulsion. Dread.

Sylas's heart thumped like a drum. He steadied himself and opened his thoughts to the kye he could hear just beyond his reach. Let me change, he implored the Lady. Let me change and fly away from all this. But he had marked too recently to respond to a call, even if one so distant could have reached him. He had no choice but to see this through.

Skarai whispered in Fienne's ear and she smiled anxiously and held out her hand to Sylas. He could not move. Frozen to the spot, with his blood chilling in his veins, he stared at her, stricken.

"I'm sorry," he whispered.

His father jerked his arm and pain shot through shoulder muscles strained from wrestling.

"Take it. Take her hand, damn you."

"I can't. Fienne, I can't. I'm sorry."

He had seen both men and women overcome with nerves at betrothals before. One or other often hesitated before the joining of the hands. But the villagers stirred restlessly as he stood frozen, the blood rushing in his ears.

"Please, Elder Skarai. Don't do this to her. Take her back to your wife. Say it we made a mistake. Say she refused me. Say she loves another. Please don't do this."

Fienne's lips trembled. "But I would not refuse you. You are the gentlest man in the village. I would have you as my husband before any of them. When my father asked me I agreed straight away."

His throat clenched; this would hurt her. Sylas looked across at his mother. She stood perfectly still, her face drawn and sad, but over her shoulder he could see the Aerie's peak emerging from the mists, and it was beautiful. He strained his ears for any hint of the pipe, but it did not come.

"I cannot marry you, Fienne. I will not." He raised his voice. "I will not take her, do you hear me? I will go back to the Aerie. I cannot marry. Not Fienne. Not anyone. I mean to be a changer."

"You'll do as we say, young Sylas!" Skarai said, pulling Fienne's hand out in front of her and motioning Craie to do the same. Sylas had never seen a couple's hands forcibly joined, but that was what they intended. Thoughts flashed through his head. Would it be binding, if forced upon him? It would be the elder to whom he would take any grievance, in the normal run of events, yet the elder appeared as intent on forcing the match as Craie. Of course, Sylas thought absently, he is ridding himself of a barren daughter. And he can blame her childlessness on my preference for men, and none of the shame will attach to his family.

"No," she said, her voice choking in her throat. "If he does not want me, I would not have you force him."

"He will do as he is told, girl, as will you," Skarai said. "Do you want your brother in the desert when Sylas could take his place? Your brother, who is meant to lead the village after me?"

Craie's hands were clamped around Sylas's wrist, trying to force his hand out to Fienne's. All Sylas could think was that this could not be right. How could they enforce a betrothal enacted in these circumstances? Couldn't the onlookers see that it was nothing but a sham?

He raised his voice. "They try to trick my father. The girl is barren. She has had no flows. She should never have had the bead. I will not marry her."

Silence fell. Craie's hands fell to his sides and his mouth hung open. Skarai's eyes bulged with fury, his face reddening and his hands clenching in front of him as if aching to pummel Sylas into the dust.

Fienne stared at him, her wide eyes tear-filled.

"Who—Who told you?" she said with a gasp. "They said it was a secret—that no one beyond family knew of it. How could you do this to me, Sylas? In front of everyone. Omena's wings, but I thought you cared for me a little." And she fled across the circle towards her parents' house, evading her mother's attempts to stop her. Her sobs filled the air as she ran.

Craie watched her go. When he turned back to his son, there was murder in his eyes.

CHAPTER 9

"IT IS KIND OF YOU to see me, Master Donmar."

"I think we can dispense with the formalities, Jesely," said the leader of the changer council. He poured some tea and pushed a cup towards Jesely. "Try this. It's a herb Ayriene brought back from her last journey. She hopes it will establish in the gardens, and has spared some to make me this delicious tea. She says it has calming properties. I think she's trying to tell me something."

The pair chuckled and settled back in their chairs with the familiarity of long acquaintance. Jesely of course had grown up at the Aerie, whereas Donmar had come from one of the desert villages, but despite the eight-year difference in their ages the pair had become good friends. When Jesely began the change, Donmar was well on his way to the mastery, and when Jesely joined the council, Donmar was strongly tipped as the next leader. These two, and later Cowin, strengthened the Chesammos representation on the council. Donmar had been instrumental in increasing the Aerie's food production to compensate for the reduction in tribute from the holdings.

Donmar blew across the surface of his tea and

Jesely inhaled the steam from his own cup. It had a pleasant fragrance; he could well believe it had calming effects. With luck, it would settle the nervous churning in the pit of his stomach.

"So?" Donmar prompted. "I doubt you came here to sample Ayriene's tea."

Jesely took a cautious sip before replying. "I need to talk about something that happened a long time ago. Something I should have asked about then, but I was a young man and not as good as expressing myself as I might have been."

Donmar raised an eyebrow. "Sounds ominous."

Jesely set his cup aside. "I need to know what happened to Shamella." He studied his friend, watching for any response. None came.

"Shamella? Now that was a long time ago. I'm not sure how much more I can tell you. I told you what I knew at the time."

A face danced in Jesely's memory. A young Chesammos girl, a year or so younger than him. Girls tended to come to their change later than boys, so Jesely was an apprentice and controlled changer by the time she came to the Aerie, but she caught his eye straight away. Fewer girls than boys became changers, so female changers were always in demand with the young men. Shamella captivated them all, but she won Jesely's heart.

"I need to know how she died."

This time he saw an instant of alarm before Donmar schooled his features back to their usual neutrality. "She died on a visit home. You know that."

"But what killed her? It's important."

Donmar sipped at his tea, fingers wrapped around the cup as if to warm them, although the day was mild. Jesely wondered if Donmar, like himself, was reliving Shamella's last days. Donmar had just become a master when Shamella came to the Aerie. She had no talent, but a lively disposition and a caring nature. When Donmar asked the council if he might take his first apprentice, and they agreed, he approached Shamella, who accepted his offer without hesitation. But on a visit home not long after, she had died. To the best of his knowledge, no niche had been dedicated to her on the island—almost without precedent—and her name went unmentioned, so that quickly it was as if she had never existed.

"Jesely, I—" Donmar waved a dismissive hand as if to say the matter was over and done, but Jesely interrupted him.

"I have a student. He hears many kye, as Shamella did. I need to know if that killed her—if there is anything I can do to protect him."

That got Donmar's attention. The man paused, cup halfway to his lips, then set it on the table. His hand shook as it did so, Jesely noted. So much for calming effects.

"Who is it?"

So the multiple kye was significant. "Tell me what happened."

Donmar shook his head, composure returning. "She went home. She died of an illness that had taken several others from her village. Nothing more than that."

But Jesely was an empath, and while Donmar

had been talking, he had been carefully extending tendrils of aiea-dera to read the man's reactions. Donmar lied; of that he had no doubt. So what had really happened to Shamella? And how did this affect Sylas? Then the fist of Jesely's heart gave one powerful punch against his ribs. Sylas had gone home a day or two before. It could be nothing. The timing of his visit to his village, when he had admitted to Jesely that he heard many kye in his head, might be coincidence, but that was as it had happened with Shamella. If anything happened to Sylas on his visit home, Jesely would feel responsible for the rest of his life. He had to be sure Sylas was safe.

As soon as it became clear that he would as likely get information from the Aerie's stone walls as from Donmar, Jesely left to find Sylas. He had a sudden pressing need to bring him back where he belonged.

Sylas's father hadn't made good on his threat to remove every strip of skin, but it felt like he hadn't failed by much. Craie had laid into Sylas with the blade grass switch, leaving his back bloodied and striped, his face and chest bruised where his father had used his fists when the switch finally shredded. Sylas hadn't tried to resist. He had shamed Fienne; he deserved it.

When Sylas left the village no one called or lifted a hand in farewell. Those out in the open had averted their gazes and hurried into their houses. What he had done was unforgivable, whatever the rights and wrongs of the arrangement, and although some might have some sympathy for him, he was outcast. He left without a word, although it would have pained him to speak. He suspected his nose was broken; one or two of his teeth felt loose. At least his father hadn't written a curse tablet against him. He still might, but Craie couldn't write well enough to inscribe his curse, and Sylas doubted he could raise the money to have someone else write it for him.

After the beatings, when Kael managed to persuade Craie that Sylas would die if he took much more punishment, Craie ripped the earring from Sylas's lobe and threw it in the dirt. "You said she did not deserve her bead," Craie shouted. "Said she was no true woman and should not wear it. Well, you are no true man. You are weak—have always been weak. You are not fit to wear the bead. I only wish I had never given it to you in the first place."

The pain of the wire being torn from his ear was nothing to what he had already suffered. But walking alone from the village with his shirt hanging in shreds on his back and blood running down his neck from the wreck of his earlobe—that was the worst pain of his life.

His mother pressed a water skin into his hands before he left. Craie glared coldly, but not even he would see a man go out into the desert with no water. Stumbling and shambling, his back throbbing as if he were freshly flogged with each step, Sylas knew it would be a long, agonising walk. Even fully fit, he had expected the walk back to take him several days.

He did not know how long he walked across the miles of ash and dust, but the sun passed its zenith before he slumped to the ground. Flies buzzed around him, drawn by sweat and blood. Sylas fumbled with the stopper of the water skin, hands shaking with shock and exhaustion. He allowed himself two mouthfuls only, holding the second and swilling it around his mouth. It was warm—little relief for the pain in jaw and face—but it moistened his parched tongue. He shook the skin; less than half left and the ash still stretched out before him. His water would run out before he reached the scrublands. Unless he could find plenty of swanflowers, he would be in big trouble.

Sylas tried to get to his feet. In the distance he could see the tall spiny outline of a clump of swanflower plants. At least their bitter pulp would supplement his water supply. It was also a simple treatment for cuts and stings. When one smeared the pulp over a wound, the water evaporated to leave a clear film which helped to keep flies off and dirt out. It might be too little, too late, but he would do anything to get a little relief from the pain.

He suspected once he reached their shade that he would go no farther. Even with the additional water and the meagre nourishment the pulp would offer, he was utterly spent. In the sky above him, carrion birds circled: crows and ravens and magpies, sensing death approaching. He glared up at them.

"Not yet, brothers. You shall not have me yet." But without help, he knew he would die. He ate as much of the pulp as he could keep down, then smeared more over his back, face, neck, and earlobe.

Forlornly, he stared at the mountain peak of the Aerie so far in the distance. When he did not return would they think he had decided to stay in Namopaia? He squinted up at the birds. If he had learned to control his changing, he could be up there now, although his poor physical condition meant that he would probably fly himself to death before reaching the Aerie. A bird—a hawk of some sort, he thought—made a wide arc as it circled. Bolder than the others.

Seeing if its meal was ready.

"Shoo! Go away!" Waving his arms split and cracked the congealing pulp, tearing his wounds open anew. He sobbed, fire burning the length of his back. The last things he saw was a hooked beak, designed to tear flesh, before he slid into blessed blackness.

Ayriene slumped against the infirmary wall. One of the healers brought her some bread and cheese and fruit juice, and she ate and drank automatically without tasting. Throughout the night there had been a constant stream of people to Sylas's bedside: changing dressings; giving him spoonfuls of water; checking for signs of fever. Streams of morning sunlight now poured through the room's high windows. She had watched over him all night, only now considering him truly out of danger. The food helped, but what she wanted most in the world was a bed.

How Jesely had found the boy, the Creator only knew. He had flown out, spotted him under a swanflower, and trickled the last drops of water from the semi-conscious lad's water skin between his lips before flying for Ayriene. The two of them had flown back and commandeered a wagon from the nearest village to carry him back to the Aerie.

"How is he?" Casian spoke from the door. He had been there nearly as long as Ayriene had—banished from the room itself to keep him out of the healers' way.

Ayriene jerked awake. Not the first time she'd fallen asleep propped against a wall. When a patient needed care one's own needs took second place, and food and rest had to wait.

"He'll be fine, I think," she said. She knew Casian; an Irenthi of such high standing at the Aerie hardly went unnoticed. But she couldn't understand why he was so interested in a Chesammos. "It's a good thing he knew to cover the wounds with the swanflower pulp."

One of Ayriene's first tasks when they got Sylas to the infirmary had been to strip away the tattered remains of his tunic and bathe his wounds. The swanflower pulp had dried and cracked, sticking the fabric to his skin. Gentle as the healers were, the wounds had nevertheless reopened as they worked. Still, it would have been worse without his impromptu treatment.

"He's Chesammos. He knows things like that."

She looked at him curiously. "Did Jesely tell you to wait here?"

"No. Let's just say I have an interest in him."

"Does your interest extend to sitting by his bed while I take a nap? Getting as much water as you can into him if he does wake?"

"Of course." Casian came to the bedside and looked down on Sylas's still face. "What happened out there? You and Master Jesely left in a rush and no one knew what was going on. Then when you came back it was clear Sylas was very sick, but no one would tell me anything."

Ayriene was surprised to hear a catch in his throat. Good friends then, these two. An unlikely combination, but nothing really surprised her any more, here at the Aerie.

"He was in a bad way. Drifting in and out of consciousness. He'd lost a fair bit of blood, and there wasn't much of his back left intact. It was like raw meat." She shuddered at the recollection. "When I got to him he was dehydrated. Delirious. Convinced carrion birds were coming to eat him."

Casian shuddered. "Could he have died?" His fair skin bleached whiter, all blood gone. If Ayriene hadn't been accustomed to Irenthi and their sickly pallor, she would have thought him on the verge of fainting. Maybe he was, at that.

"Yes, he could. I couldn't heal him until we'd got the wounds properly cleaned. Jesely and I had carried a few salves but there was a limit to their usefulness. We managed to get some more swanflower into him before the wagon arrived with water and my healer pack, but he could have died, certainly."

"His bastard father did this." The young man's

mouth set into a fine line.

In the wagon, Jesely had used his empath talent to send encouragement to the unconscious boy. She was sure that had kept him alive. Shock and blood loss could have killed him, if not for the mental support.

Once back, Ayriene had been able to treat him more effectively. The wounds were closed, and after a sleep she would channel more aiea-dera to heal them completely. He would have hardly a scar to show for his trauma. She had fixed his jaw, and would heal the broken nose later. She had hesitated before healing the earlobe, knowing what store the Chesammos set by their earrings, but the lobe had been a torn and bloody mess and the linandra bead nowhere to be seen. She had searched Sylas's clothing, but had not found it, so had healed the ear, figuring it would be easier to repierce it once healed rather than try to mend the flesh around an ear wire.

"If he wakes, water first, remember. Then if he seems distressed, put this powder into the water and get him to drink as much as you can."

"For the pain?"

"That, and a sedative to help him sleep. That is what he needs right now. Can I trust you with this?"

"Of course."

The healers wouldn't like it, a changer coming into their infirmary and administering remedies, but he had waited there for hours with no sign of leaving, so he might as well make himself useful. She turned the corner. A six-bed room with only four occupants. She lay on the nearest empty bed.

Just a nap, she told herself. Just a few minutes.
And she slept.

Casian waited until Ayriene left before slipping
into the chair by Sylas's bed. Sylas rested peacefully,
propped on his side with pillows supporting him.
From what Casian could see, the healers had done
a good job. Casian had seen the bloodied remains of
his shirt, and the reddened bowls of water carried
in and out. He knew it had not been pretty.

He mopped his friend's forehead with a cool cloth,
then stroked damp hair away from Sylas's face.

"You stupid bloody Chesammos," he muttered.
"I take my eyes off you for a couple of days and
look what happens. How did you manage to get
into this much trouble in your own village, for the
Creator's sake? Lucky Jesely found you." And why
Jesely had been flying over the desert road at just
the right time, Casian couldn't think. It was as if he
had known. As if fate intended him to save Sylas.
Casian shivered. Maybe that was true. Sylas had
to be there when Casian became king. He couldn't
die yet.

Casian wondered about seeings. Did the act
of seeing mean that the event would take place,
or could things still change to prevent it? He was
beginning to believe that the event was made certain
by the seeing; otherwise why would the changers
store all the fragments of past predictions? If they
had been made long ago, the chances of random
events changing the path of history were huge.

Sylas had survived; Jesely had found him;

Casian still had the possibility of the throne of Chandris in his future.

"I need you, Sylas." He found he meant it. Not just for the promise of the crown, but for Sylas's own sake. Casian had never been in love—swore he didn't know what love was—but the fear he had felt when he thought Sylas might die had made him wonder if he might not love this man.

He could not risk Sylas again. He would make Sylas go to his mother's house—keep him there until Casian could work out how the crown was to be his. If the Chesammos unrest grew, he would be out of the way—safer even than in the Aerie with its seeings and intrigues.

He thought Sylas stirred—that a ghost of a smile crossed his lips.

Casian bent to kiss Sylas's brow. "I will keep you safe, my love."

CHAPTER 10

WHEN JESELY ARRIVED, CASIAN MADE his excuses and left. Sylas had regained consciousness for a few minutes, the young Irenthi said, his face drawn. He had taken a little water and then the healers had given him more sedative to try to keep him still while Ayriene's healing took effect. Casian seemed disinclined to wait with Jesely; he excused himself to get some food and rest. Jesely was not unhappy with that arrangement. Relations had been strained between Casian and him recently, and his friendship with Sylas was only a small part. Casian considered himself ready to study for the mastery; Jesely did not. Harsh words had been exchanged on both sides and their once amicable relationship had all but fallen apart.

Ayriene slept next door. Transforming took its toll on a changer, and the healing Ayriene had managed on Sylas's beaten body sapped still more of her strength. The healers were attentive in her absence. They flitted around, always seeming busy, although Jesely could not have said exactly what they did. He felt a little purposeless, sitting by the bedside, but he felt a responsibility for the boy that he could not explain even to himself.

Maybe an hour had passed when Ayriene came to the door, bleary-eyed. She smiled when she saw him. "Anyone would think he was your apprentice, the interest you take in him."

He felt it like a punch to his chest. It had been said before that he favoured the boy, but he was drawn to him. Not just because he was Chesammos. Not just because he struggled in his studies and it came naturally to Jesely to help the less fortunate. But something else. Something Jesely could not quite identify.

"He's sleeping peacefully."

"Good." She lowered herself into a chair with a sigh.

"Still tired?"

"Sore." Ayriene stretched out arm and shoulder muscles. "Healers don't fly often, since it would mean leaving our packs behind. We're not easily parted from those."

Healers built their packs up over many years, accumulating their preferred remedies. A pack became as personal to a healer as a journal to a diarist. Ayriene's leather satchel had been new when Jesely had first known her. Now it was battered, the leather worn in patches, but she would no sooner replace it than she would set aside her own right arm. She had even been concerned about leaving it with Miralee while she flew for Sylas. Ayriene rummaged in the satchel, drawing out a small pot and removing the stopper.

"Luckily, being a healer means I always have relief to hand." She scooped out a blob of waxy salve on her first two fingers and smoothed it into shoulders and upper arms, sighing as it took effect. "Ah, that's better. Numbstem. Wonderful stuff."

"Have you eaten?"

"They are bringing something for me, I think. They said you were here, so I asked them to bring extra. I doubt you've eaten much, either." She finger-combed her hair, pulling it to her nape and twisting it up, securing it with a single pin in that women's way that always seemed somewhat magical to Jesely. "I bet I look a sight. I haven't washed in two days."

"I'll watch him while you bathe and change, if you want."

"I might take you up on that. I'd feel better if I could get clean." She studied him. "So are you going to tell me why you were flying so near his village? If I didn't know you better I'd think your personal interest in him was getting a little... unhealthy."

How to tell her he had been drawn there by memories of a woman long dead?

"I don't know. Lucky I did, though." He shifted uncomfortably under her stare. She didn't believe him. By the Lady, would he be the subject of gossip now? He would have to come up with a better reason for being in the right place at the right time.

Ayriene tucked the pot of salve back in her pack, wiping her greasy fingers on her clothes. Then she pulled a torn piece of parchment from the pack's front pocket. "I'd almost forgotten about this."

The side of the parchment facing Jesely had odd fragments of words, one marred by a large ink blot. Ayriene looked at the reverse, though, a thoughtful expression on her face.

"What's that?"

She handed it to him. The parchment was torn from top to bottom, and there were traces of writing—if one could call it that—near the ripped edge. The hand was childish and clumsy. In contrast, the pictures drawn in the margin were of the highest quality.

"That one on the top—that's a medelerinn. We use it to help with mild pains. I don't recognise the other. It doesn't seem to be in my herbal. It's likely of no medicinal value. I wish I could show you the pictures of medelerinn in the commonly used herbals. They are so crude compared with this. I could give this picture to anyone—even the newest apprentice healer—and they could find the plant from it. The ones in the herbals are barely recognisable."

"Who did them?"

Ayriene shook her head. "I don't know. Miralee found the parchment left on a table in the library and gave it to me when I left my pack with her. It went out of my mind, with Sylas and all. Miralee knows Adwen and I had talked of rewriting the herbals to include the plants that have been brought from the mainland in the last few years, common names, Chesammos names, that sort of thing." She paused, biting her lip and her mouth twisting as she tried to hold back tears. The loss of her son still showed on her face. When she spoke again, her voice thickened with grief. "Miralee thinks it might take my mind off things. I had given up on the idea—it wouldn't be the same without Adwen— but with someone who could give me illustrations like these, it might be worth it."

"If Miralee found it in the library, then Gwysias might know. There's not much happens in there that he's not aware of."

"That's a good idea, but I won't get away from here today. If Sylas is going to succumb to fever it will happen soon, and I need to give his back more healing now that I have recovered. It will scar if left too long."

"I'll go. I need to talk to Gwysias anyway."

Jesely had a fair idea who might have drawn the pictures. At least, he had a good idea whose scrawling writing it was—Gwysias had complained about Sylas's penmanship often enough. But Sylas had never given any indication of any artistic talent. Jesely imagined his lessons gave him little opportunity to show it off, since they centred around more academic pursuits. The boy must be a natural artist, if they were by him, for the Chesammos had little use for drawing. And if the drawings *were* Sylas's work, and if Ayriene was looking for an illustrator for her book... Jesely's hopes rose. He had never approached Ayriene about Sylas, although the Lady knew he had asked nearly all the masters if they would take him as apprentice. He had assumed she would be looking for someone with an aptitude for healing, if she ever took on another youngster. Ayriene would be perfect. She was used to dealing with teenage boys and able to teach him a trade he could follow even if he were not allowed to stay in the Aerie. When he left Sylas's bedside, Jesely felt a lot more optimistic about the boy's future than he had in a very long time.

꩜

Jesely spotted Gwysias on the path alongside the library. An unremarkable man, the small, grey-haired master split his time between the library and the scriptorium, where he oversaw copying of precious books and taught penmanship to novices. No book eluded his notice, and there were few references he couldn't find. His arms were overloaded with parchment rolls, books, and brushes, and as usual his spindly fingers were ink-smudged.

Jesely fell into step beside him. Gwysias gave him no greeting but Jesely did not take it amiss. The scribe spent much of his time deep in thought.

"A moment of your time, Master Gwysias."

"If it's about young Sylas you're wasting your time, Jesely. Boy's a lost cause."

Jesely faltered, stopping in his tracks and staring after the shorter man, before trotting to catch up. "What do you mean?"

"What I said. Might as well stop trying; spend time on someone more deserving. The boy is irredeemably stupid."

"When did you start to learn to read and write, Gwysias? How many languages do you speak?"

"I? Just Irenthi, of course. What else would I speak? And as for reading and writing—well, I suppose six or seven years of age. Why? What has that to do with Sylas?"

"The boy's father actively tried to prevent him learning. He had scarcely any education before coming here, and yet see how fast he has picked things up. When he speaks to you in Irenthi, do you notice any errors in his grammar? Is his vocabulary lacking? His native tongue is Chesammos, you know, so he is speaking his second language, to say nothing of reading and writing in it. And yet you think him irredeemably stupid?"

Gwysias grunted, unconvinced. "Still, you spend too long with that one. I know you feel some kinship with the boy, him being Chesammos, but Casian needs some attention. It's not just me who's commented on it."

The barb stuck, lodged in the space between Jesely's conscience and his better nature.

He had neglected Casian recently; he knew that. The Irenthi had been a pleasant enough boy, but the adult he was becoming made Jesely deeply uneasy. Changers served, seeking no personal advancement. If they took on high office, it was to enable them to serve more completely. But Casian had been raised as heir to the second most powerful house on Chandris; ambition and intrigue were in his blood. Sylas was a wounded bird, desperately fluttering towards a better life for himself and his loved ones. Casian would thrive with or without Jesely. Sylas needed him.

"Do you really need to switch him? He is doing the best he can."

Gwysias sniffed. "He is lazy. He lacks application."

"He is raw and untutored and he uses the wrong hand to write with, but I'll not believe he is lazy. All the other masters say he tries hard at the tasks he is set."

"If he wants to stay among us he needs a basic level of education; you know that as well as anyone. But I cannot make a swan out of a sparrow, and as it stands you would be better off seeing that he achieves control and sending him home."

"That appears to be out of the question, after what has happened."

Gwysias stopped abruptly. "What has happened?"

For a moment Jesely regretted his hasty words, but the Aerie was a close-knit community, and even if the changers could be trusted to hold their tongues, there were servants who could not. Chances were that the story of Sylas's arrival had already spread, and that only Gwysias's naturally cloistered existence had stopped him hearing the news.

"He came back from his piercing ceremony beaten half to death. It's only thanks to Ayriene's talent that he still lives."

Gwysias let out a long low whistle, then pursed his lips and nodded. "The lad's options are closing around him, it seems. What if he cannot be trained, Jesely? The council are running out of options."

Jesely nodded. "Burning, which I doubt Ayriene would agree to, or blood elder for the rest of his life, which can't be allowed to happen for all the usual reasons. He has already marked for longer than I'm entirely happy with. He may have several years before the worst of the side-effects begin, but begin they will, and then his life will become increasingly uncomfortable."

"I still don't understand why you spend so much time with him and neglect your own apprentice so shamefully. I mean, I know that we need to encourage Chesammos to stay—they are the source of our communication with the Lady, after all." He honoured Jesely by using the Chesammos term for Mount Eurna. "But is this one lad worth all the work you are putting into him? Everyone notices how much he has your favour. It is not just me asking questions, Jesely. Many others wonder what is so special about Sylas that you spend so much of your time and effort on his behalf."

Jesely closed his eyes. It was so hard to explain, but the boy had something about him. Something that flitted on the edge of Jesely's mind like a thought half-forgotten.

"He says he hears many kye," Jesely said at last, reluctant to break a confidence. "I have not heard of anyone who claimed that since Shamella."

"Shamella," said Gwysias. "That explains it, at least a little. But she is dead, Jesely. I know you and she were close, but you must not let what happened to her cloud your judgement."

"If this lad has the same ability—or handicap— as she, I want to understand it, if I can. Try to save him from the same fate that befell her, if indeed it was the kye that caused her death."

Jesely had hoped he might marry Shamella someday. His family had stayed purebred through three generations of changers and he had hoped to continue the tradition. Her loss so young had been a tragedy, and for all Donmar's evasion, Jesely was sure he knew more than he was telling. If this was something that afflicted Chesammos changers, even only once in a generation, the Aerie should understand it.

"Please, Gwysias, if you know anything about Shamella's death, tell me. I worry for Sylas."

Gwysias shook his head, but to Jesely's empath senses it seemed he had softened somewhat. An air of sympathy surrounded him. "I know no more than you. I have never been on the council, so if anything was discussed in meetings about her then I never heard it. But I will help the boy, if I can, for her sake and yours. If he deserves a switching he will get one, mind, or I do an injustice to all the other novices who have received a stripe or two from me over the years."

Jesely pulled the parchment from his belt. He was sure he knew the answer, but he asked the question anyway.

"Before you go, do you know who drew this?"

Gwysias scowled, wagging his finger in mock rebuke. "You sweet-talk me into treating your pet better and then you go and remind me of one of his recent misdemeanours. It is Sylas's work, as you might tell from the daubings beside it. And, yes, I did punish him for it. Why do you ask?"

"Because it might give him the future he needs," said Jesely. He had the oddest impulse to hug Master Gwysias, but imagined the landslide of books and brushes that would result and limited himself to a quick grasp of the forearm instead. Yes, this unlikely talent of Sylas's might be his salvation.

"I've hardly seen you in the last week," said

Miralee, throwing herself into a comfortable chair in her mother's bedchamber. She pulled a cushion from behind her back, landed two sound punches on its feathered middle and replaced it, leaning back with a sigh. "That's better."

"I've been busy. And you've not been about much yourself, I gather." Ayriene had slept soundly the previous night, going to bed before sundown and not waking until the Aerie had been about its business for a good two hours.

"I heard. A novice, wasn't it?" Until a few days before Miralee had been a novice herself, but Mistress Yinaede had ended several years without an apprentice to take her on.

"Sylas. Chesammos lad. You know him?"

"To nod to. Garyth knows him, I think."

Ayriene lay sprawled on her bed, her hair loose about her shoulders, damp from her bath. Never had hot water felt better. She had fallen into bed dirty and aching, but the bath had worked miracles. She hoped the food that should be on its way from the kitchen would complete the transformation.

"How are your lessons going?"

"Better now."

Ayriene caught the implication that all had at some point not been well, and raised an eyebrow. "Now?"

"Probably me overreacting." Miralee tossed her hair back over her shoulder in a dismissive gesture.

"But?"

"But... well, Casian started coming to Mistress Yinaede's classes a while ago."

That was strange. "He's not a seer, is he?"

Miralee pulled a face. "He's a talent, but no one knows quite what his talent is. Mistress Yinaede didn't want him there. She suggested he pay you a visit to see if he was a healer. At least that would keep him away from me for a while. He could sit too close to *you* and see how you reacted."

She forced herself to sound calm. "Has Casian shown an interest in you?"

An expression of horror crossed her face. "Mother! An interest?"

"You know what I mean. He's an attractive man, and he's not averse to using his attraction. He's involved with Sylas, but he also doesn't seem to place too much importance on faithfulness, from what I'm hearing."

"Sylas is welcome to him. He makes my skin crawl. I told Mistress Yinaede I didn't like him near me and she moved our lessons to the library. He must know what we've done, and why, but he's never asked. Too proud, I expect. You know what the Irenthi are like."

Casian was the only Irenthi Miralee knew, but Ayriene let it slide. "At least Yinaede took it seriously."

A knock sounded at the door. Miralee answered it, taking a tray of food from an Irmos servant and setting it on the bed.

Ayriene patted the covers. "There's plenty for two. Sit here and help me with it."

Miralee perched next to her and smeared butter thickly on a piece of still-warm bread. "Yes, she was good about it. I don't think she likes Casian much either. Anyway, there's a part of the library where the seeings are recorded—seeings and parts of seeings. Yinaede showed me how and where to record mine—the one I told you about, with the man who looked like Casian, and the Chesammos."

"I remember. That can't have taken you long, though. Garyth says you've been shut in there for hours at a time."

"There's more to it than simply recording. It's part of the seers' job to try to piece them together—link them up and make sense of them. It's fascinating."

"So did you link anything with your seeing?"

Miralee beamed. "Yes! That made me feel so much better. Just knowing that other seers recorded the same event I did makes me more confident that it wasn't just a weird dream. And that it's important, you know? All the other seeings about it were old—twenty, thirty years ago, some of them—but they fitted. Same Irenthi with the linandra crown. Same Chesammos man and girl."

"Girl?" Ayriene hadn't heard that part.

"Yes. She was there in mine, but I didn't see her well. She was more of a feeling, if you know what I mean. I thought she might be Chesammos or dark Irmos, and the other seeings describe her as Chesammos. The fragments we found thought the king might be Deygan—they were seen before he became king—but Yinaede says they can't be since I've had the same seeing. People only see things forwards in time, she says, never backwards. Makes sense, I suppose. What use would it be to see things that have already happened?" She hesitated, making a face like someone eating sour fruit. "I still think he looked a lot like Casian, but I don't like the thought of that roach becoming king."

"Deygan is healthy, and he has three sons. One of them will follow him. Jaevan, Creator willing. He will make a fine king. Did the other fragments shed no light?"

"A little. One of them said they had heard the Chesammos man say 'You cannot hold your throne without me' and 'Without me you will fall. You need me.' That's odd, don't you think? How could a Chesammos help an Irenthi hold the throne? I wonder if I'll ever know what it was about. I expect a lot of seers never know why they saw what they did." She seemed a little morose at the thought. "They said the Chesammos was clean-shaven too, so I think he must be a changer, don't you?"

If the Irenthi were Casian, Ayriene reasoned, then that could make Sylas the Chesammos. But how would he be in a position to help a king, and how would Casian have come to be king in the first place? She shook her head. Miralee was right. Chances were neither of them would ever know the circumstances of the conversation. She made a mental note to talk to Jesely about it, and settled back as Miralee reminisced about Adwen. For the first time in ages, Ayriene's thoughts were with a teenage boy who was not her lost son.

"What news?" The man's voice was gruff, hoarse from being caught in a vent during an eruption in his youth. He had escaped with his life—he had been young and strong then—but his voice had never recovered and it still hurt him to eat or drink. Only sheer determination to bring down the Irenthi made him carry on, made him keep fighting when every day was a struggle to overcome pain.

"Namopaia are with us," said another, younger man, his skin showing the effects of being one of a dig team. "We sent Neffan to wrestle at a wedding there and he made contact with their rebels."

"Any fighters among them?"

The second man snorted. "You know Namopaia. It's a wonder they have committed at all, although I get the impression most of the village are unaware or pretending it's not happening."

"So we aren't likely to get anyone willing to take direct action from there." Hoarse-voiced man coughed, doubling over at the pain it caused him. "Damn me, but it's bad again. The Lady grant I live to see our efforts rewarded."

"Maisaiea-yelai," the other echoed, bringing his fingertips together in the sign of the mountain.

"What other news?"

"Sennak and Diprit have gone to the city. They heard news of a sympathetic linandra singer who will cut the stones and trade them for us—for a price. If he proves reliable, they will bring back whatever weapons the stones have bought."

A grunt of satisfaction. "Good. Anything else?"

"We have been talking, Sennak and Diprit and I. What about the feast day of Deygan's ascension? If we could attack the procession, maybe kill Deygan or one of his sons, then even if we died in the attempt they couldn't cover it up. The Irenthi would have to take notice. And it's a few months off yet—gives us time to gather arms, make plans."

Silence settled while hoarse-voiced man digested this thought. "Would that lose us followers? There is much love for Deygan and his family among the Irmos. He has provided well for them. You need only look at how many of our young people marry outside our race. They believe they are better off having Irmos children."

"But it would show we mean business," the younger man said, his eyes shining with zeal. "What does it matter if we have weapons if we don't intend to use them? A guardsman here, a minor lordling there—it will all come to nothing unless we can show Chandris that we are not to be ignored."

He had always thought himself an opponent of the Irenthi, this gravel-voiced veteran of the mines, but the thought of killing children sickened him. Yet with their boys up for selection for the pits once they had their earring, and the earring being given earlier and earlier in an attempt to bolster their numbers, what were many of the lads sent to the pits but children themselves? They died the slow death of the linandra digger. At least Deygan's boys would die quickly, maisaiea-yelai.

He nodded slowly.

"See to it," he said.

CHAPTER 11

WITH THE CHANGER COUNCIL CONVENING, Jesely was concerned to see Master Olendis waiting outside the chamber. A changer could attend part of a meeting in order to contribute, but would then leave so the council could speak freely on the other topics on the agenda. Jesely could only conclude that while he had been concerned with Sylas's recovery, Olendis had raised the subject of the problem novice with Donmar, who had promised to bring it before the council.

The main item on the agenda was the planned visit to the Aerie by King Deygan and Prince Jaevan. Most kings, and high holders before them, had kept to the business of ruling Irenthi holdings, and left the Aerie to itself. Deygan, by contrast, tried to restrict the Aerie's power, reducing the changers' perceived importance in the eyes of the holders. With the tributes reduced, the Aerie relied on what the changers could grow on the mountaintop or catch in the lake, or what they produced on the few farms the Aerie owned outright. With that, and the money brought in by masters tutoring the children of nobility (both from Chandris and overseas), they managed to feed and clothe themselves and send any extra to the desert Chesammos. If Deygan meant to exert more control over the Aerie's operations, that could mean increased hardship for the desert dwellers. With rumours reaching the Aerie of skirmishes between Chesammos malcontents and Lord Garvan's men, Deygan was unlikely to look with favour on their continued shipments of food and clothing into the desert.

They spent much of the afternoon considering Deygan's likely strategies. Despite the seriousness of the debate, Jesely found his attention wandering to the master sitting outside. His presence had to be bad news for Sylas. If he failed to change for a time, the trauma of recent events could be blamed, but Olendis's patience grew thin. Nausea rose in Jesely's stomach. He had the feeling Sylas was running short of time.

When he was called in, Master Olendis recounted the events of three days before Sylas's trip home, when he had once again tried and failed to transform.

"I have given him ample opportunity. The boys who joined around the same time all learned in the usual timespan. Only Sylas has failed to transform even once," the elderly master concluded, licking his lips nervously and looking around the table.

"Are we certain the boy is even a changer?" That was Fennoc the herbalist, a fair Irmos.

"He had the physical symptoms," said Jesely, "and from his description of the aiea and the kye, I believe he has the ability."

"He could have heard the others talk about these things," Olendis observed sourly. "Maybe the boy has been hoodwinking us all this time."

"I don't believe he would have endured the beating he did in order to come back, if he was faking," observed Ayriene dryly.

"Is there any precedent for a late change among Chesammos? We know girls often change later than boys. Do Chesammos boys change later than other boys? Learn control more slowly?" Fennoc again.

"Girls change later, but then learn at the same sort of speed. Maybe faster. This applies across the races. We would expect girls to have control within a year of their change." Olendis had taught several female novices; he knew what he was talking about. "As for Chesammos, we have some here. Shall we ask them?"

"I changed at thirteen," said Donmar. "I had controlled the change and been apprenticed by fourteen. Cowin here was exceptional; in fairness, we can't compare Sylas with him. He changed first at nine, but I've never heard of another child of any race changing that early."

"Master Jesely?" Olendis turned to him. "When did you change?"

Jesely squirmed in his seat. It felt like a betrayal when he said, "Much like everyone else. Thirteen, fourteen, and it took me three or four months. Sylas was a little late even showing signs of the change. But I was raised here. I grew up hearing talk about changing." It sounded a poor excuse even to him, and he thought he caught a hint of pity in the faces around him. Many of the council members knew he had been mentoring Sylas.

"So what do you recommend, Olendis?" asked Donmar.

"It is not for me to decide the fate of a novice, but if you were to ask me if he would ever learn to change, I would have to say it looks unlikely. Not only that, but the boy doesn't even have the wits to come up with a convincing excuse. If he could not hear the kye at all I might believe him, but this story of hearing many kye voices. Utter nonsense."

Jesely had shifted his gaze to Donmar's face when Olendis spoke of the kye, and he saw it where others did not: a twitch of the cheek and an involuntary glance, first at Jesely and then at Cowin. Cowin's hands were clenched into fists. A muscle twitched in his cheek.

"What do we know about the boy? What is his background?" Cowin's voice was strained.

Master Donmar raised a hand from the table. "This isn't the place for that line of questioning. Unless you have some particular insight, I fail to see what his background will reveal. What we need to decide now is what to do with him."

Cowin subsided, but Jesely could tell the answer left him dissatisfied. Cowin definitely had more interest than Jesely could account for.

"Sylas has faced extreme opposition from his father," said Jesely, "and he lost his brother only a few months ago. Could he have raised some sort of mental barrier to changing?"

"That sounds like your line of work, Ayriene." Donmar deferred to the only healer at the table.

Jesely gripped the edge of the table. He was not

sure it would do Sylas any good to have the council think him mentally unstable in some way, but it might make Donmar defer the suggestion Jesely knew he worked towards.

"Ailments of the mind are difficult," she said slowly. "There is little we can do with herbs except administer calming draughts. I cannot use my talent on such sicknesses. Without a physical injury to treat I am a mere herbalist, like any common healer. There is nothing my kye can help me repair. Even if it were true that he resisted the change, there would be little I could do."

Jesely took in a deep breath. He had known that, of course. One changer several years ago had become so disturbed in her mind soon after the birth of her first child that she tried to throw herself off one of the towers. Ayriene had given her sedatives of the sort she mentioned, but had been unable to heal her with the talent. The woman recovered several months later, but was so shaken by it all that she had not dared to have another child, blaming the birth for her sudden instability.

Ayriene continued. "There may be repercussions from the past few days, but he shows little sign of trauma. In fact, he has proved remarkably resilient. He is sitting up when he is able, talking with visitors. Casian spends a lot of time with him."

"Yet there is another way to make the boy safe if he cannot control the change," said Donmar, "and it is one to which we must give serious consideration."

"I know where this is leading, and I would oppose such a move," said Jesely. "If he cannot change with the pipe then he is in no danger of changing to a call not intended for him. To make doubly certain, he can continue to mark as he has done between flights up to now."

"If the boy were an exceptional student, then maybe that would have been a possibility, Jesely," said Donmar. "But he shows no particular aptitudes. In fact Master Gwysias has come to me several times complaining of his lack of application. Personally, I know what I would do, although it is an extreme step to take."

Several of the council shuffled uneasily. Burning the ability from a changer was indeed an extreme step. The process involved all the aiea-bar a changer could hold being channelled through that part of another changer's mind that accessed the kye. Even the changers did not understand fully how it worked, and as such it held many risks. It would keep Sylas safe from involuntary changing, or from answering any calls that he might hear from the Aerie or elsewhere, but it would be an admission of failure. Their failure, not his. Failure to teach him to use his skills safely.

Jesely thumped the table with his fist. "We cannot do that! It was always a solution of last resort, even when there were changers who knew how to do it safely. How can we justify doing it to a boy whose only crime is learning more slowly than we would like?"

Donmar leaned forward. "The only other changer who could hear many kye died suddenly, as you yourself pointed out to me. What if burning him would save him from this fate?"

Jesely read Donmar as the leader spoke. Not

his thoughts—no empath could do that—but his emotions, his reactions. He was frightened. Of Sylas?

"And what then? Send him home to a father who beat him so badly he could have died on the journey home?" Jesely did not want to be the one to tell the boy that he had to return to Namopaia.

"We could keep him on here. Hire him as a stable hand or a kitchen boy or something. Something that suits his abilities," suggested Fennoc.

At least he was sympathetic to the boy in his own way, Jesely thought. But while others who could change laboured at the Aerie—Ayriene's own son Garyth worked in the gardens—turning a potential changer into a kitchen boy struck Jesely as little more than scandalous. Still, rumbles of agreement circled the table, several masters turning to discuss this suggestion with their neighbours.

Ayriene's voice broke through the discussions. "You said that the boy had no aptitude, Master Donmar. I believe you are wrong. Jesely, do you have the parchment?"

He did. He had it tucked in his belt pouch, entirely forgotten. He pulled it out, waving it toward Ayriene.

"Yes! It was him. It was Sylas did this. You say he has no aptitude for anything, but look at how the boy can draw!"

Donmar protested that drawing was of no use to the Aerie. Maybe they could find someone in need of a draughtsman in Banunis or Adamantara, but first the boy must be burned. Jesely found himself in the grips of a wild optimism. Ayriene had not volunteered to apprentice Sylas, but had prompted Jesely to show the pictures. Would she take him? Use him for this herbal of hers? Jesely prayed so.

Cowin slipped away after the meeting before Jesely could confront him. Something was going on that Jesely didn't understand: something that affected Sylas. People were keeping secrets, and Jesely didn't like secrets.

"Are you meant to be up?" Casian rushed to Sylas's side, grasping his forearm. Sylas was still wobbly after days spent confined to bed, but he shook off Casian's support.

"I can do it. I just got up too fast and my head started spinning."

"But what are you doing up at all? Did Mistress Ayriene say it was all right?"

Casian guided him back to the bed and Sylas sat. He just needed to take it a little slower, that was all. He'd be fine. "Of course. You don't think I'd be disobeying my mistress this soon after she took me on, do you? I'll wait till I'm outside the gates at least." He grinned.

My mistress. Sylas said the words over in his head. *My mistress.* True, when he had thought about it, he had always imagined he would be saying "my master," but to be apprenticed to Mistress Ayriene was better than he had ever dreamed. The only healer talent in the whole of Chandris had apprenticed him. He wanted to pinch himself to make sure he wasn't dreaming.

"So it's true then? I heard it in the refectory just

now, but I told myself not to listen to idle chatter. That my good friend Sylas wouldn't have me find out from gossip. That he'd want to tell me himself."

Casian's hurt tone was a punch to the stomach. "I was going to tell you myself. That's why I'm up—to come and find you. They'd taken my old clothes away, and no one had thought to leave any fresh. It took them a while to fetch some from my room and—"

"Doesn't matter." Casian waved a dismissive hand. "I just wanted to be sure you weren't jumping to any stupid decisions."

Sylas wasn't sure what reaction he'd expected from Casian. He had hoped that his friend would be pleased for him. Supportive would have been even better. He would be learning a trade, seeing parts of the island he had never visited—maybe going to the mainland, if Mistress Ayriene wanted it. But he would come back. He hoped Mistress Ayriene would continue trying to teach him to fly. Master Olendis might have given up on him, but Sylas was convinced he could learn, if only those voices in his head would quieten. Then maybe he could fly back to see Casian from time to time.

He hadn't expected Casian to call his decision to accept her offer 'stupid.'

"But you know it's all I've ever wanted."

"To traipse around the island drawing plants? Since when? You never mentioned that as your ambition before."

Casian was so much smarter than him, so much quicker. If they got into an argument Sylas would likely end up agreeing that black was white before he knew what had hit him.

"To be apprenticed to a master. To be taught to manage the transformation. To be with someone with enough patience to actually help me to transform. The Lady knows Master Olendis won't, but I think Mistress Ayriene might."

"Ayriene." Casian's lip curled. "You know she lost a son about your age not so long ago? You'll find yourself with a mother, not a teacher, if you go along with her."

"That's rubbish. There's not one person in the Aerie who would believe she was trying to use me to replace her son." The look on Ayriene's face when she had spoken of Adwen had resembled the one his mother had worn after Lynto. He thought Ayriene brave to take him on, and was determined to do his best to deserve her trust in him.

"Do you really think this is the right thing to do?"

"Yes!" Sylas took Casian's hand and stared intently into his face. "I think it's *exactly* the right thing to do. I will learn a trade. I won't have to go back to Namopaia, and I can learn to be a changer without Aerie tutors on my back. Maybe I'm just slow. Maybe it will all come if I can give it time. It's perfect for me, can't you see that?"

"But what about me?"

"I'll miss you, but I won't be gone forever. We'll come back to the Aerie every now and then—I asked Mistress Ayriene about that—and I'll be safe, don't you see? I worried they would send me away. Now my future is secured." The threat of dismissal had always hung over Sylas. But Casian looked so lost at the prospect of him leaving that Sylas wondered for the first time if he *had* done the right thing in accepting.

"I made those arrangements for you, and you ignored them. You would be safe at my mother's house and we could see each other whenever we wanted." Sylas hesitated at the slight note of petulance in Casian's voice. He was used to getting his own way, Sylas reminded himself. He answered more softly, tried to sound as persuasive as he could.

"And I'd be a servant all my life. I'd never learn to change or make anything of myself. Just learn how to carry a tray and serve wine. If it doesn't work out then I can go to your mother's, but this way I have the chance to be someone on my own account, without always relying on you and your family's favour."

Casian stood. "Fine. But when you come back the offer might not still be open."

"What?"

"If you can go off with Ayriene so bloody easily then maybe I don't mean as much to you as I thought I did."

"Don't say that." Sylas stood also. He tried to embrace Casian, kiss him to show him how much he cared, but Casian pushed him away.

"You won't get around me that way."

"You're being unfair—thinking only of yourself."

"*I'm* thinking only of myself. When it's you saying you want to 'be someone' and 'make something of yourself.'" Casian sneered his words back at him. "You're a Chesammos. There's only so much can be made of a Chesammos." And he turned on his heels and stalked out.

The words hit Sylas like a face full of cold water. He knew Casian used words to wound, make people change their minds and agree to what he wanted. There had been something else, too. When Casian stared him down, it had been like fingers squeezing his skull and a voice whispering inside him that he should do as Casian said. That he wanted to. That it would be best for him.

Was he being selfish? He hadn't thought of it that way, but maybe he was. Deep inside he held the conviction that he would not be content as Casian's mother's servant unless he had no other options. His only route to self-respect was to have some measure of status on his own account. He would never have Casian's titles, but he wanted to be more than just a whore, kept in the household for Casian's benefit. What would happen to him when Casian married to breed heirs for his house? How would a wife react to Sylas's place in her husband's affections? No, he had to follow this course, whatever the result.

Even if it meant losing him?

That thought came close to breaking his heart.

CHAPTER 12

SYLAS ATE HIS EVENING MEAL in the refectory, sitting at one of the long trestle tables with some of the other novices. He hoped he looked more at ease than he felt; he was never entirely comfortable around the other youngsters. Set apart by race or ability, he always had something to be awkward about, slights to be taken whether intended or not. But soon he would be on his way. Mistress Ayriene had been happy with his progress, and they were to leave in two days. His few belongings were packed and ready. He just hoped he could reconcile with Casian before he went.

The Irenthi had left the Aerie shortly after his conversation with Sylas, and Master Jesely was livid. Rumour had it he had gone home to Lucranne to see his father this time, not the mother in whose service he planned to place Sylas. Once their changing was controlled, apprentices and journeymen were allowed occasional trips home, but leaving without permission was a breach of protocol which Jesely would not readily overlook.

"Good evening, Sylas. May I join you?"

A dark-skinned man stood opposite him, across the table. He swung his legs over the long bench, reached for a bread roll, and tore off a chunk. Lifting it to his nose, he sniffed appreciatively.

"I missed fresh bread on my travels. I lived for so long on waybread and what passes for bread on the mainland that even the overcooked stuff they serve you youngsters seems good. You'll find the same on your own travels, I daresay. Nothing like fresh-made Aerie bread."

Sylas knew who he was; how could he not? There were not so many Chesammos masters that he would not know Master Cowin, if only by name and reputation. He had been in the Aerie briefly when Sylas first joined, then had gone off on one of the journeys so many masters seemed to take to further their knowledge of the world or changer lore. He had returned to marry Mistress Elyta, and the match had set the Aerie buzzing.

Sylas bowed as best he could sitting at the refectory table. All he could do was incline his head and make the sign of the Lady, forefingers and thumbs pressed together, and hope that Cowin understood what he intended by it. The other novices nudged each other, gathered up the remains of their meals, and left.

"Forgive me for interrupting your meal," said Cowin. "I have been hearing a lot about you."

Hearing a lot about him? Not much complimentary, he would guess. Around them, people cast covert glances in their direction. Masters ate on the dais or in their rooms, not in the lower refectory. Sylas fidgeted. He didn't like being the subject of scrutiny.

"You caused quite a stir, you know, coming

back in the state you did." Cowin popped a piece of bread into his mouth and spoke around it. "And I expect you're still the talk of your village. Where are you from, boy?"

He would never have called him 'boy' with the bead in his ear, but Mistress Ayriene's healing had worked so well there was no sign it had never been pierced. Sylas fought down a feeling of mistrust. There was no good reason Sylas could think of for Master Cowin's interest. He didn't know what made him lie to the master, but lie he did.

"Cellondora, Master." The village Pietrig had mentioned as at the heart of the rebellion.

"Cellondora, eh?" Cowin's dark eyes were penetrating and Sylas had the uneasy feeling that Cowin knew he was not telling the truth. "What was your birth name?"

Few at the Aerie realised that the names used by Chesammos were not their full names. Full Chesammos names were rarely used except on ceremonial occasions. A male child's name was chosen by his mother, female by her father. All were shortened, the first part of the name typically taken for everyday use.

Should he give Master Cowin his real name? Casian would urge caution, but the Irenthi smelled deceit on everyone. Surely Master Cowin would mean him no harm.

"Erden-sylassan, Master."

"Erden?" Cowin looked thoughtful. "Interesting that you go by Sylas, then."

Sylas hesitated. "My name was picked by my mother, but my father... My father would not have me use it."

"And he didn't like Erden because...?"

Sylas was not sure, exactly. He had grown up being called Sylas—was used to it. No one queried why he used his secondary name rather than his first. The first was usually in deference to some male relative, or person to whom his parents owed a debt. He had wondered who this Erden might be, but both his mother and his father became tight-lipped when he asked, and soon he learned not to ask.

"I believe there was someone of that name whom he did not much like, Master." That was as close as he had ever come to the truth.

"I can believe that." Sylas was not sure Cowin was aware he had spoken aloud. Then, more urgently, he asked, "And you are not a talent?"

"No, Master." He was scarcely a changer, far less a talent. Cowin's face showed his disappointment, and Sylas felt his shortcomings keenly. He had let the master down in some way he could not guess. "I am sorry."

"You have brothers and sisters?" With the current Chesammos emphasis on producing many offspring, that was a reasonable assumption.

"A sister."

"Just one?" That disappointment again.

He nodded slightly. "I had a brother. He died several months ago. There was to have been one between my brother and me, but the baby came too early." And so didn't count, by the Chesammos reckoning. Another thing for Craie to hold against Zynoa.

"Your sister. She is older? Younger?"

"Older, Master. By two years."

Cowin gnawed his lip. "Probably too old to show signs then. She is not a changer? Did not come to the Aerie while I was away?"

"No, Master."

"So there are none in this generation," Cowin muttered. "But She is quiet, for now. That may not be of consequence. There may be grandchildren yet. They may come in time to save us." He roused himself, aware of Sylas's curious gaze on him. "Your mother, is she well?"

Sylas's mother was always a mystery to him. Clearly not from Namopaia originally, she had no family nearby. While his friends had cousins by the armful, Sylas had only those on his father's side. He knew nothing of his grandparents on her side: nothing at all. Now, looking at Cowin, he wondered.

A forbidden love?

Sylas felt sick. Could she have been sent away for loving someone her family deemed unsuitable? He had often thought there must be something secretive about her marriage. Why would she accept Craie, much less travel far from her home to take him? Could Cowin have been the reason?

"She is well, Master. Thank you."

No, it couldn't be. He studied the master more closely than he had had opportunity to do before. His mother was approaching her fortieth year, and had been married at nineteen or twenty. Cowin did not look more than twenty-eight, thirty at the outside. That would have made him a child when

Zynoa married. Even if Sylas had underestimated by a year or two, Cowin still would have been too young for his mother to look at in that way.

Master Cowin rose to go. Sylas got to his feet too, grateful that the master was leaving, aware of the curious faces wondering what they had been speaking about.

"If you see your mother..." Cowin caught himself, bit back the words he had been about to say. "Work hard, young Erden-sylassan. Work hard and achieve your potential."

As Master Cowin left the dining hall, Sylas stared after him, once more running through the numbers in his head. Could Cowin be so much older than he appeared? He had waited longer than most men to marry. Maybe he had held onto the last crumbs of hope that long. The son of his lost love appearing in the halls of the Aerie as a novice might well have been enough to make him accept that what was past was gone. Had he married Elyta, finally accepting that Zynoa was beyond his grasp? The idea made Sylas feel ill.

Conversation resumed once the master was gone. Casian would hear of this; he would want to know what Master Cowin had asked Sylas. Ambition and pride drove Casian. Whatever information he could glean would be stored away for future use— assuming Sylas even saw him again. The thought of leaving without saying goodbye to Casian filled him with sadness, but right now that took second place to his anxiety about Master Cowin and his strange questions. Sylas's departure could not come a moment too soon.

Casian did not fly to Lucranne often, but when he did it was usually at night, as his owl kye preferred. He could fly by day—the majority of his training at the Aerie had been in daylight, since owl changers were rare—but it drained him more than a night flight. His father's staff hardly batted an eyelid when he emerged from his rooms in the morning, not having been there the night before. He asked a servant to enquire of his father if it would be convenient to speak with him, then broke his fast with his younger brother.

Yoran, at nearly seventeen, had been raised with the hope, if not the expectation, that Lucranne would come to him, and that became clearer to Casian with each visit. Even before Casian's changing, and the possibility that he might choose life at the Aerie over a political future as a lord holder, Garvan had preferred Yoran. It was by no means strange that Garvan gave Yoran the same training as Casian; a lord holder needed more than one heir. The Creator might strike any man at any time, and even Deygan, with his three sons, would be hoping for more from his current wife. But it was more than that. Casian had realised since he had gone to the Aerie that Garvan subtly encouraged Yoran's belief that he would be the next lord holder of Lucranne.

The brothers had never been close, and Garvan's actions had removed any chance of them becoming so. Casian treated Yoran with caution, not knowing what promises their father had made to him, and Yoran treated Casian with a coolness bordering on contempt. Being a changer among the Irenthi was a stain on a house's honour, and Yoran clearly thought that Casian's hated ability rendered him unfit for the title. He must have had a few uncomfortable years, Casian thought with bleak humour, wondering if one day he would wake up with the pains in his limbs and the cramping in his stomach that signalled the onset of the change. Yet Yoran had come through those years unscathed. Most boys changed in their fourteenth or fifteenth years, although there were a few exceptions. Now nearing his eighteenth, Yoran was safe.

Over a light breakfast, Yoran probed gently for hints of the purpose for Casian's visit. He must hope that I've come to tell Father I intend to stand aside as Lucranne's heir, Casian thought ruefully. According to the laws of Chandris, an heir, once acknowledged, could not be set aside. He could abdicate his position of his own volition, but family squabbles or preference for a younger child would not be allowed to cause an heir to be supplanted. Fortunate for Casian, in the circumstances.

Garvan did not appear surprised to see Casian, but then not much surprised the lord holder. He was a man of even temper, his anger slow to rise although fierce once provoked. Not even Garvan could entirely hide his surprise, though, when Casian announced he had left the Aerie.

"Did none of the masters try to persuade you otherwise? I would have thought they would be keen to keep their only Irenthi."

"None of them pay me much attention, least of all the one who should nurture me most. But

I left without seeing anyone. Why should I be accountable to them?"

The only person he would have wanted to see before leaving he was too proud to apologise to. For most of the flight home he had struggled to understand Sylas's decision. Why destine himself to months, if not years, of trekking around Chandris at Ayriene's beck and call, rather than the luxury of Casian's mother's house? But he would come, eventually. Once he realised that his life would be more comfortable as a valued servant than spending his time knee-deep in blood and vomit as a healer. Casian shuddered. Even the smell of the infirmary when he had visited Sylas had made his stomach roll over. The miasma of sickness and decay and death had hung in the air. And Miralee had seen them together, a few years from now, Casian wearing the crown of Chandris. Sylas's future was set, however much he squirmed on the hook in the meantime.

Garvan's face hardened. "Common courtesy, for one thing. Respect. Realising that there may come a time when as lord holder of Lucranne I may need the goodwill of those at the Aerie."

No mention of Casian as lord holder. Strange. His father was normally all too keen to tell him how a lord holder should behave when Casian's own deeds did not live up to his exacting standards. Would his father make him go back?

"I tell you, Father, Jesely wants to keep me down because I am an Irenthi. It does his Chesammos heart good, I think, to lord it over one of our race."

"I think you do Master Jesely a disservice."

Garvan put a slight emphasis on the title, as if to show his son that he was prepared to give the master his correct respect, if Casian was not. "He has never been anything but courteous and attentive when I have spoken to him."

"So why is he not letting me study for the mastery?" Casian felt as he had as a small boy, being reprimanded by his father over some misdemeanour.

"Have you met all the requirements?"

"I believe so, yes."

Garvan studied his son carefully, and Casian felt himself wither under his stare. He had an aura about him that made people take him seriously. Casian had done his best to watch and emulate, but despite his efforts had not cultivated a fraction of the lord holder's presence.

"It is not something he would do from spite, and if he did, there are other masters at the Aerie who would ensure that your best interests were met. There must be a good reason. And now you run away, like a sulky boy who is not allowed to win at every game. Will you discredit our house by giving up when you fail?"

Casian certainly felt sulky, with his hands balled into fists and his mouth fixed into a petulant pout. He forced himself to relax, performing the first stages of calling the kye, letting himself float. His kye stirred, ready to evoke his owl form.

We fly, changer?

In irritation, he pushed the kye to the back of his mind. Not now, he thought. Damn me, why did I ever think being a changer could give me an advantage? But it did. He could travel alone and without fuss; could observe events from the sky with no one giving him a second glance; could access that strange and wonderful talent that made people do his will.

"I have hardly failed. I am a changer, and I can resist the call and transform at will. There is one in the Aerie now who cannot even master those simple steps." He felt a brief pang of guilt in his chest at using Sylas for such an unfavourable comparison.

To his surprise, his father frowned more deeply. "Do you compare yourself against the weakest now, Casian? There was a time when you would measure yourself against the best and work to improve if you found yourself wanting."

Casian realised he had clenched his jaw again. He should have known his father would not approve of his sudden reappearance. How disappointing to have his true heir back with him, preparing to assume his position, rather than the favoured younger brother.

"Maybe if you spoke to them? Pointed out to them that I am more than ready for mastery. You might have more influence than I."

"And if I try to bring my position to bear on them it goes against the independence of the Aerie from the nobility. It also makes you look like a petulant child, running home to get his father to intercede for him. You need to stand on your own feet, Casian. Prove yourself to them. Make them respect you, if they do not. Show you are worthy of your blood."

"So you want me to stay? Keep working for

the mastery?"

His father poured a cup of water and sipped at it thoughtfully. "I had hoped you might rise high within the changers, make a place for yourself there."

"But I am heir of Lucranne."

"And I may not displace you; it is our law. But you can stand down. Yoran stands ready to replace you. He would make a worthy lord holder, and you would make a fine master changer. Maybe even a councillor in due course. An Irenthi on the changer council would be of great benefit to us. It would give us an influence we have lacked since the last time Lucranne produced a changer."

But that had been centuries ago, when Lucranne had been the ruling house. The first two sons of Lucranne had changed and the holder council had overthrown the lord high holder, putting Banunis's holder in his place. Their fully human younger brother had been allowed to become holder, but Lucranne was reduced to the second house. Of course the holder of Banunis had voted for Lucranne's removal, and he had plenty of support. Once Banunis was installed as the new high holder the law regarding abdication had been passed, since all the holders were now nervous about an unfortunate outbreak of changers in their own families.

"So you want me to renounce my claim on the title?"

Garvan avoided Casian's eyes for a while, staring fixedly into the bottom of his cup, then sighed.

"That would be the ideal situation, as I see it. Chandris passed the law allowing an heir to stand aside for a reason. We have never had a changer head of house in all the centuries the Irenthi have ruled in Chandris. I would not have Lucranne be the first, if I can help it."

Casian felt as if he had walked off a cliff. To lose Lucranne was inconceivable. It was undeniable that being a changer had made his position difficult for a while, but he had received no challenge. It seemed that the passage of centuries had led to a more enlightened nobility. Or, more likely, the other holders could not see any benefit in causing trouble for his house. Most of Lucranne's lands were desert, with the responsibility for linandra production and managing the Chesammos that entailed, and Garvan had handled both duties with extreme efficiency. It was in the other holders' best interests to leave things in Lucranne as they were.

Garvan was a wily man: an astute politician who had raised his sons to be like him. He would not be swayed by emotion, or be persuaded into revealing anything he did not want known. Casian knew that he would learn exactly what his father intended and not one whit more. Casian's understanding of his talent was a recent thing, and he had never had the opportunity to use it on his father, had it even crossed his mind. But now he reached for the aiea-dera, extending the streams of it towards Garvan. Tiny tendrils of energy, cautiously used, for fear his father would realise what he did. He pictured them creeping towards Garvan, like vines twining around his head, exerting their control.

"Why do you want me to stand down, Father? Why do you prefer Yoran for your heir over me?"

Garvan's eyes widened and Casian withdrew a little. Could he feel it? Did he know what Casian intended? His father laid a hand on his forehead as if massaging away a headache. He shook his head; he could feel something. Casian had noticed this when he tried his talent on other people. If they were in any way inclined towards his way of thinking, extending his influence went smoothly. If the person was against him, or resistant to his ideas, the compulsion generally failed.

"Is there some reason you think me unsuitable to be Lucranne's heir? Is it the changing?"

The aiea snapped, like a too-taut bowstring, Garvan slamming the door closed on Casian's talent. But for a moment, Casian had had him. Each time he used his talent he learned a little more, both about the talent itself and about those on whom he tried to use it.

"Go back to the Aerie before you are missed. You are a promising young man. You could rise far. Go back and accept their discipline and work hard. If you are still dissatisfied, come back in three months and we can talk again. But you must leave with Master Jesely's permission and all proprieties observed. No sneaking off in the night like a thief."

"But—"

"Deygan visits the Aerie soon, with Jaevan accompanying him. He has always been uncomfortable dealing with Irmos and Chesammos, although he met with Master Donmar many a time during the Lorandan invasion. Having an Irenthi there will make the visit go more smoothly. The council may see what an asset you could be and overrule Master Jesely. And you may make an impression on Deygan. No harm in making connections with the king, eh?"

Garvan's voice made it quite clear there would be no discussion. Casian could tolerate another three months, he supposed, but if Jesely still dragged his heels he would insist his father either take him back or give him a good reason why he would not. And an opportunity to make himself known to Deygan and Jaevan—maybe to see how responsive to his talent the pair of them were—that would be worth something.

Three months. No more. He would be master changer or heir to Lucranne.

He was not prepared to give up both his ambitions.

CHAPTER 13

ANY VISIT TO THE AERIE by King Deygan was noteworthy. Great political importance always accompanied the meeting of Irenthi rulers with the undoubtedly influential changers. But this visit was even more remarkable. Not only was Chandris uneasy—the first hints of dissent among the Chesammos were spreading—but Prince Jaevan accompanied his father for the first time, and everyone was keen to make a good impression on the young heir. He was widely rumoured to be a supporter of both the changers and the Chesammos, and many laid their hopes for the Aerie's survival on the boy's slender shoulders. It was an open secret that his father barely tolerated the Aerie, his decision to have his son tutored by some of its finest minds notwithstanding. And Deygan's intolerance of the Chesammos was well-known.

When the royal party arrived, the courtyard was four deep with changers, apprentices, and novices, to say nothing of cooks, maids, and the like. The procession came through the main gate, Deygan looking straight ahead. He made a point of not showing emotion in front of the common folk. In particular, to display any pleasure at being here would be both false and politically unwise.

He had been at odds with the Aerie for some time, and Deygan tolerated his annual visits rather than enjoying them. He scarcely acknowledged the crowd, who sensing his mood hushed into an uncomfortable silence. Jaevan rode by his side, his head twisting this way and that, attempting to take in every detail. Deygan tolerated the boy's enthusiasm. His intention for the rest of his reign was to reduce the Aerie's power, if not disband it completely. Let his son rule an island where full control was with the Irenthi, not shared with some hocus-pocus band of magic-doers.

Formalities bored Deygan. Master Donmar greeted the king, and Deygan spouted some equally bland and meaningless words back. Donmar had aged. So had he, Deygan supposed, but grey showed in dark Chesammos hair where it did not in Irenthi white-blond. They had known each other many years. Donmar's knowledge of Chesammos lore had given Deygan a deadly edge when the Lorandans invaded the island the year Deygan succeeded his father. Jaevan also greeted the master changer, in a clear voice which as yet showed little sign of breaking. Deygan noticed his son scanning the crowds, and for the first time appreciated that Jaevan was not the youngest here, as Deygan had expected.

Most boys began the change at thirteen, though it varied. Girls did not begin their change until fifteen, or even later, so most novice classes were a strange mixture of young women and boys barely into adolescence. There were younger children too, offspring of the Aerie's inhabitants, only some of whom would prove to be changers themselves.

After Master Donmar, the king was greeted by Master Jesely, and Deygan noted his son's beam of pleasure at the sight of the Chesammos master. At least the boy had some familiar faces here. As did he, Deygan realised, recognising the young man at Jesely's shoulder.

Casian took hold of the king's palfrey's bridle while Deygan dismounted, bowing in the Irenthi fashion to the king and his son. It was interesting that the Aerie chose to have Casian so in evidence at their arrival. Were they trying to make the point that the Aerie was no longer the sole preserve of Irmos and Chesammos, and thus Irenthi had less reason to see it as a threat? Casian was an embarrassment or an opportunity, depending on how one looked at him. He was an embarrassment to his father, certainly. Irenthi nobility still regarded changer children as an unfortunate accident, and one as highly-placed as the heir to Lucranne was hard to cover up. Garvan had chosen to embrace it: to encourage his son to learn changer ways and make up his own mind which path to follow. Deygan was not sure he would be as broad-minded, in similar circumstances.

"Master Jesely," said Deygan. "It is good to see you. My son has been in a fever of excitement to see you again." Jaevan's broad smile was unreserved. The boy would need to learn to disguise his emotions—he could hardly play politics with his feelings writ large across his face. But he was young yet. Let him be a boy for a while longer.

"Casian," Deygan acknowledged the elder son of

his friend and rival. Casian dipped another quick bow. He was graceful and smooth, born to privilege.

"Your Majesty. Welcome to the Aerie." Although Deygan expected that being a changer would be a matter of embarrassment to an Irenthi, Casian gave no sign of awkwardness that the changer city had been his home for the past—what—four years? Five? Soon it would be time for him to decide where his loyalties lay, then, and either commit to the changers and set aside his claim to Lucranne, or renounce his abilities and return to prepare for his inheritance. Deygan couldn't help but study the young man a moment, as if by that scrutiny he might determine which way his decision would tip.

"But you are Irenthi. Are you really a changer?" said Jaevan, blurting the words out. Deygan hissed his irritation. Jaevan might be a boy, but he needed to learn when to hold his tongue. Casian smiled and inclined his head.

"Indeed I am, Your Highness. The only Irenthi at the Aerie at present. I am something of a curiosity, which I think is why I am here to greet you. If your father allows, I would be happy to show you around and answer any questions you might have."

Deygan felt a strange prickle in the back of his mind, like a troublesome fly on a hot afternoon. He rubbed a weary hand across his forehead. It was not a long distance from Banunis to the Aerie, but the terrain was arduous, and he felt as though he had been in the saddle all day. What was it Casian had said? Show the boy around? He could see no reason why not. Better an Irenthi to take care of him than one of these damned Chesammos the

Aerie kept harbouring. He waved a gloved hand.

"Yes, of course. Excellent idea. See to it, will you, Jesely?" Deygan could not understand the look of displeasure that flitted across Jesely's face. That prickling feeling itched at the back of his skull, then vanished as quickly as it had come. "Maybe we could go inside. I, for one, could do with a wash and a bite to eat."

Deygan might have been mistaken, but he thought Casian flashed Jesely a look of satisfaction as the royal party headed for the great hall. Politics. Always there was politics.

Jaevan started the changer council meeting well enough, clearly understanding what was being said, asking pertinent questions when his father allowed him to speak. But as the second hour dragged into the third his face grew paler, and his well-trained erect posture became a weary slouch. The boy was flagging—anyone with eyes in their head could see that.

Much as the king might want him to sit through entire council meetings, ones such as this with the Aerie's policy on the Chesammos people being put to debate were torturous enough for the regular participants, much less a twelve-year-old boy. Jesely thought no one but him had spotted it, but Ayriene caught his eye and raised her eyebrows. Yes, she would notice. She would be the one called upon to revive the lad if he passed out at the table. Jesely gave the slightest of nods. He would call attention to the lad's plight.

"Sire, if I may make a suggestion, should we not take a short break to refresh ourselves? His Highness looks tired." There were refreshments available, and Jaevan had taken some fruit and a cup of wine, well watered, but it seemed to Jesely that wine might make him sleepy rather than give him the injection of energy he needed to get through the rest of the meeting.

"I am all right, Master Jesely. Really, I am," Jaevan said, trying to sit more upright in his high-backed chair, but the hand that reached for his cup trembled, and the boy's naturally pale Irenthi skin seemed almost translucent.

His father studied Jaevan's face, taking in the boy's pallor, the tired droop of his shoulders.

"Maybe a walk around the courtyard, Sire? I would be glad to accompany His Highness, since he knows me a little."

The lad clearly did not want to lose face in front of the council, but he brightened at the suggestion. He was trying so hard to be a man, and doing remarkably well for his age. He had the willowy look of all the Irenthi, as if a strong gust of wind would take his legs from under him, but he had the steel and determination of his father. Not many would cross Deygan, and the council was getting a grilling that Jesely would be glad to escape, if only for a few minutes.

"Please, Father? You did say I could look around. The Aerie buildings are older even than Banunis, my books say, and I'd like to see some of them."

Jesely pushed back his chair, attempting not to show the relief he felt. His temper was steadily fraying as Deygan spoke of the Chesammos. The king's words were all of controlling and repressing. They were Jesely's own blood, for all Deygan clearly saw him as a changer rather than a Chesammos. He could see from Cowin's face that the other master would have escaped the meeting too, if he could have seen a way out. Jesely saw little chance of compromise in Deygan's attitude.

"No need to take you away from our discussion, Master Jesely. Lord Casian offered to show my son around. Maybe he could be prevailed upon to make good his offer?"

Jesely was not sure he liked Casian being given his Irenthi title in the Aerie. After all, here he was just a journeyman, whatever his birth. Even so, he had Casian sent for. The Lady knew he could have chosen a better chaperone for the boy—whatever reservations he had about Casian associating with Sylas applied equally to Jaevan—but Casian would be one of Jaevan's holders in time. Better the two young men had the opportunity to develop a friendship now, if only for the sake of Chandris's future. And it was natural that Deygan would want his son cared for by another Irenthi when out of his sight.

So if it were all so right and proper, why did Jesely's spirits drop at the door closing behind Jaevan and Casian? There was more to the feeling than simply the prospect of more hours in council. Jesely wished he had been allowed to supervise the young prince. Sighing, he refilled his cup and settled back in his chair to listen to the debate.

"I thought they were never going to stop talking." Jaevan flashed a smile that bordered on cheeky, sheer relief at being out in the fresh air shining in his eyes. Casian knew from experience the sort of training he would be going through, designed to produce the epitome of an Irenthi nobleman. It was nice to see a spark of individuality from the boy.

After so long surrounded by Irmos and Chesammos, it felt vaguely strange to be speaking to another Irenthi here.

"They will likely talk for some hours yet, Highness. Your father does not visit the Aerie often, but when he does he covers a great deal of business."

"That's what I said, only you are more polite. I suppose all this stuff about the Chesammos is important, but it was a little awkward with Master Jesely and Master Donmar and Master Cowin sitting there. My father does not seem to see them in the same way as the Chesammos he talks about. I suppose changers are different." The lad's brow furrowed, the mark of a boy trying to understand men's affairs.

"In more ways than you know, Highness." Jaevan seemed an open sort of lad, guileless and naive for all his training. Casian didn't think he had ever been naive. Garvan's training insisted his sons were alert for any double-meaning, any seemingly innocent question designed to extract information that the speaker had never meant to let slip. He wondered if now might be the right time to try out his talent on Jaevan, with the boy so grateful to be rescued from the council meeting that he might spill secrets in his desire to be liked.

"He doesn't like the Aerie, you know," said Jaevan. "I think if he could find a way to stop the changers having any influence he would. He says the Aerie helps the Chesammos—sends them extra food and clothing so they don't have to work as hard. Is that true?"

Casian spread his hands. "Highness, here I am just a journeyman, not even a master yet, for all my birth. You have heard more of the highest counsels than I have. It is not for me to question what my elders and betters discuss at these meetings." But it might be useful for him to know, he thought, particularly if Jaevan were to be present at many such meetings in future.

He called on his kye and extended a tiny tendril of the aiea-dera in Jaevan's direction. "What did the masters discuss today, Highness? The Chesammos question, you said?"

The boy flinched. Had he felt Casian's touch? But he had hardly started yet. Then a sensation in the aiea threads made Casian withdraw. Casian hadn't tested anyone for talent yet—that was left to masters—but he had been tested on his arrival at the Aerie, when they determined he was a changer talent. He had felt it from the other side: that merging of two changers' aiea that took place when the auras surrounding talented changers met, the feeling that led to the expression 'talent knows talent.' Casian frowned. He must have misinterpreted the signals.

"I'm sorry, Casian. I suppose things discussed in council should not go beyond the walls of the chamber."

So, a failure, if a small one. Casian took it with good grace. "Of course, Highness. I would not ask you to break a confidence. We will have to work together in the future, after all. Shall we go and look at the great hall? You said you would like to see it. You will see it at the feast in your father's honour tonight, of course, but this way you can look at your leisure without the curious staring at you."

He led the prince across the courtyard, towards the oldest part of the Aerie: a cloistered area leading to the great hall. Casian drifted another thread of aiea towards the lad, with the same disconcerting effect. If he didn't know better, he would swear the boy was a talent. This could set an interesting precedent. His father could not possibly insist on Casian standing down if Deygan's heir was also a changer, unless Deygan set Jaevan aside, and he was hardly likely to do that. Anyone could see that the king loved his eldest son.

As they walked, a shrill note sounded on the other side of the wall separating the outer courtyard from the lake and fields beyond. Out there somewhere one of the novices or apprentices was learning to change, finding their own kye in the Outlands and joining with it to transform into a bird. Not yet able to do it without the pipe, evidently—that was the next stage. Finding one's kye without it being called to you by the linandra was harder, yet most changers managed it reliably within a few weeks.

Casian turned to explain all this to Jaevan,

then chuckled quietly to himself. No need. The boy would not have heard it. Only changers could hear the call of a linandra pipe: changers and their kye. But when he saw the boy, he froze. Jaevan stood, head tilted towards the sound and his arms clasped across his abdomen. Casian did not want to believe what he was seeing.

"Are you all right, Highness? Can I get you a drink of something?" No, this could not be happening. Not here. Not now. Not with the prince in his care.

The lad's eyes were full of tears, but he blinked them away. "That noise. It cut through my head and then it hurt here." He clamped his hands tighter to his stomach.

Casian stared at the boy, hardly able to believe it. Jaevan had clearly heard the pipe and the only way that was possible was if he was a changer. Jaevan was how old? Twelve? Thirteen? On the young side for the change yet. But occasionally a youngster would have symptoms for some time before the onset of the change. Casian had experienced them himself—somewhat like growing pains, odd cramps that came and went. It could be months, even years, yet before the young prince would need to come to the Aerie to be trained. From the terrified look in his eyes, the boy had worked it out for himself. Could he have guessed before the visit?

"Please, Casian," he whispered, straightening cautiously and wincing as if in anticipation of pain as he released his hold on his body. "Please don't tell my father. Don't get me wrong; I'd love to be a changer. I'd love to learn to fly like you do. But I can't be one. It isn't possible. I'm his heir. Please promise me you'll not tell him."

Casian promised, but he thought his vow would likely bring the boy more trouble in the long run. As the change progressed, a stray call within earshot could make him transform whether he wanted to or not. Without a master to guide him he would be vulnerable to predators or to overflying. But until the boy's changing became common knowledge, as it surely would, Casian had a hold over him. His failure to compel the boy at this first meeting was just a setback. He could learn to manipulate him, he was sure, and then he would have the future king of Chandris at his command. One step on his own route to the throne.

CHAPTER 14

S EVERAL MONTHS HAD PASSED, AND Ayriene and
Sylas were settling into a routine—getting
to know each other better. So far, Ayriene
thought, it had gone well. Sylas had been quiet
for the first week or so out of the Aerie. He missed
Casian, that was clear enough, although at least
the pair had been on good terms when she and
Sylas left. Part of it was nerves, she was sure. His
confidence was so battered by his recent experiences
that he faltered over the simplest tasks. It was only
when he realised she meant to teach him, and did
not expect him to know everything straight away,
that he began to thrive.

That evening they found a place to make camp.
Rain had come and passed, and they found shelter
under a rock overhang. Sylas's skill with the sling
brought meat to eat, and a brace of skinned and
gutted dheva sizzled and dripped fat as they cooked
on a makeshift spit over the fire.

Ayriene reached behind her and grasped a
handful of spongy green vegetation. She grimaced
as it squished between her fingers.

"And this is.?"

Sylas smiled. Even while he was cooking
their dinner his lessons continued, but Ayriene

could rarely catch him out. He proved to have a prodigious memory for plants and their uses, and every night he stretched out with Ayriene's herbal and committed yet more to memory.

"Imanha moss. Low-growing plant that likes riverbanks and other damp spots."

Riverbanks indeed. It was not so long since he had recoiled in horror at a stream a mere pace across, thinking it would be like the poison rain that fell in the desert. The first time he saw Ayriene scoop water up in cupped hands he pulled her away, thinking she was certain to die if she drank it.

"Usage?"

"As a poultice for drawing out infection, or as a salve. The salve doesn't last long, though. You need to make new batches regularly, or it loses its efficacy."

"Anything else?"

He reddened slightly. "As a balm after childbirth if the mother has torn. It helps prevent infection there, too."

She chuckled, then caught the laugh back when she saw his crestfallen face. "I'm sorry. I just find it hard to believe that your family lived all together in one room, then came to the Aerie where changers appear naked in front of you when they transform back, and are still so easily embarrassed."

"I won't have to handle a birthing, will I?"

"Most villages have women who serve as midwives, but in an emergency you should know what needs to be done." She pulled off a leg of meat and handed it to him. "You did well. You have earned yourself your meat tonight."

Not that she would ever have withheld it, if he had not been word perfect on his lesson. The boy was diligent, as Jesely had said. For all his difficulties at writing, which he assured her were because he used his left hand, his reading was adequate and getting better with practice. And like every young man she had ever known, his stomach seemed permanently empty.

He had grown another finger's width in the months since they had left the Aerie, but thank the Creator he seemed to have stopped, at least for the time being. If Cowin and Jesely were typical Chesammos he still had some bulking up to do; he did not yet have their breadth of shoulder and depth of chest.

For a mercy, he did not spend his spare time chasing the girls—or boys—in the villages they passed through. She expected he had found company along the way—girls often smiled encouragement at her good-looking apprentice, and so did some of the young men. But there had been no lasting involvements, and for the time being, that suited her fine. The more attention he paid to his studies, the better the healer he would become, and the sooner he could support himself if necessary.

Towards the end of their journey, Adwen had been showing more of an interest in the local girls than she liked and she had taken pains to introduce him to the appropriate pages in the herbal. Bastards in most of Chandris's villages were known as 'changers' children,' their fathers having flown and left them. Adwen had taken her instruction on such matters with a smile and a joke, but Sylas would be another matter. As far as she knew, Sylas was only interested in male partners, but she couldn't afford to take any chances. Probably leaving a marker in the herbal for him to find would be her best option, she reflected, watching her apprentice ripping meat from bone and licking the grease from his fingers.

"We head into the uplands tomorrow. Are you ready?"

He nodded. "I want to see a forest. Wood is so scarce in the desert. I want to see trees and trees and trees as far as I can see, like Casian told me about."

"I think we can manage that." She tipped her head to one side to consider him. "You know we will most likely see upland Chesammos while we are there."

"They work in the fields. Master Jesely told me that. The upland Chesammos and the desert Chesammos have become sundered. Once we were all one race, each working according to their skill and receiving according to their need. The Irenthi changed all that, and now the uplanders and the desert dwellers might as well be different races."

He was matter-of-fact, but had an air of sadness. The Chesammos had once owned the whole island. She was not sure how their systems had worked, but he was not the first who had told her of this means of providing for everyone—a far cry from the way things were now. The Chesammos were free people who might as well be slaves, as it stood. In the lands she had visited where slavery was legal, slaves were a valuable commodity. They were well-kept, fed and clothed. The average slave lived in better conditions than many of the desert Chesammos. No wonder they had heard rumours of rebellion as they had travelled the island. Sylas had not mentioned them, but she wondered how much of it he had taken in—whether he sympathised with what they were trying to achieve. He was safer with her than among his own people, at any rate. Healers were respected; changer healers doubly so.

At least the lad seemed happy to be travelling. Chandris was not large, but it had a stunning variety of environments. From the desert of the south to the rainforests in the north, and the mountain range that formed the island's spine, she planned to visit them all. Ayriene had been stunned to discover how little Sylas knew of the island on which he lived. He knew only the area close to Namopaia, the Aerie, and the route he had to take between them. He had only seen the sea from a distance; he had never seen a forest, or a farm, or any of the other things Ayriene took so much for granted. It gave her pleasure, showing him this small part of the world and witnessing his wonder at what it contained.

"So long as you know," she said. "We will head north and east tomorrow and we should be in Redlyn the day after. Now, suppose you show me how you'll make that imanha moss salve?"

He grinned, taking a jar of oil from his pack and setting a small pot in the embers of the fire. The boy had a sure way about him, and he picked things up quickly. He was not Adwen—would never take Adwen's place—but she had to admit it was good to have company by the fire of an evening. She settled down to watch him set the oil infusing.

Sylas thought he was prepared for what he was to see in Redlyn, but when it came to it he was not. The Chesammos there looked a lot like him and had the distinctive build of his race, but there the similarity stopped.

If he had stopped to think, he would have realised that they would not live in ash brick huts. Just as wood was a prized commodity in the desert, so was brick elsewhere, used mainly for the castles and mansions of the wealthy. These Chesammos lived in houses of wood and willow, thatch and skins, as did the Irmos, of whom there were many. They wore Irenthi-style clothing, although in fabrics much less fine than any Irenthi would be seen wearing.

But what surprised him most were the earrings. The menfolk still wore the twisted wire and bead, but some wore them in both ears, not just one. The women wore them, too: simple affairs so as not to get in the way while working, but no woman would have worn an ear wire in the desert. Most shocking of all was the bead. A few wore linandra, but many more wore beads of other colours—a pink coral here, a clear quartz there—of the sort worn by Irmos for decoration. The custom of piercing had been kept after the sundering of the desert Chesammos and the uplanders, but the ritual importance of the wire and its bead had been lost.

Ayriene tugged at his sleeve. "You're staring," she warned him. And he was, but they stared back. He had stubbornly clung to his old clothes, loose-fitting, bound at wrists and ankles to keep out ash. And he was the only grown man without the ear wire. That was enough to set him apart in any Chesammos settlement.

A man approached, a few years older than Sylas, but taller. Looking round, Sylas saw that this man was far from the tallest. Better diet and fresher air made these uplanders thrive, it seemed.

"Welcome, healer. Cousin. My name is Erlach," he said, giving Ayriene a respectful bow, deeper than those accorded even the Irenthi in the south. He made the sign of the Lady to Sylas, joining thumb and fingertips and raising his index fingers to his lips. Sylas returned the salute, grateful that this, at least, was the same as at home. "We have been looking forward to your visit, healer. We have our own herbalist here, but she anticipates learning much from you. And we have a young man with a broken arm which has not healed, and one with a knife gash that has become infected. Both injured while gathering the fruit and nut crops."

Erlach had none of the accent Sylas was used to. From his voice he could have been Irmos, or even Irenthi at a push. Looking around, he saw many dark Irmos children playing in the streets, even some with fairer skins. In the desert, his people clung to the old ways, told the old stories, preserved their bloodlines. Here, with the prospect of a better life for those with some Irenthi blood in their veins, the preservation urge did not run as deep. Within two, maybe three generations, he estimated, there would be few people left here who could claim pure Chesammos blood.

Sylas shifted to Chesammos to ask their host if there were anywhere they could wash, any food and water to be had after their journey. He was aware of Ayriene's eyes narrowing and wondered if he had given offence. The man laughed nervously.

"If I understood you correctly, my house is at your disposal. You will find fresh water and food there, and beds, if you need to rest after your journey." Erlach replied in fluent Irenthi, then flushed when he saw Sylas's expression. "My Chesammos is rusty, I am afraid, and I would be embarrassed to try in front of one who obviously speaks it well. We rarely use the language now, even amongst ourselves. My parents both speak it, if you wish to converse in your own tongue."

Sylas's spirits fell. He had thought at least to speak a little Chesammos here, but the young man slapped him across the shoulders.

"When you have rested maybe we can speak a while, cousin. I would like to hear of the southlands and how you fare there. I hear there are... changes afoot." Erlach cast a cautious glance at Ayriene, but she was making a good attempt at seeming not to hear. "There will be a gathering in your honour tonight."

"Wrestling?" Sylas could not keep the eagerness from his voice. "Will there be wrestling? I am out of practice, but I am accounted good in my village. I would love to try my skills against some of your men."

Erlach moistened his lips. "Wrestling? Why... no. Not tonight. We rarely wrestle now, if truth be told, but if you enjoy sports we have a game I can show you. I will need some of my friends to come back from the fields, but we can teach you, if you wish. The rules take time to explain, but I'm sure you will pick it up."

Sylas smiled in what he hoped was a polite fashion. The beauty of wrestling was that you could practice any time, as long as you could find a man willing to be your opponent. But having to gather a group—and *rules*! How many rules could a game need?

"I think maybe I shall rest a while. On reflection, I am tired after our long walk."

Erlach brought his face closer to Sylas's and whispered urgently. "I must see you alone. I hear that Chesammos plan to rise up against the Irenthi. That they gather weapons."

"Here?" Sylas checked over his shoulder in case they could be overheard. "You have weapons here?"

Erlach looked aghast. "No, not here. We are a small community, as you see, integrated with the Irmos. There is little revolutionary spirit in this village. But one of the villages to the south of here will join, I believe. I only hope the rest of us will not be drawn into your conflicts. It cannot end well."

He showed Sylas and Ayriene to the small dwelling that had been prepared for them. They washed and lay down on their first proper beds in many days. Sylas stared at the ceiling. Sleep would not come, despite his tiredness. This place was not Chesammos: not as he knew it. But then his own people were leaving the old ways, in a far more radical way than these villagers. Weapons? He could hardly picture Chesammos men armed with daggers and knives and spears. His mind recoiled from it.

Chandris was hard for Chesammos—had always been hard. But now it was no longer safe.

They spent several days at Erlach's village so that Ayriene could monitor the progress of her two more serious patients and spend time with the village healer. Not only did she have new remedies to explain, but she left a few of her precious seeds to try to establish the new plants in Chandris. Once there were patches in strategically placed villages, she hoped, the wind and the birds would spread them farther.

Sylas became more uncomfortable as time passed. He found it hard to express, but being around people so obviously Chesammos in a village so alien to him was a disorientating experience, and their Irenthi dress and speech and manners only made it worse. By the third village he knew what it was.

He was homesick.

Ayriene continued to teach him as they moved between the villages. His most recent lesson had been on kaba sap, a deadly poison to Chesammos and Irmos, but which would merely cause Irenthi a severe stomach upset before they recovered completely. A bizarre substance, Sylas thought, that would differentiate its effects between races.

Something different in their blood, Ayriene speculated, or in how their bodies reacted. Either way, the Irenthi had the good fortune to survive it, although the effects were bad enough they might wish for death before they recovered.

From there she took him on to the importance of making potions, tisanes, and tinctures up to the correct strength. It was not enough to know the correct plant or part of a plant to use for a remedy, she stressed. Sometimes quantities were important too, and this was where the goodwife who grew herbs in her garden for their healing properties sometimes made fatal mistakes.

"Did you know that a tea of gethenee leaves is poisonous in large quantities, or if prepared incorrectly, but a weak tincture can restart a stopped heart? Something can be good for you in small doses, yet damaging if you take too much." She looked straight at him when she said that, and Sylas wondered if she were trying to tell him something. Was Casian a poison, did she think? Was it safe for Sylas to see him occasionally, but damaging if he saw him too often? Or was he reading too much into a seemingly innocent observation?

Mulling over these uncomfortable ideas made him slip deeper and deeper into one of his dark spells. By the fifth village Ayriene was struggling to get any conversation out of him. He walked resolutely, head down as if on some marathon trek, and when they worked he scarcely spoke except to confirm instructions or check that he was making up a remedy correctly. More and more she was allowing him to make decisions, offering suggestions and stopping him if he went drastically wrong, which he rarely did, but letting him be a healer in fact as well as in name.

Finally, as they sat resting with tea brewing in a pot over the fire, rolling strips of torn linen for bandages, she turned to him.

"Are you all right? You've been moody these last few days. I know young people can be that way sometimes, but it's not like you. Is there anything I should know?"

"I'm fine." He rolled bandages as if it were the most important task of his life, resolutely watching his hands moving and not meeting her eyes.

"I'm not going to try to be your mother, because I'm not, but if there is something amiss I need you to tell me. If anything is troubling you—something about your studies, or if you've decided healing isn't for you or..." She stopped and studied him for a moment as if something had occurred to her. "You didn't meet someone, did you? Back in one of the villages? I mean—it would be understandable. I don't know if you would fit in here in the uplands— from what you've said, things are very different here—but we could go back and you could talk to him. Or her. Whichever."

He sighed and put down the neatly rolled material. Lifting the pot from the fire, he poured two cups of the steaming tea and handed one to Ayriene. Just for an instant he made eye contact and the genuine concern in her face touched him.

"It's nothing like that. But being around Chesammos—even ones who aren't like me—made me realise how much I miss my family. Well, my mother at least, and my sister. She has been married a few months now. She might be pregnant, for all I know."

Ayriene packed the bandages into her healer pouch and checked the pots and vials, making notes of supplies that were running low.

"I ordered some flowers and seeds harvested and dried for me, and by my reckoning they should be coming into season round about now, so with drying time and shipping they should be in Adamantara in two or three weeks. The merchants will hold them for me, so I don't need to be there the day they arrive. I was going to stay in Adamantara once the supplies are on their way to the Aerie—there's always plenty of call for a healer with the ships in and out—but there's no reason why we shouldn't go to the desert for a while instead. I'll fly to the Aerie for a day or two to make sure the healers there know how to use the new supplies. If you stay in Adamantara, that will be quicker than us both walking there—even quicker than riding in the wagon. Then we can carry on into the desert."

It felt as though a weight had lifted from his shoulders. "Thank you, Mistress. The men of the villages have told me dreadful things about the south planning rebellion, although the Lady knows how stories have spread so far. I would like to see for myself what is happening. Maybe I can help my family if things are getting bad." Would the Aerie take his mother in, if he pleaded her case? She was a good weaver; she could weave for her keep. Or cook. Or clean.

The news he had heard in the second village, of

an attack on Lucranne by a party of Chesammos, preyed on his mind. Most of the desert fell into Lucranne's holding and Garvan had always been a fair holder. The villagers had not been able to tell Sylas the outcome of the attack, except that the perpetrators had been executed. But if any harm had come to Lord Garvan, then Casian was lord holder now. And if any harm had come to Casian... His stomach clenched. If harm had come to Casian surely he would have known.

He had to admit to himself that it was not only his family he missed. Deep inside he yearned to see Casian again. Even enduring his taunts would be preferable to not seeing him at all. He wondered if Casian missed him, too.

"There is something else, Mistress."

She regarded him silently.

"When I agreed to become your apprentice, you said you would help me learn to fly. Would you train me? Then if I needed to see my family, I could go to them without us having to completely change our route." He bit his lip. Not entirely the truth. What he wanted was to fly to the Aerie, to Lucranne, to wherever Casian was. The excitement of leaving with a new mistress, of learning new skills—that had overridden the pain of leaving Casian, at least at first. But it was there now, in his chest: a dull ache like the pain of bereavement, reminding him of what he had left behind. He wanted to ask to go to the Aerie with her when she went, but who knew if Casian was even there? He had been disenchanted enough when Sylas last saw him to have quit the place for good. And she was right; she would move faster without him.

"You know why healers rarely fly?" she asked him.

He nodded. "Because we have packs of supplies too heavy for a bird to carry, and too precious to be left behind. And because it is tiring, and we owe it to those who need our care to be as rested and healthy as we can, lest we misdiagnose them or do not treat them to the best of our ability." It was the unofficial creed of the healer. "But I would not do it often, Mistress, and when we return to the Aerie you know Master Donmar will ask if I have made any progress. If I have not, might they not forbid you to have me as your apprentice, when there are so many promising young changers who might benefit from your tutelage?"

When she had taken him on, it had been with the proviso that she would not bind him. Normally a master would bind an apprentice—a contract on both sides that forged certain links between them using their kye. With doubt hanging over Sylas's abilities, Ayriene had declined to make that link, and she stood by that decision. Part of it was due to her son, he knew. In some way she seemed to think that binding Sylas would be displacing Adwen; Sylas understood that. But the threat of his ability being burned away hung over him.

Ayriene fixed him with a stare that seemed to see into his soul. At last she nodded slowly. "Very well then. I am no flying tutor, like Master Olendis, but I will try. We will make a bird changer of you yet."

CHAPTER 15

THE DOMED HOUSES WERE VISIBLE from some distance away, goosebumps on the skin of the desert. As they approached, Sylas was amazed to see how small they were, their single rooms hardly bigger than Master Jesely's study at the Aerie. Namopaia. His home.

No, not his home any longer. That was the road now: wherever he and Mistress Ayriene ended up. A fitting solution for a man who did not fit in either of his lives. His one attempt at transformation since his plea to Ayriene had once more ended in frustration. All the planning and preparation—making their belongings safe so that no one would happen upon them while Mistress Ayriene accompanied him on first flight—all wasted. First flight, Sylas thought bitterly. Just being around a master changer wasn't going to teach him to fly. Deluded fool!

He hoped seeing his mother and sister would bring him some peace—enough for him to carry on with his aim of becoming a healer, at least. Maybe if he could manage that, he could take his mother away from here. The healer way forbade taking more for a healing than the patient could afford, and in most villages, that was little enough. Even

Mistress Ayriene did not earn much—he had seen the few smallcoins in her hand after a morning of consultations—but at least it gave him hope that someday he might support himself and his mother. Maybe not in comfort, exactly, but anything would be an improvement on Namopaia and his father.

Dark gazes followed them suspiciously as they made their way into the village. Irmos faces, especially ones as fair as Ayriene's, were a rarity here. Ayriene as usual greeted everyone with a smile, introduced herself as healer, showed her pack. In each village, she would set up by the well to allow people to come to her. Sometimes it took a while for the first person to come, but then others would approach, encouraged by the first. Her customers fell into two types: those simply wanting her advice about one ailment or another, and those prepared to pay what they could afford for salves or teas or tinctures. With Ayriene's unique talent, she made it known that she could offer healing for physical hurts also, and linandra diggers often came to have fingers broken in the mines made good as new.

If no invitation to stay was extended to them by the time she had seen all who came to her, Ayriene and Sylas would quietly pack their bags and set off along the road. Healers never stayed where they were not wanted.

A trickle of Namopaians came to them, most averting their faces to avoid making eye contact with Sylas. They knew him, yet gave no sign of recognition. His father was known for his temper, and few would cross Craie without good cause.

In the distance he saw Ilend and his hopes rose. If Ilend was here, then the dig team were in the village. Pietrig was home.

He recognised the woman coming towards them and his heart lurched. It was Aithne. He had hardly dared hope that one of his family would approach them, yet here she was. As the others had done, she avoided looking directly at Sylas, but greeted Ayriene with a bob of the head and a timid sign of the Lady as if unsure what was the accepted courtesy for a healer.

"Healer."

His heart sang at the sound of her voice, and his throat ached with the need to speak to her.

"How may I help you?" said Ayriene.

The words seemed to want to jump from Sylas's throat: to ask if she was all right; to ask after his mother. But he had to hold his tongue until she spoke to him. Until she acknowledged him as her brother, he was the healer's apprentice, nothing more.

"I am pregnant, Healer. I am getting bad sickness—not just in the mornings, but all through the day. I worry for the child. Do you have anything that can help me?"

Sylas struggled to keep his face composed, to keep the healer's mask firmly in place over his features. She was pregnant. It had been likely, given the pressure she and Kael would have come under, but to have it confirmed was a joy. A smile tugged at the muscles of his cheeks and when he looked up Aithne was beaming at him, her eyes twinkling with happiness.

"Sylas," she said. "It's good to see you."

Now that he was permitted to speak he couldn't find the words, but he could feel the happiness spread across his face. She turned back to Ayriene.

"Healer, we would be honoured to offer the use of our house for you and your apprentice."

Ayriene inclined her head graciously. She handled these conversations regularly, but made each person feel they were the first ever to offer the use of their home. Sylas wondered if he would ever treat people with Ayriene's ease, and doubted it.

"We would not put you to any trouble. If you are pregnant, maybe you and your husband should not disturb yourselves."

Aithne shook her head. "We can stay with my husband's parents for now. They have room for us. The baby is not due for a while yet and we will be quite comfortable."

Her husband's parents. That made sense. Craie would never let Aithne and Kael stay with him and Zynoa if he knew it was for Sylas's benefit. Aithne and Kael were making a stand in front of the village doing this, and Sylas knew and appreciated it. They were saying that they would accept and welcome Sylas, no matter what the circumstances of his leaving. Although, if he had come back with anyone less than a healer—and a changer healer at that—he might not have been able to expect the same outcome.

Aithne's offer of accommodation also helped with the awkwardness of payment. Sylas knew only too well that the desert Chesammos had little with which to pay a healer. Ayriene had graciously accepted food and ale from their previous customers. However, since Aithne was providing a roof over their head for the night, Ayriene could legitimately wave her offering away. Aithne turned to leave, clutching leaves to make a tea which would help with her sickness and a tonic to boost the health of the baby she carried. Sylas took her hand.

"Come to the house tonight. Please. I need to talk to you."

She nodded silently and left, and his cares lifted like a weight from his shoulders.

Sylas fretted until Aithne's soft knock sounded at the door. She slipped inside at Mistress Ayriene's call.

"Are you comfortable? Did you get enough to eat? Can I get you more water?" She had annoyed him as a child. She had been every inch the big sister, keeping her little brothers in line, and they had clashed many times. But at that moment the habit seemed endearing, not irritating. He had missed her more than he cared to admit. He held out his arms and she hugged him, then pushed him away, slapping his shoulder and dashing tears from her eyes.

"Where have you *been*? We've been so worried. We didn't even know if you were still alive. Mother insisted if you hadn't made it back the Aerie would have sent someone to look for you, but it was still in the back of our minds. You could have let us know you were all right."

Ayriene cleared her throat. "I'm sorry. That was

partly my fault. I should have seen to it that you had news of your brother. Sit down, Aithne. Sylas has been on eggshells waiting for you. Can you stay a while?"

Sylas squeezed Aithne's hand, but her nervous glance at the door spoke volumes. "I can't be long. It's all round the village that you are back. I'm surprised Father hasn't tried to make Kael stop me seeing you."

So Kael was allowing her to see him. That was a comfort. He didn't want to come between his sister and her husband. He remembered Kael calling him brother, Kael stopping his father beating him to death. She had married a good man.

"Does Mother know I'm here?" He had half hoped to see her at the door with Aithne, but of course his father would never permit it.

"She knows. She says if you can be at the well at sunrise she will meet you there."

Tears pricked his eyes. She would risk his father's anger to see him. His voice was husky when he replied, "I'll be there. Is all well with her?"

"You can ask her yourself in the morning, but she is as well as may be. She misses you, of course."

"Father?"

Aithne glanced towards Ayriene.

"She knows," he said. "You need have no secrets from Mistress Ayriene."

"He is much as he ever was. Pleased about the baby." She laid a hand on her belly in the protective gesture of the expectant mother. "He never speaks of you, except to curse you, but you probably expected nothing else."

Indeed he had not. On an impulse, he decided to ask her something that had been preying on his mind since his conversation with Master Cowin. "Aithne, do you know what our grandfather's name was?"

She flashed a look at him. "Why, Bairyn. You know that. He only died a few years ago. Is your memory so short?"

"Not Father's father."

She swallowed hard; she had known which grandfather he meant. Silently, she shook her head.

"Don't you think that's a little strange?"

She gathered their supper dishes, stacked them on the table ready to take away. He knew this simple action was to give her an excuse not to meet his eyes.

"I always thought it might be Erden. You know, because of your name."

"Me too. Didn't you ever wonder why we never knew anything about Mother's family?"

She looked up then, pain in her eyes. "Of course. But you know why we didn't ask."

If Craie had got even a hint that the children were asking questions, or that Zynoa was telling them things he didn't want them to know, they would all have suffered. He wanted to ask her if their mother had ever mentioned knowing someone called Cowin, but could not bring himself to—not with Ayriene there. As it was, she was learning too much about his family, and little of it was good. There was something else he needed to know.

"Has there been any trouble recently?" The uplanders had spoken as if the desert villages were about to erupt into violence, yet Namopaia seemed much as it ever had. Sure, there was a little tension in the air, but that could be accounted for by his presence. She chanced another look towards Ayriene, then shrugged her shoulders.

"I suppose some of it is common knowledge now. There was an incident a few weeks ago. Some of the villagers from Cellondora attacked an honour guard of the lord holder's. They were carrying his standard, and the villagers thought that meant the lord holder himself was with them."

"They attacked soldiers? With what?"

"They had their hunting slings." Aithne hesitated, taking a quick look over her shoulder at the door. Sylas glanced that way too. Had she heard someone? He crept to the door and opened it, looking this way and that for eavesdroppers.

"There's no one there, Aithne."

She covered her face with her hands and he saw that they were trembling. "I'm sorry. It's all been very difficult here. A lot of men are joining the rebels, and I'm scared Kael will get involved. It's so stupid. What do they think they can do? Some of the Cellondorans had swords, Sylas. Chesammos bearing swords. It's unthinkable!"

Where in the name of the Lady had they got swords from? A Chesammos buying a weapon would attract attention. Word of many Chesammos buying weapons would find its way to the ears of the Irenthi, one way or another. "An honour guard with a banner but no lord holder? Was it a trap?"

"Some of the men think so. They think someone is telling the Irenthi of their plans. Sylas, I'm so frightened. What if Kael gets drawn into it? I want our baby to have a father."

"You must try not to upset yourself," said Ayriene. "That's not good for the baby, whatever foolishness its father is planning."

"Are many of the men from the village involved?" He swallowed around a lump that had formed in his throat. "Is Pietrig?"

Aithne sighed, and he got the impression she had been waiting for him to mention that name. "I think so. Most of the diggers are, and I don't think he'd be alive if he wasn't at least going along with it. He avoids his father when he can. Rumour is that the elder wants him betrothed to a girl from Cellondora. Some sort of strategic marriage to ensure the two villages working together for the rebellion. Fienne is worried half to death about him." She met Sylas's eyes, daring him to ask after Pietrig's sister. He was more concerned about the news of Pietrig's imminent betrothal, and its implications, but his guilt required him to ask after the girl he had wronged.

"Fienne. Is she...? How is she keeping?"

"As well as you might expect, considering how you embarrassed her in front of everyone." That was the sister he remembered, arms folded across her chest and a glare in her deep brown eyes. "I wanted to ask the healer if she knew of anything that might help."

"For what?" Ayriene was obviously listening—making no attempt to hide the fact—although in a small Chesammos house it would be hard *not* to hear.

"A woman of eighteen who has never had her flows. Is there anything she might take to make them start? My brother here was indiscreet about her problems in a very public way and now she worries she may never find a husband. I know there are things you can take for painful flows and heavy ones. I just wondered."

"Bring her here tomorrow. I can look at her privately and see if anything can be done."

Any herbalist could give teas and potions, but only Ayriene could use the aiea-dera to look deep inside a person and see if anything damaged could be mended. Maybe that way Sylas could make amends. If he had not exposed Fienne's troubles he would not have been beaten by his father, he would not have been healed by Ayriene, and like as not he would not be here now with the best healer on the island. Sylas's guilty conscience regarding Fienne receded a little. Maybe the Lady worked through him to get a good outcome for Fienne. He hoped the Lady would be as kind to Pietrig.

Sylas was waiting by the well when the sun came up. Zynoa emerged from the little dome house he had grown up in, looked left and right, then walked towards him, her pace increasing as she got closer until she was running. He trotted towards her, breaking into a run himself to close the gap between them, catching her in his arms and hugging her until they were both breathless. His reluctance to be touched by her on his last visit home flashed through his mind and he felt a brief flush of shame, quickly extinguished by the sheer joy of being with her.

"Oh, my boy," Zynoa said through tears. He realised with a start that his own cheeks were wet and wiped them with the back of his hand, grateful that there was no one there to see.

She took a step back, her hands on his shoulders, and studied his face.

"You have got so tall," she said, stroking his hair and pulling her hand back as if embarrassed. "You are taller than your father now. Almost as tall as your grandfather, I think."

She had never spoken to him of her family, and he wondered if Aithne had mentioned his question from the previous night. He wanted to ask her more—if his grandfather had been so tall, had he been an uplander like Erlach?—but time was short. Before long the village would stir and people would emerge to go about their chores. The well was an obvious place for the two of them to meet, but also the first port of call for most householders in the morning.

"Are you well?" Had she suffered for his mistakes?

She nodded. "The better for seeing you. You leaving was so hard for me, but I see it was the right decision. You look so healthy. And apprenticed to a healer." The pleasure was written all over her face. "That is an honest profession. Are you full changer now?"

"Not exactly." How to tell his mother of failure heaped upon failure? "But Mistress Ayriene has promised I can go back to the Aerie soon to pick up where I left off. She says I am good enough to be a healer myself someday."

"Ayriene?" She seemed thoughtful.

"You have heard of her?"

Zynoa didn't answer, but took the linandra necklace from around her neck and held it out to him.

"You must take this now," she said. "I offered it to you once before, and you refused it. You cannot refuse me this time. Aithne will have told you of our troubles. It is only a matter of time before the men take the beads to pay for swords or daggers, and I will not have my necklace used for violence. Or the soldiers will come. If I am caught with these in my possession, they will think they are stolen. Hide them at the Aerie if you can, or carry them with you. But I can keep them no longer. You may need them one day, Sylas. Take them for me."

The reasons why he could not take the beads stood: they were too precious; he might be robbed; by rights they should go to Aithne. But before he could argue he happened to look out of the village, along the road he and Ayriene had travelled the day before. In the distance rose the plumes of ash and dust that announced horsemen approaching. The lord holder of Lucranne would never send his riders to Namopaia this early in the morning, unless he intended to catch everyone unawares.

Unless it was a raid.

CHAPTER 16

"SOLDIERS COMING!" CRIED SYLAS, TRYING to gauge how long they had before the horsemen overran them. They seemed to be moving steadily, more concerned about the welfare of their mounts than speed on the rough surface of the desert road. All to the good.

He looked over the rim of the well. His mother could not have linandra beads in her possession if she was searched—not with the way things stood. He could hide them in Ayriene's pack, but even a healer might not be immune to inspection. If he dropped them down the well they might never get them back. He had no idea how deep the water was, but the bucket never seemed to hit the bottom. Put them in the bucket and lower it? No, the soldiers would want water for their horses, and themselves. They would be found. Think, Sylas, think!

"Give the necklace to me. I'll hide it," he said. Zynoa nodded. She trusted him. He had failed everybody and everything, yet still she trusted him. "I need you to go. Fetch Aithne and hide in the kiln. If there's trouble, I want the two of you well away from it."

She gripped his arm, then reached up and embraced him. "I love you, Sylas. Take care."

He ran for Aithne's house, waking Ayriene as he clattered through the door.

"Get up!" he said, never minding that he was speaking roughly to his mistress. "Soldiers are coming. You must go."

"They would not hurt me," she said, instantly alert. "I am a healer. Even soldiers respect healers."

"If it is a raid I want you safe. Even healers get hurt in raids. For the love of the Lady, Mistress, you are the only living healer talent. I would not have you come to harm in my village, maisaiea-yelai."

"What will become of you?"

If he had learned to change, he could have flown with her. But they would have to return to reclaim their packs and have the whole village know him for a coward who would not face the holder's soldiers.

"I will take my chances with the rest of my people. The Lady has decided that I must be a Chesammos today."

She crouched, readying herself for the transformation; Sylas stood aside from the open door.

"Come back when the soldiers go," he said. "There may be injured for us to tend. I'll save the packs."

He never failed to be awed by the transformation. Where Ayriene had crouched was now a falcon— her higher bird form. She could circle the village, watching events unfold, and none of the soldiers would think anything of a lone bird in the sky. Surging forward, the falcon took flight.

Back at the well, Sylas looked around. People were emerging from houses, pulling on breeches and tunics and looking up the road towards the soldiers. He had to be quick before anyone noticed him. He put the necklace around his neck to keep it safe, then climbed up onto the side of the well and lowered himself into it. His arms and shoulders were still strong from the wrestling, but even so this seemed like a quick way to a long drop. With luck, he could conceal the necklace well enough to keep his mother safe, but so it could be retrieved later.

His feet scrabbled for a hold. He was tall enough that his feet rested on rock, not the ash brick of the well wall, but his hands were another matter.

Climbing was not a skill that desert Chesammos children learned, but he had seen some of the Aerie's children daring each other to climb higher and higher up the tower walls. They had reached for each foothold and handhold in turn, making sure of its safety before committing their weight. Now he would see if he could emulate them. He would have given a lot to have Benno here right now. That boy would have been over the side like a monkey.

His heart thudded, his chest so tight he strained for each breath, and bright dots swam before his eyes. Lady help him, he could not panic; he could not. If he survived a fall from that height he would likely drown. Desert Chesammos didn't learn to swim, either. He drove the picture of his body floating in the dark water below from his mind.

Happy that both feet rested securely on rock, he forced himself to let go of the edge with one hand. Reaching down inside the well, he felt for a hold with his fingertips. The ash bricks were regular, with hardly a gap between them. The well had been there before his father's birth, but he cursed the brick-maker who had done his job so diligently. Questing fingers found a gap in the brickwork, and he hoped it would hold him—that straining muscles would not fail him.

He could hear shouting above—men raising the alarm. The first job of the morning for the older children would be to fetch water. He hoped that just for once, they were being excused from their chores. With a small moan of fear, he let go of the top with his other hand, searching for another gap to cling to. His muscles were trembling already, effort and terror making him weak. Maybe he should have buried the necklace in the ash and hoped that feet and hooves did not uncover its hiding place.

Two more shuffles downward and he was satisfied that no one leaning over the edge would notice the necklace by chance. He felt around him. His hands were just above ground-level, he estimated, his feet well below. He reached about with one hand, then the other, feeling for something from which to hang the necklace, or a gap in the bricks into which he could place it.

Sylas found a protrusion—a metal peg, or similar—perhaps the remains of an earlier well structure. He looked up to the sky. It was brightening by the minute. The necklace could do with being lower still, to remove the chance of the sun at its highest glittering on the stones and betraying their presence. Still, it couldn't be helped. Most water was drawn early in the day when, Sylas judged, the sun would not have come round enough to play the traitor so. The peg was long enough to hold the necklace without fear of slipping, yet close enough to the wall that the bucket would not catch it by accident.

This would be the hard part. He had to let go with one hand long enough to take the necklace from his neck and loop it around the peg, and his arms trembled with the strain of holding himself. He felt for a better foothold, then handhold, trying to make himself more secure before letting go with his left hand. One small fearful noise escaped him as he let go, drawing the beads over his head and clinging to the bricks again with both hands. He looked nervously into the blackness. He could not see the water. It was a long way down and the sun did not yet give enough light to illuminate the well shaft. Swallowing hard, he let go, hoping his arm would hold him again, maisaiea-yelai. Once, twice, he wrapped the necklace cord around the peg, then flattened himself to the well wall, gasping with the effort.

Reaching for the handholds he knew were there, he pulled himself up, but before he could reach the top a man leaned over the side. He yelped, almost letting go in his fright, but an arm reached to grasp his hand and help pull him up and over. Pietrig. Thank the Lady.

"What in the name of the Lady are you doing down there grunting like a hog? No, don't tell me. I don't want to know. Crazy brickmaker, get out of here. The lord holder's soldiers are coming." And before Sylas could say anything, Pietrig had slapped him across his shoulders and pushed him away from the well. Trembling, dripping sweat, Sylas walked a few paces back towards the village, then bent, leaning on his knees to get his breath back. By the Lady, he hoped never to do that again!

Now he had to be a man, pierced ear or not, and stand with his people. He straightened and walked through the first few houses to where the villagers had gathered to face the soldiers. Some of the villagers cast him sidelong glances, but several moved to make room for him, and one shook his hand.

The horses clattered to a halt and the leader removed his helmet and swung from the saddle.

"People of Namopaia. His lordship of Lucranne has received information that you are withholding linandra. I have orders to search the properties of Skarai, elder of the village, and Ilend, leader of the dig team, as well as any others I deem necessary. I require those men to step forward and make themselves known to me."

Skarai stepped forward despite his wife hanging on his arm trying to pull him back. "I am Skarai. No withholding of linandra happens, or will ever happen, in my village."

"Then you will have no objection to our search. Where is team leader Ilend?"

Ilend stepped from the crowd, less confidently than Skarai had. If Pietrig had been right, Sylas thought, this was the man who had instigated the hoarding of linandra to fund an uprising. He certainly looked guilty enough, the muscles at the corners of his eyes twitching, his tongue sliding sideways to moisten dry lips.

"I am Ilend. You will find no linandra in my house."

Sylas stared across at Skarai's family. They were all there: his wife, Fienne, and his six younger children. Pietrig had rejoined them. He seemed to feel Sylas's gaze on him and slowly turned his head. If Sylas had been in any doubt the stricken look on his friend's face would have told him. Pietrig knew where the linandra was hidden. Not in the elder's house, surely. Pietrig was smarter than that.

Sylas held his breath, half expecting the officer to call his father's name. If they knew the dig team had been saving the stones, did they also know about his mother's necklace? He wondered if his mother and sister had made it safely to the kiln. If the soldiers mounted a systematic search they would be found, but if not, at least they would be safe if violence erupted.

The officer waved a hand. "Borden, take four men and search the elder's house. Sysk, take another four to team leader Ilend's."

The remaining soldiers stayed in their saddles, their horses stamping and blowing. It was a long way from Lucranne to Namopaia and the animals needed attention.

"My men and their mounts will need water. You," he pointed at Sylas, whose heart leapt in his chest at the snapped word. "Fetch water. Quickly now."

On shaky legs, Sylas moved to obey. By the Lady, had he ever thought the masters at the Aerie intimidating? These uniformed men, swords at their waists and pikes by their saddles, were worse. Pietrig moved to help him, but the officer shouted. "I never told you to move."

"The well is deep, sir. If you want water quickly for your men, he will need help. Each bucket will take several minutes, alone."

The officer considered, then nodded and Pietrig joined Sylas at the well.

Sylas turned his body slightly to shield his face from the soldiers, but kept winding the handle to bring a full bucket of water from the depths. "Tell me there is no linandra hidden in your house. Tell me you weren't that stupid."

"What were you doing down there? Is the water safe? Did you poison it with some of your healer potions?"

"Never mind that. Are those damn soldiers going to find linandra stones in your house?"

Pietrig nodded, his posture a picture of abject misery. "They might. Ilend gave them to me to look after. He said the elder's house was the safest place for them. That even the lord holder would not dare search the elder's house." He gave a short, pained laugh. "Looks like they were wrong. They wanted to keep me loyal. They knew I wasn't convinced that this whole thing was a good idea. Having the linandra hanging over me—they thought I wouldn't dare speak against them."

Behind him, Sylas heard a villager's voice, and he stiffened and stopped winding the rope.

"Who told the lord holder we had linandra here? Who has been spreading lies about our village?"

The officer looked down his nose, considering whether the question was deserving of an answer.

He stroked his horse whip, and Sylas thought for a moment he intended to apply it to the speaker.

"Lord Garvan heard there were plans to steal linandra. He gave you time to amass enough stones to incriminate yourselves before acting on the information."

Sylas's skin turned ice cold and the hairs on his arms prickled.

"What's the matter?" said Pietrig. "You've stopped winding. The officer will be wanting this water."

"I... I feel sick," Sylas muttered, leaning over the wall of the well.

"Don't throw up into the well, for the Lady's own sake. That would spoil the water for days, even if you haven't poisoned it."

"I'm not going—" Sylas broke off as one of the soldiers emerged from Skarai's house, a leather pouch in his hands. One of the four with him had a grip on Skarai's arm and a dagger at his throat.

"Omena's wings," Pietrig moaned softly, slumping against the well. He looked likely to be sick now, instead of Sylas. Sylas grabbed his shoulders and shook him.

"Run to the kiln. My mother and sister are hiding. They may not look for you there. Run!"

"No." Pietrig was as pale as it was possible for a Chesammos to be. "If they search and find me there they will think your family are involved too. And I can't hide myself while my mother and Fienne and the little ones are in danger. What sort of man would that make me?"

Pietrig pulled away, stumbling towards where

Skarai's wife and other children clutched at each other for comfort. The younger ones were sobbing, sensing their elders' fear.

"It's mine," said Pietrig, approaching the officer. "The bag is mine. It's my fault. Don't blame my father. He knew nothing about it, I swear." At Pietrig's words his mother cried out and his brothers and sisters howled all the louder.

"How did you come by them? Did someone give them to you?"

Tell them it was Ilend, Sylas thought at his friend. The bastard murdered Yestro. Tell them it was him.

"I am on the dig team, sir. It is an easy matter to hide a stone or two each trip."

Sylas screamed inside. Pietrig would end up hanged, if they even went so far as to take him back to Lucranne. More likely they would just run him through on the spot with one of their fancy swords. Had he come home just to see his best friend murdered, and likely Skarai with him?

"Dig team, eh? And these here are your family, yes?"

Pietrig closed his eyes, his chin dropping towards his chest. "Yes."

"Then to help make up for the linandra you have stolen from the lord holder, this one can join you digging." The officer pushed Pietrig's brother, Kavan, towards Ilend. "He will go to dig with you, team leader. We will see if he is more honest than his brother."

"He is only eleven," Pietrig said, looking to his father for help. "Tell them, Father. See, he does not wear the bead in his ear. It is the rule that none can be picked for the dig team until he is confirmed into manhood." He addressed the officer, "Please, sir. He is too young. He can't be chosen for two or three years yet."

It was true. Pietrig himself had his ear pierced when he was barely old enough, his father using his influence to get his son named early. Pietrig had then been chosen for the dig team in the first draw for which he was eligible, so Skarai might have been thought too hasty, but Kavan was years younger even than Pietrig had been.

"What about him?" The officer jerked his head at Sylas. "You can't tell me he isn't old enough for your earring. What are you Chesammos doing? Deliberately not piercing the ears of your boys to avoid them digging, eh? And you still keep some for yourselves and think Lord Garvan won't notice." He spat on the ground. "You people must think we are stupid. Bring him."

The soldiers dragged Pietrig towards the horses, pulling his hands together to bind them.

"No." Skarai stepped forward. "Take me. Leave my son, but take me."

"Are you admitting responsibility, elder?"

Skarai hesitated a moment, then nodded. "Yes. Yes, I am. Spare my son."

"Bind him as well. The whole family is rotten to the bone."

Pietrig's mother clung to him, crying. "You cannot take him. This must be another's doing. My son would not steal from the lord holder."

When they led the two men away, a stone

whistled past the head of one of the soldiers. Then another. And another. The menfolk of the village had come with their slings, and were prepared to use them in defence of their people. Before Sylas registered what was happening, a fight had broken out. The Chesammos were at a disadvantage, as always, slings and fists against swords and daggers and pikes, but they fought with what they had. More than one soldier crumpled to his knees with a handful of ash flung in his eyes, and several riders lost control of their horses when their mounts suffered similar treatment.

The usually disciplined soldiers of Lord Garvan's guard were unsure of how to respond to an enemy who used ash and stones as weapons, particularly since many of the assembled villagers were women, children, and the elderly. More men joined the fray and Sylas saw the gleam of sun on steel. Please the Lady, not a blade in Chesammos hands. He groaned aloud at the thought.

A soldier came at Sylas and he dropped, using the loose surface to slide into the man's legs and avoid the sword strike that would have gutted him. He brought his knee up into the man's groin and the soldier fell into the dust, howling and clutching himself. Blows were not permitted in Chesammos wrestling, but even so Sylas clasped both hands together and crashed his fists onto the back of the man's neck. Not enough to kill—Lady help him, he was a healer—but enough to put the soldier out of action for a time. In the back of his mind he hoped Ayriene was not watching from on high, but he was in no doubt that he was fighting for his life.

He saw Skarai go down to a helmeted soldier's sword and heard a woman's scream. Despite everything, he knew Fienne's voice. Omena's wings, he could not let Fienne be hurt. He followed the sound, saw Skarai motionless on the ground with blood pumping from his chest. Even if Ayriene returned when the fight was done she would be too late. Skarai was losing too much blood, too quickly, even for Ayriene to save.

Pietrig had heard his sister scream too. The two men faced each other in the chaos.

"They will kill us all," Pietrig gasped.

No. Not if they want their linandra dug. Garvan is too much the lord not to protect his own interests. The thoughts flashed through Sylas's mind, but he could not articulate any of them before a movement out of the corner of his eye caught his attention. A soldier with a pike thrust towards Pietrig's gut. Sylas yelled and threw himself at the pike, pushing it up, and the point impaled itself in Pietrig's shoulder rather than his stomach. The soldier stumbled and fell to his knees, losing his grasp on the weapon.

Sylas threw himself to the ground beside Pietrig; blood flowed steadily from his wound. Not as fast as his father was bleeding, but enough to be mortal, if left untreated for too long. Pietrig smiled weakly at Sylas.

"So, healer, something for you to practice your stitching on."

Omena's wings, but he needed more than stitching! He needed Ayriene. Sylas scanned the sky, looking desperately for the falcon, but if it had not been safe for her here before, now it was ten times worse.

"Save my family," Pietrig said, his face paling as his body went into shock.

Through the chaos, he heard Fienne's voice again, screaming for help. Sylas looked wildly around, and spotted her kneeling beside Kavan's slight body. The lad appeared unharmed, but when he dashed to her, dropping to his knees at her side, she looked at him numbly.

"He's dead. A stone from a sling hit the back of his head and he has no heartbeat. What have we come to that we are killing our own?"

"Come with me," he said urgently, but she shook her head. "I won't leave Mother, and she won't leave Father."

He pulled her to her feet. "What good does it do them if you are killed? This is carnage, Fienne. For the love of the Lady, let me help you. Let me put something right."

She let him guide her to the outskirts of the village and into the building that housed his father's kiln. Tapping on the door he called, "Aithne. It's me. I have Fienne here. I'm going to open the door." The last thing he needed was one of them thinking he was a soldier come to take them.

Terrified eyes looked back at him from the darkness. The women's clothes were black with soot, but they were safe, thank the Lady.

"Are you all right? Can you breathe?" The flue would to give enough air for two, but with three, it would get stuffy quickly.

She nodded shakily. "Have you seen

Father? Kael?"

He hadn't, and he had to get back to Pietrig. Surprisingly, he was worried for Craie. It made no sense. The man had made his life a misery, but it seemed blood made a difference after all.

"I'll look for them. Stay quiet. I'll come back when the soldiers have gone."

Sylas crept along the side of the kiln. The fighting was dying down. Now there were shouted orders and sobs of women and children instead of screams of men and horses. He stepped away from cover only to find himself slammed against the ash brick wall. Craie stood there, blood-smeared, his fists on his hips. He grabbed Sylas's shoulders, bringing his face so close that Sylas could feel his breath.

"I might have known you'd skulk here till the fighting stopped. You don't think this has anything to do with you any more, is that it? I don't suppose I can thrash you now you've taken up with a healer, but I can do this. Let her heal you if she will." He drew back his fist and punched Sylas full in the face. Sylas felt his nose crunch, tasted blood in his mouth, trickling down the back of his throat. Craie spat, all his venom behind the gesture. "I meant what I said last time. You are no fit man, and no son of mine."

Craie stalked away, back towards the well, where the soldiers were calming panicked horses, mounting up, and preparing to leave. If the worst he came out of this with was another broken nose and a face full of his father's spittle, that was probably better than he deserved. He had to get to

Pietrig. Sylas scanned the sky for a circling falcon, hoping desperately that Ayriene could get back in time, but there was no sign of her—just blue sky and a few wispy clouds.

Someone had put Kavan next to his father's body, and covered them both with a blanket. There would be a funeral pyre that night, and not just for Skarai and Kavan. He could hear sobs from other clusters of people. Other families had lost loved ones in this skirmish. Then he heard Pietrig's mother's voice, thick with tears.

"You have killed his father and his brother. His sister is nowhere to be found. Do not take another child from me."

Pietrig had been dragged to his knees, and was being held between two soldiers. His tunic was soaked with blood, and he was unable to stand by himself.

"He should hang at the gates of Lucranne, by rights, but he'd not live to get there," said the officer. "I'd hang him here, if there were any bloody trees to hang him from. Seems to me this is doing him a mercy."

The officer drew his sword. Pietrig's mother screamed and made to run to his side, but other villagers held her back. Sylas felt like he was in the middle of a nightmare. The air around him seemed to thicken and he struggled to breathe. His feet felt rooted to the spot, the horror of what the soldier was about to do leaving him frozen. Then he heard his voice screaming, "No!" and he was sprinting towards where the man stood over the helpless Pietrig. Hands grabbed for him, tried to hold him back, but he shook them off, running as if possessed for his friend. He barely registered the flash of the blade in the morning sunlight as it slashed through Pietrig's throat.

A red torrent. Pietrig falling to the ground, his blood spilling into the ash.

Sylas cried out again, the sound torn from him in an agonised scream. From the corner of one eye he saw a pike descending. Then all he knew was a blinding pain in his head, the ground spinning beneath his feet, an overwhelming nausea in the pit of his stomach, and an enveloping blackness.

CHAPTER 17

SYLAS CAME ROUND WITH A thundering headache, an inability to breathe through his nose, and the vague realization that he had expected never to wake up at all. Voices haunted the air around him, but like the shadow of a dream, when he grasped at the words they seemed to drift away. He tried to open his eyes, but the command didn't reach his eyelids, so he concentrated on trying to understand what the voices were saying. He knew they were familiar to him, and let them swirl around him until they resolved into three: Mistress Ayriene, his mother, and Aithne. A hand rested on his forehead.

"I think he's waking up."

The hand was replaced with a damp cloth, cold with well water. He managed to open his eyes a crack.

"Can you hear me, Sylas?" Mistress Ayriene's face leaned over him, her eyes red-rimmed.

"Thank the Lady; he's awake." That was his mother. No surprise that *her* eyes were red.

He looked back to Mistress Ayriene. Were her tears for him? A hand clasped his; he couldn't tell whose. He tried to speak, but the words caught in a throat dry as desert floor. Cool water passed his lips, acrid with the taste of sulphur.

"Take it easy. Don't rush."

Sylas remembered the pike swinging towards him and raised his hand to where it had struck.

"All healed," said Mistress Ayriene. "It took a lot of aiea, and others needed me, so I haven't seen to your nose yet. I assume you want me to make you pretty again. Although, if you'd rather leave it like that, let me know. I'm getting a bit bored with fixing your nose."

He snorted. Damn. Bad idea. His nose throbbed.

"You are lucky the healer stayed nearby," his mother said. "The pike broke your skull. I was afraid we would lose you." Her voice shook, and the pressure on his hand increased. His mother's hand, then. "What were you thinking, going for the soldier like that?"

Despite her words, he thought she sounded proud.

"I thought I might lose you," said Ayriene, and her voice also trembled. "Lucky he decided to crack your head and not spit you. Damn you, Sylas, if you'd died I'd never have forgiven myself."

"Not your fault," he whispered. He had been lucky. She had come too late to help others: Skarai, Kavan, Pietrig.

"Pietrig!" He tried to sit up, but couldn't. Pietrig was dead; he had to be. Even if Mistress Ayriene had been there when it happened, she could not heal a cut throat fast enough to stop a man bleeding to death.

"I'm sorry," said his mother. "We all saw you try to save him. His family is grateful to you."

"Fienne?" For the Lady's own sake, let Fienne

be safe.

"She is as well as can be expected. I've had a quick look at her. She's unharmed from the fighting, of course—you got her away in time—and from what else I found I think I can help her with her other problem."

Thank the Lady; Ayriene could cure her. She could find a husband, have a family of her own in time. But Pietrig... The pain of his loss stabbed through his chest and he closed his eyes. Then a sudden thought had him trying to sit up once more.

"The necklace. It's in the well. I tied it to a peg inside, so the soldiers wouldn't find it."

"Then it can stay there, for now. Ilend has been casting greedy glances my way. I can tell him you took it with you."

Ayriene pushed him gently back.

"Drink this. While you are sleeping I'll fix your nose so you will breathe more easily when you wake."

"Mother, did you ever know anyone called Cowin?"

Ayriene and his mother exchanged glances. It was that look. The one women gave each other when a man asked something they didn't want to answer.

"Whatever put that into your head? Drink, Sylas. You need sleep to recover fully, even with my healing."

He downed the draught, working out in his head what combination of ingredients she had given him as he drank. It was a potent mix and he drifted quickly towards sleep, aware of the women leaving his bedside, speaking in hushed tones at the doorway.

"It would be best if you left sooner rather than later, healer," his mother said. "His father has got it into his head that it was Sylas told Lord Garvan about the linandra. Not everyone believes him, but enough do that it could get difficult."

"I find it hard to believe anyone would think that, but I will heed your warning. We will leave as soon as Sylas is fit to travel."

A door creaked and he wondered who was leaving, which of them would watch him while he slept. His mother, he thought. Ayriene will see to any others injured in the fight, then maybe she can put Fienne's mind a little more at ease, despite her grieving for a father and two brothers. He heard more words, softer still, and his sleep-befuddled mind fought to understand them.

"Thank you for taking care of my son, Ayriene."

"If I had known he was yours, I might have taken him on sooner. Can I tell Jesely? He still mourns for you."

"No. I am no longer who I was and it must stay that way. I must be Zynoa, Craie's wife, and be content that my son, at least, is a changer. Besides, if it got back to Donmar that I lived..." Her words faded away, and he slipped into a deep and peaceful sleep.

Sylas stood vigil with Pietrig's family later as the funeral pyre for those killed in the attack crackled and spat into the night sky. One of the little ones swore he saw a kye rising, but with so many bodies on the pyre it was impossible to tell whose soul had risen to join them. Sylas saw nothing, but clung to the hope that his friend could join the bird spirits, closer to the Lady than his earthly form. He would not have seen anything, anyway, through the tears that stung his eyes.

Smoke, he told himself. Just woodsmoke.

A few hours later he had recovered himself enough to tell his shocked mother and mistress, "I'm staying."

Ayriene and Zynoa stared at him, then at each other. Neither spoke. They both had authority over him, in their own ways. He wondered if each was deferring to the other. As the silence continued he said it again, more forcefully this time. "I'm staying. My father thinks I'm a coward, so I'm going to volunteer for Ilend's rebellion. I'm going to fight with the men."

The women exchanged another look, and this time it was clear enough. They thought the blow to his head had shaken his wits loose.

"I mean it. You saw what they did to Pietrig. To Skarai. They can't treat us like that. We have to stand up to them."

Them. The Irenthi. Casian's face swam before his eyes and he dismissed it angrily. Casian wasn't like them.

"And you think you can make a difference?" Ayriene spoke softly, sadly.

"I think I can show them I'm not the coward they all take me for," he said. "They expect me to run away. Well, I won't. Not this time. This time I owe it to Pietrig to fight. I want to find the bastards that killed him."

"You stood to fight and the healer had to save you," his mother said. "If she'd not been here we'd have lost you—likely some of the others she healed, too. More pointless deaths."

"What if it were Casian?" Ayriene's thoughts had gone in the same direction as his own. He could see his mother mouthing the name. She knew there was someone he cared for at the Aerie. It had probably never occurred to her that it could be an Irenthi, far less Lord Garvan's son. "What if the rebellion brings you face to face with Casian, each of you with a sword in his hand. Could you kill him?"

"What are the chances of that happening?" He could feel himself becoming defensive. Ayriene had targeted his weakest point, as he might have known she would.

"Probably slim," she acknowledged, and he thought he had made his point. Then she added darkly, "His honour guard would kill you before you got close." His gaze snapped to hers. He wasn't stupid; why was she treating him like a child? "Be reasonable. You have trained to save lives. The Irenthi's soldiers have trained to take them. Could you kill someone, even an Irenthi, in cold blood? Could you take up a sword or a spear and take a life?"

"If it came to it, I could," he mumbled. "Mistress, they killed my best friend in front of me—in front of his mother and his brothers and sisters. They thought no more of doing it than they would of crushing an insect. We are nothing to them. Less than nothing."

"You cannot fight," Zynoa broke in. "You have to listen to the healer, son. Would you repay the work the Aerie and Mistress Ayriene have put in to train you like this? Would you rather throw Mistress Ayriene's efforts back in her face than be thought a coward? I have had many people tell me how you tried to save Pietrig, risking your own life. No one who saw that believes you craven, whatever your father might say. The more Craie says on the matter, the more he proves himself a fool." Zynoa's tone softened. "You are no killer. Killing destroys what the Lady created. It destroys a man's soul piece by piece. It eats him from the inside, like esteia's poison."

"What do you know of killing?" he said bitterly and again, that strange exchange of glances caught his attention.

"More than I should," his mother said. "But I paid for what I did with the things that meant most to me. I replaced them with you and your brother and sister. I have lost your brother. Do not make me lose you, too. Do not make the mistakes I made."

They left him deep in thought, trying to make sense of what she had said. His thoughts and feelings were jumbled, like one of the streams Ayriene had once had to coax him to cross. They tumbled over each other, and when he thought he could see the way of them, the flow crashed over a rock and was broken.

He slept uneasily, and when he woke, his way seemed clearer. He packed his bags, methodically checking the healer pack as Ayriene had taught him. She had used many of her preparations, and he made notes to himself of what needed to be replaced.

His mother's words bothered him. When had she ever killed? How was her life here in Namopaia a punishment? And Cowin and Donmar—what was their part in this? He might not be able to fight, but he would have answers.

Sylas and Ayriene took their time travelling to Adamantara. Sylas grew stronger each day, but Ayriene didn't want to push him. She was confident of her healing. His skull had fully healed, and although he still tired easily, she expected no long-term effects. So with no deadlines to meet, and Sylas subdued by the loss of friends and the manner of their passing, they made an easy pace.

Adamantara shook Sylas out of his low spirits. He brightened when the desert land became scrub and then rough pasture, with seeds and leaves and bark and roots to identify, store, label, and add to his pack, but not before a drawing of the plant found its way into his book. Ayriene considered sending the sketches to the Aerie for safe-keeping. The bundle of parchment was heavy to carry, and the scribes could start copying the new text for Ayriene's herbal. It also represented several months' work, and she was acutely aware that it could have been lost in the attack on Namopaia.

The town itself was a bustling port, at the mouth of the island's only true river. Sylas was a little overwhelmed at first, both by the number of people and by the sight of the sea. The sea never failed to raise Ayriene's spirits. She loved the smell of the salt, the swoops and cries of the gulls—a form rarely taken by changers—and the slap, slap of the waves on the quay. It took some persuasion to get Sylas down to the shore, but once there he sat for hours, watching the waves rise and fall, mesmerized by a body of water the size of which he could never before have imagined, and even now only barely comprehended.

Ayriene pronounced herself delighted at the quality of goods shipped in from the mainland, and busied herself finding a wagoner prepared to transport them to the Aerie. She took care of that while Sylas explored. She was not sure where he roamed, in truth. The lad was still reserved after the events in Namopaia. Ayriene had seen sword wounds before—had healed her share—and had seen men killed and injured by violence. But for a Chesammos to witness such things was all but unheard of. She knew he worried that the violence would spread. From what she heard, that was inevitable.

Gossip in Adamantara was that Chesammos had come to the town to buy weapons—not the hunting slings that they habitually carried, but bladed weapons. And not belt knives, or knives that would skin and gut the animals the slings killed, but ones designed for use against men. Word had got back to the king, she was told. All merchants were now forbidden to sell a Chesammos a blade longer than the length of a man's hand from heel to fingertip, and the lord holders had introduced searches in their capital cities. Any Chesammos found with a blade longer than those permitted was liable to be executed. An Irmos buying a blade on behalf of a Chesammos would suffer the same fate.

At this news, Sylas admitted he was glad he had stayed with Ayriene. She was pleased to hear it. She understood his anger and frustration, obviously, but rebellion was not the path he should take.

On the evening they left Adamantara, they sat together by the fire. The wagoner saw to his horse and sat a little apart. He had made little conversation on the journey. Many people were uncomfortable around changers, and he preferred his own company.

The only dry kindling Sylas found nearby was squealwood, and the fire let out eerie wails that set shivers running down Ayriene's back. Sylas had told her once before, sitting by a squealwood fire, that the Chesammos told their children stories of a lost spirit. One of the kye had crossed from the Outlands and could not find its way back, becoming trapped in the thorns of the squealwood bush, and the noise made when the wood burned was the kye shrieking in agony. Sylas had proved a surprisingly good storyteller; she had hardly slept that night, thinking of the tortured spirit. Now, sitting at the fire hearing the shrieks, she felt as if she turned her head sharply she would see it out of the corner of her eye.

"Tell me another story," she said. "Not the squealwood one. Another one. A story your mother told you."

He thought a moment. "I don't know which one to tell."

"Is there one about the Lady? She's obviously important to you."

"She made us. The Chesammos. The Irenthi. The Irmos, I suppose, since they are a mix of the two. Although I'm not sure if they would count as one of her peoples."

Ayriene drew her blanket closer about her shoulders, ignoring the questionable status of her Irmos people. "You believe she made the Irenthi? Even though they came to the island only a few hundred years ago?"

"They left, and came back. They were her first people."

He felt awkward talking about his beliefs, she could see, and tried to steer him away from them. "What about that oath you use? 'Omena's wings.' Is there a story behind that?"

"Omena Stormweaver saved the island. She was a Chesammos changer. The Lady grew angry—she does sometimes, making the ground shake and the mountain spit fire."

She nodded. "You're too young to remember the last time that happened. It was soon after Deygan became king. The Lorandans threatened to invade. They managed to land a couple of troop ships north of Adamantara. There were earthquakes then—smoke and dust from the mountain. It looked like we were in for a full-scale eruption." Ayriene hesitated. She had never understood what happened next. "It just stopped. We've not had any trouble since."

"When it happened that first time, Omena sang to the Lady. She heard the Lady's song, the one she makes with the aiea, and she sang it back to her to make her be at peace. My mother tells the story well. You should have asked her to tell it when we were in Namopaia."

Ayriene sat up, staring at him. "Wait. You believe the aiea comes from the mountain?"

"Where else would it come from? It is only on the island, you said. Once you are out of sight of the land, you can no longer feel the aiea, no?"

"No, but it comes from the island. That's what I've always been told. Why would it come from the mountain?"

Sylas smiled. "Because we came from the Lady—all of us. Maybe you need to believe that to believe the aiea comes from her."

Ayriene pondered on what he said and a dozen questions bloomed in her mind, but she did not want to get into a debate on Chesammos religion, if a religion it was. Not with the two of them so tired with travelling, and the wagoner a few paces away. She reached for her pouch, drawing out a tiny linen-wrapped package.

"I almost forgot. I bought something in Adamantara." She felt strangely awkward holding it out to him. "Take it. It's for you."

Nearly losing Sylas in Namopaia had made her realise how attached to him she had become. In any Chesammos village they visited, one thing set him apart from the other men, and she had contributed to it, albeit inadvertently. She would take the opportunity to make amends.

"A present?" He untied the thread and the cloth fell open to show a tiny linandra bead on a thin metal wire.

"I know you don't have the hole since I healed your ear, but I have a tokai needle. Piercing it would be an easy enough job."

He tried to pass it back to her, the bead still resting on the linen. "I can't take this."

"It didn't cost that much. I only got a small one, and if you look carefully there's a flaw in the stone, but I thought... I thought that would be best."

She knew by now that Chesammos pride could be prickly, so she had chosen a small stone of low quality, guessing that the one he had been given at his ceremony would have been similar. She had not wanted to cause him shame. Except, from the look on his face, she had. She had thought she would make him happy with her gift, but it seemed she had missed the mark.

"I can't, Mistress. Don't ask it of me."

The boy sounded wretched. Did he think she would order him to do something that was clearly causing him distress? She poked the fire and the wood shrieked, the eerie wail appropriate to his mood.

"When we've been around Chesammos you've been the only man without one. I've seen people noticing, so I'm sure you have as well. I thought maybe it was time you had yours back."

"The linandra can only be given by a Chesammos, Mistress—a man's father, or an uncle if the father is dead. Or the village elder if the man has no living male relative of sufficient standing. It would not be proper for you to do it."

She could feel her cheeks reddening. Of course, she should have guessed there would be rules and rituals to be obeyed. The Chesammos did so love their rituals.

"I have embarrassed you. I'm sorry. That was not my intention." And now she was embarrassed, too. She had offended him when she had simply wanted to give him a gift.

"I know it wasn't. It was a kind gesture, but I would not pretend to have been given an honour that I have not. My father took the bead from me and will never give it back. His brothers would not go against his wishes. I don't know who the elder is now that Skarai is dead, but I doubt he would either." He rewrapped the bead and wire in the linen and tied the thread, frowning when his bow was not as neat as the original.

"I know nothing of my mother's family, but even if there was a suitable man among them I would not go begging a stranger to give me the bead. Maybe you can get your money back."

"Keep it. Maybe an opportunity will arise when a Chesammos of suitable status can confer the honour on you. Maybe Master Jesely? We'll be at the Aerie in a couple of days; he could do it for you. Or Master Cowin." He had asked after Cowin, she remembered—asked her mother if she knew him.

"With respect, Mistress, Master Jesely was born and raised in the Aerie. I could not ask him to perform a traditional Chesammos rite. Master Cowin I scarcely know." He seemed nervous when he mentioned Cowin. She wondered if he knew something she did not. Had the boy worked out that his mother had been at the Aerie, many years before? Ayriene should have been surprised to see her in Namopaia, but she had guessed something strange was afoot when Donmar had her heal Shamella and then word of Shamella's death had come so soon after.

She curled his fingers round the package. "Keep it for now. There may come a time when you can wear it honourably. And if not, it may pay for a bite to eat or a roof over your head if you are in need." Ayriene held his gaze, leaving her hand around his until he nodded minutely and tucked the bead into his pouch.

"Thank you, Mistress," he said.

CHAPTER 18

"SIT DOWN, CASIAN."

Casian eyed Garvan edgily. He had rehearsed his opening speech on the way to Lucranne, and he launched into it, rather than play around with social niceties.

"I gave it three months, like you said. I spent time with Prince Jaevan, and now the king won't be back till next year, so I'd be better off in Banunis trying to consolidate the relationship. Master Jesely still has no interest in me. I don't think he wants to help an Irenthi, and even with Sylas placed with Ayriene, he mostly ignores me."

"Sylas? That's the Chesammos you were friends with?"

Casian could feel his cheeks heat. Though they had reconciled before Sylas left, it still smarted that he had taken off with Ayriene rather than going along with Casian's scheme. The damn Chesammos wasn't meant to think for himself; that hadn't been part of the plan. Casian missed him. The Creator only knew how much.

"Our paths cross from time to time," he said, wincing at the note of defensiveness he heard in his voice.

"I know things are different at the Aerie,"

Garvan said, pouring wine into tall silver goblets and pushing one across the table to Casian. The nobleman drank, holding the vessel in long slender fingers. "I'd prefer if he were not Chesammos, but Master Jesely explained that all are equal in the changers' eyes. All the same, we have to talk about his status."

"Status?"

"Clearly you cannot marry as long as you have him. No self-respecting Irenthi woman will marry a man with an acknowledged Chesammos lover. So the title will pass to your brother after you, we must assume. Or his children, if you outlive him. It would be tidier if it were all settled well in advance of that, of course. So I will have the documents drawn up to make it official that you are standing down as heir. Then your way will be clear to acknowledge this Sylas as your partner." Garvan juggled Sylas's name on his tongue like a hot coal. It sounded as if it pained him to say his name.

"Standing down? I have no intention of standing down." So his father was still plucking at that harp, was he? Garvan had clearly made enquiries about him at the Aerie and decided that Sylas was his key bargaining point. Casian loved Sylas, but he would not set his title aside for him. He wondered what Jesely had said to give his father that impression.

Garvan frowned. "Then he will have no more status than a common whore. Chesammos may be lowly, but they can be touchy, you will find. Sometimes the most base are the most sensitive about their honour."

It had not even occurred to Casian that he acknowledge Sylas, or that his father would take the prospect of him having a male lover—a male Chesammos lover—with such equanimity. In fact, he would have bet a hefty sum that his father would have laid about him with the flat of his sword if he had suspected such a thing, foaming at the mouth about the honour of Lucranne. Garvan seemed to be refusing to meet his gaze. Casian swallowed several gulps of wine and wondered what he was missing.

"I... think you have misunderstood the nature of the relationship, Father," he ventured at last.

"He is not your bedmate then?" Garvan's ice-blue eyes narrowed. "I was led to believe it was common knowledge." He too raised his goblet, taking careful sips and licking his lips. "A pity. My informant seemed to think you were well suited."

Talking to his father sometimes reminded Casian of a particularly intense game of towers. As fast as Casian built one tower, Garvan laid waste to another and set siege on a second. He had rarely beaten his father at any game of strategy. Garvan was as determined as ever that Casian should abdicate, then. Casian poured himself another cup of wine, but cradled it in his hands, taking occasional sips and rolling the taste around his mouth. If his father were playing politics with him he would need a clear head. This was one game Casian intended to win—or at least not lose.

"Is something the matter, Father?" Casian asked. "You seem to have a lot on your mind."

Garvan swirled his wine, then tipped the

remainder down his throat and pushed the goblet away. His face hardened and he locked eyes with Casian, forcing him to maintain the contact.

"No more dancing around, then. You will stand down as my heir, Casian. You will abdicate your position and Yoran will succeed me."

If Casian had not known better he would have thought his father possessed of the compulsion talent, but this was simply the sheer force of Garvan's not-inconsiderable will. He blinked, trying to regain possession of his wits, and spoke carefully, determined not to falter.

"Didn't you hear me say I was leaving the Aerie? That's what you've wanted, isn't it? You've trained *me* to inherit Lucranne, not Yoran."

Not entirely true, and they both knew it. Certainly Casian had the training in his early years, but there was probably less difference now between him and Yoran than Casian liked to think. His brother was a capable man, more than able to make a good lord holder. But why?

"I have known since your birth," said Garvan. "I chose not to make it public, for various reasons."

Casian felt the game pieces shifting around him. His tower was in danger again, but he lacked the subtlety to understand his father's move.

"Known what?" Casian's mouth was dry, and he gulped a mouthful of wine. Although a fine vintage, as always at his father's table, it tasted like vinegar.

"Your mother came to me on our wedding day pregnant, Casian. She claimed you were born too early, but anyone could see you had gone the full time. And your eyes, Casian. When your eyes turned green that left me in no doubt."

"But you told me—" Casian stopped, swallowed hard. "You said my grandfather had green eyes. Mother's father, who died when she was a baby. You told me that was where they came from."

"And I made sure that everyone heard that your maternal grandfather had green eyes, so anyone who queried it got the same story. Your mother's father did one great thing. He died so long ago no one can remember *what* colour his eyes were. I loved your mother, then as now. I wanted no shame cast on her."

"So why did you name me your heir if you knew me to be a bastard?"

"Our laws do not allow us to remove a son from the line of succession, to prevent fathers passing over less promising boys, or boys who resist moulding by their fathers in favour of a better candidate or one who will more closely adopt his father's ideas. I declared you my heir when I acknowledged you as my son, and I acknowledged you as my son to spare your mother. I must stand by that decision."

"So denounce me now. Save yourself the trouble of an abdication."

"If I did it would cast doubt on Yoran's parentage, and still bring shame on your mother. I still love her. I would see no man speaking badly of her for a mistake made many years ago."

"So you hoped that I would stay at the Aerie, stand down of my own accord, and neatly solve your problem for you? And now I'm back, and the problem remains." Casian was surprised how calm he felt. At least it made more sense now. His father's preference for Yoran. His mother compensating for his father's distance. But never a word said to him or his brother of why.

"And if I refuse to stand aside? What then?" He knew the answer before it came.

"I have come to think of you as my own, but even lord holder's sons have accidents. Do not put me in that position. It would break your mother's heart to lose you."

Casian set the cup down deliberately, forcing his hand to remain steady in case the rattle of cup against table should betray its shaking. He shook with rage, not fear, but his father might not see the difference. He rose, taking his leave with as much composure as he could muster.

"Don't take too long reaching your decision," Garvan said. "If you are to return to the Aerie I will need to take action quickly. Your decision to leave has doubtless angered many people."

Casian nodded curtly. He had not endeared himself to the council when he left. Harsh words had been spoken. Most he had believed true at the time, but many he would retract now, given the chance.

"Who was he?"

Garvan shook his head. "I have my suspicions, but I will not name a man without proof, and I never asked. I tried to deny it to myself for so many years the time to ask her passed, and she never told me, although from things she has said she knows I know the truth. If you want to know, I suggest you ask your mother."

Which Casian would hesitate to do, for the same reasons as Garvan. It would risk hurting his mother, and she was the only constant he had left. Ambitious he might be, but Casian was not totally without a heart. So, he had no mastery, no place on the changer council to look forward to, and now no inheritance. Casian did the only thing he could think to do in the circumstances. He flew to see his mother.

Casian's mother was not surprised when he knocked, asking to speak with her. Her servants would have told her of his arrival, and Boreana, lady of Lucranne, was as imperturbable as her husband.

Boreana and Garvan were a good match, as arranged marriages went. It might have been several years since Boreana moved her household from the city of Lucranne to a manor on the edge of the desert, but that was no reflection on their relationship. She wilted in the desert, like a flower deprived of water. She needed trees and plants around her, and the smell of fresh, clean air. Lucranne sapped her spirit with its miles of ash and tainted air. Had it not been for the linandra stones, no great house would have built its seat out there in the desert. Lucranne might not be the most hospitable city on Chandris, but it was undeniably the wealthiest.

Casian had flown by day, ignoring the discomfort of his naturally night-flying owl. His father's news had upset him more than he wanted to admit. He was not the rightful heir of Lucranne. His entire life had been built upon a lie, and both his parents had gone along with the deception. Where he had been confident and brash, now he was battered and bruised. He needed to talk to his mother, needed reassurance that he could still be who he had dreamed. That he was not destined to be an unknown man's bastard son.

As he flew, he mulled over his options. He could refuse to stand down, as he had threatened, but his father would never let another man's blood inherit Lucranne. If he persisted with that route he would have an unfortunate accident, or succumb to a particularly virulent fever, or meet one of any number of convenient deaths by which Irenthi lords saw off their rivals. Should Casian try to preempt him—by ensuring his father's role would be discovered in the event of his death, say—this would not save him. Indeed, it would likely make Garvan see him disposed of sooner rather than later. It would embarrass and degrade his mother, and threaten Yoran's position. His brother—half-brother, he reminded himself—was an annoying prig at times, but Casian could not find it in him to want the whole Lucranne dynasty brought down.

She had guessed the purpose of his visit. He saw it in her face as soon as he entered the room. They sat opposite each other in her chambers, and she regarded him, lips drawn tightly together, before she spoke.

"You know." It was part question, part statement.

He nodded.

"He told you, or you guessed?"

"He told me. I wanted to leave the Aerie. He told me if I did, it left him with an heir too many. He set out my options."

She jerked her head to one side in the gesture that served her in place of a shrug. "And I suppose you want to know the details?"

He stared into her face, seeing for the first time fine lines around her eyes, like cracks in ice. The first signs of age—or were they caused by pain and secrets? Maybe it came to the same thing.

"Not especially."

Her head twitched upward, the suggestion of surprise in her features.

"Just tell me, was he true-blood?"

"I might have known that would be your main concern." There was a hint of amusement in her voice. "Your father was pure-blood, Casian. I was young and he was persuasive. You've inherited that part of him. I've seen you sweet-talk people into things they had no intention of doing, many times."

Talents often amplified traits present before the person became a changer, he knew. No one was surprised that Miralee was a seer. She had been unusually insightful, even as a child. The changers had debated for years whether that meant a talent was fixed from childhood, maybe from birth, or whether it built on an existing characteristic. Casian wasn't sure whether he liked having inherited his ability from his unknown father. It was useful, certainly, but for Boreana to see his father in him—it made him uncomfortable.

"Was the changing from my father, too?"

"As far as I know there is no changing in your

father's family."

Would she tell him if he asked, he wondered. He could compel her. He had never had cause to try to compel his mother, and the idea made him uneasy. A part of him wanted to know—he would be a liar if he claimed otherwise—but he had to maintain the pretence of being Garvan's son. It might be simpler if he didn't know, given the risk of encountering his real father someday. As it was, he would be looking at any Irenthi of his mother's age and older, and wondering.

"So, what do you do now?" she said.

"What do you mean?" He pushed away the idea of using a compulsion on his mother. He had to keep the urge to use his talent under control if he was to keep it secret.

"Are you going to let Garvan dictate your life? Go back to the Aerie and quietly disappear, as he would prefer?" She had said 'Garvan' instead of 'your father,' he realised. His mother's gaze remained fixed on his face, and he became aware that his jaw had tightened. She nodded, satisfied. "Don't forget I am the king's cousin. The blood of Banunis runs in your veins, if Lucranne's does not. Never forget that."

It was as if she knew of his thoughts about the kingship. His bastardy would need to be concealed for him to have any chance at the throne. That, or he would have to find a way around it.

"I will remember, Mother."

She folded her hands in her lap. "That Chesammos lad hasn't arrived yet. Do you still want a place for him?"

He had almost forgotten Sylas in all this. "He has other plans for now, but I still intend for him to come here. He may need a bolt-hole in due course."

"If your plans are as ambitious as I think they may be, you may wish to think carefully before encumbering yourself. I am not criticising, or advising, merely making sure you think of all the possibilities." By the Creator, if he didn't know better, he would think his mother was an empath talent herself. The uncanny way she seemed to read his mind would make Jesely envious. She continued, "I would never pry; you know that. But I must admit, I am intrigued to meet this man who has held your interest longer than any woman ever has."

"You will," he promised.

"Remember what I said. You can do anything you set your mind to. Your father and the others see changing as a problem to be overcome. You and I see its possibilities, I think. You can be anything you want to be, my son. Leave Lucranne to your brother and look for your own path. Then both my sons may achieve greatness."

At least his mother believed in him, he thought, as he kissed her cheek and took his leave. And sometime soon Sylas would take up his place in her household. Gradually all the pieces of his plans would fall into place.

CHAPTER 19

W HEN THEY REACHED THE AERIE, Ayriene got caught up in teaching healers and herbalists on the storage and preparation of her supplies, and had little time for anything else. She sent Sylas to the gardens to deliver seeds and seedlings and to instruct the gardeners in their care. On their travels, she had spotted that he had an eye for which environment suited which plant. His grasp of herb lore was uncanny in a desert-dweller, although now she had met his family, she understood that better. The boy had inherited more from his mother than his father, for which Ayriene was thankful.

For the past three days, Ayriene had felt pulled in all directions. There had been time for a quick talk with Miralee and a quicker one with Garyth, but now she had a few minutes to herself to catch up with an old friend. But she realised, with dismay, she was anxious in his company. What she had discovered in Namopaia—and that she could not tell Jesely without betraying Shamella's confidence—left her uneasy. There were too many secrets these days, even between changers. Even between friends.

She leaned back in the chair opposite Jesely

and sighed. Her feet hurt and her back hurt and her head hurt, and the pain-relieving tea she had drunk had not yet had time to do its work.

Jesely pushed a cup of water towards her.

"I would offer you wine, but I might have to carry you to your bed after."

She took the cup and drained it. "You might be right. The infirmary are so excited about the new ingredients they've had me up there instructing them on their use since I arrived. I swear this is the first time I've been off my feet in three days, except to snatch a few hours sleep."

"I've heard great things about what you found. You are quite extraordinary, you know."

She did not feel extraordinary; she just felt tired to the marrow of her bones. "With such a rare talent I feel I have to push myself further. Try to prepare the island for when I'm not here any more and they have to do without me."

Jesely frowned, leaning to look deeply into her face. "There's nothing wrong, is there? You're not sick?"

"Creator, no! Did I sound maudlin? I didn't intend it that way. It's just that I feel such responsibility."

And she had been unable to secure a talented healer for the next generation. If Adwen had been alive she doubted she would have felt the need to push herself so hard. Sylas learned fast, but he would never have her talent. It all seemed so futile.

As if he read her mind, Jesely asked, "How is Sylas progressing? You seem to get on well with him."

A smile swept across her face despite her

tiredness. "He is a gem, Jesely, if a little more emotional than I am comfortable with. But you were right; he learns fast and we are a good match. He will make a competent healer, in time. He's working with the herbalists, learning from them and drawing. He's missing Casian, though. Has he left for good, or will Sylas have a chance to see him before we leave?"

Jesely frowned. Ayriene knew what Jesely thought of that relationship, and while she was sympathetic to his objections, she wouldn't forbid Sylas to see Casian, even if she could. The lad needed some free time, and he'd enjoy it more with a friend.

"He went to see his father. Or maybe his mother. Anyway, he's due back tonight."

"I'm glad. They are of an age that we can't dictate their friendships any more. And Sylas is sensible enough to make his own mind up about whom he mixes with."

He poured them each a cup of the herb tea that had been brewing on his desk. "I suppose you're right. There's little I can do now to influence Sylas, even if he were not your apprentice. I'm glad he is doing well. I always thought he would thrive, if I could find the right place for him." He glanced across at her. "He came to visit me, you know. We talked for a long time about what happened in Namopaia. About what it might mean for the Chesammos. He thinks deeply about things—more deeply than you might expect."

She knew that. She wondered if he had told Jesely that he had almost joined the rebellion.

AC SMYTH

"The raid shook him. It made him question what it means to be a Chesammos, especially with his friends and family getting involved. Did he tell you they are buying weapons? The lord holders have put searches in place on the city streets."

"It's insanity," said Jesely, shaking his head with its shock of dark waves just beginning to be touched with grey. "They have never handled swords before, and they are up against trained soldiers. What can they hope to achieve?"

As far as Ayriene knew, Jesely had never seen bloodshed like the raid on Namopaia. He had spent most of his life safe inside the Aerie walls. Even Sylas in his short life had seen more bloodshed than Jesely. Ayriene had seen the results of skirmishes over the past year, but the worst destruction she had seen was during the Lorandan invasion when Deygan was new to his throne. The invading forces and their ships had been wiped out by a massive fireball. Ayriene had never found out how that fireball happened. Respar, the council leader before Donmar and Ayriene's own master, had cut off all her questions, and sworn her to silence. All she knew was what she had seen—the Lorandan troops wiped out, and burns on Shamella's hands. Donmar knew what had happened, she was certain, but he had been sworn to secrecy as she had been.

"Namopaia could have been wiped out, even with such a small troop. I'm sure Garvan's men only stopped the killing to restrict the damage to their lord's workforce," she said. She had seen little of the actual fighting, but had seen the aftermath: eight men, women, and children dead, including

Skarai and his two sons. Many others injured.

"Two of the other holders have made an announcement," said Jesely. "Half of all Chesammos young men and women in their holdings must marry an Irmos. They mean to wipe the Chesammos out by degrees, I fear."

"Where do we stand on this, Jesely? The Aerie, I mean. We try to protect the Chesammos as best we can. We send them food and clothing, visit their villages to try to find their changers to make sure they get an education here. If Deygan and his lords clamp down on the Chesammos, we will find our aid opportunities reduced. Any help we give the Chesammos will look like an attack on Deygan."

Jesely let out a long sigh. "I feared it might come to that. Part of the Aerie's original purpose was to handle distribution of assets so that none went without. But gradually the lord holders have taken on that task, trying to isolate the Aerie from any sort of political power. If it comes to it we must either make a stand against the Irenthi or hand over all rights to help those in need—Chesammos or Irmos."

"Then I am torn," she said. "My heart wants the Chesammos to stand up for themselves—to say they have been badly treated all these years. On the other hand, my head tells me that they should back down. Accept what comes. Make the best of what Garvan and his ilk offer them."

"And do you think either will have a happy conclusion?" Jesely studied her carefully and her heart sank. She knew the only possible answer to that question.

"No," she said. "I do not."

Casian had found a flask of wine somewhere, and his fair cheeks were pink-tinged. Sylas drank more moderately, as usual. He found it took much less wine to have an effect on him, and after several attempts in the past at matching Casian drink for drink, he knew the brief pleasure was not worth the pain.

Casian waved his glass for emphasis as he spoke. "So I have told the council I'm leaving, not that they took it well. But if Jesely doesn't see my potential, then I'm wasted here. My father says he can get me a position at court. Maybe something military. I think I should enjoy the military. I spoke to my mother and she thinks I can do better than Lucranne. Maybe some position high up within Deygan's aides."

He seemed to have been spending a lot of time with his mother recently, from what Sylas could make out. Casian had always had an ambitious streak, but his mother was encouraging it. Sylas could tell that Casian had fallen out with his father over something, although the Irenthi was cagey when Sylas tried to establish what had happened. The falling out was sufficiently severe that Casian had muttered something about standing down as heir to Lucranne while in his cups the night before. While it occurred to Sylas that their relationship might come under less scrutiny if Casian were no longer heir to a great house, surely no falling out was as final as to mean him giving up his title? Then he thought of Craie. If Casian's bitterness towards Garvan was only half what Sylas felt towards Craie, there would be no going back for them.

Sylas had some news for Casian, too.

"I may see you in Banunis, then. A message came late last night. Ayriene has been called to Banunis and I am to accompany her. She is packing her supplies now. Master Donmar offered us horses. Can you imagine me on a horse? But Mistress Ayriene is not a good rider, and I've never ridden in my life, so we are taking a wagon."

Ayriene had called for him when the news came. He had been with Casian, of course, but if she noticed his dishevelled appearance and the flush to his cheeks she knew better than to mention it. She asked him if he would rather stay at the Aerie to continue his lessons or go to Banunis with her. He had been to Master Olendis once and while the master seemed as displeased with Sylas as he had ever been, Sylas at least thought he was making progress. He could hear one voice above the rest now, and it had spoken to him, or so it seemed. It called him "Crowchanger" and asked "We fly, changer?" but try as he might, Sylas could not manage the exchange of energies that was needed to transform him.

So he would be a crow when he changed; he could have wished for better. Crows were carrion eaters, reviled by most of the people of Chandris. But many Chesammos took the crow as their first form, and certainly he could not have hoped for Casian's magnificent owl form. It seemed only right that an Irenthi lord should become a great white owl. He was tempted to stay and see if he could complete the change, but a trip to Banunis was not to be missed. Maybe he could persuade Mistress Ayriene to pipe for him, once they were there and their supplies were safe. He felt so close to a breakthrough.

A smile split Casian's face. "You are going to Banunis? Then I shall certainly persuade my father to arrange a post for me. We could have good times there, you and I. Much better than under the disapproving noses of the masters here. The two of us loose in the big city—imagine it!"

"I've never been there. Is it as big as they say? Adamantara was enormous. Is it true that Banunis is bigger?"

"Adamantara? Big?" Casian laughed. "Oh, you are such a child sometimes. Banunis is the largest city on Chandris, the seat of the king. Once Lucranne was bigger, when it was the high holder's seat, but Banunis has expanded since. Yes, my love, Banunis is much bigger than Adamantara." Casian laid a hand on Sylas's cheek and Sylas felt a warmth that had nothing to do with the wine. Casian stroked the side of Sylas's nose with his thumb. Sylas's breath caught in his throat.

This was the son of the man who had ordered his soldiers into Namopaia. The son of the man whose troops had killed Pietrig, nearly killed Sylas as well. By rights Sylas should hate him. By rights he should be joining his people and taking up arms against the Irenthi. But those thoughts were overwhelmed by the touch of Casian's hand on his skin.

"Is it true your father broke your nose again?" Casian murmured. "If so, Ayriene did a good job. Two breaks without a healer talent on hand would have made you look like a tavern brawler. It would be a shame to spoil such a face." He trailed his finger across Sylas's lips. Sylas swallowed hard.

"I've missed you," said Casian. "I didn't think I would, but I have. It has been lonely here without you."

"You have plenty of friends. And many willing and eager to be much more. I've seen the way women look at you." He winced at the petulant words. He tried not to be jealous, really he did, but everywhere he went, Casian drew people's stares.

Casian's fingers grasped Sylas's hair and pulled him closer. "I don't want them, my beautiful Chesammos." Casian leaned forward to crush Sylas's lips beneath his. "I want you."

Ayriene folded the few spare clothes she carried when she travelled. They made a small bundle— little enough to show for her nearly forty years on Chandris. She carried her pack of remedies and her herbal, a sleeping mat and blanket, water skin and basic provisions. She considered the dress she held, weighing its usefulness against the need to carry it on her back when they left Banunis. The temptation to put in one more was great—they would be travelling to the city by wagon, after all—but she learned long ago to travel with as few personal possessions as possible. Reluctantly, she set the dress aside.

Her chamber door flew open and she took an involuntary step back. Few people would enter a master's chamber without knocking, even in direst emergency, but the figure who shot through the doorway was one of those who could enter her rooms as they pleased. Her daughter entered, her face flushed, golden hair in disarray as if she had been running.

"Thank the Creator you haven't left yet," Miralee gasped. "I've had the most dreadful seeing."

Ayriene sat her down and handed her a cup of water. Miralee drained it, shaking visibly from head to foot.

"I wouldn't go without saying goodbye; you know that."

"You must not go at all! You must stay here where you are safe. Or at least go alone. Please, Mother. It's Sylas. Creator, but I wish I had never shown you that drawing." Miralee sobbed and grabbed Ayriene's arm. Ayriene winced. Her daughter's fingers were tight enough about her flesh to leave a mark; whatever the girl had seen had left her terrified. Ayriene sat beside her and pulled her close, as she had when Miralee was a child.

"Calm down and tell me what's wrong." She smoothed a strand of hair away from Miralee's face, wet with tears. "You had a seeing about me?" And Sylas, evidently.

Miralee wiped her face with the sleeve of her dress, fighting back the sobs that threatened to rip from her throat once more.

"There is danger coming. Great danger for the

Aerie—for all of us. The whole island, I think—it wasn't clear." She covered her face with her hands. "I saw fire flying through the sky. The library burning." She gulped and looked up at Ayriene, eyes red-rimmed, cheeks blotchy and tear-streaked. "I know it sounds far-fetched, but I didn't see images this time—not like other seeings. This one was more like... knowing. Like I'd always known it and was remembering, like when you go somewhere new and have a feeling you've been there before, you know?"

"What did Mistress Yinaede say? Have you told her?"

Miralee nodded, wiping her eyes again.

"It happened in her class. She was showing me a different way to call on the kye: one she uses sometimes to try to have a seeing about something. I was to use it and think about something."

"And what did you think about?"

Miralee sucked in a quick breath and for a moment Ayriene thought she might cry again, but she bit her lip to force the tears back and then answered.

"I thought of you. I didn't know not to think of a person; she didn't say."

"And you saw Sylas?" And fire in the sky. For a moment Ayriene remembered the invasion. The fireball engulfing the Lorandan army, burning men and boats in a huge conflagration.

"You told Sylas that he had to live—that he had to save the island. That there was something coming that only he could stop. And then you were lying on the floor and there was a bloody wound in your chest. I think—I think you were dead."

There was no holding back the tears now, and Ayriene held Miralee while her daughter cried like a little girl. Ayriene had been so proud when her daughter had shown talent when she changed, and thrilled she was a seer. Seers were almost as prized as healers among the changers, and Miralee's talent was strong. Now she wished her daughter could have been as blessedly untalented as her elder son. Garyth had laughed off being the only member of the family with no talent, saying he was happy enough without the responsibility. He had been the wisest of them all.

"Hush now, my love. Why would Sylas do me any harm?"

"I don't know, but please, Mother. You cannot be with him. I know it. I know it like I know my own name. Please don't take him with you when you go. He may not mean to harm you, but he will. He will."

Whatever had happened during the invasion, Sylas's mother had been involved. And now Sylas was involved in something not of his making. She could not leave him in the Aerie. If Ayriene could work out the connection between Shamella and Zynoa, then so could others. And that, along with his hearing of multiple kye, as his mother had before him, might seal the boy's fate. When the wagon left for Banunis, Sylas would be on it. Whatever Miralee had seen, he deserved that much.

"So, I take it that my information about the

Chesammos village was correct?" Casian once more sat before his father at the castle in Lucranne. No, not his father, he reminded himself. Just the man who had raised him.

"It was." Garvan's admission seemed grudging, as Casian had expected. "We found a bag of uncut linandra stones in the elder's house. The man's son confessed to the crime and was dealt with." Garvan pushed a bowl of cherries across the table. "Have some of these. They are good."

Casian could feel a subtle shift in their relationship since his last visit. Garvan no longer spoke to him as a father to a son, but more man to man, albeit as an older man to one of considerably less experience. It had been a gamble, telling Garvan what Sylas had said in his sleep in the infirmary. It could have been nothing but the mutterings of a sick man, but Sylas had been agitated about this Pietrig—clutching at Casian's hand and begging him not to hide linandra, as if Casian were the Chesammos Sylas addressed in his dreams. Casian had gathered something else from the ramblings, too—that Pietrig had meant more to Sylas than Casian had suspected. If that one were dead now, so much the better. Casian wanted no rivals for his lover's affections.

Casian selected three of the blood-red fruits, pulled the stalk from one, and popped it into his mouth. "I have a proposition for you," he said around the sweet flesh. He might as well launch into his plan. If he tried to play it clever, Garvan would cut him to ribbons. He realised with a shock that he thought of the man as Garvan, not Father.

The shifting attitudes were not all on one side, it seemed.

Garvan raised an eyebrow. "I'm listening."

Casian spat the stone into his hand, licked the juice from his lips. Then meeting Garvan's eyes he said, coolly, "I do not intend to stay at the Aerie. No, hear me out," he added quickly, as Garvan opened his mouth to protest. "I have proved my worth to you with my information about Namopaia. Think how much more use I could be to you at Banunis. You said once that every lord holder worth his salt had a spy in every other lord holder's castle. Did you ever manage to infiltrate Deygan's staff?"

The irritated twitch of Garvan's jaw told him that the lord had not, and it clearly rankled.

Casian leaned forward, matching Garvan eye for eye. "If you procure me a position in Banunis I can feed back information of relevance to Lucranne's interests. I will not spy for you in the conventional sense, but I will act to support your house." Not so long ago he had thought it was his house too. He had still not entirely adjusted to that loss.

Garvan grunted. "And the succession?"

"I will not stand down."

Garvan slapped the table with the flat of his hand. "And I will not have you inherit my title. It's out of the question."

"I will not stand down, but I will not hand the title on. Yoran can have it after my death, if he outlives me. And his sons will inherit after him. If I achieve a position equivalent to Lucranne then I shall stand down at that point and let him have the title he has coveted for so long—and that you clearly raised him to believe would be his someday."

"And your children?" Garvan ignored Casian's barbed comment.

"I will pledge never to marry. I will have no legitimate heirs to follow me." He might be planning to move Sylas into his mother's household, once the stubborn Chesammos was done fooling around with this plan of his to work as a healer, but Casian did not intend to abstain from female company altogether. He had been careful. There were no bastards of his to complicate the Lucranne succession, at least none that he knew of. But never marrying was the easiest way to win Garvan over.

Lucranne's holder considered the offer. "What is to stop you going back on your word? Doing away with your brother once I am dead?"

"By then, Garvan, I shall be the king's right-hand man, with your help. Why would I want Lucranne? You see, you have an incentive to help me progress."

The lord holder of Lucranne made a face as if the cherry he had bitten contained a worm. His mouth pinched and twisted, he finally said, "I will help you, if you sign your name to that agreement. But you will never, ever, call me Garvan. As far as the world is concerned, you are still my son. You will address me as Father, sir, or my lord, as the situation demands. Do I make myself clear?"

He did. Perfectly. For a position at Deygan's side and the opportunity to make a bid for the throne, that was one sacrifice Casian was more than prepared to make.

CHAPTER 20

THE CITY OF BANUNIS WAS not impressive by mainland standards, but at several times as big as Adamantara, it was the largest Sylas had ever seen. It sprawled across the hillside like a great grey-brown scab, walls of stone and ash brick slashing through the lush green of the surrounding woodland. The city rose in tiers and terraces, fitting itself to the landscape as if conceding that much to nature. The castle itself occupied the highest tiers, with a view out across the sea in one direction and towards the Aerie in the other.

The seat of House Banunis was not beautiful. Built mostly of ash-bricks formed in the desert by previous generations of brick makers, it was more functional than attractive, but its high grey walls dominated the surroundings. The towers rose so high that as Sylas craned his neck to see the top they seemed to lean towards him, and he lowered his eyes hurriedly as nausea rose in his stomach.

He stayed close to Ayriene, a knot of anxiety gathering deep inside. He remembered his first sight of the Aerie. To a desert boy, raised where the only hills were the rise and fall of the desert rocks and the ripples in the ash caused by ash storms, the mountain had seemed to go up forever. Despite Sylas's eagerness to become a changer, his father nearly had to drag the reluctant boy up the hillside. Sylas remembered thinking that not smelling the sulphur of the vents meant there was no air—that his father was taking him to die on the mountaintop. The Aerie's buildings seemed giant-built to him after the dome dwellings of the Chesammos, and Banunis Castle dwarfed even the Aerie. He would never find his way around a place so vast.

A queue had formed to enter the city. Pedestrians, people pushing carts or driving pack animals, and wagons pulled by horses or cheen all jostled through the huge wooden gates. Sylas found himself surrounded by the smell of animals and unwashed bodies. Once he was inside, he saw trinket-sellers with trays hung around their shoulders, and tradesmen wheeling handcarts and crying their wares. Farther on the scent of spices and fresh fruit rose from a marketplace. A Chesammos labourer unloaded kegs from a wagon and carried them into the cellar of a tavern. Another Chesammos shovelled horse dung into a barrel which he rolled along the street, stopping at each steaming pile.

Ayriene saw Sylas watching. "The tanners will pay him in smallcoins for a barrel-full. Not a job many would wish for, but it will keep him in food and shelter." Sylas was unmoved. Shovelling shit in Banunis, labouring in the fields in Redlyn, or digging linandra in the desert—Chesammos always got the hardest and dirtiest jobs. It came as no surprise, just a vague disappointment that even in the king's city things were no different.

From one of the side streets, the chink-chink of a hammer beating iron and the smell of charcoal and burning hooves proclaimed a smith's forge. Men's voices rose in dispute over some imagined slight. A boy snatched an apple from a stall and ran, the fruit-seller shouting after him and shaking his fist. Sylas's head swam, trying to take in the sounds and smells, wishing he could find a quiet spot to hide from the madness. Even in the vastness of the desert, he had never felt so insignificant.

He lagged behind, part reluctant to commit himself to the noise and bustle, part edged out of the flow by locals with no patience for strangers who stood and gawked like simpletons. Ayriene took his arm and pulled him into a side street to let him catch his breath.

"It's something, isn't it? I grew up here, so I know it well, but a person can easily get lost in this place. We are heading for the castle, so if we get separated, keep moving upwards. There are three more gates. If I lose you I'll stop there. You can't get to the castle without passing them, so I'll find you, never fear."

He nodded, his mouth dry. The words meant little to him. Panic had muddled his wits and already he could scarcely remember what she had said. She slapped his shoulder. "Come on. Once inside the castle it will be quieter."

"Are all cities like this?" he asked, his boots

slipping on cobblestones wet with rain and horse piss.

"Some are worse," she said with a rueful smile. "On the mainland they have cities that make Banunis look like a village."

He swallowed hard. Then he would never go to the mainland. Banunis felt like being lost inside a madman's skull; worse than this would drive him insane. How could people live, crushed together in the noise and stink? He would sooner have the sulphur smell of the desert gases.

Through the next gate the congestion eased a little. Sylas watched wide-eyed as a juggler spun a stream of leather balls. He tried to count how many there were and failed, the motion reduced to a blur. The juggler pocketed the balls with a flourish, calling out, "Coppers for your entertainment, ladies, gentlemen? Any spare smallcoin?"

He felt for the pouch at his side, but Ayriene dragged him away. "If you leave money, even a smallcoin, in the purse of each juggler or acrobat or tuppenny bard you pass you will end with nothing, and you have little enough to start with." That was true. Ayriene had given him a few coppers for his work, but he feared he had done little to earn it. "And watch out for that pouch," she said sternly, and he noticed that she had tucked hers out of reach. "These crowded streets are a haven for cutpurses and worse. If caught, they are strung up as a deterrent to the rest, but there are still people desperate enough or quick enough to try, however small the reward."

At the next gate most of the people milling

around were soldiers of the king's guard or Irenthi. Some of the Irenthi had servants in their train, all of them Irmos. It occurred to Sylas that the better dressed the Irenthi, the fairer skinned the servants. He wondered how Casian had persuaded his mother that she needed a Chesammos to wait on her. Someone as high-placed as the lady of Lucranne would have fair Irmos servants, surely. Looking around, he could see no Chesammos here at all. The farther in, the higher up, the lighter the skins of the occupants became. Sylas became aware of people stopping to watch him pass.

"You are a changer and a healer, Sylas. You have as much right here as they do," Ayriene said in a tone meant to be overheard. Sure enough, eyebrows arched but no one challenged him and they carried on quickly through these streets and up to the third gate: the one that opened in to the castle itself.

A guard in the livery of House Banunis stepped forward.

"All Chesammos to be searched, by order of the king."

The man's hand rested on his sword hilt, the threat unmistakable. Behind him two guards with pikes moved to block their way. Sylas's pulse quickened; he knew from experience how much damage a pike could do.

"He's my apprentice. I vouch for him."

The soldier's gaze took in her healer pack—the large leather satchel healers carried—and he shuffled awkwardly.

"No offence meant, Mistress, but I have my

orders. All Chesammos searched, no exceptions."

"I don't mind," Sylas said. The last thing he wanted was to cause any trouble.

"It's for weapons, like. Easy done and on your way." Sylas glanced at Ayriene and she raised an eyebrow, then nodded. Searching Chesammos for weapons would have been unnecessary a few months ago. He wondered if the rebellion had spread to attacks within Banunis itself, for King Deygan to offer an implied insult to Ayriene.

The guard was quick but thorough, making Sylas take off his cloak and boots, going through his bedroll and his pack. He offered his hunting sling, but the soldier passed it back with no comment. Sylas was glad his linandra bead was safely wrapped in its folds of linen and stashed in his pouch, away from the guard's prying eyes. Satisfied that he posed no threat, the guard called to a servant passing inside the gates, and gave instructions for them to be escorted into the palace.

When the gates swung closed behind him, Sylas forgot his feelings of displacement and stared in awe. If on the outside Banunis Castle was an unprepossessing lump of a building, once inside it was every bit a royal palace. He stared around him, mouth agape. What was he doing in a place like this?

Ayriene chuckled. "Come on. We need to get washed and into clean clothes if we aren't to look like we've been brought in to clean the chimneys. And for the Creator's sake hold yourself like a changer. You look like you are expecting to be taken by the ear and thrown out at any minute."

Which, it had to be said, was exactly how he felt. He squared his shoulders, set his face to what he hoped was a look of confident determination, and followed her.

The interior of Banunis Castle left Sylas more than a little confused. He had felt the same way in his first days at the Aerie—walking the flagstone corridors wondering if he would ever find his way out; late for lessons more than once because he had taken a wrong turn. The labyrinth of passages had been utterly bewildering for a boy who had grown up in houses which each had one large circular room. He had learned to find his way around the Aerie, he told himself. He would learn to navigate the castle too, if he didn't stumble into the king's apartments and find himself frogmarched to the dungeons in the meantime. He tried to memorise landmarks—a small window of coloured glass here, a cracked paving slab there—and gradually the place seemed less formidable, if never exactly familiar.

Lonely with no company, and Ayriene being closeted away with Deygan as often as not, he asked after Casian. Lord Casian was not expected at Banunis, the servants told him. His scheme to land a position here must have failed.

Left to his own devices, he found his way to the library. Banunis Castle proved to have an extensive selection of books, with an entire section of changer lore and history. This was a subject he had not covered in his lessons, and from the dust on the volumes no one here studied it, either. The writing was hard to decipher, and Sylas's reading abilities were stretched to the limit, but he passed countless hours with the masters of the past. He worked his way through a learned analysis of talents, their variants and presumed origin; biographies of noted council members; a collection of letters and notes, frail almost to crumbling, on the removal of Lucranne from the position of high holder.

One afternoon he was reading as usual, the index finger of his left hand lightly following the words as he mouthed them. The door to the library opened, the top hinge creaking as it had every time Sylas had entered. Doors in Banunis Castle were huge, half again as tall as Sylas, and as wide as the ones on the great hall at the Aerie. It shut with a dull thump, and Sylas held his breath to listen for footsteps. The person made little sound. The library was carpeted—such luxury—and any footsteps were dulled by the woven wool. Sylas watched the aisle anxiously. He had been given the run of the library, but some instinct told him they had not intended him to go poking about in these old, and doubtless valuable, reference books.

Over the thumping of his heart he thought he heard feet moving on carpet, the shoes or boots occasionally finding a worn patch and making muffled footsteps on the floorboards below. Once he thought he smelled something, the scent of herbal soap briefly reaching his nostrils past the mustiness of old parchment wrapped in slowly decaying leather. Sylas froze. He felt hunted, like quarry driven to ground in a dead end, waiting for the hound to sniff him out. A clean and fragrant hound, who moved softly in Irenthi boots.

When the figure reached the end of the row, it uttered a stifled gasp, hand flying to a face of palest ivory. It was hard to say who was more startled, the newcomer or Sylas. The figure was slender, maybe a hand's length shorter than Sylas, and carried a fire bowl covered with a glass mantle to light his way through the gloomy stacks. Its glow illuminated his face, showing a generous nose, finely shaped mouth, and eyes Irenthi-pale. His silver-blond hair appeared to glow in a nimbus around his head, caught by the flickering light.

The moon, Sylas thought; his hair shines like the moon. He knew he stared, but at that moment he thought the boy the most beautiful person he had ever seen.

The Irenthi boy licked his lips, holding the fire bowl out in front of him. In a voice intended to be confident but missing the mark by a fair margin, he said, "Who's there? Show yourself."

Sylas rose to his feet, being careful not to make any sudden movements. Most of the Irenthi went unarmed around the castle, but he knew many of the nobility, even their youngsters, often carried concealed daggers in case of attack.

"I beg pardon, my lord," he said. "I was given leave to use the library. I did not know these shelves were forbidden." But you had a good idea they might be. Fool!

"Keep your hands where I can see them," the young man said, approaching slowly, weighing Sylas up with his gaze. He was younger than Sylas had first thought. His voice had yet to change to the deeper tones of manhood and his skin was fair and soft-looking.

As he approached, Sylas's first impressions were confirmed. The lad was Irenthi—as true-born as they came, from the looks of him. He had the high cheekbones and pointed nose Sylas associated with Casian. Green eyes like Casian's too, he could see by the flickering gold light of the fire bowl. Now the first quaver had gone from his voice, it held a quiet authority and had the air of one used to being obeyed without question.

Prince Jaevan.

The thought shot through Sylas's mind like a stone from a sling. How many errors of protocol had he committed? Should he kneel, as if to King Deygan, or was a bow sufficient? He had expected to meet the prince in a more formal environment, if at all, and for Ayriene to have briefed him beforehand. No room in these cramped aisles to kneel, he decided, and made a hurried and ungraceful bow, raising his head only slightly to make the sign of the Lady, thumbs and forefingers together to make the shape of the mountain peak.

"My humblest apologies, Highness. I did not expect to see you here. I will leave you to your studies."

He gathered up such notes as he had made, in his haste forgetting that the ink bottle was uncorked and sloshing the black liquid over the tabletop. Biting back a curse in his own tongue he looked around for something with which to mop the spillage. In his desperation he considered tearing a strip from his shirt, knowing full well that would earn him trouble from Ayriene. The ink had missed the books, thank the Lady; he shuddered to think what the punishment might have been had he damaged some of these priceless parchments with his clumsiness.

The lad smiled, showing white, even teeth. He reached into his tunic and brought out a kerchief.

"Use this. Not that the desks in here haven't seen their share of ink over the years."

Sylas muttered thanks, sopping up the ink and then holding the kerchief awkwardly. Did he return it to the prince, wet and stained, or take it and attempt to get it laundered?

"Keep it," Prince Jaevan said with another smile. "It is only a little thing."

Sylas bowed again, preparing to make his excuses and run, but Jaevan stared at the table, then at Sylas, realisation written across his features.

"I know you, I think," he said. "A Chesammos scholar, writing with a brush instead of a quill. You are from the Aerie. You must be Ayriene's apprentice. Tell me I am wrong." His boyish face lit up with pleasure at having worked the puzzle out for himself.

Sylas mumbled something about not being much of a scholar, hoping Prince Jaevan would give him leave to go before he showed himself to be a fool, or broke something, or both, but the prince waved him to a seat with an eloquent gesture of his long, thin hand. The prince himself sat across the table from Sylas, the damp, black stain between them.

"Do you know what my father and Ayriene are talking about when they shut themselves away?" Jaevan said. "They discuss my symptoms. My aches. My cramps. Mistress Ayriene tries to convince my father of what we both know is true and he still fervently denies. She tests me for this and that, at his insistence, but all the signs point to one thing, and one thing only."

Sylas stared. Ayriene had not told him why they had come, only that King Deygan had summoned her. For all he knew it was a regular occurrence. Was he understanding the prince correctly?

Jaevan scowled, a strange expression on such a flawless face. "It's my life they are talking about. It's not fair. They should listen to me." He paused, pulling on his lower lip. "Tell me, changer. What did it feel like when you first changed? Did it hurt? What is it like to fly?"

When Ayriene found Sylas later, he was sitting in the courtyard with Jaevan. The pair were deep in conversation. Sylas had Jaevan sitting cross-legged on the ground in Chesammos fashion, despite there being a perfectly serviceable bench nearby, and the two talked animatedly, their chatter and laughter echoing around the courtyard. Ayriene could not remember the last time she had heard Sylas laugh. It was a shame the circumstances were so inappropriate.

They looked odd, dark head bent close to the fair,

and they drew curious glances from passers-by. Chesammos were entirely absent from the castle—the servants were all Irmos—and a Chesammos would never be seen treating an Irenthi as a near-equal. The castle staff were unsure whether to be affectionately indulgent of their young prince, or utterly scandalised. Ayriene had no such doubts. All but dragging Sylas away, she told him in no uncertain terms that what he had done was not proper.

"But he asked me to sit and talk with him, Mistress. He says he will be king one day, maisaiea-yelai, and he wants to understand all his people, not just the Irenthi. He says his father thinks nothing of the Chesammos. He sees us as a tool by which the most unpleasant and most dangerous jobs get done. Jaevan—Prince Jaevan—wants to make things better for us."

Sylas's hopes were understandable, if unreasonable. If the Chesammos survived as a people until Jaevan took the throne, and if a changer was allowed to become king, Jaevan would find himself as hamstrung by tradition and politics as had his father.

"Idiot!" said Ayriene, giving him another cuff round his head for good measure. "Don't you think that Deygan himself spoke that way once? When Prince Jaevan becomes king he will find that ruling does not mean pleasing himself, but juggling the needs and wishes of the king's assembly, by whose right he holds the throne."

Sylas looked hurt, and Ayriene regretted her

harshness. During their travels she had become genuinely attached to Sylas, and was pleased that his eyes had lost the hunted look they had worn in the Aerie. But sometimes he had no more sense than an ash beetle. Sitting in broad daylight talking to the heir to the throne as his friend and equal, indeed. If Deygan were to hear of it he would likely order Sylas removed from the castle, or at least prohibited from speaking to the prince without proper supervision.

Sylas sat, subdued, drawing with chalk on a slate; parchment was too precious for him to practise on. His brows were furrowed and his deep brown eyes seemed even darker than usual. He drew with an intensity that Ayriene recognised. Her apprentice was troubled, and her reprimand was only a part of it.

"Sylas?" She raised an eyebrow at him, hoping he would share his thoughts. Stray fragments of chalk dust clung to his clothes and he brushed them off with a frown.

"I like him, Mistress, and I think he likes me." The frown deepened to a scowl. His Chesammos features reminded her of a storm brewing, dark and foreboding. "He has no friends his own age. He has brothers, but they are younger. The one nearest his own age is more interested in horses and archery than books and knowledge, and the next one is just a child. His father is busy—too busy to spend much time with him—and his mother is dead, so he has no one but his tutors to talk to about his interests. He is lonely, I think. And..."

he hesitated, as if reluctant to betray a confidence. "Mistress, do you and the king talk about whether Jaevan may be a changer?"

The bluntness of the question brought her up short.

"Prince Jaevan, Sylas. If you disrespect the prince it will be bad for you. Even with me, you must watch your tongue, in case you grow too used to bad habits. It is no concern of yours what the king and I talk about." She willed herself to maintain the upper hand despite his sullenness. "Has the prince spoken to you about it?"

He nodded. "He thinks he is changing. He has the pains, and he said he heard a call at the Aerie. He is frightened, Mistress, and no one is telling him anything."

He is lonely, I think.

The tone of Sylas's voice haunted her and she realised that Sylas might as well have been talking of himself. He had no one his own age, only his tutor to talk to and that tutor so busy of late that he had been left to his own devices. She had neglected him. Ayriene wondered if Jesely might be prevailed upon to make one of his visits to the castle. Sylas got on well with Jesely. But that was another tutor; what he needed was a friend closer to his own age. And at least she could encourage his friendship with Prince Jaevan. Sylas's relationship with Casian troubled her. That could only end with Sylas hurt when Casian eventually cast him aside.

"I will speak to the king. It could be that he may let you meet with Prince Jaevan, although probably in more formal circumstances than today." She smiled faintly at the recollection of the crown prince sitting in the dust in his fine clothes, throwing his head back to laugh at something Sylas had said. It could be that this unlikely friendship would be exactly what both of them needed.

CHAPTER 21

BANUNIS HAD BEEN IN A state of growing excitement about the upcoming feast day since before Sylas and Ayriene arrived. Officially the anniversary of Deygan's coronation, it had also become a celebration of Chandris repelling the Lorandan invasion. The two events had happened within days of each other, the invaders thinking to strike at a young, untried ruler.

Sylas begged Ayriene to let him go and she had intended to accompany him, but had contracted a head cold from a patient and had taken to her bed with some of her own remedies. Sylas was nervous about going without her—the city would fill with visitors for the celebrations and the streets would be more crowded than usual—but he wanted to see the procession. Jaevan and his brothers would ride in the carriage with King Deygan, and would help him throw silver and smallcoin to the populace. Sylas's main interest was seeing his new friend in his princely role, standing beside his father.

The crowds began to fill the streets early, people staking their claims to the best spots. Over the years, the places had been marked where it was easiest to catch one of the coins thrown by the royal party. Mostly the king and the princes threw coppers, but an occasional lucky person would be on the receiving end of a half-regal, or even a regal. The scrum for the silver coins often got dangerous, Ayriene warned Sylas before he set off. He intended to stay well clear.

He had no need to scrabble for smallcoins. The pouch at his belt, which he tucked carefully inside his tunic before he passed the castle gates, held a few more coins than when he arrived. On occasion, encouraged by Ayriene, Sylas had set up in the courtyard of the castle, waiting for customers to come to him as they did in the villages. He had earned a little extra from that, enough to buy himself some ale and a pie or two at today's festival. He had no personal expenses, as his food and lodging were provided by House Banunis. He might be sleeping on a pallet at the foot of Ayriene's bed, a curtain pulled across the room to give a little privacy, but it was better than most nights on the road.

He exited the castle gateway and went out into the streets that led to the lower city. A storm had passed over the previous night and Sylas had sat at his window, unable to sleep as the thunder rumbled its way over the castle. Lightning had forked, slicing the air to crackle through the ash-brick towers, and the rain had lashed the streets and houses of Banunis City.

His feet slipped on the smooth, wet cobbles, the leather soles of his boots worn thin from travelling. One leaked, the cold damp seeping through to his feet; he examined the boot with annoyance. Then he chuckled. Desert Chesammos wore no boots. The soles of his feet had themselves once been as tough as leather.

The crowds grew denser as he made his way down the hill, the press of bodies jostling him, making him uncomfortable. He saw more Chesammos faces than usual—men, women, and children joining the crowd in the hopes of catching one of the regals to sustain them through the lean days of winter. Here and there a cry went up when someone discovered the cord of their belt pouch had been cut. Sylas tucked his purse deeper inside his tunic and considered returning to the castle. The smell of old sweat turned his stomach, and his pulse raced at the unfamiliar feeling of being carried along by the press of people, sometimes entirely against his will and into areas of the city he did not recognise. He had thought to stay in the main street, since that was the way the king's procession would come, but for respite he took himself into a side road, leaning in a doorway to regain his composure.

The smell of fresh-baked pies drew him to a small stall set away from the main throng. The pie-man was doing good business, even off the main thoroughfare.

"I didn't fancy my chances out there," the man commented. "If my stall wasn't overturned in the press, I'd have lost pies left and right to the street children instead. The little buggers are quick enough to dart in and take one while my attention is with a genuine customer. At least this way my proceeds feed my own children, not some guttersnipe."

Street children? Among the Chesammos even the poorest were cared for. Even in the worst of times, none need steal or beg to support themselves. Sylas munched thoughtfully on his own pie, good and hot and spicy, with a flavour he thought he should know but was unable to identify. He wondered if Jaevan knew that children right on his father's doorstep were having to steal to eat.

A hubbub from the main road announced the approach of the procession. Soldiers beating drums marched ahead of the parade to clear the way and streets that had already seemed crowded to Sylas became more so as people squeezed to the sides to let the carriages through.

Clashing cymbals and blaring trumpets preceded the king's carriage, and then Sylas could see him. Jaevan stood at his father's side, resplendent in red robes and with a circlet around his head, a linandra stone in the centre of his brow. Deygan wore the king's coronet—a more ornate version of the one Jaevan wore, set with the biggest linandra Sylas had ever seen. The two younger boys must have been perched on stools to see over the sides. Their white-blond heads were bare, but they wore the same red robes as their father and brother. The king and the three princes dipped time and again into the baskets of coins. Deygan's arm arced outward like a farmer sowing seed and people plucked the coins from the air or scrabbled for them on the ground. Jaevan and Marklin copied Deygan, and little Prince Rannon did his best, although his coins dropped far closer to the carriage than those of his brothers.

Jaevan's eyes seemed to search the crowd. Not looking for Sylas—he could never have spotted

Sylas in all these people—but as if he sought the neediest. The king's blessing, they called these alms, and people snatched the coins from the air, clutched them in their fists and kissed their fingers. Sylas's heart swelled with pride watching Jaevan. He would make a fine king one day and maybe, if Sylas succeeded in his training, he could be court healer. Then they could be friends always. His determination flared into passion. Whatever it took for him to succeed, he would be a healer and serve Jaevan.

An instant later, Sylas noticed stones flying towards the carriage from all directions. The street here was narrower than most other roads in Banunis—the perfect place for an ambush. The stones flew so fast that no arm could have thrown them. They had come from slings: the weapon of the Chesammos.

The two guards riding on the back of the carriage leaped in beside Deygan and his sons, pushing them to the floor and protecting them with their bodies, but not before Sylas saw one of the younger boys fall under a stone and Jaevan with blood streaming from a wound to his forehead. Sylas's stomach lurched. He could help; he was a healer. But the carriage driver whipped up the horses, and the soldiers in the front of the procession pushed the crowd out of the way to get the carriage back to the safety of the castle walls. People screamed. It seemed the carriage driver was not too particular about people being out of his way as he whipped the horses forward. Sylas wondered how many were being brought down beneath pounding hooves.

Sylas scanned the crowd. One attacker was behind and to the right of him. He caught a glimpse of golden brown skin and dark hair as the man turned to flee. Elsewhere, others were overcome and handed over to the king's guard. Sylas tried to push through the throng to the man who had been behind him. He had hurt Jaevan. He could not be allowed to escape.

"Here's another. Take him."

Rough hands grabbed him, pinning his arms to his sides. His first instinct was that of a wrestler. He broke the hold, taking a grip on his assailant's shoulders in turn. In a fair fight, one on one, Sylas would have had the measure of this man. He was no wrestler; he stood too heavily on his feet. Sylas turned, tripping the fellow, who landed on his back in the dirt. Another man grabbed Sylas's shoulder and he whirled, landing a punch to the second man's chin. By the Lady! A healer should not be brawling in the streets. The thought had barely crossed his mind before a blow to the small of his back from a third man dropped him to his knees, sobbing for air, streaks of light splitting the blackness that gathered before his eyes.

Sylas was hauled to his feet, one man twisting his arms behind him and another holding a knife to his throat. The man he had dumped in the ash took the opportunity to exact his revenge. A punch to Sylas's gut doubled him over as best he could under restraint, coughing and wheezing as the breath was knocked out of him. The man rubbed his knuckles grimly and looked to be considering which part of him to hit next.

"Leave him be." A man wearing the livery of the city watch strode forward and the two men not holding his arms fell away, abashed. "We'll take it from here. All the bastards who attacked His Majesty have been taken. Next you'll see of this fellow, he'll be swinging at the end of a rope."

Sylas tried to protest. He was no rebel. He was a changer of the Aerie. A healer. A man was allowed to protect himself, wasn't he? A few of the city folk spat at him, but mostly he heard voices muttering "Chesammos scum" and "hang the filthy bastard." They would listen to him once he was back in the castle. There they must recognise him for who he was and release him.

He was bound, hands behind his back, and bundled like a sack into the back of a wagon with four other men. He knew one by sight: Neffan, a wrestler from Cellondora. One of the men had taken a wound to his right side, and blood soaked through his homespun tunic. He looked about Sylas's own age, with his beard only soft fuzz on his cheeks. Sylas kicked the driver's platform to attract attention.

"Guard, there's a man hurt back here."

"Keep it down, you." A soldier leaned from the bench and jabbed Sylas with the butt end of his spear.

"What will happen to us?" He was sure he knew the answer.

"You'll be imprisoned, tried, and then strung up by the city gate, as you deserve. Your filthy Chesammos heads'll be stuck on pikes as deterrent for any of the rest of you who crawl out of the desert to threaten the king."

"I'll not be hanged," said Neffan grimly. Sylas saw that Neffan's hands were bound in front of him, not behind, and that he had managed to work his pouch free of his tunic. From the pouch he drew a stone, all sharp edges like a flint, and drew it across his wrist. Fool man. He would not draw enough blood like that to kill himself. Droplets of blood formed on the golden skin, and the man smiled with satisfaction. His friends stared in horror at the welling blood.

"By the Lady, Neffan, you know what you've done?" One of his fellows hissed at him, his face drawn.

Neffan nodded. "Four hours, maybe five. But a death of my choosing, not of the king's."

Sylas stared from one to the other. They knew something he didn't. The man tried to throw the stone at one of the guards, but with his hands bound he could get no force behind it. It bounced harmlessly off the guard's boiled leather jerkin and out of the wagon.

"What is he talking about? What has he done?"

But none of the men said a word. The wagon shuddered to a halt, and they were manhandled out into the courtyard of Banunis Castle. The guards were none too gentle, and the occasional fist or boot found flesh if the prisoners did not move fast enough for their liking. Sylas found himself in a part of Banunis he had never seen, nor ever thought to.

The castle prisons.

∽∾⊙∾∽

The prisons were as grim as Sylas might have expected. The smell of a thousand men held there over the years made him gag—the combined stench of sweat and vomit and human waste. A few handfuls of straw had been tossed on the stone floor, and the only light came from a barred window high above. Around the walls, metal rings hung at intervals. Either he and the others were too unimportant to be shackled, or the soldiers didn't expect they'd be there long enough to warrant the effort. Sylas wasn't sure which option was preferable.

The injured young man's legs gave out once they were through the door, buckling under him so that he dropped as if felled. Sylas crawled to him, pulling the fabric away from the dark stain on his tunic. A knife or sword had pierced his side, beneath his ribs.

Sylas went to the door. Made of stout wood, it had a small, barred observation window. He shouted between the bars, "Hey! We need help here. One of these men is injured." There was no response. He shouted again.

"Don't care, as long as he lives long enough to be hanged," came the answer from outside.

"I need a message taken to Mistress Ayriene."

"Mistress Ayriene? The changer?"

"That's right. I'm her apprentice."

Sylas could hear footsteps along a flagstone corridor. The gnarled face of a man with close-cropped greying hair and several days' growth of stubble glared through the window. When he spoke, Sylas could see gaps where teeth had been, and smell the rankness of his breath.

"You a changer, boy? Turn into a bird and fly away, then. You could get through the bars up there, I reckon." He cackled unpleasantly.

It came as no surprise that the jailer didn't believe him. With dirt on his clothes from the street, muck from the prison floor and stains on his tunic, he looked every bit the Chesammos criminal.

"I can't change, but I swear to you I am her apprentice. My name is Sylas. Please, you have to tell her I'm here."

The man spat between the bars. "Don't have to do nothing. Just take you to the king's justice when I'm called to, and with a bit of luck get to help with the stringing up too. You had a bit of sympathy up to now. Stoned the king and his boys, and you lost it. Who uses stones, unless children pelting rats and dogs in the street?"

"At least bring me water and bandages, and untie my hands so I can tend him. If one of us dies then that's one fewer trapdoor for you to open beneath our feet." It made Sylas sick to his stomach to think of the five of them hanging from ropes, but the fellow needed convincing.

It worked. The bandages the guard passed through the door soon after had been used and washed many times, but at least they were clean. The water smelled of the taint of the Lady's breath, so it had come from the common well, not been filtered through sand, but it was better than nothing. For a moment, while the door was open, Sylas was tempted to run. If he took the man by surprise, landed a lucky blow or two, he might make it—to the next locked door at least. He didn't want to think what would happen if his way was barred. The man didn't seem the type to laugh off an escape attempt. And that would leave the wounded man with no caregiver. Sylas sighed. He had to do his duty.

"Please send word to Mistress Ayriene. I'm telling you the truth."

The man grunted (or it might have been a short laugh—Sylas wasn't sure) and turned the key in the lock. His footsteps faded along the corridor, and Sylas dampened one of the cloths and wrung it out. If he was lucky, he might keep the man alive long enough to be hanged. The thought gave him no comfort.

CHAPTER 22

SYLAS DID WHAT HE COULD for the injured man, washing and binding the wound and using what water was left to sponge his face to make him more comfortable. Soon after, it became clear that Neffan was also sick. Sylas could not understand how or why. He was uninjured, apart from the scratch from the flint. The conditions were bad, certainly, but the stale air and stench would take several days to make any of them unwell. Neffan had not been here long enough for the watch bell to sound, far less sicken with anything.

His words ran through Sylas's head.

Four hours, maybe five. But a death of my choosing, not of the king's.

Sylas took Neffan's hand and turned it wrist up. Around the scratch the skin had bruised, a livid red-blue clearly visible on the golden-brown of the man's skin. He felt Neffan's forehead. The man was feverish, but how had he become ill so quickly?

"What have you done?" Sylas grabbed Neffan's shoulders and shook him. "The princes—two of them were hit. Will they be sick now, too?"

Neffan said nothing, but a smile curled the corners of his mouth and his eyes took on a satisfied gleam.

Deygan would have called for Ayriene as soon as he and his sons reached the safety of the castle, of that much Sylas was sure. Even sick herself, Ayriene would heal the boys' wounds. Sylas wondered how long it would take before someone noticed that the princes were not recovering as they ought. They were probably getting worse by the minute, if Neffan's symptoms were anything to go by. Ayriene would have sent for Sylas by now, particularly if she was no better than she had been in the morning. But when he was nowhere to be found, she would assume that he had stayed in the city. Celebrations would go on well into the night, and the taverns and brothels did a roaring trade on feast days. She probably thought he was out drinking or whoring; there were men as well as women to be had, if you knew who to ask. The castle dungeons would be the last place she would think to look.

Think, Sylas, think! He sat where floor and wall met, knees drawn up to his chest, hands in fists on either side of his forehead. He was missing something. They had chosen slings over daggers or swords or bows. He would bet that Chesammos entering the city for the feast had been searched at the main gates, so they could not have brought in anything larger. That made slings the obvious weapon choice for the would-be assassins. But over those distances, through a crowd, a man would have to be inhumanly accurate or have the Lady's own luck to land a killing blow. And Neffan was dying from a scratch.

He rolled to hands and knees and crawled

across to Neffan, whose cut arm was now covered with bruises. Despite the man's protestations Sylas investigated further, finding the first pale purple splotches oozing into the skin of his chest.

"It's poison, isn't it?" he said, his face close to Neffan's. "You coated the stones with poison. That's why you threw stones, hoping to break their skin." The image of Jaevan with blood running from a wound on his forehead haunted him. "What did you use, damn you?"

Neffan refused to speak—or could not.

Sylas settled back against the wall once more. Ayriene had taught him about the poisons which were toxic at a high level but had healing properties in smaller quantities. He thought he could ignore those. Poison on a flint would deliver too small a dose to be effective. That left three that he knew of, none of which Mistress Ayriene had ever mentioned. She might know of them, but two were from plants found largely in the desert, and which had no medicinal uses.

He could eliminate the one that killed in minutes—Neffan had already survived longer than that—which left kaba sap and esteia. They had similar symptoms, both starting with a fever. Kaba sap caused bleeding from the eyes and nose and mouth in its later stages, but by then the patient was too far gone to save. He could not afford to wait that long. Esteia was eaten by people tempted by the nut-like seeds. Then another thought occurred to him. Irenthi were immune to the effects of kaba sap. Well, not immune, exactly. It would give an Irenthi an unpleasant stomach upset, but not kill him. So if it was kaba sap, then Jaevan was safe, but he couldn't imagine that Neffan and his gang would have made such an elementary mistake.

Most cases of esteia poisoning were by ingestion of the seeds, but Neffan had not eaten anything—just scratched himself. Unless they had found a way to extract the poison from the nuts. Could they be ground up, maybe boiled to make a liquid poison with which to coat the flints? He had never heard of it being done, but that didn't mean it was impossible. Skin contusions were a symptom of esteia poisoning, and as far as he remembered, kaba sap left no marks. A better death than the rope? Maybe. Neffan had chosen his own way to die, but Sylas did not intend for him to choose Jaevan's. How long had it been since the parade? How long did Jaevan have before the antidote would be futile?

Sylas went to the door, banging with his fists, yelling as hard as he could manage. He heard grumbling. The guard who had brought the bandages shambled his way to the window and scowled through.

"What's the matter? Your friend died, has he? Can't say I'm sorry."

"He's not dead, but another is sick. Very sick. And Prince Jaevan will be soon, if he isn't already. The stones were poisoned. You must get word to Mistress Ayriene."

The guard scratched at his scalp. His hair was close cropped, a precaution against the lice that were surely rampant in the cells. He didn't look to Sylas as if he was very bright, and Sylas fretted at any delay.

"We don't have any time. They have used a Chesammos poison and Mistress Ayriene may not know of it. Let me out so I can help her. Or at least tell her what I've said."

"Poisoned, you say? Your stories are getting better, I'll give you that. First you're a changer and now Prince Jaevan is poisoned. Very creative. Maybe I'll give you another couple of hours—see what you come up with then."

Sylas shouted in frustration. "The Lady burn you for a fool! I am a changer, and the prince is in danger of his life. If he dies, I'll tell the king you ignored my warnings if I have to scream it out to him with a noose around my neck." He pounded on the door with his fists again. "Listen to me, flames blind you! You must tell the healer it is esteia. Esteia!" He slammed his shoulder to the door in sheer desperation, never expecting it to give.

The jailer looked as if Sylas's sudden passion had almost convinced him. "Why should I stick my neck out for you? I go to this healer and you're not who you say you are, I don't just look stupid, I likely lose my job as well. You going to make it worth my while?"

Sylas had little money, certainly not enough to make this man step out of line. He felt a pang of regret at pies eaten, ale drunk, and coins casually tossed to street performers. But he did have one thing that might win the man's attention. He pulled out his pouch and opened the drawstring. The little package was safe inside. He drew it out and untied the thread, linen draping his palm, the linandra bead sitting in the centre. He held the bead up to the bars between finger and thumb. It was a poor stone, and if the man looked closely he would see the flaw running through it, but it might be enough to appeal to his greed.

"This for you, if you take my message."

The guard's eyes glittered. "Say now, is that linandra?" He licked his lips, glancing over his shoulder down the corridor. "What's to stop me coming in there and taking it?"

"You try and I'll swallow it. You can check the slop bucket for the next couple of days, if you're that desperate. Now go and tell the healer." He surprised himself with how firm his voice remained when inside he was quaking with fear. Jaevan had already lost so much time.

And then he heard it, faint as if far away, almost beyond hearing.

We fly, changer?

Had he truly heard it or was his mind playing tricks? The linandra between his fingers took on the same faint glow as when he was tested for sensitivity. He could hear the other kye too, but this one was stronger than the others—clearer. His heart thumped like a punch behind his ribs. There was a moment where it seemed to stop beating altogether, and then it raced with excitement. Was it here, now? Had his true kye shown itself in the king's dungeons? He wanted to laugh with relief, with despair. Even if he changed here he could not escape—the bars were too close to let all but the smallest of birds through.

He felt it. The lurching, twisting, giddying

sense of part of himself being left in the Outlands, the awareness that his mind was shared with something other than himself, the stomach-churning sensation of falling as he transformed. Sylas looked at the bottom of the door from scarcely a handspan off the ground. His clothes lay around him, the linandra bead nestled in their folds. Instead of feet he had claws that scraped and clicked on the stone floor. He spread his wings and turned his head to see them move at his command. Shiny, almost oily in appearance, and blue-black. He was a crow, then, as he had thought he might be. Sylas fought down a glimmer of regret. He was a true changer at last; he should be elated at his success, not disappointed at the form he took.

"Hey! Where'd he go?" He heard the jingle of keys, the creak of the door opening, and then he was back, a human, crouching on the floor of a dank prison cell beneath Banunis Castle. The guard stared down at him, mouth open, eyes wide. "By the Creator! You really are a changer. I saw you. Just for a moment, like, but I saw."

Sylas fell to his knees on the floor. He was naked, his clothes scattered at his feet. Bent double, he retched miserably, bringing up the remains of his pie. Had anyone told him that changing could nauseate him? He didn't think they had. He spat, wiped his mouth, and plucked the bead from the pile of clothing, making sure it was firmly in his grasp.

"Take a message to Mistress Ayriene. Tell her it is esteia that ails the prince. Take the message for me and the bead is yours."

The man licked his lips as if considering a juicy steak, then turned and ran. Sylas could hear his booted footsteps thumping up the steps to the castle.

Sylas found the piece of linen and wrapped the bead once more, taking care not to touch it with his bare hands. It had glowed before he transformed. Was linandra the key? If so, why had no other Chesammos needed a bead? Master Cowin had changed at nine years old. He would not have been close to having the piercing at that age. But enough for now that he had done it at last, and without a call to help him.

The other men watched him silently as he dressed himself.

"It is esteia, isn't it? Tell me now, before I have Mistress Ayriene give the prince the wrong treatment."

Neffan stared sullenly back at him, but the young man—the one whom Sylas had treated—nodded. "No harm, since you've guessed. It was our only hope of getting Deygan or one of the princes. We will hang for it, but I don't regret trying. I never wanted anyone else mixed up in it, though. I hope your healer can convince Deygan you weren't involved."

Sylas was less worried about that than about saving Jaevan. His only knowledge of esteia was of ingesting it, not putting it straight into the blood. If Ayriene did not know of esteia, as seemed possible, then she would not know the antidote. The guard had to get to Ayriene and make her listen. And then she had to make Deygan listen to her. He sat by the wall again, chewing on his thumb knuckle. Even if Ayriene managed to secure his release, they might already be too late.

Ayriene's mind raced, even as she held the contact with the kye that gave her the healer talent. The king had sent for her as soon as the royal party returned and she quickly assessed the damage. Prince Jaevan's temple and a gash on Prince Rannon's forearm were healed in a few moments. Prince Marklin had been pushed into the bottom of the carriage by a guard, and was shaken but unhurt. King Deygan had been struck on the chest but was only bruised, saved from worse injury by the leather tunic he wore under his robes. Ayriene gave Marklin a sedative to help calm his nerves, and as an afterthought made one up for the other two boys as well.

News came that the attackers had been apprehended and were in the castle prisons. Ayriene would not have been surprised if Deygan had ordered them hanged there and then, such a rage gripped him. Five men, all Chesammos, the soldiers said: one injured, but the others fit to stand interrogation, should His Majesty want them put to the question. The rebellion was spreading, then, if they felt confident enough to attack the king in his own city.

It all seemed routine at that stage. The injuries were healed and the boys given a herb tea to settle them; she had no need of Sylas. But when, inexplicably, Jaevan and Rannon showed other symptoms, she had a messenger sent to summon him to the king's chambers. When the messenger returned to say there was no sign of him in the castle—that he had been seen since leaving for the procession—she was surprised but not concerned. Maybe he had been in the lower part of the city and was unaware of the attack on the king's party. Or had overcome his usual preference for solitude and found some part of the city where celebrations and carousing were in full swing.

Now she *really* needed him, and no one had seen him for hours. Damn the man! Where had he gone off to?

Rannon and Jaevan both developed a fever shortly after. Some sort of infection from their wounds was possible, certainly, but she would not have expected it so soon. Rannon had the more delicate constitution so she concentrated on the younger prince first, linking with her kye to try to support his healing. No matter what she did, she could not bring the fever down, and when Rannon and Jaevan were both bathed in sweat, she had to resort to the more traditional method of sponging them with cold flannels. King Deygan called in a servant to assist. Sylas was still nowhere to be found.

Soon, Prince Rannon moaned and thrashed in his fever. Bruises formed on his chalk-white skin where no stone had struck him. Ayriene had to admit she was baffled. If she had had time to collect her thoughts then maybe she could have made sense of it, but two royal princes growing sicker by the minute under her care left little time for anything but keeping them alive.

The king's apartments became a sick-room. Prince Marklin retired to his own room with a nurse to keep him out of the way. Ayriene was considering a second dose of sedative for the boys when a knock came at the door.

"Who is it?" Deygan barked.

Ayriene did not raise her eyes from Rannon. The child was failing. His skin was almost entirely covered with bruises, and they were spreading fast. His heart beat fast but more faintly by the minute. She could help steady a failing heart, but the boy's body was collapsing and she could do little more for him. And Jaevan was fading too, despite his greater strength. It would not be long before Ayriene would have to choose to abandon Rannon to help Jaevan. As crown prince, his needs took priority, but it broke her heart to leave Rannon to die. Where in the Creator's deepest hell was Sylas? There was little enough he could do, if a healer talent was failing, but his absence was inexcusible.

"Beg pardon, Your Majesty. Madam healer," a nervous-looking servant said. "This man would not be put off, Sire. Says he knows what is wrong with the young prince." She cast a quick look at Jaevan, his face slick with sweat, tossing and moaning and trying to shake off the blanket that Ayriene had pulled up around his shoulders.

"And is my son the talk of the castle now?" Deygan shouted. "Who has been gossiping? Was it you? I'll have your back striped for you if it was."

"No, Sire, no," she said, eyes darting from Deygan to Jaevan and back. "I swear I said not a word to anyone. But he came here saying it was poison, Sire. I thought maybe the lady healer should hear him, in case it was important."

"Send him in," said Ayriene, before Deygan could say anything. She would listen to anyone who had a hint of what was wrong with the boys.

He was an unsavoury looking man, with battered leather jerkin and equally battered boots, and he smelled of sweat and old food and latrines. His hair was close-cropped, and by instinct she noted the broken veins on his face. He drank too much, like as not, and limped like one who was afflicted with gout.

"Your Majesty. My lady," he said gruffly. "There is a man in the cells claims to know her ladyship." Ayriene was anything but a lady, but few knew how to address changers, and giving her a rank to which she was not entitled was safer than giving offence.

"In the cells?" Ayriene could not think who she might know who had been consigned there, or how he might have any inkling that Jaevan was ill, or what ailed him.

"Aye, m'lady. Brought here with the Chesammos as attacked His Majesty, he was. He says he's a changer and..." he looked uncertainly at Deygan, "he did change. Just for a few moments, like, but he did it, by the Creator. He really did."

"Sylas?" she breathed.

"Aye, m'lady, that was the name he gave. There was poison on the stones they threw, he says. He said I must be sure and say to you that it was esteia."

"Esteia?" Ayriene said, scrabbling for her herbal.

It was not a name she was familiar with, but Sylas had all but memorised the tome. She would not be surprised if he now knew more plants than she. "Is he still in the cells?"

The man nodded, seeming unsure if he should bow when spoken to, and settling for ducking a nervous half bow to each of them when addressed. "My lady, he is tending two of the men what were brought in. One was hurt when they were captured and one has some sort of fever, by the looks. Yon changer man says he is innocent, Sire. But he was arrested along with the others. He didn't have a bag of stones as they did, right enough, but he did have a sling and—" His eyes dropped and his battered boots shuffled uncomfortably, smearing the Creator knew what onto the carpet. "He said he wasn't one of them, Sire, and if her ladyship knows him then maybe he was picked up by accident, like."

"No stink without shit," Deygan said darkly. Ayriene knew Deygan did not like Sylas being in the castle. It was no accident that there were no Chesammos in Deygan's household, and Deygan heartily disapproved of his eldest son's more liberal approach.

For a moment Ayriene wondered if Sylas might have sought out the rebels, remembering his reaction to the Namopaia raid. Just a moment, then dismissed. He would not do anything to harm Jaevan. And if he had—well, she would meet that possibility later. Right now, she needed him.

"If you want me to save your sons, I need my apprentice here. If he is right, and the Creator knows *I* think the boy is onto something, then I can keep the princes stable in their present condition a little while longer. If it is this poison, as he claims, then he needs to find an antidote and make it up." Her herbal had no mention of esteia, far less an antidote, but she would not admit that in Deygan's presence. It could be Sylas knew it by a local name.

"Can't someone else do it? Under your instruction?" Deygan's white eyebrows drew together in suspicion.

"Does anyone in your household know how to make up an infusion, Sire? And if they do, can they recognise medicinal plants reliably? If they bring back the wrong one they will waste valuable time, or worse, make the princes sicker. Sire, your sons' lives are at stake. I need you to trust me and let me have my apprentice, even though he is Chesammos."

The king harumphed and stroked his beard. "Very well, then. But he will be your responsibility. There will be guards on the door and in the room, and if he lays a finger on any of my sons I'll have him killed without question."

"Agreed." She turned to the guard. "If there is an antidote nearby, tell him to fetch it. If not, bring him straight here. And hurry, man. We have little time."

She turned her attention back to the princes. Jaevan held his own, but she was losing Rannon. Even if Sylas knew the antidote and could find it quickly she was afraid it would be too late for the younger boy. She very much feared Deygan would be short an heir by nightfall.

CHAPTER 23

S YLAS BURST THROUGH THE DOOR a few minutes later, not stopping to consider that the room he entered in such an unseemly fashion formed part of King Deygan's personal apartments. He registered the silver-haired man almost too late to skid to a halt and effect a rushed and hardly adequate bow.

"Your Majesty," he acknowledged the king, who watched him with narrowed eyes and no attempt to disguise his contempt. "Mistress, I think I know what ails the princes." On the way up the guard had confirmed his suspicions that two of the boys had been hit and were now sick, and that the healer didn't seem to be making them any better. His eyes flickered to Jaevan, then to Rannon. He gasped at the sight of the younger boy, and Ayriene moved smoothly to block the child from his sight.

"Esteia, the man said. Do you know of an antidote?"

"Yes, Mistress." If it is not too late. That thought rose unbidden in his head. Jaevan had bruising on his face, but it didn't seem to have spread beyond his neck and shoulder. Rannon was a mass of bruises, his torso almost completely purple. "Mistress, when the bruising has spread so far—"

She cut him off. "Do you know where to find it?"

"It grows near the esteia. I'd know where to find it in the desert, but here... I would not know where to find it in Banunis, Mistress."

"Then you must fly," she said.

His jaw dropped.

"Me? But I can't change."

"The jailer said you changed in the cell. Was he lying?"

He hesitated. He had changed back in seconds, but he had changed, there was no doubt about that. "No, Mistress. But you can change better and fly faster than me."

"And the time you would waste drawing the plant for me would use up any time I gained. To say nothing of the risk that I might bring back the wrong plant, even with a drawing."

First flight was always accompanied. There was too much risk of an untried changer losing their bearings and flying beyond the reach of the aiea-bar, or overflying themselves and dying of exhaustion, or becoming prey to one of the real hawks that lived on the island. "Will you come with me?" He knew what the answer would be.

"I cannot leave the princes, Sylas. I am giving them what strength I can through the aiea-dera. Without that, they might succumb to the poison so fast that even an antidote would not help them."

He had given the jailer his linandra bead, as promised, but now had the sinking feeling that the bead might have been the key to his changing. How could he admit to Ayriene that the price of his freedom had been her gift to him?

"Sylas?" When she spoke, he realised he had fallen into thought. "I can pipe for you."

"I... I don't know if I can do it again. In the prison I was angry and desperate and..." And he had had the linandra.

"Look at Jaevan, and ask yourself if you are desperate enough."

His heart bled to see his friend. The boy dozed fitfully, the fever making him restless and pale as death around the blotches that marred his fair skin. "How would I carry it?"

She rummaged in her pack and handed him a pouch. "This is what changers use to carry things in bird form. You'd need to be careful not to stretch yourself, but leaves—leaves?" She raised an eyebrow enquiringly and he nodded confirmation. "Leaves wouldn't weigh too much. You should be safe enough carrying them back." Ayriene grasped his wrist. "I know you've got it into your head that you can't change and you're probably nervous about flying alone, and I don't blame you. But I wouldn't ask it of you if I didn't think you could do it. Will you try?"

Sylas risked a glance at King Deygan. He and Ayriene had been talking in hushed voices and he wasn't sure how much Deygan had overheard, but he looked older, his face drawn with worry. He stood to lose two of his three children if Ayriene and Sylas failed. As a Chesammos, Sylas should probably be supporting the rebels and refusing to help save the boys, but he saw a father anxious for his sons, not a ruler—not an Irenthi. And Jaevan was his friend, whatever the gulf between them.

"I'll try."

She took her pipe from her pouch and blew it, the strong pure note subtly different from Olendis's, but causing the same stirring of the kye in his head. He heard the same familiar insistent clamour but now he knew which voice he was listening for. It came through clearly.

We fly, changer?

No, not yet. But don't go. What do I need to do?

His voice sounded breathless in his own head. He must not lose contact.

I will wait for you in the Outlands.

Sylas loosened the collar of his shirt and untied his breeches.

"You hear it?"

"I hear it." She blew again, and Sylas felt the twisting shock of transformation. He picked up the pouch in his beak and hopped towards the window.

"You'll need to change back to fill the pouch," said Ayriene. How did he understand her, as a crow? This was all so new and strange to him. "I'll call regularly. If you are in bird form it won't affect you, but if you are in human form it will prompt your change so you can fly back. I don't dare give you long. Fly hard, Sylas."

And she threw open the window shutters to let him out. His first flight, alone, and on a desperate mission. A part of him wished Master Olendis could see him now. A part of him wished Casian were here.

He was too late to save Rannon. The frail six-year-old's condition had deteriorated too far by the time Sylas returned with the leaves and boiled them to make the antidote. Although Ayriene dribbled the liquid past his lips, hoping against hope that he would rally, the child died in his father's arms less than an hour later.

Jaevan was stronger, and managed to drink a cup of the potion. Soon after his little brother gave up the fight, Jaevan's fever broke and the bruises stopped spreading. By evening, Ayriene declared him out of danger. If the antidote had come but a few minutes later they would have lost him, but he lived, though weak as a newborn. Sylas sat by Jaevan's bed, determined not to move despite Deygan's disapproval. Just after nightfall, he opened his eyes, and reached one hand out to his father and one to Sylas. A tearful Sylas dropped to one knee by his bedside and swore that as long as Jaevan needed him, he would be there. Deygan pursed his lips in annoyance, but Jaevan smiled and squeezed Sylas's hand, touching the back of Sylas's bent neck in the Irenthi manner of accepting an oath.

Lucranne held some of Sylas's heart, but Banunis held the rest. As he swore his loyalty to Jaevan, he was aware of how the Chesammos would perceive his actions. He was a traitor to them now. A loyal Chesammos would have held his tongue, let the Irenthi brats die, and gone to the gallows proud of his race and his heritage. If he had not been an Irenthi's pet before, that was certainly how they would see him now. But his choice was made. He was changer and healer first, Chesammos second.

He would serve Jaevan, if Jaevan wanted him. He would serve Jaevan for as long as they both lived.

~~~∽∽∾∾~~~

King Deygan attended the hanging of the three Chesammos in person. Neffan was long dead of the esteia, and the man who had been injured seemed barely conscious when they put the noose around his neck.

Prince Jaevan attended the king at the executions, to show the crowd that he lived. Rumours had run wild after the assassination attempt, and Deygan knew the importance of quashing them. Jaevan had to force himself to keep watching, but he stared resolutely at the gallows until his father allowed him to leave the balcony overlooking the courtyard where the scaffold had been erected.

To Deygan's mind, there should have been another man hanging beside them. When it became obvious that they had failed to kill the king, the conspirators had Sylas send word to Ayriene of what ailed his sons. How better to grant a Chesammos traitor access to the king and his family—to put him in a position where he could strike again? How convenient that the apprentice knew the poison used and where to find the plant to save Jaevan, where the master healer did not. It stank of conspiracy to Deygan. The healer's boy was implicated and up to his neck in it.

Jaevan still looked as if a gust of wind would carry him away. He had taken to his bed after his brother's funeral two days before, saying he felt unwell, but each day he grew a little stronger, and Ayriene pronounced herself content with his recovery. The bruises had faded, and his appetite had somewhat returned. As he grew stronger, so did he grow more persistent in asking Deygan's permission to meet with Sylas.

"Just to talk to, Father," he begged. "After all, he did save my life. It is churlish not to thank him."

King Deygan did not voice his suspicions to his son. Jaevan had taken such an interest in the Chesammos youngster that he would have denied his father's fears without a second thought. Ayriene also maintained that he owed a debt to Sylas, but it all seemed a little too convenient. If Sylas were indeed part of the conspiracy to kill the royal family, best he not know that Deygan's mistrust of him went any deeper than his known dislike of his race. He had ordered Chesammos entering the city searched and still they had killed his son. The guards had not queried a pouch of flints, never thinking that they could be used to kill one prince and bring another to death's door.

"I have had word from Lord Garvan," he told Jaevan. "He asks permission for Casian to attend court to learn statecraft. I have agreed; he will be a suitable companion for you. He knows the Chesammos from the Aerie, I believe, so I will agree to you meeting with the healer lad, but only in Casian's company. He will be your companion and protector. For as long as this so-called rebellion lasts, your safety is of the utmost importance." If Jaevan persisted in asking for Sylas, let him at least have an Irenthi companion: one in whose loyalty Deygan had no doubt.

Once back in his apartments Deygan received a messenger bearing alarming news.

The killers had been from Cellondora, and the central role of that village in the rebellion was confirmed by Deygan's own intelligence. Since the village lay in Lucranne's territory, Deygan had sent a message to Lord Garvan asking for its destruction. The lord holder had complied. In the short term, Garvan would compensate the lord holder for loss of income due to the loss of a linandra team. In the longer term, Garvan could make other villages increase the size of their teams to redress the balance.

A night raid by three companies of soldiers, two of Garvan's and one of Deygan's, should have left the villagers dead and the houses razed to the ground. But reports coming back from Cellondora spoke of people escaping—trained changers taking to the air to elude the soldiers. The messenger estimated up to fifteen escaped that way, and possible unpunished rebels among them.

Deygan sent back a message. The escaped Chesammos must be hunted down. There must be no survivors.

"And where is Master Donmar now?" Jesely rubbed sleep from his eyes as he followed a novice along corridors towards the council chamber.

"He is in the chamber, Master," said the young girl brightly. "I think he has sent for the other councillors."

"In that case, you do not need to accompany me," he said. "I can find my own way to the council chamber, and you must have tasks to be about."

A flicker of disappointment crossed her face. The council being called at this time in the morning was an unusual occurrence. Jesely guessed she would have been hoping for some snippet of gossip to carry back to the other novices. "You have done well, Kote. Go back to your work now."

Other masters arrived at the chamber, most bleary-eyed or arranging their tunics. Only the earliest risers looked as if the summons had not caught them unawares.

Master Donmar sat at the head of the table, eating chunks of fruit with a fork and taking sips of tea. The centre of the table held fruit and cold meat and bread fresh from the kitchens. Donmar was uncommonly good at remembering the comfort of those called to council, and Jesely's stomach growled. It would have been a long meeting indeed with no breakfast. Jesely picked up a roll, breaking it open with his thumbs and pushing a slice of cold beef inside.

"No sense asking what this is about, Donmar?"

The council leader looked less composed than Jesely had first thought. He was unshaven—unusual in itself for a man so careful about his appearance—and his eyes were bleak.

"I'll wait for the others," he said. "That way I only have to tell you once. There will be questions, and I'm not sure I have the answers."

Each councillor took his or her usual place at the table. No places were allocated, beyond that of the leader, yet changers were creatures of habit. Donmar waited until all were settled with food and drink before speaking. An expectant hush fell across the room.

"Just after daybreak, changers whom I have not seen for a long time arrived at the Aerie. Some of the names may be familiar to you: Artem, Nyniss, Pabori, Grygg, Sabelan, a few others. Eleven in all."

Donmar paused, waiting to see who would work it out. Pabori had only left the Aerie two or three years before. For Artem, Nyniss, and Sabelan somewhere between three and ten years had passed since they were changers. Few around the table would remember Grygg. He had trained at about the same time as Jesely himself—going on twenty years before.

Jesely frowned. "All Chesammos?"

"Not only that, but all from the same village—Cellondora, one of the linandra-digging villages under Garvan of Lucranne."

"How did they get here?" Fennoc the herbalist asked.

Donmar's gaze swept the table. All the council members were present except Ayriene, who was in Banunis, and Narais, who at eighty-six years of age still clung to life, but only barely.

"They flew. They represent a large proportion of the changers Cellondora has produced for the last two generations. Most of them had not transformed since they went home, but they were desperate enough to try."

"Desperate?" Yinaede prompted.

"Their village was destroyed in the night.

Everyone was slaughtered; their homes burned out. They report seeing the liveries of Lucranne and Banunis among the soldiers."

Jesely's mouth was as dry as ash. "Do we know why?"

Donmar wet his lips. "Three days ago in Banunis, there was an attempt on the lives of King Deygan and his sons. His youngest boy died. Prince Jaevan was only saved by Ayriene's skill. The perpetrators were from Cellondora. This seems to have been in retribution for the assassination attempt."

"A whole village?" Yinaede pressed her hand to her mouth. All the colour had drained from her face and Jesely thought she might faint. He poured her a drink and passed it to her. She gulped a few mouthfuls but it hardly seemed to help. Jesely stared at his hands. They were shaking.

"Deygan cannot be allowed to get away with this," said Cowin. "His hatred for the Chesammos is clouding his judgement. A whole village for an act of rebellion by a few men? That's outrageous."

"Were the assassins caught?" Jesely asked.

"Yes. They were caught and hanged. I heard..." Donmar glanced at Jesely, "I heard Sylas was involved."

"Sylas? But he wasn't from Cellondora."

"He told me he was, a few months ago," said Cowin. "At the time I thought he wasn't telling the truth, but..."

"Was he—" Jesely's words caught in his throat. "Did they hang Sylas?"

Donmar looked troubled, but shook his head. "I did not hear that he was among those executed. I have sent to Ayriene for clarification, but I do not believe Sylas to be dead."

Jesely could not believe it. Would not. Sylas was a peaceful man. He wouldn't get caught up in rebellion, whatever the provocation. "So Deygan cannot even claim that his son's killers had fled back to their village. This is wanton destruction, not justice at all."

"Indeed," Donmar sounded tired, and Jesely understood the pained look in his eyes. "But these changers have put us in a difficult position. The soldiers saw them go. They shot at them as they took flight. Several were killed as they tried to escape, I'm told. In fact, Nyniss took an injury and it escapes me how he managed to fly all the way here. By now, Deygan knows that some eluded him and has probably guessed where they fled to. The question is, what do we do with them?"

"You can't be thinking of handing them over?" Yinaede looked aghast. "Donmar, if he would kill a village to get revenge for his son, being changers won't save them."

"Quite the opposite," Donmar agreed. "In fact, I had some news from Ayriene a day or two ago that makes me wonder if Deygan may not become even less fond of changing. She reports that Prince Jaevan himself is showing signs of the change. Not only that, she believes him to be a talent, although she has not yet established its nature."

Stunned silence settled, then all the councillors seemed to speak at once—shock and excitement in their voices. Donmar held up his hand.

"First we must decide about the Cellondorans.

They left years ago, not wanting to commit to the years of study it would take to become masters. Yet we clearly cannot send them away. They have no homes to return to, and even if another village would take them in, it would put that village at risk of similar treatment. I daresay Deygan would claim that they were sympathisers or collaborators or some such. But I will not allow them to stay without the agreement of the council. Do we keep them here and give them shelter from Deygan, or not?"

It was unanimous. They were changers; they could not be turned away in their need.

Before they left, Donmar told them that he had asked Ayriene to come to a special meeting of the council to discuss Jaevan. The crown prince would need training, for his own safety if nothing else, but Jesely had a feeling that dealings with Deygan over the matter would be anything but straightforward. Deygan and Donmar had worked together to thwart the Lorandans years before, around the time that Shamella died, but relations had been strained between them ever since. Something had happened over that time that had left the two forever estranged.

Jesely looked forward to seeing Ayriene. They had been friends a long while, and he was keen to see her and to quiz her about this wild rumour of Sylas's involvement with the rebels. But he could not decide whether, with the Chesammos situation blowing out of control, Banunis was the safest place for the lad, or the worst. One thing he was certain of: the Aerie was no longer safe. Not while they harboured the Chesammos from Cellondora.

All the councillors were silent as they left the chamber, some deep foreboding haunting them all. Jesely at least had the feeling that this might give Deygan his excuse to move against them. Forces were shifting on Chandris, and he could not tell how they might play out.

CHAPTER 24

"Now I want to see you do it alone," said Ayriene, leaning back in a horsehair-stuffed leather chair in her room. One end of the room looked like the Aerie workshop, equipped with pans and burners, mortar and pestle, jars and pots in all shapes and sizes, and a selection of roots, leaves, and berries that would not have looked out of place in the palace kitchens. "Make up another bottle of the infusion of leaves, so you will have plenty to mark with while I am away. Creator willing I will only be two days or maybe three, but this is the sort of discussion that could rumble on longer. And a batch of Jaevan's potion, so I know I can leave that in your hands, too."

"Will you take him on, Mistress?" Sylas bit back the begging 'please' that he longed to put on the end.

"I told you," she said, "the life of a healer is not appropriate for the heir to the island. Would you have him walk with us the length and breadth of Chandris?" Her tone softened as she saw the disappointment he knew was etched into his features. "I know you would enjoy company, Sylas, and I'm sure Jaevan would love it, getting to travel about and meet all the common people he is so interested in. But think of the danger. He never leaves the castle without two bodyguards, sometimes more. We would turn into a wagon train if we took enough guards to satisfy Deygan. No, he must study at the Aerie, or here, and that rules me out, I'm afraid."

At the Aerie. Safe behind the high brick walls. He might as well be a thousand miles away for all the times Sylas would get to see him. He and Ayriene had visited the Aerie once in eight months of travelling. He would have to learn control before he could fly to visit him, and Sylas still could not transform without the aid of a pipe or linandra. He had not admitted to Ayriene the role linandra had played in his changing, nor that he no longer owned the bead she had given him.

Casian had arrived the previous day and had lost no time in taking up his position as Sylas's caretaker. While Sylas remained in Banunis, he had to be under the direct charge of either Mistress Ayriene or Casian, on pain of imprisonment. Already he chafed under the restrictions. Casian intended to make himself indispensible at court, one way or another, and seemed determined to resume his role as Jaevan's mentor. Deygan would place no barriers between Casian and Jaevan, as he had between Jaevan and Sylas. It did not take much thought to work out what would happen. Casian would attach himself to Jaevan like a leech to a swimmer, and Sylas would lose them both. That it was entirely appropriate for Casian to be Jaevan's mentor only made the potion more bitter for Sylas to swallow.

"So," Ayriene said, gently breaking his train of thought. "Begin. Which of these do you need?"

That at least was easy. "These, Mistress." Sylas selected a bulbous root, about the size of his clenched fist and the colour of a new bruise, and a bunch of leaves, long and slender, with fine downy hairs on the surface and red veins thick on the underside as if bulging with blood. He squeezed one of the leaves and the juice stained his fingers. "Blood elder leaves for the infusion for me and the root of the plant for Jaevan's decoction."

"Good. Now show me how you prepare each."

Tearing the leaves roughly to release the juice—no knife to taint it with its metal—he placed the leaves in a bowl and poured boiling water over until all the leaves were covered. He stirred vigorously, the sap staining the water a dark pink. "That's all I can do for now, Mistress. I'll put it in a jar and shake it every day for a week. Then the liquid will be blood red when he held up to the light. It's strained through fine linen, then heated again to boil off most of the water." Now that he had shown himself responsive to the call, Ayriene did not dare leave him unprotected until he learned to resist.

"Side-effects of the blood elder leaf when used for marking."

Ayriene had warned him before he started what he could expect. A lot of the side-effects began only after many years, and he would not be marking that long, maisaiea-yelai. When Ayriene came back she could work on his control. Then he could resist the call, change at will, and finally stop marking.

"After many years, pain like the eating away of

your joints. Also itching and crawling of the skin so severe that a man may scrape his own skin off with his fingernails trying to escape it. In the shorter term—" He flushed furiously. "In the shorter term, it can cause impotence. Mistress, it does wear off, doesn't it?" He would not mark long enough to experience the other side-effects, but it would be a cruel joke to be with Casian at last, but unmanned by the blood elder leaf.

"No one has used it so long that it has not," was her carefully worded reply. One man might respond differently than another. A woman might use a salve that a hundred others had used without problem and come up in weals. A healer worked on likelihoods, not certainties. "Once we can work on your control, with luck you'll only need to mark for a few weeks—three or four months at most. Now the decoction."

This differed from the infusion only in a few details, but he was to administer this potion to Jaevan. The responsibility frightened him, however much Ayriene told him it was safe and however many times he had prepared such potions for the people they had treated across the island. A man might be adversely affected by a decoction that a hundred others had drunk without problem. She had just said as much.

"I peel the skin off, so, and chop it." He cut the root into pieces the size of his first thumb joint. No avoiding the metal knife for this; the root was too woody and tough to be torn apart with fingers. He took a scant handful of the pieces and tossed them into an enamelled pan. When Ayriene had shown him she had taken a full handful, but her hands were smaller. Covering the pieces with water, he put the lid on the pan and set it to heat. "It will take two hours," he said, "and then I leave the pan with the lid on until it is cold. It will have changed colour from red to bluish-purple."

"So you *have* been listening," she said approvingly. "And how much must Jaevan drink?"

"A goblet each evening before he retires. This will keep three days, no more, and then I must make a new batch. But you will be back by then, won't you?"

"I hope so. You may add honey to it, or mix it with wine if he prefers. It has a bitter taste and he may wish to disguise it. Wine hides the colour too—some people find purple off-putting. Now you must show me that you can mark yourself and then I must go. The message said 'with all haste,' and although I had to make sure you could care for yourself and Jaevan I cannot delay further."

The marking hurt, though not unbearably, and he pricked the skin neatly enough for even Ayriene's approval. The marks on his chest now covered a patch a little smaller than his palm, and they would never leave him—a permanent reminder of how slow he was to learn. But he *was* learning. He would be a healer, and then the Aerie could never cast him out again.

❧

"Lord Casian."

A servant's voice hailed him along the corridor. Casian gave a vexed acknowledgement. When would the staff here learn that he was a man of importance, not to be hailed like a fishwife across a market? "Lord Casian, you have a visitor. We weren't sure where you were, my lord, but we showed him to your apartments."

"My apartments?" An unknown visitor had been left unattended with his possessions? He mentally scanned his antechamber, wondering if he had left anything unattended he would prefer other eyes not to see.

"Yes, sir. He arrived by unconventional means, if you understand me, sir. I thought you would want him shown to your chambers."

A changer? A visitor from the Aerie? Not Jesely, surely? They had parted on bad enough terms that he thought never to speak to his old master again.

"You did well. I'll go there directly."

"I had food and wine delivered, my lord. And clothing."

Casian half smiled. Of course. His mysterious visitor would have arrived without a stitch. He wondered how scandalised the castle was at a naked man being shown to his rooms. Not the naked man he would want in his rooms, sadly. He was shut up elsewhere in the castle.

Having mentally reviewed a list of who might pay him a visit at Banunis, he was unsurprised to find Gwysias in his room, enjoying a hearty meal. He greeted Casian with a wave of his knife, cutting a chunk of a fine-smelling goat cheese and popping it into his mouth.

"Good day, Gwysias. To what do I owe this unexpected pleasure?"

"I have information for you. Although if I had known what fine fare I would be offered, I might have paid you a visit sooner."

Casian took a chair opposite Gwysias and poured himself some wine. He sniffed speculatively at it. The wine was strong and dark, and he topped up the cup with water. It was early yet.

"Information?"

Gwysias swallowed, washed the food down with a goodly gulp of wine, and nodded. "Your father had something to do with destroying Cellondora, I assume?"

"My father and the king combined to eradicate a dangerous nest of rebels and revolutionaries," Casian said, schooling his face to stillness.

"And did you hear that some escaped? *Flew* to safety?"

The emphasis on the word left Casian in no doubt what he meant. "There were changers among them?"

Gwysias raised an eyebrow. "Of course. It would be hard to go to any town or village and not find changers, I imagine. I also suspect more perished there, either caught by surprise by the raid or trying to protect friends and loved ones." He pointed his knife at Casian. "But some flew. About a dozen, I believe. And would you like to guess where they flew to?"

"The Aerie," Casian breathed. "Does the king know this?"

"The soldiers presumably saw them escape, and if they saw them, Deygan will know." He gave Casian a shrewd look. "I wondered if maybe he would have told you—if my information would be of no value to you—but I see he has not. I wonder, though, if he knows where they are."

Casian clenched one hand into a fist. Damn it all. He didn't like Gwysias being better informed than he was.

"If I have brought you valuable news, my lord, may I make a request of you?"

Casian noted the form of address. In the Aerie, Gwysias had been Casian's superior; outside, Casian outranked the Irmos changer by a large margin. "Ask."

Gwysias twisted a ring on his finger. "With Chesammos claiming sanctuary the Aerie may no longer be safe. I request to serve you here, in Banunis."

"What use have I for a scribe or a librarian, Gwysias? I have no staff—not even a manservant. I have no need of one with your skills." The man's face fell. He was genuinely worried. "What makes you think the Aerie is not safe?"

"The girl, Miralee, she had a seeing. I saw it entered in the records."

"A seeing? What about?"

"An attack on the Aerie, by an army of the king. Death. Destruction."

Casian all but held his breath. Deygan would lead an army against the Aerie? Gwysias watched him, hope in his eyes.

"And that was entered into the public record?"

Gwysias shook his head. "No. Miralee and Yinaede came to the library, and asked for entry to the secure area where only seeings likely to cause unrest are held. I read it after they left. They had made other entries lately, but in the open area. That's why I looked specifically at what they wrote that last time—to see why they thought it worthy of concealment when their others were not."

"What else did they enter?"

Gwysias gazed steadily at Casian. "My lord, I have helped you. I have always been your friend."

"Very well," Casian said, "I will give you sanctuary if you need it, for a time. Now tell me what else they entered, before I change my mind."

"The girl had a seeing of an Irenthi king and a Chesammos who appeared to be some sort of advisor."

"Yes, yes," Casian waved his hand dismissively. "I know about that one. What else?"

"They studied the archives and linked that to other earlier seeings of the same king and Chesammos. There was a young girl there, too."

This was more like it. "And?"

"The Chesammos said something along the lines of 'I can keep you on your throne' and 'Without me you will fall.' I don't remember the exact words. My memory isn't what it was. But that was the gist."

Casian considered. How could Sylas be that key to his position? "You are sure they were linked?"

"The evidence strongly points to the seeings being linked, yes. I believe Miralee and these earlier seers saw the same event."

So whatever else, Sylas must be there when Casian took the throne, and would play some part in him keeping it. And a girl—but she was of no consequence yet. That would be explained when it happened. Sylas had a sister, he vaguely recalled. Maybe his sister would be involved too.

"Very well, friend Gwysias, I will help you. If the king marches on the Aerie and I am there, fly to me in the king's army." He downed the rest of his wine. "I must tell the king what you have told me, and you must return to the Aerie before you are missed. Remember, if you are attacked, fly to me. I will keep you safe."

⁓⚬⚭⚬⁓

"They are at the Aerie?" Deygan's voice was steady, but Casian could detect a hint of anger in his tone.

"So my informant tells me, Sire."

"And he is reliable?"

Casian took a moment, as if giving the question careful consideration. "He has been in the past. He has grudges against Master Donmar, but I cannot imagine him inventing a story such as this. Not when so many people in the Aerie would know the truth or falsehood of it."

"And you came straight to me? You told no one else of this?"

"Of course, Sire," Casian made his voice soothing, let his aiea-dera extend toward the king. He had certainly not told anyone else. Information gave him power; he was not about to share that with anyone else. Strictly speaking he had not brought the information straight to Deygan, but had sat a while, wondering how best to use it— what the implications might be if he did.

"What do you intend for the Aerie, Sire?" It would

serve him well if the Aerie became less powerful. If they had any inkling of what he intended they would surely try to stop him. Those bloody women and their seeings. And decades of seeings in the library, too.

"I will see it destroyed." Deygan's words brought Casian's head up as if jerked on a rope. Destroyed? Casian's heart hammered. The Aerie had always been there; it was hard to imagine the island without it. And yet, if the institution Sylas so much wanted to be a part of no longer existed, Casian might find him easier to convince. He had his healer training, certainly, but with the changers in disrepute, a changer-trained healer might find himself less in demand.

And yet...

"Might it not be better to allow the Aerie to survive, but with its powers reduced? With a council made up of changers beholden to you for their existence, any decisions they made would be a sham, their power illusory."

"You see yourself at the head of the changer council?" Deygan quirked an eyebrow at him. The king had spotted his ambition, yet he encouraged it, in his own subtle ways, where Garvan had always discouraged him. Casian would find more fertile soil here with the like-minded Deygan than he had in Lucranne.

"No indeed, Sire. I see myself at your side. Yet there are men in the Aerie who have been passed over because Donmar did not see their true merit." Gwysias would make an admirable head of council. He would owe Casian his position, and he would be easily compelled by Casian's aiea.

"Donmar." Deygan's face twisted in disgust. "Scheming Chesammos. He served me well enough in the invasion, but he has been deliberately obstructive since. As if he could make up for what he did then by opposing me now. Pah! I'd like a reason to take him down a notch, and that's certain."

"Send them a message, Sire. An ultimatum. They hand over the Cellondorans or you will send troops to seize them, and you will not be responsible for any damage or loss of life that might result."

"You think they would listen?"

Casian spread his arms in an eloquent gesture. "It is worth a try. If they hand the traitors over, that suggests they are willing to listen to your authority. If not, at least you know you cannot trust them."

"See to it. Have the message brought for my seal. It can go with Ayriene. In the meantime, tell the captains to ready their men. I want the ballistas prepared and their crews rehearsed. Put the armies on war footing. Say nothing of this to Ayriene, or she will take word to the council of our preparations. The Aerie will regret playing politics with me."

CHAPTER 25

AYRIENE LEFT BANUNIS AS A falcon. Sylas envied the ease with which she transformed—the grace with which her bird form took to the air. He would be happy with his lower form, if only he could do at will what she seemed to take for granted.

Casian was in charge now. Deygan's rules required Sylas to be always in Casian's sight or be arrested again. The king's suspicions were undiminished, and Sylas's chances of becoming royal healer grew less by the day. Deygan had damned him by association, and he knew how close he had come to feeling a noose around his neck.

"So we have plenty of time to ourselves, with no masters here," Casian observed, watching Sylas with lazy green eyes. "Can you think of any way we could amuse ourselves?"

Casian's lascivious look made Sylas shiver with unease and desire. He felt the stirring that told him that the blood elder's side effects had not yet taken hold. The Irenthi sat beside him, close enough that their thighs touched and Sylas could feel the heat of Casian's body. He eased his neck inside his collar.

"Are you too hot?" Casian untied the laces that

held Sylas's collar closed. He slid a finger down Sylas's neck, lingering over the pulse point as if to feel Sylas's heart hammering faster. "You need to relax."

Casian stroked Sylas's cheek with his fingertips, dragging them up into Sylas's hair. Despite his worries about his future, it was all Sylas could do not to turn into the caress. He had dreamed of this—guilty, restless dreams. Pietrig's face turning into Casian's; his father's face turning into Ayriene's as she beat him bloody; Jesely, wearing his mother's linandra necklace, begging Ayriene to stop the beating. He swallowed hard.

"You are shaving," Casian said, stroking the roughness of Sylas's cheek, where the mirror told him a dark shadow now showed. "I wondered if you would bother while you were travelling. Jesely follows the Aerie custom of keeping clean-shaven, but Cowin wears a beard from time to time. He says it is because it is easier when he is on the road, but I think some of it is wanting to feel like a Chesammos, even among changers. I think I should grow a beard. What do you think? Would it suit me?"

"I..." The words caught in Sylas's throat. He tried to steady his voice. "I think if you do, you have decided you are Irenthi, more than you are changer."

Casian frowned, his fingers stopping their stroking. Sylas was glad they had stopped, and yet wanted them to continue.

"So you are changer more than you are Chesammos? Do you feel forced to choose?"

"What do you think?" Sylas winced at the bitterness in his voice. "The Chesammos are going against the king, trying to kill his sons. They are causing trouble between the Aerie and the lord holders. I am damned by the colour of my skin as soon as I walk into a room. If I can be a changer, I can escape that. I can be accepted. At least as much as a changer *can* be accepted."

"But you have such lovely skin," Casian said, his fingers wandering once more, loosening the ties further to reveal Sylas's chest with its dark red markings. "It is the colour of dark honey heated slowly over a flame. And your eyes—your eyes are like knotted braele wood. You are such a beautiful man." Sylas shivered as Casian's fingertips made their way down his chest, tracing the red dots of blood elder. Casian smiled at the expression on his face.

"And you, you have hair like the moon." The moment he said it he felt he had betrayed Jaevan. That was what he had thought about Jaevan when they first met. He had sworn Jaevan his loyalty, but Casian had his love, his heart, his desire.

Sylas had a momentary feeling of disquiet. Ayriene had only just left. She trusted him. But oh, the feeling as Casian's lips caressed his skin. It was so warm in their room. His skin heated and he could feel the beginnings of a sheen of sweat, the moistness of Casian's breath. He had a momentary pang of guilt as Pietrig's face swam before his, then a moan caught in his throat as Pietrig was forgotten. Casian's hands and mouth coaxed the response from him; he let instinct drive him. It would be so sweet to submit. So sweet.

⌘

If Sylas had not needed to give Jaevan the potion that evening, he would have stayed curled up beside Casian, enjoying the feel of skin on skin. As it was, he had to wash and dress before attending the prince. Casian would have to go with him—Sylas was not allowed out of the room by himself, far less to see Jaevan—but Casian was sound asleep when Sylas rolled out of bed and studied himself in the mirror above the wash bowl.

He poured water into the bowl and examined his reflection more closely. The marks of Casian's nails showed red on his shoulder. There was salve in his pack that would help them heal, but they would do as they were for now. He lathered the soap, then paused before applying it to his face. Casian said he was beautiful—if that description could even apply to a man—but when Sylas looked in the mirror all he saw was the hated golden skin. Yet Casian cared for him and he—his stomach turned over—he loved Casian.

He glanced at the bed. It was empty, the covers pushed back. Casian stood behind Sylas in a silk robe, watching him in the mirror. He rested his hands on Sylas's hips.

"You've been looking at yourself for ages. I never took you for the vain type." He kissed the nape of Sylas's neck. The fabric felt smooth and sheer against Sylas's back. He had never owned a garment so fine, and for it to be a chamber gown, not to be worn outdoors, made it all the more luxurious.

"I was thinking."

"About me?"

Sylas snorted. "Now who's vain?" Casian's face in the mirror took on a look of disappointment. "Of course about you. Who else would I be thinking about?" Other than Jaevan, maybe.

"Did you miss me?"

What sort of question was that? "Of course."

"You could stay here, you know. With me."

"I'm not going anywhere. Not for a while, anyway."

"No, but when Jaevan is being tutored and does not need his potions any more, you will be off. You have been here, what? Ten days? Two weeks? When did you last stay so long in one place with her? When will I see you again?"

It was true. They rarely stayed more than a day or two in any one place, and Ayriene preferred towns and villages over the cities. She preferred to tend those folk with no regular healer than city dwellers with ready access to herbalists and apothecaries.

"I am an apprentice healer. I go where my mistress goes."

Casian looked at him in the mirror, watching the blade scrape stubble from his face.

"I came to Banunis with no servant. My old servants were taken into my father's household while I was at the Aerie, and he did not offer me anyone when I left. It is not seemly that a man of my status should be unattended. Stay with me. Be my manservant and let us be together."

Sylas splashed cold water onto his face, turning this way and that to check he had not missed anywhere. "I have an obligation to Mistress Ayriene."

Casian snorted. "And has she let you tend to anyone yet? Or do you just carry her books and boil leaves for her?"

"I do what I am capable of. I still have much to learn."

"And in the meantime you draw her pictures. Does she mean to make you a healer, or are you with her to get you out of the council's sight?"

That plunged a blade deep into Sylas's own insecurities. He had stitched and bound wounds, and applied poultices, but little more. Did Ayriene not trust him with anything more complex? He shook himself. She trusted him to give Jaevan the elder root potion; she must trust him. But yet, he only had to give a goblet of potion once a day—a potion he had made with her watching for errors.

"I want to be a healer. I want to show the council that I am good for something."

"Oh, you are good for something. I can vouch for that." Casian's eyes twinkled in the mirror and Sylas let his gaze fall to the wash bowl. He was flushing again; he could feel the heat in his cheeks. Was that all he was to Casian? A willing bedmate? Whenever Sylas mentioned *his* ambitions, *his* desires, Casian laughed them off as unimportant.

"I want you to stop marking. I have taken careful inventory of all the marks on your chest, so don't think I won't notice. I don't want to risk those side-effects you mentioned, not now I have you to myself at last." The heat spread to Sylas's neck and Casian laughed out loud. "Will you never grow out of that? Not that it's not endearing, in its own way."

"What about your father?"

Casian shrugged. "I told you. He does not want any child of mine to inherit Lucranne, and he encourages our relationship since no potential heirs will come of it."

"I will think about it," Sylas said. He really did want to continue studying with Ayriene. A trade of his own would make him more secure than being Casian's bodyservant, especially since he was afraid Casian would tire of him in time. The novelty of a Chesammos lover would fade and then Sylas would be left in service with no prospect of anything better. Maybe turned out of Lucranne service altogether and forced to take whatever menial job he could find to keep himself. He would not end up shovelling shit in the streets of Banunis, not if he could help it.

But that churning feeling in the pit of his stomach told him that he loved Casian and wanted to be with him. With Casian's arms around him he felt secure—as if he were where he was meant to be. So why did the thought of staying with Casian make him so uneasy?

He turned, brushing Casian's hands from his hips and offering the Irenthi a quick kiss. "I have to get dressed and go give Jaevan his brew. And so must you, since I am not trusted beyond the doorway on my own."

And as he tugged on his homespun tunic and breeches, he wondered how his life had taken this strange turn. And where it would end up.

Sylas and Casian went to the royal apartments, Sylas's mind still spinning with unfamiliar emotions and future possibilities. His dream of staying at Banunis seemed a heartbeat away, but only at the cost of disappointing Ayriene, giving up his healer training and ultimately his dreams of becoming a changer. If he completed his training, would Casian be waiting when he came back, or would a new toy have taken his place?

As if Casian could read his thoughts, the Irenthi laid a hand on his arm. Sylas jumped, and the potion slopped around the goblet, a drop or two escaping and running down the edge of the goblet to stain his hand. In the dim light, it looked like blood. Sylas shuddered. Next time he would bring it in the stoppered flask. In his current mood, he was all too likely to spill it. He remembered the ink in the library. It seemed Jaevan made him prone to spilling things.

He observed Casian out of the corner of his eye, the Irenthi's movements silky and catlike, the beginnings of a beard on his cheeks. Sylas would have thought him unattainable, this heir to a great house, had he not just spent the last several hours in his bed. Casian caught his eye and smiled. Omena's wings, maybe the man *could* read his mind. Was it certain Casian was not an empath, or were Sylas's thoughts so obvious?

Jaevan's face lit up when he saw Sylas. The young prince was truly worthy of being described as beautiful, but still a boy. Casian was a man, taller and broader, if not as stunning in looks.

"It is time for the blood elder, Highness." Casian

was always so proper. Sylas would have used Jaevan's name and Casian likely knew it. He could not resist emphasising the differences between them, and Sylas's disregard for propriety made him look like an ill-mannered oaf beside Casian. But at the Aerie, Casian had made a point of using the masters' names without their titles whenever he could get away with it. With the masters, Sylas had always minded his manners.

"Can I try it first?" He took a sip and pulled a face. "Ayriene warned me it was vile. I'm going to add some of this," Jaevan held out a pot of honey with a wooden honey-dipper. He added a *lot* of honey, stirring with the dipper. He still had a boy's sweet tooth, and he licked the drips from his fingers like a child. "Marklin says he wants to be a changer too, but I've told him he has to drink nasty medicine each night if he is. I think he's reconsidering. Father would certainly prefer if he were not a changer, I think. Especially after Rannon." His face clouded at the thought of his little brother, and Sylas thought he saw a hint of tears in his eyes. "Is Father still keeping it secret about me?"

"I think so," said Sylas. "Although if you go to the Aerie to study, he may not be able to."

"Many children from the noble houses of the mainland come to the Aerie to study, Highness, and they are not changers," Casian said. "It is a sign of high social status for them to finish their education there. Your father will have it be known that you are building diplomatic ties, and no one will think any different. Or if they suspect, they will hold their tongues for fear of causing trouble between your houses."

"I suppose so," Jaevan said, raising the goblet to his mouth and taking a mouthful. He winced, then drained it, wiping his mouth with the back of his hand. "It is still vile, even with honey. Maybe I should give Marklin a taste to put him off his wild ideas. But I think it would be worth it, to fly like a bird." Jaevan became wistful. "Tell me what it is like to fly."

Casian told him. He had flown many more times than Sylas, and his first form of a great white owl with a stripe of dark grey across wings and feathers was truly remarkable. If that were his lower form, Sylas wondered, what would his higher form be? An eagle, maybe? Sylas was sure Casian could be one of the great changers given the chance. Sylas could not comprehend why Jesely had held him back.

Sylas offered a few comments, but mostly Casian spoke, with Jaevan dreamily speculating what his bird form might be. He would like to be an owl like Casian, he thought, but if that was as rare as they said, then a crow like Sylas might not be so bad. It was with Casian telling him of swooping and soaring and joining with the kye that the young prince's eyelids drooped and finally closed altogether.

As they crept out of the prince's bedchamber, nodding to the guard on the door when he asked if Jaevan slept, Sylas hoped that Ayriene would be back soon. For his first experience of acting as a healer without Ayriene's supervision to be on the crown prince of Chandris was intimidating, to say the least. Even with Casian there, Sylas was uncomfortably aware of the responsibility.

Three days at the outside, she had said. He hoped she was right.

CHAPTER 26

THE AERIE'S REPLY ARRIVED IN the afternoon while Casian and Sylas were otherwise occupied. Casian had bribed the messenger to convey the message only to him, and so it was late evening, after they had administered Jaevan's potion, when Casian called at Deygan's apartments.

"How dare they refuse me?" The table shook under Deygan's fist, sending ripples across the surface of the red wine in his goblet.

Up till now, Casian had thought Deygan not weak, exactly, but certainly not anyone to fear. Now, standing before him and feeling the blast of his anger, he knew Deygan was not to be trifled with. He still thought the plan might work, however. A tired Deygan intoxicated after his nightly flagon of wine should, in theory, be more easily compelled than one in full possession of his wits.

"They say changers are always welcome in the Aerie, Sire, and that those who sought sanctuary from Cellondora denied any involvement in the act against you and your sons."

Casian had heard the accounts of the destruction of the village from the messenger's own lips, and they had turned his stomach. The survivors told of children spitted, women with their heads dashed open, bodies strewn through the village. Elyta had used her talent to truth-tell them, the messenger told Casian. It had happened as they said.

"They would deny it, wouldn't they? I gave orders for the whole bloody village to be killed as an example. What sort of an example does it give if I allow them to hide at the Aerie?"

"There were old people and women among the survivors, Sire. I am sure they had no part in it." Two of the escaped changers were far advanced in years, and had spent time in the infirmary recovering from the flight. One of the changers who had left Cellondora had never reached the Aerie. She had been old, too. The survivors believed she flew herself to death crossing the desert.

"No part, you say? Yet were they ignorant of it? If they knew of it and did nothing, they are as guilty as the rest. The whole damn village was a rats' nest of rebels. The Aerie cannot do this with no fear of retribution or they make a laughing-stock of me."

"The Aerie are arrogant, Sire. They believe they have as much influence over the island as you do, maybe more." Casian hesitated. This next step would remove him from the changers forever. "Your people mutter that the Aerie were behind the attack on Your Majesty and his sons, Sire. They ask how simple desert Chesammos could have sufficient knowledge to use poison against you. They look at the healer in your court, and they ask questions."

Deygan's eyes hardened and Casian wondered if he had pushed his talent too far. The king was open to suggestion against the Chesammos and the Aerie, and Casian's compulsions found fertile soil. He had not as yet established how far Deygan had turned against Ayriene, but the king absorbed the idea that Ayriene plotted against him like water into cloth.

"My people ask this? They think I am being duped by the healer?"

Casian spread his hands in a helpless gesture.

"What do they know, Sire? If you believe in Ayriene and her abilities—believe her to have acted in good faith towards you and your sons, then you know best, of course. But they wonder that she had with her a Chesammos who knew the attackers. That the Chesammos had knowledge of the poison used—"

"Enough!" Deygan roared. "The Aerie think they can outwit me. Well, I won't have it! I won't, I say!"

"Indeed, Sire. It does seem to me, though, that Sylas was used as a dupe in this. He has a genuine affection for your son, and I do not believe him directly involved."

Deygan waved his protestations away. "The boy is of no importance. If he pleases you for the moment he can be dealt with later. It is the masters who are a danger to me. Do you have the men ready, Casian? Are they ready to march on the Aerie?"

"They are, Sire. Three companies of foot and horse will be ready to march in the morning, and the machines with them. If the Aerie will not hand over the traitors we will take them by force."

"Thank the Creator I have a loyal liege man who

has set aside his own unfortunate nature to serve me. If they surrender, Casian, you shall lead them. I will have Donmar's head on the Banunis city gates and you will lead an Aerie loyal to me, and answerable to the King of Chandris in perpetuity."

Unfortunate nature, indeed! Deygan had tried to persuade Casian to renounce changing altogether. While Casian had, he hoped, given the indication of agreement, he had stopped short of promising that he would no longer transform. It was too useful to him, and besides, he enjoyed it. The sensation of flight, as he had explained to Jaevan, was truly indescribable to one who had never experienced it. He did not intend to set it aside, even for Deygan, but he would have to be discreet about its use. Everything was coming together nicely. Very nicely indeed.

The banging on the bedroom door came in the middle of the night, and at that time it was bound to be bad news. Sylas was first to wake.

"Just a minute!" he called, extracting his arm from where it had wedged between his body and Casian's and shaking it back to life. He grabbed a sheet and wrapped it around his waist. Rubbing sleep from his eyes, considering lighting a fire bowl and thinking better of it, he went to the door and unlocked it.

A pair of guards stood there, the one at the back with a lantern, both with unsheathed steel in their hands. The three-quarter swords the king's guard used in the castle, not the broadswords worn outside and on ceremonial duties, but no less lethal.

"We are to take you to the king, changer," the man at the front said. "You too, Lord Casian." His voice was deferential towards Casian, but the tone he used with Sylas implied trouble.

"What's the matter?" asked Casian, finger-combing his hair and rubbing a cloth damp from the pitcher of water at his bedside over his face.

"Something wrong with Prince Jaevan," said the guardsman. "King said to bring you right away. Don't know any more than that, sir." He looked past them to the crumpled bed behind and Sylas had a feeling he knew exactly how things stood. Doubtless they thought he was Casian's whore. The difference in social status between them would make the alternative almost incomprehensible. But Casian loved him; he was sure.

"Can we at least dress? Make ourselves presentable for the king?" Casian's tone altered subtly and the guardsman shifted from one foot to the other.

"Don't see why not," he said. "Your lordship and his friend will hurry though. The king will not be kept waiting."

They tugged on smallclothes, breeches and tunic, and Sylas too drew a wet cloth over face and neck. He would have liked time for more before seeing the king, but from the guard's manner speed was required, especially if there was trouble with Jaevan. Sylas's stomach felt like he had swallowed a rock. His legs were heavy walking to the door, weighed down by a leaden mass of dread, and his fingers could barely grasp the door handle for shaking. Casian squeezed his shoulder.

"It will be fine. Probably Jaevan had a nightmare and the king is overreacting. Too much wine before bedtime." He smiled weakly. Sylas wasn't reassured. Casian didn't believe that any more than he did.

The guards fell in behind them for the short walk to Jaevan's apartments, Sylas as acutely aware of the weapons as if the points were pricking the small of his back. His stomach rolled and he tried to swallow past a lump in his throat. Casian gave him another encouraging look. "Fine, remember," he said.

Sylas would have liked a touch to reassure him, a squeeze of the hand or Casian's hand laid on his shoulder, but he would not dare with the guards there. Sylas took what comfort he could from Casian's presence—his confidently erect posture at Sylas's side.

When they entered the room it was clear things were anything but fine. Jaevan thrashed on his bed, sobbing wildly, while a pair of servants tried to restrain him. Deygan took two quick strides to stand squarely before Sylas. For a moment Sylas thought the king might strike him, but his long pale forefinger stabbed towards Sylas's face.

"What did you give my son, damn you? You and your friends didn't manage the job last time, so you've had another try, isn't that it? You should have swung along with them and damn what the healer said. Tell me what you've bloody given him, or Creator save me, I'll strangle you myself!"

When Sylas protested that the potion was completely safe—that he had prepared it under Ayriene's supervision—Deygan swore so loudly that Sylas was scared he would carry out his threat. Casian moved smoothly past Deygan, talking reassuringly to Jaevan, trying to comfort him, but Deygan rounded on him next.

"Do you think I haven't tried that? He won't listen to me. His own father. Just wails and throws himself about. Damn me, I'm not even sure he can hear me. He's gone mad, Creator save him." Deygan collapsed into a chair and buried his head in his hands. "My boy. My dear boy. What have they done to you?"

Sylas tried to go to Jaevan, but before he could reach him Deygan was on his feet. "Don't touch him! Don't go near him! Don't you think you have done enough damage, Chesammos bastard?"

It was on the tip of Sylas's tongue to remind King Deygan that he had helped Ayriene save Jaevan from the esteia—that without Sylas's intervention, Jaevan would have died days before. He bit back the words. The king was hardly rational at the moment, and reminding him of the poison incident, and Sylas's supposed part in it, might not be wise.

"Then why did you call me from my bed?" said Sylas, as calmly as he could manage with the weight in his stomach growing heavier by the moment. "Did you bring me here to shout in my face? I am a healer. Am I to watch him suffer, or try to help him?" He pushed past the stunned king to Jaevan's bedside. Kneeling, he took Jaevan's head in his hands and made the prince look into his eyes.

"Hush, my prince. Whatever ails you, I am here now. All will be well, trust me."

Jaevan's sobbing lessened somewhat, and he settled, his eyes fixed on Sylas's face. Crooning as if to a child, Sylas shushed him, waving the servants away. They backed off, exchanging nervous glances. Sylas wrapped his arms about the boy, marvelling at how slender his body was, how frail he felt. Jaevan had eaten only lightly since Rannon's death, but Sylas had not appreciated how thin he had become, until now.

"Get your filthy hands off him, you—" Deygan began, but broke off, Sylas vaguely aware that Casian had moved to interrupt him. He could hear Casian's voice speaking softly, but urgently, asking Deygan to at least let Sylas try.

Jaevan gradually calmed in Sylas's arms until his crying stopped, apart from occasional wracking sobs from deep inside. His body still shook, but little by little the trembling diminished until the prince regained control. Sylas reached for a cup of water and held it to Jaevan's lips, ignoring the renewed protest from Deygan. Sylas accepted a damp cloth offered by one of the servants and wiped the tear streaks from Jaevan's face. "There now, my prince. All will be well. It was just a nightmare."

No nightmare Sylas had ever heard of would produce that sort of reaction. A child, tormented by monsters and unknown fears alone in the dark would have been comforted by his own father. Jaevan had been hysterical. Beyond hysterical. He had been scared out of his wits. Sylas needed all his concentration to stay calm, or he would have caught Jaevan's mood and whimpered like a child.

Jaevan shook his head, his face still terrified, his skin paler than pale.

"No," he whispered.

"What was it then, if it wasn't a nightmare? Was it that Destroyer's brew the Chesammos gave you?" Deygan loomed over the other side of the bed.

The prince cringed away from his father, pressing himself back into his pillows. "No," he repeated.

And however much they encouraged him to tell them what had brought on such an extreme reaction, that was all they got out of him. His lips pressed tightly together, he refused to utter another word. Only when Deygan tried to send Sylas away did he respond with tears, threatening to repeat the hysterical sobbing when his father ordered the guards to take Sylas from the room.

Finally, reluctantly, Deygan allowed Sylas to spend what was left of the night in the chair beside Jaevan's bed, dozing sometimes and waking often to check on the prince, who cried out several times in his sleep, seeming to see again whatever had caused him so much distress. Casian and a guard remained too, and before dawn a second guard came to the room. The two soldiers escorted the dazed Sylas away—to where, he did not know.

CHAPTER 27

JAEVAN STIRRED AS THE CASTLE returned to life. In the courtyard two storeys beneath his window, servants fetched and carried, stable boys mucked out horses, and weary guards were replaced by fresh, leather-tunic-clad and helmeted colleagues. Jaevan's green eyes opened, then glanced towards the chair where Sylas had been when he fell asleep. They widened at the sight of Casian alone there, and he lifted his head from the pillow to scan the room. When he looked back to Casian, his eyes asked the question.

"The guards took him an hour or so back."

Alarm crossed Jaevan's face and he sat up. "Why?"

"Don't worry. Your father won't harm him—not yet. He sent orders that if you were peaceful, Sylas was to be taken away. I don't think he wants Sylas around you any more than he can help."

"I see." Jaevan's voice was hoarse, and he was more subdued than Casian had ever seen him. The boy was exhausted.

"Do you remember anything about last night?"

Jaevan swept shoulder-length silver hair back from his face. His eyes were still reddened and bloodshot, and his face was puffy. His gaze sank to the coverlet. "Yes."

"Your father thinks Sylas did something to harm you. He is still suspicious of him after the assassination attempt. Sylas is not in a cell, but he is under armed guard in a room somewhere. One with no windows, I'll be bound. Your father wouldn't risk him transforming and escaping."

Jaevan licked his lips, held out his hand towards his water jug. Casian poured some and passed him the cup.

"What... will he do with him?"

Casian was concerned about that himself. Sylas occupied most of his waking thoughts. Was this what love felt like? Casian had thought himself incapable of it.

"I don't know. I think he will hold him until Ayriene returns. If there was something wrong with the brew, it was Ayriene taught him how to make it. There is always the chance that it was she who planned against you and Sylas was just a dupe."

Ayriene had plenty of opportunity many times to do Jaevan harm and not taken it. Even from where Casian stood, Sylas seemed the more likely to have tried to hurt Jaevan. Not that he believed he would, not for an instant. Casian could see his concern for the young prince was entirely genuine— genuine enough to arouse jealousy in Casian's mind. If Sylas was attracted to one Irenthi, might he not be to another? Jaevan was too young yet for him to act on any attraction, but Casian would watch how the relationship developed.

Casian leaned closer. He was in a perfect position now for Deygan to choose him as a mentor figure for his son. The heir of Lucranne would be an ideal person to introduce the prince into society, teach him how a young man of his position would be expected to conduct himself. If Casian had been a master, he might have been put in charge of Jaevan's training. Jesely had thwarted that possibility, but Casian could still take advantage.

"If I am to help Sylas, I need to know exactly what happened last night." Jaevan turned away from him, but not before Casian saw the pained expression on his face. This had been no nightmare. The aiea swirled about Jaevan like a mist. Talent knows talent. Could the boy be a seer? Jaevan had the air of one who had been shown something by the kye that he had not wanted to see. Ayriene must have spotted Jaevan's talent too, and that would make the council all the more keen to get Jaevan into their clutches. Casian must act quickly.

Casian laid a reassuring hand close to Jaevan on the bed, careful not to touch him—that would be presumptuous, although Sylas seemed to get away with much more. He worked hard to make his voice earnest.

"The kye showed you something, Jaevan. I can tell. I know of these things. I have a little of the seeing talent, although I can tell that yours is much greater than mine. Maybe sharing it would help?"

The boy turned back, his face so gaunt and miserable that Casian felt for him. "You see things? Like I did?"

His shot in the dark had hit its target, then. "Sometimes. What did you see?"

Jaevan's lip trembled, his eyes glittering with

tears. Angrily, he raised a hand to dash the tears away. The boy was still young enough to cry, but old enough to be ashamed.

"I saw people dying. They were screaming. Trying to escape. Turning into birds to fly away and being shot out of the air by archers. They turned back into men and women when they died. One of them had an arrow through her throat." Cellondora? But that had been days ago. Was that even a talent? What point would there be to a talent that showed things that had happened already?

"Was it a Chesammos village?"

Jaevan gulped, gripping the edge of his blankets as if he could hide beneath them from the things he saw. "No. It was the Aerie. The walls were falling in. Ballistas were throwing balls of fire, and the buildings were ablaze. It was a battle, Casian. It was war."

The Aerie? Casian's stomach knotted. "Who? When?"

Jaevan nodded, his face showing his distress. "I don't know when. Soon, I think. I saw my father there and he looked the same as he does now. But he looked frightening, like he was mad. And..."

"Yes?"

The boy looked down, staring fixedly at his shaking hands. "I—I can't."

"Tell me. I need to know everything so I can help Sylas. You do want to help Sylas, don't you?"

Jaevan nodded, biting his lower lip as tears rolled down his cheeks.

"Tell me, my prince." He had heard Sylas use that term for Jaevan—an endearment the way Sylas said it. He hoped it would make Jaevan trust him.

Jaevan looked up, green eyes despairing and fair eyelashes wet.

"You were there, Casian. You helped my father lead his soldiers against the Aerie. Promise me you won't. You mustn't. I want to be a changer and make the Aerie strong again when I am king. If it is destroyed, I won't be able to learn. I won't be able to help the Chesammos. Promise me you won't do it."

Casian smiled. "I am a changer myself, my prince. Why would I lead an army against them?"

His mind raced. He would lead the army? Beside King Deygan himself? For that privilege, he would sacrifice every changer on the island if he had to. He reached to the Outlands, drew to himself the kye that held his compulsion talent. Then he leaned close to Jaevan, so that he could speak in little more than a whisper.

"You must tell no one else of this, do you understand? You must say nothing to anyone. No letters. No journal entries. No telling anyone anything of what you know." He felt his compulsion meet its target and he released the kye, satisfied that he had done what he intended.

The prince lay back on his pillows, sighing wearily. Casian left instructions with the guard at the door that the prince had not yet woken after his upset of the night before and was not to be disturbed. Casian allowed himself a satisfied smile as he headed for the royal apartments. Only a few days in Banunis and an opportunity had already presented itself. If this continued, his brother could have Lucranne and welcome to it. Casian had a bigger prize in his sights.

❧

Casian requested a meeting with King Deygan as soon as he left Jaevan. He meant what he had said to Jaevan about helping Sylas—he loved the man, after all—but this opportunity to advance himself in the king's eyes was too good to miss. And if it led to the downfall of the Aerie, then so be it. They had overlooked him—passed him over for Elyta, who was only two years older. Clearly she would be elected to the council because she had manipulated Cowin into a marriage. He wished her well of him. Casian had a Chesammos changer of his own.

The sooner he established himself in Deygan's court, the sooner he could have Sylas freed. He had meant what he had said to Sylas. House Lucranne had a healer, and a good one, but Casian could always find a place for a good bodyservant. Now he was at court he would need an attendant. No need for Sylas to go to his mother's after all. His pulse raced at the thought.

Permitted entry to Deygan's anteroom, Casian bowed deeply. He could be a courtier, when required. Plenty of courtiers achieved high position, with power and wealth at their fingertips. If Garvan was determined to displace him in favour of Yoran, Casian would show them both that he could rise higher. If he played his cards right he could become wealthier and more influential than Garvan.

"Casian," Deygan acknowledged his bow with a

wave of his hand. "If you have come to ask mercy for your changer friend then you may as well hold your tongue. The man is as clear a traitor as I have seen in many a year."

Casian's heart sank. If Sylas were to stand accused of treachery then his job might be harder than anticipated. Although, Jaevan would plead Sylas's case—and Jaevan generally won his father round in the end. And inasmuch as Casian didn't intend for Sylas to be hurt, Miralee had seen Sylas with Casian as king. So whatever Deygan threatened, Sylas would live. Maybe he would be imprisoned until Casian could overthrow the Banunis line, but if he had been in Miralee's seeing, then at least Casian knew he would not die.

"Sire, I come to offer my service to House Banunis." Another accomplished bow. His father would be proud of him. All that education, finally making itself useful.

Deygan's brow furrowed. "You haven't come to plead for your friend?"

"Sylas must be dealt with as you see fit, Sire. But I am confident you will decide that he meant Prince Jaevan no harm. He saved him from the assassins' poison, after all; why should he wish him harm now?"

"He was in a prison cell charged with being associated with those who poisoned my son, that's why. He got himself out of being hanged as an accomplice. The man will have been looking for an opportunity to harm the prince ever since."

Deygan's face was reddening and Casian could see there would be no arguing. Sylas would hardly try to kill the prince when he had been known to have made and administered the potion. Not without fleeing the castle after. He certainly would not have spent the night in Casian's arms, had he just plotted murder.

"As you say, Sire. The truth will be brought to light when Mistress Ayriene returns." The Creator will it so, for Deygan seemed set in his mind that Sylas was guilty. The first flurry of doubt scattered across Casian's mind. What if he couldn't convince Deygan that Sylas was innocent, even with his talent? What if a seeing was not set once it was seen? What if Sylas's death meant Casian would not become king, after all? He dismissed the thought. He was too far along his route to change course now.

"Sire, I have had a seeing. May I have your permission to share it with you?"

Deygan scowled. "Seer, are you? I had not heard that. You are proving a useful man to have around, Casian of Lucranne. There has not been a seer at court for many years."

"My talent is weak, Sire. Nothing to compare with Mistress Yinaede, or others at the Aerie, but I believe this seeing will be of interest to you."

He recounted what Jaevan had told him, of the burning and the killing, and that Deygan himself had led the destruction, with Casian at his side. He made no mention that it was Jaevan who had seen it, of course, passing the seeing off as entirely his own.

"And what will prompt me to take this action?" Deygan asked, a thoughtful look settling on his face.

"I do not know," Casian had to admit. "I see what I see, and it is rare for all the background to be revealed to me."

"And it was soon, you say?"

"You looked as I see you now, Sire, in the full prime of your manhood."

Deygan sniffed and Casian wondered if he had pushed his flattery too far. The king mistrusted flatterers, preferring men to speak their minds—as long as what they said broadly agreed with him.

"I had not thought to destroy them yet. They are a thorn in my side, and their sheltering of the Chesammos rebels verges on treasonous, but I was not sure I had enough justification. I had thought intimidation—an army at their gates—would be sufficient. Maybe I was wrong. Maybe nothing short of destruction will suffice. Leave me, Casian. I must go and see my son. It is good to know that I have a loyal servant in you, even if you do have the misfortune to be one of the tainted."

How easy to plant the idea of destruction in the mind of a man already partly controlled by the aiea-dera.

Deygan rose, wobbling as he got to his feet. Casian suspected the king had slept little, troubled by what had happened to his son, yet unprepared to admit the depth of his concern by returning to Jaevan's bedside overnight.

"Is he any better?"

"Prince Jaevan was sleeping when I left him, Sire, but I am sure he will have recovered from whatever ailed him last night."

That had gone reasonably well, Casian reflected, returning to his room. The question of recruiting Sylas to his household remained, but Casian was confident he could persuade Deygan it was for the best.

The maids had tidied; his bed was made up, the pitcher of water replenished. Sylas's belongings were gone, his few possessions removed from the room. Whether those were now in his guarded room or with the king to be searched for evidence of his supposed treason, Casian did not know, but the room felt empty without him. He wondered again about the permanence or otherwise of seeings, and for the first time he wished he had paid more attention in Mistress Yinaede's lessons.

This time, when the pounding came on the door of Casian's bedchamber, he was alone, fully dressed and lying on his bed. His Majesty required him in His Highness's chambers, the guard said. Deygan didn't waste long telling him why.

"He can't say a word!" Deygan raged. "What in the Creator's name was in that bloody potion?"

Creator! What had he said to the boy? 'Say nothing to anyone.' Something like that. And he had said it under the compulsion of the aiea-dera, while Jaevan had been susceptible to suggestion. A laugh threatened to bubble up in Casian's throat, wholly inappropriate in the circumstances, and he forced it down. The lad was doing exactly what he had been told.

Casian looked into Jaevan's eyes. He knew.

He knew what Casian had done and he would tell Deygan, if Casian ever released him. His talent would be revealed. His passing off of Jaevan's seeing as his own. His ability to coerce and manipulate the king and his son. Deygan would not let him stay in his service. In fact, Casian thought, it would be a wonder if he didn't have him quietly done away with. Deygan would never let a man live who had such power over him and his son.

"I... I don't know of any potion that could make a person mute, Sire."

If Jaevan remained silent, the blame would have to fall on either Ayriene or Sylas. Casian had no argument with Ayriene—she had always treated Casian decently enough when their paths had crossed—but if forced, Casian would sacrifice her to save Sylas.

"Of course you don't!" Deygan shouted. "You're not a bloody healer! It's that Chesammos has done it. Probably at the Aerie's instigation. I've already lost one heir and they mean to take another from me. How can a mute rule Chandris?"

He couldn't—a thought that hadn't escaped Casian. Had another of the Banunis dynasty been conveniently removed from his path?

"Can he write his thoughts, Sire?" This was a risk, and Casian knew it, but someone would suggest it sooner or later. His mind whirled as he tried to remember how exactly he had bound the prince—the precise words he had used to seal his compulsion. Creator, but he was in deeper than he had planned to be. If Deygan ever found that he was behind this...

"Excellent idea," said Deygan, snapping his

fingers at a pasty-faced servant skulking by the door. "Bring ink and parchment."

When the implements were brought it was as if Jaevan had never seen them before—never written a word in his life. He would hold the quill if it was placed in his hand, but made no effort to dip it in the ink, nor any attempt at writing if the quill was dipped for him.

"That's it!" said Deygan. "No more delays. The army leaves tomorrow. I'll raze that accursed nest of traitors to the ground. They think they can take my sons from me one by one and then they'll strike at me. Well, they'll soon learn who rules on Chandris when their precious bloody Aerie is in ruins."

Sylas spent the day under guard in the castle library, searching old herbals for any mention of blood elder root and its side effects to no avail. He was amazed he wasn't in the dungeons, but Deygan had agreed to give him access to the books, to see if he could find a cure for Jaevan.

"I must have done something wrong," he said, when Casian managed to slip away from the king to come see him. "The Lady help me, Casian, but I can't find a mention of anything like this in any of these." He indicated the books, then clasped his hands together, gnawing on the knuckles. He pushed dark curls away from his face. "How is Jaevan?"

The truth was, he was getting worse. Each time Casian went to his room, the prince had retreated further and further into himself. Casian had seen something similar in men who had experienced something profoundly disturbing, but Jaevan's decline was so swift it frightened him. How much of it was the seeing, he wondered, how much the compulsion, and how much damage to the boy's mind from the trauma of recent days?

"Just don't say it's your fault," Casian urged. "Ayriene must accept the blame. She supervised you making up the potion. If the amounts were wrong, it was for her to correct it. If you so much as hint it was you, he'll kill you." Casian could try to influence Deygan, but from experience he couldn't make the compulsion work unless the subject at least partly agreed with the thought or belief Casian was implanting. There was not a morsel of Deygan that did not believe in Sylas's guilt. He would have Sylas's head, and Ayriene's too, if the master healer was foolish enough to return to Banunis.

"She mustn't come back." Sylas took Casian by the arm. "Send a message to the Aerie. Tell her not to come back."

"You know she will. She wouldn't abandon Jaevan in this condition. Or you. And if he recovers, someone has to train him."

"They can send someone else. Olendis. Gwysias. Anyone. Anyone Deygan doesn't have a grudge against. But he can't kill the only healer talent. It's Ayriene, Casian. He can't kill Ayriene."

Casian snorted. "I don't think there *is* anyone at the Aerie that Deygan doesn't have a grudge against right now. With the harbouring of the Cellondorans, I think he regards all changers with equal hatred." When he told Sylas about the slaughter at Cellondora, Sylas had confided in him what he had seen at Namopaia. The friends he had lost. When he spoke of a man called Pietrig his throat closed and his voice choked up.

"It's a mess," said Sylas. "Just one big mess. If I went to Deygan, admitted responsibility and let him kill me, do you think I could end it? Would that put it right?"

Casian sighed and shook his head. "I don't think it would. I don't believe anything can put this right."

CHAPTER 28

THE FORCE LEFT BANUNIS EARLY the next morning, horse and infantry by ranks, ballistas on their massive wagons pulled by long-legged cheen. Deygan intended to destroy the Aerie—to leave no legacy of the changers who had attacked his son and challenged his authority so openly. If he had his way, scarcely one stone would be left atop another.

If Deygan wanted that, Casian intended to see he got it. Once he had aspired to a council position, but at Deygan's side he would learn statecraft, gather allies, and grow in influence. If he intended to stand in Banunis Castle and claim the throne for himself one day, as Miralee had seen, it would be from Banunis, not the Aerie's council chamber. With the changers brought down, there would be no one to recognise the true extent of his talent, and to burn it from his mind.

When they left Banunis, Casian rode at Deygan's side, as heir to House Lucranne. The details of his arrangement with his father would remain secret as per their agreement, so to the world he was still Garvan's son. A pity Deygan had fathered three sons, he thought. Marriage to a daughter could have bound Casian to the crown with ties of blood as well as loyalty. No matter. If Casian played his part here, Deygan would raise him to more influence than he had ever dreamed. Deygan was right; in his current condition Jaevan could not inherit Chandris. Now Marklin was the only Banunis heir. Should Deygan make a slip in years to come, when Casian had proved himself, why then, Casian would not be beyond taking advantage.

The Aerie would regret slighting Casian.

⁓⊱◈⊰⁓

Ayriene wondered if she could pretend not to have heard the knock on her study door. She had spoken to Miralee and Garyth since returning, but had hoped for a rest before the council met to discuss Jaevan's changing. She discounted the idea as quickly as it had come. Healers didn't get time off. If someone needed her, she made herself available whatever the hour.

"Come in," she called, straightening her dress and trying shake off some of her tiredness.

Master Cowin poked his head around the door. "Excuse me, Ayriene." He frowned as he took in her appearance—obviously she *did* look tired. "I'm sorry. I shouldn't have come. I'll come back another time."

"Sit down, Cowin," she said, gesturing to a chair. The Chesammos master rarely sought her out. In fact, she didn't think he had been to her study in the nearly fifteen years she had been a master changer. "How can I help you?"

He lowered himself into the seat. He was a tall man—even taller than Sylas and he was tall for a

Chesammos. Probably an uplander, she thought, remembering Erlach from Redlyn. His knee twitched restlessly. Ayriene couldn't remember ever having seen Cowin so agitated. She sat too, and waited for him to speak. He licked his lips.

"I need to talk to you about Sylas."

"Sylas?" Ayriene's weariness disappeared in a wave of anxiety. "Is there a problem? The council aren't showing an interest in him again, are they?"

"By the Lady, no," he said, "And if what I suspect is true, the longer we can keep it that way the better. Is he with you?"

She shook her head. "I left him in Banunis. He can fly now, if not spontaneously, but I needed someone I trusted to administer Jaevan's blood elder. And Sylas preferred to remain in Banunis, now that Casian is there."

Cowin sucked in a long breath. "Changer blood in the line of Banunis. We live in strange times."

"It seems so. Jaevan shows many of the signs. Strange, though—there is no hint of changing on either side of the family, any more than there is in Casian's. It seems to have appeared from nowhere."

"Kiana has a theory about that." Cowin's foot stopped bouncing and he leaned forward. "She speculates that it is not a matter of blood inheritance, at least not entirely. She thinks being on the island causes some sort of modification in humans. The modification is passed on and increased in each generation, until at last the ability to reach the kye and manage the change becomes evident. She thinks more and more Irenthi will become changers from now on, as more of them adapt to hear the kye, but they will have no Chesammos blood in their veins." That was the origin of the stigma against changing among the Irenthi: the assumption that Chesammos blood was to blame.

The theory had much merit, and was not dissimilar to Ayriene's observations of slight differences in the same plant species on Chandris and on the mainland.

"So the Chesammos are more likely to become changers, since their ancestors have lived here for generations, and this mutation is fixed in their bloodlines. Interesting." She would like to discuss it with Kiana, but right now she had other concerns. "And Sylas?"

"Ah, yes." Cowin smiled, and Ayriene appreciated why so many female hearts had been broken when he married Elyta. "It's a little... personal." Her face must have shown her first reaction, for he laughed. "No, Casian need not worry I'm going to steal him. Not when—" He broke off, fidgeted again. "Not when I think he may be my nephew."

Ayriene stared, unable to find the words to encourage Cowin to continue. It was all she could do to stop her jaw hanging open. He smiled sheepishly at her reaction, cleared his throat, and continued.

"I wondered about him at that council meeting, when Olendis said the boy claimed to hear many kye. There is a Chesammos story..." He rubbed his face and stared out of the window towards Eurna. This was totally unlike Cowin. She had never known him to be tongue-tied. "I don't suppose you want to hear Chesammos folklore, do you?" Again the sheepish grin.

"Just start at the beginning."

If Cowin was Sylas's uncle, then it had to be on his mother's side. There would be no need for secrecy on his father's side, and Craie was desert Chesammos where Cowin looked every inch the uplander. Cowin closed his eyes for a long moment before continuing. "When I was six years old, my sister left home to come to the Aerie. She was sixteen."

"And her name was Shamella."

He started. "You knew her? You would have been close in age, I suppose, but how did you guess?"

Her memory flashed to a terrified young woman she had healed of terrible burns to her hands, at a time when she was still Master Respar's apprentice, and just learning her talent. The changers were told Shamella had died on a visit home, and Respar, then the head of the council, had impressed on a terrified seventeen-year-old healer that she must not speak of what she had seen. Shamella would have been eighteen or nineteen then. Cowin's relationship to her had clearly been kept quiet, but by whose orders? Was this something Cowin himself had done, or was there involvement at council level?

"I healed her once. Go on. I'll tell you my part of the story when you've finished yours."

"When I was eight, Master Donmar came to our village. This was before he was council leader, of course, but he was newly-elected to the council. He said there had been an accident and Shamella was dead. This was just after the invasion, around the time Deygan came to the throne."

She nodded. It all linked together. Cowin knew some parts of the story; she knew others. Maybe they could piece it together between them.

"The following year I began to change. I was only nine. My parents didn't want me to come to the Aerie—they had already lost one child there, after all—but the Aerie insisted. Changing so early was unusual, they said. They wanted to watch how I developed. Master Respar interviewed me as soon as I arrived. He said I must tell no one that I was Shamella's brother. I didn't know why, and I didn't ask. I was only nine and scared to be away from home. They had me use my secondary name, in case Shamella had mentioned me to anyone." He stopped and smiled sadly at Ayriene. "Did you know that Sylas doesn't use his true name?"

"Really? No. Why not?"

"Because his father wouldn't let him use the one his mother chose for him. Which, incidentally, is my true name too. We are both named for my father. I'd have noticed him a lot faster if he had been called Erden. And so would others, I imagine. As it was, he was just another Chesammos boy, at least until Olendis mentioned the multiple kye." He stared out of the window to the herb garden beyond. "Shamella heard many kye too."

"I know," said Ayriene. "Jesely wondered if that contributed to her death. He was worried for Sylas, in case something happened to him because of it."

"Did Jesely have any grounds for believing hearing many kye was dangerous?"

"I don't think so. I just think he was making

sure Sylas was safe. After all, he was told Shamella died suddenly. No explanation. He was fond of your sister. He never really got over her."

"I didn't know that. She and Jesely would have been a good match, I think. But if I'm right, she didn't die, but was hidden away somewhere. Long enough to have a son, anyway, and Sylas told me he had a sister too. I need to know why they lied to my family. I don't believe Sylas knows any more than I do—probably less, from the brief conversation I had with him. But it seems you know a little about what happened to my sister."

She rested her hand on his forearm. "I know that the changers were told she died at home, and you were told she died here. I know that Master Respar made me swear silence and that Donmar was appointed to the council shortly after, and to the leadership not long after that, for all that many of us thought he was unsuited to the post. I know that I healed her of burns just after the invasion was repelled, and from the way Donmar looked at her something dreadful had happened. And I know she is alive, and living in a little village called Namopaia, under the name of Zynoa."

And then she watched as Master Cowin cried.

A changer returning to the Aerie thwarted Deygan's surprise attack. She raised the alarm as soon as she landed, giving the Aerie at least some notice of what was coming.

The king rode at the head of a column of foot and mounted soldiers, with strange machines carried on huge wagons pulled by cheen. The Irenthi rarely used cheen, the long-legged, flat-hooved beasts used to haul wagons across the desert, but horses could not have pulled those weapons of war up the side of the mountain on which the Aerie perched.

The island hadn't seen this many weapons in centuries. The Chesammos were peaceful, the past few months aside, and squabbles between the lord holders were addressed across the council table, or settled by duel. The island had never seen a battle, let alone a war, although the Lorandans had brought them close. The mysterious contraptions on the wagons were ballistas, Master Flain surmised from the witness's account. He had seen pictures in books in the Aerie library.

The Aerie was thrown into confusion. Such defences as it had were to protect against wind and weather, not an army bent on destruction. And they had axes and knives, but those were for splitting logs and butchering cattle not splitting heads and butchering people. Anxious parents, changer and human alike, badgered the council for news. What were their plans? Would the women and children be allowed safe passage if Deygan attacked? How would they be evacuated? But the council, Jesely included, had no answers.

"Master Jesely!" A voice behind him made him turn.

The speaker was a young changer called Deckhan—untalented, but a hard worker and recently raised to the mastery. A friend of Cowin's, if Jesely remembered correctly. The man was dark Irmos, almost as dark as Jesely himself. Not much

Irenthi in that one.

"Deckhan?"

"The council is called, Master Jesely. Master Donmar asks that you attend."

Better be a quick meeting. The king was barely an hour away, if the rumours were true. In the streets, the people milled about, exchanging news, indulging in wild speculation, casting fearful glances towards the main gate, which stood open as it always did at this time of the day.

On his way he heard mutterings, hastily hushed when he was noticed. Speculation was rife that the attack was because they harboured the men and women from Cellondora, and general opinion seemed to be in favour of handing them over to save trouble. Most of the Aerie's inhabitants were Irmos of one shade or another, and many laid the Aerie's present problems firmly at the feet of the Cellondorans.

Twelve of the thirteen council members assembled at the table; Tomas the historian was absent from the Aerie. Fennoc the herbalist had come straight from the garden, if his dirty shirt and fingernails were any guide. He sat miserably brushing at his clothes and picking earth from beneath his nails. Normally smartly turned-out in public, he was clearly ill-at-ease at this hurried call to council without time to change and wash. Caiet looked to have been supervising a flight, and wore only a gown pulled over a hurriedly knotted caigani. Unlike Fennoc, Caiet presented himself as calmly as if he were in his courtliest outfit. Flain had brought a book from the library, and was showing the people on either side of him the picture of the ballista. They did not seem comforted by the image.

The changers settled to Donmar's rap on the table, all eyes turning to him and staring intently.

"The king marches on the Aerie, ladies and gentlemen. In a short time we may be under attack."

Murmurs rippled around the table. Elyta, newly raised to the council since the death of Narais, edged closer to Cowin and took his hand in one of hers, the other resting protectively on her stomach. She was pregnant; it did not take an empath to recognise that gesture.

"Surely it won't come to that?" Flain protested. "He is angry that we helped the Chesammos. It can be settled around the council table, as we have always settled our differences."

"He will destroy us," Yinaede muttered. She wrung her hands. Sweat beaded on her upper lip and Jesely wondered if she were having a seeing there and then. The seeing talent was unpredictable. Those blessed—or cursed—with the talent could not choose what to see, nor when to see it, and stress seemed frequently to bring them on.

The other changers debated how to approach Deygan, but Jesely kept a careful eye on Yinaede. Things she saw in her trance might be useful to them later—if any of them survived. He was vaguely aware of raised voices around the table, but only paid full attention when Donmar pounded on the table and bellowed, "Enough!"

The chamber subsided like a roomful of rowdy children reprimanded by a teacher, gazes furtively scanning their fellow councillors, feet shuffling awkwardly beneath the table.

"He will save us," Yinaede whispered, but the councillors seemed oblivious to a seeing going on in their midst. Jesely noticed Ayriene listening to Yinaede. Did she, like Jesely, wonder if she spoke of Sylas? Stupid thought, but he could not shift it from his mind. But 'he will destroy us' followed by 'he will save us' was cryptic, to say the least. Who would destroy? Deygan?

"We must shut the gates, Donmar. We must stop him entering." That was Stretham. The fair Irmos twisted his hand into the front of his shirt, unmindful of the buttons that threatened to pop as he wrenched his fist through the fabric.

"No!" said Jesely, palms flat on the table before him. "If we shut the gates he will destroy the walls with those machines of his."

"What are they, Jesely?" asked Donmar. "Do we know?"

"Flain has a book," said Jesely, and Flain pushed the volume across the table to the head of the council.

"This is an old book of warfare, Master. I believe these are the machines. They are called ballistas and are for flinging projectiles—like slingshots, but much larger. Capable of hurling heavy objects— rocks and so on—over long distances."

"No shortage of rocks on the mountainside," said Donmar, looking in the direction of the mountain road as if he could see through the walls to the twisting road beyond.

"Shall I order an evacuation?" Hollin had a gift

for organisation and logistics and had played a key part in getting supplies out to the Chesammos villages over the past months. "There are many changers who could fly to safety before Deygan has a chance to attack."

Donmar chewed on the end of his thumb and Jesely eyed him carefully. Once Donmar had made a decision he rarely backed down from it, but he preferred time to fully consider all options. Making decisions under pressure was not his strength. Jesely could see the stress in his shoulders.

"I don't think that's wise. If we evacuate the changers we leave the humans behind, and that says to them that we are abandoning them to their fate. We could have widespread panic, even have the human servants and tradesmen turn on us in their fear. The trust between the changers and the people necessary to our functioning would be lost. No, we stay, for as long as possible. If Deygan breaches the walls, then we may have to reconsider."

Jesely nodded. No sense in making hasty moves while there was a chance of negotiation. If the Aerie let down the people who formed their support system, it might take years to repair the damage.

"Might I make a suggestion, Donmar?"

Donmar seemed relieved that another was prepared to offer ideas.

"Speak, Jesely."

"If the worst happens and the Aerie falls..." he hesitated, aware of another wave of mutterings and nervous shiftings around the table, "we would need a place to gather—to regroup. I think this should be off the island. If Deygan launches a full attack, he might order a complete purge of the changers on the island."

"Where do you propose?"

"Maldahur. When Tomas travelled there, he said the potentate of Maldahur was keen to align himself with the Aerie. The people of the area are not of Irenthi origin and have no allegiance or particular sympathy to the Irenthi. In fact I think if origins were studied, the people of Maldahur are probably more closely related to the Chesammos. We may find sanctuary there for a time."

"Very well," Donmar said. "If things go so badly for us that we have to leave the Aerie, you are to make for Maldahur. Some few may be capable of flying all the way, although it is beyond the range of most. But it may be possible to buy passage from Adamantara or to fly out to sea and roost on a ship until it is impossible to maintain bird form any longer. How you then appease the captain of the ship is up to you, but the Aerie has always recompensed help more than generously. A captain may be prepared to accept a letter of credit."

A letter of credit issued by an establishment that may not exist by the time they try to redeem it. Still, it was their best chance, if things went that wrong. Jesely hoped this contingency would not be needed, but it was best to be prepared.

"There is another thing," said Jesely. "Many of the Aerie, changers and non-changers alike, are blaming this current state of affairs on the Chesammos from Cellondora. It might be an idea to keep them safe somewhere for now, in case any attempt is made to hand them over to Deygan. For similar reasons, they should perhaps be among the first to fly if we leave the Aerie."

Donmar nodded. In stressful circumstances even changers and their employees could resort to violence, and it was perfectly possibly that the survivors might become victims.

"See to it, Hollin. The Cellondorans must be protected."

"And the humans, if we fly? What is to happen to them?"

"See if Deygan will give them safe passage," said Donmar. "They have done him no harm—his quarrel is with the changers. But if he will not listen to reason, have them use the gate beyond the lake. It is a steep path and treacherous, and Deygan and his men may harry them, if they are seen trying to escape that way, but it is their best hope if all other avenues have failed."

"So do we go to meet him?" Jesely asked.

"I go to meet him," Donmar said grimly. "If one of us cannot convince him then twelve will not, and it may be that he receives a single ambassador more readily than a group."

The council erupted in a storm of protest. He must not go alone, they said. Deygan might be more inclined to listen to a single person, but he was also more likely to kill or capture one alone, where a group might command more respect.

None of them expressed what Jesely was thinking: that however many of them went out, the Aerie had no soldiers, no one able to bear arms to protect themselves. If Deygan chose to wipe them out, he could do it with little resistance.

They compromised. Three would walk out to meet the king: Donmar, Jesely, and Ayriene. Jesely spoke against Ayriene's presence. They should not risk their only healer talent, he said. Ayriene countered him, saying that there should be at least one woman in the group, and she knew Deygan better than most. She exchanged significant glances with Donmar, and again, Jesely realised there were undercurrents he was missing. He wondered what hold Ayriene had over the council leader.

If it all went wrong, Donmar told Hollin, he was to get people to safety by whatever means were at his disposal. Jesely found that he had small hope of a peaceful conclusion. The Aerie and its people faced their greatest peril yet.

CHAPTER 29

THE THREE CHANGERS WALKED IN silence down the mountain road. It was one of the few paved roads on Chandris—evidence, if needed, of the Aerie's former affluence. Ahead of them, Deygan raised a hand and the troops and horsemen came to a halt. Deygan and another rider continued on a few yards before also reining in.

The other rider bore the device of Lucranne on his breastplate. Ayriene was struck by how quickly Casian had risen through the ranks of Deygan's advisors. Even for the heir of Lucranne, his ascension had been dizzyingly fast. Once more it occurred to her to wonder about his apparent charisma—Jesely seemed immune to it, but so many others had fallen under Casian's influence that it hardly seemed natural. Sylas too, although that didn't explain the evident attraction in the other direction.

They stopped a few paces from the king, who dismounted. Casian did so too, holding both sets of reins and positioning himself a respectful few steps behind.

"Your Majesty," said Donmar, inclining his head. A full bow was not required from the leader of the changers—the difference in rank did not warrant it—but both Jesely and Ayriene gave deeper bows, as was proper.

"Donmar." Deygan's acknowledgement was barely there—a dip of the head that could have been a gesture of irritation at a buzzing insect. "Master Jesely. Mistress Ayriene." She might have imagined it, but she thought he sneered slightly saying her name. His animosity was unconcealed, and she flashed a glance at Casian. Was Sylas safe? Surely if anything had happened to him Casian would not be standing there so calmly, beside the man who meant him harm. She should not have left him. Creator! The boy was her responsibility.

"I have not seen such an array of force since we faced the Lorandans together, Sire."

Ayriene knew what Donmar was doing, and admired his approach. He reminded Deygan of their shared past—the time they had stood shoulder to shoulder against a common enemy.

A flash of light in the distance. A young changer with burned hands. The Lorandan army repelled.

"Do you have another such among your number? Would you send her against me, if you did? I don't believe you do, Donmar. I see fear in your eyes. She was unique, that girl of yours, was she not?"

That girl. Shamella. The only changer who could hear multiple kye until Sylas... her son. Ayriene risked a glance at Jesely—wondered how much of this he had put together.

A changer able to hear multiple kye. A weapon? A weapon so fearsome it had wiped out the Lorandan invasion force and which Deygan feared being turned against him. A girl given out to be dead and hidden deep in the desert under a name that was not her own.

"Send him away." Donmar's voice was rough as he nodded towards Casian. "I have things to say to you that are for your ears only."

Deygan raised an eyebrow. "And Jesely and Ayriene are to remain?"

Donmar eyed them. "I can send them back, if you would prefer."

Deygan's laugh boomed out across the mountainside. "It is the changers that have been secretive. I have no secrets from your colleagues, but maybe you do."

"Ayriene was there. She may have guessed by now. And if Jesely does not know, he deserves to be told. I will earn his hate, I expect, but this has gone on too long."

More than ever, Ayriene was sure this was about Shamella. Did Donmar know Sylas was her son? If he did, would he have allowed him into the Aerie? That increased the risk of exposure of—whatever had happened. Cowin had been admitted, but that was because of his exceptional ability. Had Donmar expected Sylas to be in some way exceptional too? Did that explain Donmar's impatience with the lad, especially when he admitted to multiple kye like his mother?

"My apprentice," she said, the words leaving her lips before she could stop herself. "Is he well?"

Deygan turned his gaze on her, his lips and mouth twisted with hate. "Your apprentice," he almost spat the words, "has done something to my son. Jaevan is almost an imbecile—mute, unresponsive. Hour by hour he draws in on himself more, while your *apprentice* protests his innocence and hides away with his books in a pretence of seeking a cure." Deygan glared at her, green eyes cold as polished linandra. "He failed at his first attempt to kill Jaevan, but my son is as good as dead now, as far as the succession is concerned. Your Chesammos has done what the rebels tasked him with."

Shamella saving the island from the Lorandans. Yinaede in the meeting gasping 'he will save us'. Sylas and Shamella, both hearing more kye than they should.

"No," she whispered.

"I should have my men seize you now, healer," said Deygan. "Have you taken back to Banunis to stand trial. But we meet under parley, and I will not break my bond." He turned back to Donmar. "I would not have it end this way," he said in a soft voice, so that only the four of them would hear. "I thought that when Respar sent you and the girl to me to repel the Lorandans that this could mean a new understanding between Banunis and the Aerie."

"It was not the Aerie broke it," said Donmar, equally quietly, genuine sadness touching his face.

Deygan spread his hands. His voice stayed soft, but there was a hard edge to it. "As you wish. You put me on the throne and you kept me there, as you promised. I am sad our friendship will end this way. Go back to the Aerie. I mean to destroy it and any who resist me. Hand over Ayriene and the Chesammos changers, and I may let the innocent go free."

Ayriene barely heard him. 'You and the girl'? Respar had sent Donmar and Shamella to Deygan to offer her ability as a weapon? The seeings had been of Deygan and Donmar in the assembly chamber, then, not Sylas and Casian. And Miralee—Miralee saw the past, not the future? A rare talent, but not unheard-of. They had got it wrong. So terribly, horribly wrong.

"He will save us," she said to herself in little more than a murmur. But he must not. If Sylas blasted Deygan's army as his mother had destroyed the Lorandans, how would her troubled apprentice ever find peace?

Jesely was lost in thought, apparently trying to make sense of what he had heard.

"We offered her as a means to soothe the mountain," Donmar said, as if to himself. "We would have used her as a true stormweaver. It was Deygan twisted her ability—turned it into something it was not intended to be. It was then he turned the Chesammos into a people to be feared and repressed."

As they returned up the mountain road, the order to advance sounded behind them. Overhead an owl rose into the sky, joined soon after from the Aerie by a hawk of some kind. The two flew for the king's lines and disappeared among the soldiers.

'He will save us.'

Ayriene hoped he would not. Not if it meant him being used to kill, as his mother had been. Not if it meant Sylas becoming a weapon.

They returned to the Aerie a more sombre trio than they had set out. Deygan would destroy them, whatever they did; Jesely was sure of that. The resentment brewed over many years had become anger at the safe haven given to the Cellondorans, and now rage at what had happened to Jaevan. But what, exactly, *had* happened to Jaevan?

Jesely remembered the intelligent, engaging young man and offered a prayer to the Lady that it was nothing serious. He ran the words Deygan had used around in his mind: 'mute,' 'unresponsive,' 'imbecile.' It had to be serious; Deygan was not one to overreact.

They made their way to the main building, shouting for the gates to be closed behind them. Unmindful of the stares from the people they passed, they ran inside, up the stairs to the council chamber and sent a young novice scampering to find the other councillors.

"Deygan is determined to destroy us," Donmar said to a stunned gathering. "Hollin, you must evacuate as many of our human staff as you can."

"It will not be easy. The path from the back gate is narrow. It will be dangerous if too many try to descend at one time. And we must avoid panic, if we can. If we have people pushing and shoving to get out, that will be a catastrophe in the making."

"I must leave it to you," Donmar said. "Tell people as you will, but word will spread, once people notice others leaving by that gate."

Hollin nodded grimly, then without waiting to hear the rest of the discussion, he rose to go.

"Masters and full changers may leave on the

wing. Again, send them off a few at a time if you can, to avoid panic. Cowin, can you see to that?"

The Chesammos changer's head snapped up. He had been talking softly to his wife, Jesely noted. Elyta was in tears, her hand resting just below her breasts. Yes, she was pregnant, he was sure, and likely scared for the child's safety as much as for her own.

"Remember to tell them our meeting-place. It could be that Deygan is merely blustering and will back down, in which case they may return here. But if he does as he says and destroys the Aerie, we must make sure that all know the agreed meeting-point."

Maldahur. A destination that would stoke Deygan's paranoia all the more. A city in a land no friend to the Irenthi. Jesely could have wished they had chosen another destination, but done was done. They could hardly meet in a country ruled by Irenthi, for fear of another king finishing what Deygan had started.

Jesely's empath talent was on full alert. He could feel the rising tide of panic among the councillors and from the people outside. Soon it would overwhelm him. He would have to leave or lose his sanity in the cacophony of other people's thoughts. He put his hands over his ears and Ayriene—blessed Ayriene—spotted what was happening. She laid a hand on his arm.

"If it comes to it, you must go. Sylas trusts you. If you can rescue him from Deygan, do it. Take him with you."

He patted her hand gratefully, then voiced

the concern that had been building in him. "The novices. How do we get the novices out?" There were dozens of novices to get to safety, some of whom had never flown alone.

Donmar's face paled. "We must send a master with a pipe to Adamantara. He can call, Those at the right part of their marking cycle will respond. Some part way through the cycle may respond to a full master's call. The rest can go with the servants."

There was a crash like booming thunder and screams of people in the distance. How had Deygan got the ballistas set up so quickly, damn him? Clattering masonry fell as the first breach in the wall erupted. Then another crash, and another. Three ballistas, then, and a short respite now while the crew dragged more rocks from the mountainside to send hurtling towards them.

"Go," said Donmar to Ayriene. "There will be people hurt—trapped in rubble, maybe. Go and do what you can. Call any healers and healer apprentices you can find to help. Send me a master—any you trust with getting the novices to safety and who takes a second form large enough to carry a pouch with a pipe."

She ran towards the sounds of destruction— shouts and screams, people calling to loved ones, and the sickening grating of walls collapsing as now-unstable stonework lost its bid to stay erect.

A few moments later a young man entered the chamber. Deckhan was a new master, but a steady sort—not one to panic. He took an owl as his second form, Jesely remembered.

"Master Donmar, Mistress Ayriene sent me.

She said you had a task for me and I should come right away."

Donmar nodded approvingly at Ayriene's selection. "You have your pipe with you?"

Deckhan patted his belt pouch. "Always, Master Donmar."

"I need you to fly to Adamantara. You'll need to carry the pipe. Take that and a caigani and as much money as you can safely carry in your pouch. When you get there, call and keep on calling. We will send as many of the youngsters to you as we can get transformed. After that, it is up to you. If things go badly here, get them to Maldahur. Sell your pipe if you have to. You may be the only hope our youngsters have."

A flurry of wings announced the first flight of changers taking to the wing to escape the carnage. Those who were able had taken their second form, trusting the power of hawks, falcons, and owls to take them higher and faster, but there were crows, sparrows, swallows, and others, all straining upwards to escape the attack on their home.

From over the wall Jesely could hear the thrum of many bowstrings, all releasing at once. Arrows fell into the courtyard and people ran for cover; an arrow is no less deadly for not having been aimed directly. Some found a target, the sickening thud as arrow point met flesh seeming to rip a hole in Jesely's heart. As the first changer bodies hit the ground, their bird forms reverting to human as they died, three thumps in a row told him that the ballistas had unleashed another assault on the walls, one missile sailing higher than the others to break through the vaulted ceiling of the great hall.

This was no mere attack. Deygan meant to raze the Aerie—to make an example of them.

The next projectiles were bundles of rags soaked in pitch and set alight. They flew higher and faster than the rocks. One lodged in the roof of the dormitory block, another hit the library, and the third crashed through the hole in the great hall ceiling to set tapestries and paintings on fire. What little reserve of calm the people had had evaporated with those flaming fireballs. People ran, screaming, some with children in their arms and others with what few possessions they had been able to snatch up. And above them, changers took to the air, some winging their way high enough to be beyond the range of the bowmen, others plummeting to the earth, their flesh pierced with archers' arrows.

And Jesely crouched on the ground, his hands clasped over his ears, trying to shut out the screeching of everyone's thoughts, hardly able to comprehend what he was feeling.

Sylas could not have said how he knew something was amiss. While the king was away from the castle, he was confined to his tiny, windowless room, and he spent his time lying on his pallet, enveloped in misery. Running what had happened through his mind over and over and over again. Obsessively worrying whether he might have done something wrong. Deciding it was impossible. Going back to the beginning and rerunning the whole sorry affair.

He pounded on the door.

"Step back," the guard on the other side ordered before opening the door, sword in hand. "What's all the noise?" At his belt the guard carried a net of fine mesh edged with metal beads, designed to be thrown over Sylas if he showed any sign of trying to transform. Deygan had ensured that Sylas mark with the blood elder before he left. He was taking every possible precaution to ensure Sylas did not fly away from justice.

"I need to walk."

The guard checked the room, his gaze scanning each corner. It was sparsely furnished with nowhere to hide anything or anybody from the guard's eyes.

"You're meant to go in the morning. You didn't." His tone was accusing.

"I am allowed one walk each day. The king said so. I didn't want to go out this morning, but I do now."

The guard scowled. Sylas could almost see the thoughts trickling through his head. If the prisoner escaped on his watch...

"It's not like I can climb down without you noticing. And I'm not about to jump off the ramparts." Although that would be—what had Neffan said?—a death of his choosing, not the king's.

"Move then." The sword point pricked his shoulder. "And don't try anything stupid."

Up on the wall walk he could see it—a glow on the horizon like a beacon fire, but larger. He checked the direction of the sun, dropping away to the west behind the main tower of Banunis Castle. It was sinking; the sky in that direction would soon take on the reds and oranges of a Chandris sunset. But these flames were to the north-east—the direction in which the Aerie lay. The flames moved on the horizon as if they lived and breathed.

"What's happening over there?"

The guard spat off the wall. "The changers, ain't it? The king took soldiers out there. Said he would demolish their halls for supporting the Chesammos rebellion. About time too, you ask me. They've been getting too proud, them changers. Think they're too important, can do what they want."

The Chesammos rebellion was an excuse, Sylas was sure: a reason the lords and commoners alike would swallow, that would free Deygan from having to admit his son was a changer and was in his rooms, unable to speak. Had Sylas brought this fate down on all of them?

He stared, horrified yet fascinated, watching his dreams burn to dust. He would never be a changer. Not now. If some survived—even if they all did—their influence would be gone. The Aerie would be gone. The people would not regard them with such superstitious awe once they were reduced to poverty and with no place of their own. The wind blew about him, coming off the mountains and chilling his face. He thought he could smell woodsmoke, and his face was cold from the breeze chilling the tears that streaked his cheeks.

Were they flying? The changers that could escape—were they flying, or were they trying to save their home? Instinctively, he reached for his kye, but even if he could change now, he would have nowhere to go.

Despite the blood elder, he felt the kye

stirring—not just his bird form, but many others, all clamouring for release. It built up, throbbing inside him. Their energy grew in his chest until he felt he must let it go or be consumed. But it died away, the suppressive effect of the blood elder juice flowing in his veins. In the distance he heard a call—a strident master's call, not a muted training pipe—but the blood elder restrained him. He could not become a bird and fly away from his guard and Banunis. And he would not. He would not leave Ayriene to her fate, and he would not abandon Jaevan—not while any hope remained of restoring him to health.

He had responsibilities.

As the red flower blossomed on the horizon, he knew he would stay. The clear note of the changer pipe rang out once more and he wondered how many novices flew towards its call and their hope of safety.

His own kye fell silent. He did not hear it again.

CHAPTER 30

ODIES LITTERED THE GROUND. OLD and young alike lay there, pierced with arrows, crushed by masonry, dead or dying. It broke Jesely's heart to leave them, but he could not stay. As people rushed past, trying desperately to find friends and family, navigating the rubble-filled streets and falling masonry, he could not help but scan their faces.

There was the novice who had called him to council earlier, her face grimy and tear-streaked. She had not responded to Deckhan's call and would have to take her chances down the mountain path.

There was Benno, the child to whom Sylas had taken such a liking, blood pouring from a head wound. The boy crumpled to his knees, then fell face-down in the ash. Jesely wanted to go to him, but he could not. Donmar had set him to see that as many as possible escaped the carnage. He had to try to save the majority, not tend one child who might already be past saving. A young man, of an age with Sylas, stooped, flung the boy over his shoulder and took off at a run. Guilt flooded him like a red wave. The youngster had acted, but the crowd's churning emotions had left Jesely almost paralysed.

Elyta stood holding a sobbing Irmos girl of seven or eight years old in her arms. She handed the child to Cowin, exchanged a few words and a snatched kiss, and her husband rushed towards the north gate. Elyta stared bleakly after him, her hand resting on her still-unswollen stomach. Jesely's gut twisted. So many trying to save the weak and the helpless, and all he could do was shout the occasional order and try to block out the mayhem. It felt as though he heard every scream, lived every thought of panic or hope or despair.

He pulled himself together, finding it harder each time to find himself in the ruin of his mind.

"You must fly, Elyta. For your own sake and that of the baby you carry."

She stared at him, her fair skin smudged with dirt, blonde hair ragged over her face where it had come loose from its braid.

"How did you know?"

"There are some who say empathy is nothing to do with the kye, just reading signals that people cannot help but give out. Whatever the truth of it, you have been giving signals that a man with one eye could read, if he were watching."

Tears streamed down her face and she looked the way her husband had gone, but the crowds had swallowed him. "I thought my child would grow up here, Jesely. Learn our ways from the day of its birth. Be greater than either Cowin or myself. What future will it have now?"

"Our ways?"

"The child is a talent. I can feel it already. Talent knows talent, they say."

"But... you are scarcely showing yet."

"Then how great a talent must it be if I can feel it already?"

He took her arm, pulled her into shelter as more arrows flew overhead. The ballistas were silent for the moment, and Jesely hoped Deygan had decided they had taken enough punishment.

"Then you must fly, Elyta. Get to Adamantara and find Deckhan. He called the novices and some of them answered. Some had never changed before—fear gave them wings. I do not know how many will arrive—I saw some killed almost as they cleared the wall walk—but some will. You must help him get them to Maldahur. He will need you. He cannot handle all the young ones by himself."

"I will wait for Cowin. He promised to come straight back."

Maybe he was hoping to hand the child over to someone else to take to safety. Maybe he knew who the child's parents were. The Lady grant that she find safety.

Dimly, in the distance, he heard a changer call. Deckhan did his job well. Jesely had told him to call and keep calling and he was doing just that. He wondered how many novices had managed to reach safety. Vaguely it occurred to him that in his efforts to call as many from the Aerie as he could, Deckhan might have called young boys and girls not yet known to them—not far enough along in their change to have attracted notice but able to be called by a pipe, if the call was strong enough. Deckhan would have to take them, too. No time to see them safely back to their families and no one left to train them if he did.

What a mess. What a bloody mess.

The sounds of crying came to him over the shrieks and crashes. In the courtyard, in the pose taken by most changers before the transformation, crouched a young boy. He raised a tearstreaked face.

"M- Master Jesely," the boy stammered, wiping his eyes with the back of his hand and straightening, flushing to be found sitting and sobbing.

Jesely wracked his memory for the boy's name. He knew most of the novices. With his empathic talent and his easy way with people, he was the obvious choice to help settle the youngsters into their new lives, but for the life of him he could not remember this boy's name and it troubled him more than was reasonable. He put an arm around the boy's shoulders.

"Come now, lad. Let's get you away from here."

"Why could they do it and I couldn't, Master Jesely? I could hear the call but I couldn't hear the kye. The noise and the screaming. I—" He wiped his face with filthy hands, leaving smears of dust and ash on his damp skin.

"Not a good time to have to learn, son," Jesely reassured him. "Run for the north gate, now. Find Master Hollin. He will show you the way to go."

He gave the lad a nudge and he trotted in the direction Jesely had pushed him. Then a thump sounded from beyond the walls, and a rush of wind fluttered Jesely's hair. A rock hurtled through the air.

"Meneas!" The name and the warning came too late. The rock smashed one of the few remaining intact walls and the boy disappeared under an avalanche of ash brick. Sobbing, Jesely tried to pull the bricks from him, but it was an impossible task. As fast as he pulled one away, two more fell to take its place. There was little chance the boy had survived, but Jesely dug with his bare hands, desperately trying to shift enough bricks to at least see him, feel for himself whether there was any life left in the young body. The rational part of him knew it was hopeless—that he should not be expending energy and endangering himself for one novice. But still he dug.

Choking smoke threatened to overwhelm him. Another burning projectile had landed in a woodpile stacked up against the smokehouse wall. Woodsmoke stung his eyes and threatened to clog his lungs. He coughed, eyes streaming with tears that were not all from the smoke.

Hands pulled him away from the collapsed wall, pressed a skin of water into his grasp. Yinaede looked at him with concern in her eyes.

"Why are you still here? I thought I told you to go. Sylas will need you."

"These people need me."

She cupped his cheek in her hand. "Go."

"But—"

"Sylas will need you. I saw it. You must survive to help Sylas in what is to come."

The hairs on the back of his neck stood up. What had she seen, exactly? Why was it so crucial to her that he left? No time to ask, not with the Aerie tumbling about them.

"Please."

He nodded, dropping into a half-crouch, then standing again. "Elyta! She is here somewhere. She is pregnant and—"

She laid her hand on his lips. "Elyta and Cowin flew a few moments ago. They used the smoke to cover their departure and as far as I know they got away safely."

"Ayriene?"

"Donmar asked for Ayriene to attend him, but I told her to leave as soon as they were done. Now will you go, you stubborn fool?"

An almighty bang and the crash of splintering wood sounded over the other noise. Then another—bang. A battering ram on the main gates—gates that were never meant for defence against an army. Gates that would never hold.

He crouched near the pile of rubble that would be Meneas's grave.

"But you—" He knew from the look on her face that she did not expect to survive.

Soldiers poured into the Aerie through the breach in the gates, and as he circled, he saw Yinaede brought down by a soldier's sword. She crumpled, blood spreading from a wound in her chest. If she had not stopped to speak to him, maybe she could have reached safety. Or perhaps she had seen her own death and embraced it. Jesely struck out for Adamantara, arrows whistling harmlessly past him. If a hawk could have cried, he would have been crying.

Donmar hardly looked up as Ayriene approached.

He seemed stunned—his eyes unfocussed, distanced—and blood stained his tunic in several places. She reached by instinct for her side, but her healer pack was not there. She had left it in Banunis for safe-keeping, her falcon unable to carry the heavy satchel such a long way.

"It's not just the Cellondorans and whatever has happened with Jaevan, you know," he said with no preamble. "I don't want you blaming yourself. Don't let the boy blame himself, either. This was set in motion when I went to Respar to tell him what I knew of stormweavers, and of my suspicions that Shamella was one."

"Stormweaver? That's how she let loose the firebolt on the Lorandans?"

"Stormweavers can draw energy from the volcano—far more than a normal changer can. If the mountain is becoming unbalanced—there are too few changers, or they aren't drawing enough aiea—a stormweaver emerges who can drain the energy away to keep the mountain safe. Another example of the mountain and the changers working together. Stormweavers have always been Chesammos, and nearly always women. They aren't talents, although Shamella somehow ended up an empath afterwards. Deygan wouldn't let his sword or his coronet be used as focus but we found her a linandra necklace from somewhere. Instead of releasing the energy safely through her, Deygan had her let it build up and up and then direct it at the invading army. I hope she has found some peace in her life. I know I haven't." He covered his face with his hands.

Ayriene had only seen the flames from a distance, but could imagine what it must have been like—men consumed by fire. She hoped for Shamella's sake that the empath talent had come to her afterwards. That she had not felt those people die.

"It could have destroyed her," she said.

"It nearly did," he agreed. "Not just her body, although you saw the damage to her hands—but the knowledge that she had killed all those people. I wish the healing talent worked on minds too; then you might have been able to save her some of the distress. I'm sorry you got mixed up in this, Ayriene."

And of course Shamella could not return. Probably mentally shattered, with a newly-acquired talent that would have been too hard to explain, Respar and Donmar had found her a new life. And such a husband that would have completely broken a weaker spirit than Shamella's.

"And now Deygan has her son."

Donmar's head jerked up. "Sylas? I thought he might be, when he heard the kye. But if I had gone probing it would have raised all those old awkward questions. How did you work it out?"

"Cowin," she said. "He had one part of the story and I had another. I still don't know if we know it all."

"If we survive this, I will tell you everything; I promise." He flinched as another volley of arrows flew overhead. "For now, you must go to Sylas. He carries the blood of Omena Stormweaver, and that is almost as rare as a healer talent. You must see him safe, Ayriene. I want you to go to him. If Deygan learns who he is, he will try to turn the boy into a weapon against us."

"And you?"

He gave a sad smile. "I led us into this. I will stay to the end. If Deygan spares me, I will do what I can to make amends."

Out of the corner of her eye she saw two birds take to the wing—two swallows, one flying as if to protect the other from the arrows. Ayriene covered her mouth with her hands. "Garyth and Miralee. Creator, my children!"

Donmar transformed and took to the air, Ayriene a heartbeat behind him. A hawk and a falcon, flying hard and fast towards the swallows, trying to shield them until they got high enough to be out of arrows' reach. Another volley followed them, the shafts hissing through the air close enough to ruffle wing feathers. But four birds together made a tempting target. A thud told Ayriene that one had reached its target, and Donmar dropped, an arrow through his throat, losing his bird form and falling to the ground. Another heart-stopping, gut-wrenching sound and Miralee fell away. Both Ayriene and Garyth made to follow, but the arrows were too dense. As she watched, a soundless scream ripping through her head, she saw Miralee change. Her daughter's still, naked form lay on the slabs of the Aerie courtyard, not far from where Donmar had fallen.

Ayriene yearned to go to her—to hold her tight even if her healing talent would do no good. But she must think of the living. That sight—that blood-covered body—would haunt her always, but she had to get to Sylas. Every second she delayed gave an archer the chance to nock an arrow and take sight at the falcon hovering above.

Garyth circled higher, too far up for the bowmen's arrows to reach him. *Go*, she signalled, using the shake of the wings changers used to communicate simple messages in flight. *Go*. He turned and flew for Adamantara, following Deckhan's call. These youngsters were the Aerie's future, she thought, climbing until she herself was safe from arrow shot. Maybe he would follow her onto the council. A council in exile, likely, but the changers' only hope if they were to survive.

Reluctantly she turned away, breaking out of her hover to set course for Banunis. For Sylas.

Ayriene returned to Banunis alone and sick at heart, and was placed under guard in her quarters. Deygan and his army had not yet returned from the Aerie. She was not allowed to see Sylas, nor to send him a message. She was angered by news of Sylas's imprisonment, but she had to tread carefully. If Sylas were as important to the Aerie's future as Yinaede had implied, and carried a bloodline as vital as Donmar made out, then Deygan must uncover no hint of it. He was perfectly capable of killing Sylas to ensure the changers never recovered.

Her thoughts returned to Miralee's death, and to her daughter's impassioned plea that Ayriene not return to Banunis with Sylas. Her daughter had been convinced that Sylas would cause Ayriene's death. But now two of her children were dead, the third dead or lost to her. If it took her own life to save Sylas, she was ready to make that sacrifice.

She heard the commotion when the army returned two days later: hooves on stone, shouted orders, jingling of harness. But still the king did not summon her. He meant to let her suffer, it seemed. It was not until the following day that she was called to his presence.

"I'm surprised you came back. You stand accused of destroying my son, yet you have the nerve to return. You are braver than I thought, or more stupid."

She wanted to lash out at him—to scream that because of him *she* had lost a daughter, and maybe a son as well. Sylas, she told herself. Think of Sylas. She would do him no good by antagonising the king.

"Destroy? He is not dead. I don't know what has happened to Prince Jaevan, Sire, but-"

"He cannot speak. He shows little, if any reaction when spoken to, even when it is his own father that speaks." Deygan's voice became a choking gasp. He raised his hand to clasp his throat as if throttling the voice that betrayed his weakness.

"I gave him nothing harmful. Blood elder has been used to suppress the change for centuries. Sylas himself uses blood elder to prevent him being called since he does not yet have control."

"The same as he gave my son?"

"He uses the leaves, piercing his skin with the juices. A piercing lasts a week, maybe more, when it is first used, before the body builds an immunity to it. The potion I prescribed for your son is taken once a day."

"And how does this blood elder not affect your apprentice, when it paralyses my son?"

"It does not paralyse your son, Sire. That is impossible. Whatever has happened to Prince Jaevan is entirely separate, and I will get to the bottom of it. Believe me."

"And the Chesammos uses the same thing, but once a week, but my son was to drink your potion every night? How is that right?"

"Prince Jaevan uses a decoction of the root, Sire. That is milder. It holds off the onset of the change a short while, as we needed time to discuss his training with the council. Sylas needs stronger medication now that he is fully through the change. It mingles with his blood, introduced through his skin by the needles. That is the only way effective enough to prevent changing to a call once changing has run its course, but before the changer achieves control of their own transformations."

Deygan grunted, clearly unconvinced by anything Ayriene said.

"So why do you not use the same method on my son that you do on your apprentice? Why do you keep your own safe and jeopardise my boy?"

Ayriene closed her eyes, willing herself to stay calm and patient. "It is Sylas who takes the riskier route, Sire. His dose is less frequent but stronger. The way he uses blood elder can cause side effects, and if used for too long they become permanent. And of course there are the marks. The introduction of the blood elder juice through the skin leaves a red pin prick of colour on the skin, somewhat like a rash."

The marks were shocking enough on the golden skin of the Chesammos but on Irenthi skin they would stand out all the more. Deygan had been adamant when she put the methods to him; his son's skin would not be permanently marked as Sylas's had been. Casian had one or two, put there by Jesely when he was at his most vulnerable. Most changers had one or two, for that matter—it was almost a badge of belonging. Jaevan would never belong. He was crown prince. He had to learn what he needed but never truly cross into the changers' world. Never become one of them.

A thought occurred to her.

"Has the prince taken his potion since the attack which you believe left him mute, Sire?"

"Of course he bloody hasn't! What sort of a fool do you take me for, woman? Why would I give him *more* of something that so clearly poisoned him? Do you think I'm mad?"

"And he showed no discomfort during your attack on the Aerie?"

"Discomfort? No. He has barely said a word since he took that Destroyer-cursed filth of yours. He stares into space. That is all."

So he had not reacted to Deckhan's callings? He should have been able to hear them at least, and she would have expected him to show some physical reaction, maybe discomfort. She had never come across anything like this before.

"May I see him?" The sooner she saw Jaevan, the sooner all this could be resolved.

King Deygan was not a man given to flights of fancy, and his anger and worry sent chills into Ayriene's heart. What if the blood elder had truly harmed Jaevan? What if it was irreversible?

"I'll take you to him. Pray that you can cure him, healer, for it will be your head—yours and the boy's—if you cannot."

CHAPTER 31

NOTHING HAD PREPARED AYRIENE FOR what she found in Jaevan's bedchamber. She had left an intelligent, spirited prince on the verge of young manhood—keenly interested in the world, observant of details, determined to right wrongs he saw around him.

Not anymore.

Jaevan sat in an armchair, face pale and drawn like one who had suffered a long illness. Brown shadows lurked beneath his sunken eyes like smudges of long-dried blood. When she entered he barely registered her presence—maybe a slight movement of the eyes, a momentary hint of recognition, then nothing.

Acutely aware of Deygan's gaze on her, Ayriene tried to conceal her shock at the sight. Overwhelming pity, followed by fear for herself and for Sylas. This was none of Sylas's doing, she was certain. Nothing she had left with him could do this, and although he devoured books, she doubted he would have found anything to produce this effect in any of her herbals. Ayriene herself could think of nothing—no combination of things—from her years of experience that would leave a person in this state. Dead, yes, or sedated, but not this... emptiness.

She knelt beside Jaevan, feeling his heart beat, his skin temperature. She looked into his eyes, examined his tongue, bared his chest to check for rashes or bruises. Nothing. No signs or symptoms, no hints or clues. Just a boy staring out through dazed eyes, distant and shocked as if he had seen things beyond his comprehension.

"Prince Jaevan?" she said, hoping for a reaction, anything to show that his mind was undamaged. "Can you hear me, Highness?"

Behind her, Deygan puffed out his chest indignantly. "Is this the best you can manage? Feeling his forehead like a nurse with an infant? He is not sulking, woman. He has been like this for three days now—not speaking, not moving."

"Is he eating? Drinking? Does he sleep?"

Deygan frowned. "There's the strange thing. Put food before him and he will eat, if he's hungry. Same with water, or ale. He will go and relieve himself. He will take himself to bed and dress and undress himself. But he makes no sound and scarcely reacts if spoken to."

"Can you bring me a quill and ink?"

"Your apprentice tried that." Deygan's voice was brusque. "It didn't work."

"Indulge me, Sire. I would like to see for myself."

Writing materials appeared as if by thought. Deygan expected an instant response from his staff, and generally got it. Ayriene set a sheet of parchment on Jaevan's knee, dipped the quill in the sooty ink and pressed it into his hand.

"Can you write what happened, Highness, even

if you cannot tell me?"

He held it without protest, but no more. No effort to bring quill to paper, far less write. No motion. Not a flicker of a muscle. He might as well have been carved from stone.

She moved a cup of water within his reach and he turned to look at it, reached out, raised it to his lips and drank, setting it back down as naturally as he ever would have. No hesitation. No feeling of unnaturalness. In that few seconds he was himself again, slipping back behind his mask as soon as the cup was back on the table.

"He will turn the pages of a book, but with no sign that he understands. He will not communicate with so much as the twitch of a finger. Tell me you can reverse this, healer, or you must face the consequences."

She shook her head. "I doubt I can, Sire. This seems to me more like an affliction of the mind, not the body."

"Are you saying my son is mad?" Deygan's face twitched.

"No, Sire. Say instead that His Highness has shut himself off from the world. It may have been his choice initially, or it may not, but I think he could not come back now even if he wanted to."

"But you can cure him?"

She drew in a long, slow breath. Healers could not cure minds, only bodies. She could pretend to minister to him, to draw the charade out for another day or two until Deygan lost patience—but after all, what would be the point?

"No, Sire. I am afraid I cannot."

The look on his face was as clear as any death sentence.

～ა๑ია⌒

Sylas was led from his room, barefoot, his hands bound behind him. This was it, he told himself; he was going to die. He hoped he would make a good end—wondered if anyone would tell his mother. Word of the Aerie's destruction would have reached the desert by now, and she would be beside herself with worry.

When he entered Jaevan's chambers, Ayriene knelt on the tiled floor of the anteroom with Deygan looming over her. Jaevan was to one side, with a middle-aged woman in attendance. At his age, Jaevan should have progressed to a manservant. King Deygan obviously felt he had regressed to a nurse.

"This is none of Sylas's doing, Sire," Ayriene said. "If Prince Jaevan has indeed been damaged, though in truth, I cannot see how, then the fault is entirely mine."

He could not let her do this. "No! Mistress Ayriene, I must have done something wrong. I must—" Guards pushed him to his knees beside her. The floor was cold and hard.

"Silence!" Deygan shouted again, drops of spittle catching on his moustache. "If you speak unbidden, Chesammos, I shall have you gagged. Do you understand me?" Jaevan whimpered and the woman shushed him. At a gesture, the guards withdrew, leaving the five of them alone.

Sylas bowed his head. "Your Majesty, I beg your

pardon." His knees hurt already. He wondered how long Ayriene had been kneeling, how much her knees must ache. Could a healer heal herself? Maybe she could heal the bruises as they formed. A strange thought. Fear made his mind distance himself from the gravity of the situation.

"Your concern for your apprentice is admirable, Mistress Ayriene, but his guilt cannot be denied. He only narrowly escaped punishment over the attempted poisoning; you can hardly expect me to be lenient."

Jaevan whimpered again and Sylas held his breath. With his eyes, he implored Jaevan to speak, only speak and make his father be merciful. But Jaevan's eyes were sad and dull, not their former sparkling green.

"Spare the boy, Deygan," Ayriene said, and Sylas froze, expecting anger and harsh words from the king at the use of his forename. "Kill me, if you must punish someone, but let the boy go."

"You are worth ten of him, Ayriene. Twenty. The boy is Chesammos, and you are a talent. For your skills, I might be prepared to keep you alive. You would have to renounce changing, of course, swear fealty to me."

"Here the boy may be nothing, but in the Aerie he was my equal. No—" She shot a sharp glance at Sylas before turning back to Deygan. "Not in ability, maybe. But at the Aerie all are equal whether man or woman, fair skin or dark. Casian never quite understood that, I fear, and sought advancement based on his skills outside the Aerie. I trust he will find fulfillment with you instead."

Casian? Was she trying to tell him something? No. Surely Casian had not been involved in what he had seen from the battlements. However estranged from the changers, he would not assist in their slaughter.

"Casian has been raised to command the king's guard," Deygan said. "The Aerie's loss is my gain. I see potential in him, even if you changers did not."

"And this advancement commenced when, if I may ask?" Ayriene's voice was cool, but polite.

"I know what you prod me for. You want to turn your apprentice against him, for some reason which escapes me. Well then, yes, he led the assault on your Aerie. Did a damn fine job of it, too. We came out of it with scarcely any damage to men or horses, thanks to him."

Sylas stared at the floor, willing his stomach not to empty. Casian had led the attack? He thought of what he had seen—the flames licking up into the sky—and what he had not seen his own mind supplied for him. Men and women running and dying. The walls of the Aerie crumbling. The herb gardens where he had spent many happy hours trampled underfoot by Deygan's horsemen. Was it all gone?

"The Aerie is rubble and the changers are slain. They deserved it, in the end. They supported rebellion and those who would harm my sons and me." He turned to address Sylas directly. "They are dead, boy. There is no Aerie any more."

Jaevan let out a low moan and wrapped his arms around his chest. Sylas was sure he understood what his father had said. Jaevan had not completely gone. He was just locked away inside himself where no one could reach him, waiting for Sylas, or someone, to find the key that would release him.

"I will have my dues, Ayriene. Your boy has taken my boy's life from him, and I will take his in return. But because he has meant so much to you and to my son, I will grant him death by the blade instead of the noose." He grasped the hilt of his sword, the pommel adorned with a single large cabochon linandra. Ridiculous, Sylas thought wryly, that he should notice such a thing when the blade could separate his head from his shoulders at any moment. The sword slid from the scabbard, the steel almost silent against the oiled lining. Sylas swallowed hard and made the Lady's sign as best he could with his hands bound. Begging the Lady for strength to meet his end with dignity, he squeezed his eyes tight shut and waited for the slash of the blade.

The air split, but it was not Deygan's sword that did it. Jaevan's voice raised in a cry that raised hackles on the back of Sylas's neck. It was a howl so primal, so heart-wrenching, that his eyes shocked open and fixed on the prince writhing nearby, his attendant trying without success to restrain him. Jaevan broke free and flung himself at Sylas, clinging to him, looking back over his shoulder at where Deygan stood motionless, sword half-raised.

"Get off him, boy," he said, "Take my son away, nurse. He does not need to see this."

The attendant knelt beside Jaevan, crooning softly like a mother to a babe, trying to prise his fingers from Sylas's arm. Jaevan's fingers gripped tighter, until Sylas was sure he bore the marks of Jaevan's fine hands on his skin.

"I...cannot, Your Majesty," she said, the colour mounting in her fair Irmos face. "I beg pardon, Sire, but he will not come."

Deygan swung the sword in irritation and the woman flinched, anticipating the edge of the blade.

"Jaevan, let go, my prince," Sylas whispered urgently, not wishing Deygan to overhear him, yet trying to make Jaevan listen over his howls of terror. "Your father is angry, and he may hurt your nurse if you continue." But Jaevan clung on, tears streaming down his face.

"Guards!" Two men-at-arms came in at the run. "My son is overwrought. Please take him to his bedroom."

They managed to drag him away from Sylas then, but Jaevan screamed, thrashing and kicking until the guardsmen had little choice but to place him on the floor for fear he would harm himself. As soon as he sensed them loosing their grip, he was back, arms round Sylas's shoulders, his body forming a barrier between Sylas and Deygan. Jaevan's eyes glittered, not just with tears, but with a steely determination.

"Damn you, Chesammos! What is the meaning of this?"

"I think he is trying to save me, Sire." Bizarrely, Sylas could hardly keep from smiling. Jaevan loved him. He loved him enough that his feelings could break through whatever ailed him to protect his friend from his father.

Deygan sheathed his sword and stepped

forward, taking hold of Jaevan's shoulders. He pulled, trying to ease Jaevan away from Sylas.

"Come now, boy. It goes with being a king. Sometimes dispensing justice is hard on the justice giver as well as the judged." Jaevan sobbed and held tighter.

Sylas gnawed on his lip. That was easy for Deygan to say. He wasn't the one kneeling on the floor waiting for his head to be severed. He shifted position. With the prince's weight added to his own, his legs were going numb.

"King Deygan," Ayriene said. Sylas started. He had almost forgotten she was there. "Your son is begging for mercy for his friend without any words being necessary, Sire. Does this not prove to you that your son is capable of understanding? Of communicating in his own way?"

"Damn it! It proves he can howl like a wounded animal. Come on, boy. Let go now!"

Deygan gave a mighty heave. For all the king's slightness he was a trained soldier, and stronger than his looks might suggest. Jaevan was again wrenched from around Sylas's neck. No sooner had Deygan pulled him away than Jaevan resumed his preternatural wailing: a sound to chill a man's blood.

Sylas swallowed hard. He had never pretended to be brave. His nerves were stretched taut and he wanted to scream at Deygan to do it—to put him out of his suspense and kill him. His gaze only shifted from Deygan's face to look nervously at the sword.

"Be quiet!" Deygan shook his son by the

shoulders. "Be quiet, do you hear me? You shame me, carrying on like this." He turned to Ayriene. "If I let you go, do you have something that can calm him? A sedative? Something to make him sleep?"

She narrowed her eyes, watching the king closely. "And what will you do when he wakes up to find his best friend dead? Do you plan to keep him sedated indefinitely?"

"He has formed an attachment to the boy that will pass. Casian is to be Jaevan's companion, as much as his duties will allow. Jaevan will soon forget about this heathen."

Jaevan's agitation increased once more. Sylas did not ask Deygan's permission to speak, but addressed the prince directly.

"Please don't, my prince. If your father has made up his mind then this will not change it. I would not have my last sight be of you in such distress."

Jaevan's breath came in heaving gasps, his sobs wrenching themselves from his chest, but he turned to regard Sylas.

"Calm yourself, Jaevan. This way time will not age us. Our friendship will always stay the same."

The prince let out a strangled whine at that and slumped to the ground, his face in his hands. Sylas considered going to him on his knees, but his legs protested, and keeping a wary eye on the king, he got unsteadily to his feet. Crossing the floor to Jaevan he squatted close by, talking softly as the prince rocked back and forth.

"Untie me," said Sylas, then as Deygan hesitated, brows drawn so far down his eyes were almost entirely hooded, he spoke louder. "Untie me. I swear I will do nothing to harm either of you, or to escape. I swear on the Lady."

Deygan drew a dagger from his belt and cut the cords that bound Sylas's hands. Rubbing his wrists, red weals showing where the cords had chafed his skin, Sylas dropped to the floor beside Jaevan, whose agitation had increased again at the sight of his father drawing his dagger. Sylas drew Jaevan's head to his chest, and the young prince sobbed his despair.

Sylas stroked the silver-white hair, and rocked the boy in his arms. Omena's wings, he was a child, for all he was a prince. Just turned thirteen, and not a man by Irenthi laws for another three years, the boy had lost a brother and now he feared losing a friend as well.

"Quiet now, Jaevan. All will be well. I will take care of you."

The prince's sobs quietened, until he was calmer, if red-faced and puffy-eyed.

"He will leave us now," Deygan said, and Jaevan drew breath to howl once more. "No! You have made your point. If you will calm yourself for him and only for him then I must rethink. But there is a price to be paid, and someone must pay it."

"Go," Sylas said gently. "I will come to you later. If His Majesty allows." He glanced quickly at Deygan, who scowled, but nodded.

"You may see him later, but first I need you here, and him elsewhere." He gestured to the attendant. "Take Prince Jaevan and see that he is bathed and given clean clothes. He needs to freshen up after this...incident. None of you will speak of this. If I hear a word of gossip about the castle, I will have your tongues cut out and then I'll hang you. Do I make myself clear?"

The guards bowed themselves from the room, and the attendant ushered Jaevan out also. He took one final look over his shoulder at Sylas before leaving, and Sylas gave him what he hoped was a reassuring smile. When the guards and Jaevan had gone, Sylas went back to his place beside Ayriene, wincing as he returned to bruised knees. Had he overstepped himself? And what did Deygan mean, he would have payment?

Deygan loomed over the two kneeling changers. "It seems my son has saved you, Chesammos. I grant you your life on three conditions." He held up one finger. "First, you will attend my son. You will be housed in a secluded hunting lodge of mine with your own small staff. You will make no attempt to leave and will communicate with no one outside the staff."

He paused, and Sylas nodded his agreement. "Of course, Sire. May I let my mother know where I am?"

"No. As far as she is concerned you died in the destruction of the Aerie. If it becomes possible later to release you, then you will tell her you escaped and hid until you deemed it safe to make yourself known."

"Sire." Sylas's stomach did a slow roll. He would cause his mother more pain, where all he had ever wanted was to make her proud and give her the life she deserved. But he had no choice.

"Second," Deygan continued, holding up two

fingers, "you will continue your studies. If there is a cure for my son anywhere in your changer knowledge, you will find it. All the books regarding changers and all the healing books in the castle library will be made available to you."

So even if he was a prisoner he could continue studying to be a healer someday. That sweetened the pill a little.

"But Mistress Ayriene would be better placed to make such a study, Sire. Will she be staying at the hunting lodge too? May she continue to instruct me?"

Deygan sniffed and scratched his forehead, which was creased into thoughtful wrinkles once more.

"You didn't understand, did you, boy? I have spared your life, but I will have recompense for my son. If it is not you then it will be Mistress Ayriene."

Mistress Ayriene! No!

When he turned to look in horror at her, she was already watching him. She had known. She had realised this would be the price of saving him. But he was not worth it.

"And to prove your good faith to me, young man, it will be you who strikes the blow."

CHAPTER 32

I T TOOK AYRIENE A FEW moments to realise what
Deygan had said. A few moments before the
fear gripped her heart and would not let go.
Not fear for her own life—that had been forfeit
when she returned to Banunis—but for Sylas. She
had been so opposed to taking him on, but over
the months she had come to think of him almost
as another son.

Miralee had warned her that Sylas would cause
her death. And there was Yinaede's seeing: 'He will
save us.' Although a tiny part of her had doubted,
she had been sure Sylas would walk away from
this, whatever Deygan threatened. But to get the
lad to do it—she couldn't believe Deygan would be
so cruel. This was a test—one Sylas must not be
allowed to fail. Whatever Deygan had promised his
son, the king would not stand for failure. If either
of them were to leave this room alive, Sylas must
do as the king demanded.

"No!" Sylas found his voice at last. "No, you can't
make me do that. I won't do it. Mistress Ayriene, I
would never harm you."

"You must, Sylas." The calmness in her
voice surprised and pleased her. "Miralee saw
this happen."

His face contorted, grief and disbelief warring on his features.

"Miralee saw me? Your daughter? But I'm not important enough to have a seeing about. Why didn't you tell me? And why would you come back, if you knew this would happen?"

Because even the lowest can change history. Because a seeing does not consider rank or skin colour. Because Sylas was so much more than he gave himself credit for. In a strange way it gave Ayriene comfort. If Miralee had been right about this, then maybe Yinaede was right too. If Ayriene's death would lead to the changers surviving, it would be worth the sacrifice.

"Because sometimes knowing your future is harder than not knowing it. And because sometimes the meaning of a seeing only becomes clear when it happens. Yinaede saw you too. She said you would save us. We need you to live."

"But, Mistress," he swallowed hard, his hands clutching at his shirt. "I am a healer, or will be one some day, maisaiea-yelai. Did you not make me swear to do no harm? How can I harm you, of all people?"

"You can, because you must. If not for me, then for Jaevan. He will need you."

She found herself fascinated by his hands, twisting and turning, leaving creases in the sweat-stained linen. The boy had the strong, capable hands of a Chesammos labourer, yet they could mop a fevered brow or make up a poultice as well as hers. Whatever Deygan made him do in this room, he could still do good in the world.

"If Jaevan is to be cared for by someone, after all that has happened to him, would you prefer it to be you or Casian? Who would have his best interests most at heart?"

He flushed, his golden-brown skin reddening, and he dropped his eyes from hers. Her heart sank. He still loved Casian, after everything. With his feelings so conflicted, who could tell what he might do. All she could do was trust. He was an honest man, this Chesammos. He would make the right choices, when it came to it, or the changers were doomed.

"You could care for Jaevan as well as I. You are a better scholar. If there is something to be found in the books, you would find it before I did. You read better and faster. And you are a talent, Mistress—the only healer talent we have."

Her heart twisted as she recalled Adwen's face. Her other children: Miralee dead in Deygan's assault; Garyth dead or exiled. Her husband. What did she have to live for?

"Sylas, grant me this." Her voice dropped to little more than a whisper. "I could not save my son, however great a healer I was. My husband and two of my children are dead. Maybe my other son is dead too. At least let me save you. Let me atone for Adwen and Miralee by saving you for whatever fate has in store."

He sat for what seemed an eternity, head bowed, while Deygan huffed and pulled at his moustache and muttered darkly about there being no decision to be made. Deygan would have killed in an instant and without a second thought, Ayriene knew. But

Sylas was no Deygan. This would leave a scar on his soul that would take a long time to heal. Maybe it never would.

At last, Sylas looked up. His tears ran like rain. He embraced her and she felt the dampness of his cheek against hers—knew that her face was wet with her own tears. She could feel him trembling, close to breaking down altogether.

"Please, Sylas. You must." And do it quickly, she thought, before we both lose our nerve.

"Mistress, I cannot. I..."

"Just do it, Sylas. For all our sakes."

He drew away from her and knelt as if in prayer. It seemed to Ayriene to last forever, but when he finally opened his eyes he seemed to have come to a decision. His face was calmer—more peaceful. He made the sign of the Lady and raised his fingertips to his lips.

"May the Lady forgive me. I am ready."

Deygan held the hilt of the sword towards him, but Sylas waved it away.

"The Chesammos never use swords, Sire, but I have used a knife on occasion."

Deygan sheathed the sword, and pulled the matching dagger from his belt. Sylas grasped it and felt its weight. The stone in the pommel was linandra, a match to the gem on the sword. A magnificent stone, and many times the size of the one Ayriene had bought for Sylas in Adamantara. She wondered if he still kept the bead or if he had sold it long since. She hoped if he had it, that he would keep it as a keepsake of her.

Sylas turned the dagger in his hands and for

one moment of blind, sickening panic, she thought he meant to turn it on himself.

"Don't make me do this," he whispered hoarsely, raising pleading eyes to hers.

"You must. Stay safe."

Again he wavered, hands trembling, and she feared he would falter. She tried to hold his eyes, to send confidence and forgiveness through her gaze. She wished she had been an empath, not a healer, that she might open her thoughts to him—show him this had to be.

Tears ran down his cheeks as he plunged the dagger into her breast, but his eyes were distant. Vacant. After the initial searing pain like a hot poker through her flesh, she could see nothing clearly. His figure swam before her eyes. She felt her kye screaming and remorse flooded her. This would send her kye into the darkness beyond the Outlands and into the true death. But it had to be.

I'm coming, Adwen. Wait for me, Miralee. I'll be with you soon, Kerwen, my love.

Blackness took her. Blackness and the cold of the Outlands.

Sylas sat, head bowed. He would not kill her. She had no right to ask it of him. Her death would not save him; it would condemn him. Chesammos did not kill. Healers did not kill. Changers did not kill. The penalty for one changer killing another was not death, but having one's arm crushed or hand cut off. That saved the kye from passing into the dark, but removed the changer's ability to fly—

the harshest punishment imaginable. He should cut his hand off now, before it had the chance to kill his own mistress.

Stay strong, changer.

The kye were breaking through. This shouldn't be possible; he had marked with blood elder. His mind raced. The blood elder stopped him being called, but did it stop the kye? The linandra on Deygan's sword was so close. Sylas concentrated, sent his thoughts questing out for the kye, and the pommel stone glowed faintly. He formed words in his mind.

I cannot. I have no strength left.

He wanted to lie down on the tiles. Feel the coldness of them beneath his cheek. Let Deygan kill him if he would. He had no strength left to fight.

You are stronger than you know. You will be stronger yet. Jaevan needs your strength.

When he looked at her she was crying. He reached out for her and embraced her as he would his mother. He could feel trembling. Him or Ayriene?

"Please, Sylas. You must." Her voice implored him, tugged at his very being. How could she ask this of him? It wasn't fair. Not even Craie had ever asked as much of him.

"Mistress..." There was so much he wanted to say to her. How grateful he was. How much he would miss her. How he would never forget her. But it all came down to that one word.

He could not, could not, could not.

"Just do it, Sylas. For all our sakes."

He closed his eyes again and reached out to the

linandra, and through it to his kye.

Can I fly? If I fly, Ayriene might fly with me.

Do you see windows, changer? To where would we fly?

It was right. Deygan would call the guards and they would be killed in bird form instead of human. The guards who had brought him both carried the weighted nets, and they would be waiting close by. He and his mistress would die naked in a net with blades through their flesh, like fish pulled from the lake.

I can't kill her.

He felt understanding through the link. Sympathy. He could feel tears running in tracks down his cheeks.

I will bring you to the Outlands. You will see nothing. Feel nothing. Hear nothing.

The coward's way out, but he could see no other. If he delayed, the kye could leave him. He might lose the contact.

"May the Lady forgive me. I am ready."

He made the sign of the Lady and kissed his fingertips, to seal the pledge. He refused the sword, but took the dagger, resting his finger on the linandra stone. With the stone in his hands, he could cross to the Outlands, return when it was all over. Like a sleepwalker, he wouldn't see a thing.

"Don't make me do this." He knew what her response would be, but he had to make one last try.

"You must. Stay safe."

He rubbed his thumb over the linandra and felt a blast of cold the like of which he had never experienced before. He knew from classes at the

Aerie that seers at least partly entered the Outlands when they had their seeings, but he had never heard of an ordinary changer making the crossing. Seers always came back. All he could do was hope.

There were places in the world, they said, where it was so cold that your breath froze like clouds in front of you; where rain fell in white flakes like ash from the Lady; where as far as a man could see was white and cold like the vastness of the ash desert. He had not believed such cold possible, but now he knew it was true. He had no body there, but if he had, his extremities would have been numb. As if in a dream he felt his arm rise and fall, heard a woman gasp and someone speaking to him. A man's voice—deeper—Deygan, calling him back.

He would stay in the cold. He would lie there until he froze. He would die with his mistress, and not be shamed.

You must return, changer. There are things for you to do. Omena's blood must save.

He stared at his hand. The dagger lay there, across his palm, and the stone still glowed. Red stained the blade, seeped onto his fingers. He suppressed a sob. There was a form on the ground, but he hardly dared look.

"I was not sure you would do it, boy," Deygan said, taking the dagger from Sylas's hand and beginning to clean it with a casual efficiency. Sylas was barely aware the dagger had gone. He stared at Ayriene lying there before him and realised the kye had told the truth. See nothing. Feel nothing. Hear nothing. Ah, Lady have mercy, he had done it. With the linandra gone from his hand, and his mind numb with shock and grief, the kye fled as if ashamed at its part in the proceedings.

He slumped to the floor, arms folded over his head, wanting to cry like a child for its mother, yet too stunned even for that.

"At least I know you will hold faith with my son," Deygan was saying. "I will have you both taken to the lodge tonight. No visitors, as I said, except Casian. You two are friends, I believe, and it may be that interaction with one of his own kind may help my son recover." The look on his face said he did not expect a recovery, but would not yet let himself give up hope. "In that event, we will reconsider your future."

He could see Casian. He could study. He could hope that the changers would return, although this story of Yinaede's was clearly nonsense. Some other changer might save them, not Sylas. Cowin, maybe. Yes, Cowin, that was it. Yinaede had seen Cowin in her vision. No one had been raised to the mastery faster than Cowin; he was the obvious candidate for the changers' saviour.

Sylas raised himself to one knee before Deygan, and his hand left bloody prints on the tiles. Restoring Jaevan was more important than anything. More important than the changers, than Ayriene, than his own life. If he did not solve the mystery of Jaevan's indisposition he would die trying. He would redeem himself.

"I swear I will do no harm to you or yours, Sire. I will not try to escape so long as you live. I will devote myself to study to restore the prince to health. I swear it by the Lady." He made the sign and kissed his fingertips. It was the most binding oath he knew.

Deygan looked down his nose at Sylas.

"Do you know, I think you believe it. Well then, I shall make a pledge to you, Sylas Crowchanger. No one will hear what happened here from my lips. As far as the world is concerned, Ayriene died by my hand, and I allowed you to live to serve my son. As far as your family and friends are concerned, you died at the Aerie. There were few survivors to know the truth of it, and even they could probably not say for sure who was there and who was not."

Deygan called for guards and the same two reappeared, their eyes flicking briefly to Ayriene's corpse, then sliding away. Their masks of disinterest never faltered.

"Call Lord Casian. I have a job for him. And take this away and dispose of it." His hand waved at Ayriene's body. "Is there anything of hers you wish to keep, young Chesammos?"

Ayriene had a pipe, but Sylas could not use it and would not dream of trying. That was for masters only. But there was one thing.

"Her pack, Sire. The healer's pack with her herbs and potions. And the herbal from her room." If he was to study healing, he would start with Ayriene's treasured book. Deygan had promised him the books from the library. Somewhere in one of those must lie the answer, and if it was there, Sylas would find it. He swore on his life. He swore on Ayriene's life.

"It shall be done. Casian will make the

arrangements for you and Jaevan to go to your retreat. You will be made comfortable, as befits a prince of Chandris and his companion."

It was only when he got back to his room that the full horror of what he had done struck him.

If he was to be shut away for the rest of his life it was no more than he deserved. He would be fed and sheltered, given clothing and books to study, where his crime demanded he should be hanged or locked in the darkest dungeon of Banunis Castle. He lay on the bed, turned to the wall and pictured Ayriene's face. His best hope of redemption lay in curing Jaevan, but Ayriene would haunt his dreams for as long as he lived.

EPILOGUE

CASIAN WATCHED THE LITTLE ENTOURAGE move away from his mother's house, setting out across the desert for the old garrison and lighthouse on the southernmost tip of Chandris. Known ironically as The Hermitage, it was as remote a spot as could be found on the island, and was to be the new home of Sylas and the still-silent Prince Jaevan.

It had taken all Casian's influence to persuade King Deygan to hide Jaevan and Sylas at Boreana's house on the edge of the desert instead of the hunting lodge as Deygan had planned. The plan served a dual purpose: it hid them from sight, which was Deygan's intention, and gave Casian easy access to Sylas, which was Casian's. But the king was nervous of entrusting such important detainees to House Lucranne. Not prisoners. Never that. The king was adamant that his son was not a prisoner, merely absent from court for the good of his health while the healer cured him. He fooled no one.

The affair had not flourished as Casian had expected, given Ayriene's absence and Casian's easy access to his lover. Sylas was withdrawn, depressed, and rarely open to the suggestion that the two of them spend time alone. With anyone else, Casian would have given up after the second rebuff, and found another, more willing partner. He rarely had to make much effort to find a bedmate, after all, and there had been others already. But Sylas's lack of interest maddened him. When Casian came to the throne Sylas was meant to be there, damn it. The knowledge that he needed Sylas itched in his mind. He *would* have him. He just needed to be patient—let Sylas get over Ayriene's death.

But however secure Casian's mother thought her household, rumours leaked out. The king's son was a drooling idiot, people said on the streets of Banunis. The next king of Chandris was a simpleton who could not wipe his own arse. Untrue, as it happened, but the stories got wilder and more elaborate. Deygan was being punished, they said, for his destruction of the Aerie, but by what or whom was never made clear. Deygan attended state events alone. That way it could be put about that the king was so wary of the threat to his sons that neither prince would be seen in public until the rebellion was squashed.

In reality, the rebellion had all but died. Cellondora had been the driving force, and with the levelling of that village, the others had gone back to their old ways. Swords had been thrown into wells or buried out in the desert.

But Deygan was left with a dilemma: Jaevan could not be passed over, according to the law that his ancestor had gone out of his way to institute. Only if Jaevan gave his assent could he be bypassed in the succession, and that he was incapable of doing.

So Jaevan died.

Not really, of course. It was a sham, from start to finish. Jaevan was said to have died of a fever, and Marklin was installed as crown prince. They held a big funeral, invited foreign dignitaries—everything the observant nobles of Chandris and beyond might expect. Even Marklin had to play a part in the charade, by his father's side at the funeral. Deygan made use of his son's pale, pinched face to convince the watchers that Marklin's beloved older brother had indeed died. No one, they said, would put a boy through that if it were not true.

Sylas kept marking. Casian told him repeatedly that he need not fear a call, since all the changers bar the two of them—and Jaevan, if he could be counted—had left the island. That was untrue, as it happened. There were three, since Casian had set Gwysias to live in the remains of the Aerie, his arm broken in three places to stop him flying, and with orders to warn Casian if any changers should return in search of survivors. Despite the mutilation, Gwysias seemed almost pathetically grateful to Casian for rescuing him. A small compulsion had helped instill that gratitude, but it would not have worked had the feeling not already been there in some measure.

So Sylas kept marking, terrified that a call would take him away from Jaevan. The effects of the marking took their toll, as Ayriene had warned, and that left Casian more frustrated than ever.

When Casian tried to stop the supplies of blood elder reaching him, Sylas took it straight to the king, who instructed that Sylas should have whatever books and supplies he needed to continue his studies. In time, Sylas could not have responded to Casian's advances, even had he wanted to.

Casian could hardly bear to think of it—his golden youth, locked away with a mindless boy in a lighthouse at the far end of the desert. Still, he thought wryly, at least he would know where Sylas was when he needed him. Sylas would be kept safe until Casian was ready to make his move. And blood elder was reversible, when that happened.

And Casian—well, he had his women, and his men—but Sylas held his heart. And his mind, for Sylas would make him king.

The remnant of the changers departed the island shortly after the destruction—what was left of them. A rag-tag band of masters and apprentices and novices with hardly a smallcoin to their names, once the passages to the mainland were paid. Jesely stayed, found himself a Chesammos village in the desert where they asked no questions. With the money he had managed to take from the Aerie, he bought himself a rickety wagon and an aging cheen with which to earn his living.

His heart sank when news of Jaevan's death reached him. Such promise lost.

He asked for Sylas in Banunis, drinking in ale houses the lad had frequented, talking to stall holders whose acquaintance he had made. Sylas had died at the Aerie, he was told. Shame. He'd been a nice lad. Yet Sylas had been in Banunis, not at the Aerie. Jesely knew that for a fact. Someone was putting out lies about Sylas, and if that were so, might not the story about Jaevan be a lie, also?

Jesely was one of the faces lining the streets when the funeral procession passed. Marklin was white and drawn—the picture of a boy who had just lost a second brother. Deygan was almost unnaturally composed. Even if he was king first and father second, Jesely would have expected more emotion in his face. And Casian... If Jesely had to describe Casian's appearance at all, it would have been 'satisfied.'

He risked everything to let out a tendril of aiea-dera as they passed. His empath talent confirmed his suspicions: raw, visceral grief from Marklin; a certain smug assuredness from Casian; and from Deygan, no hint at all of any loss. A king might school his face to stillness, but he could not hide his emotions, not from an empath.

If Sylas and Jaevan were alive, he would find them. He owed them that much. And if he could be the instrument by which Casian fell from grace, so much the better.

It was almost a relief to Sylas when the blood elder did its worst. Casian saw no reason why they should not carry on the way they had been, but Sylas could not forget what he had done. He loved Casian, but whenever he allowed the Irenthi to take him to his bed, the grief and guilt killed his desire. When he slept, he saw dying changers and Ayriene lying in a pool of blood.

Deygan had ordered the destruction, he told himself. Casian was obeying his king, as he was bound to do. There was nothing evil about Casian. He refused to blame his Irenthi lover for the Aerie, but he could not treat his own crimes with the same leniency. He had thought there was nothing evil about himself either, and yet he had killed Ayriene to save his own skin.

It was hard, living with Jaevan. Every day, seeing that shell of a man and knowing that it was his fault. Jaevan was changing—becoming a man. He had put on several fingers' width of height while they had been shut away, and his shoulders and chest were broadening. His voice should be deepening too, but the only time Sylas heard his voice was when he screamed.

He had done it once, at Casian's mother's house—waking in the night from some dream or nightmare, sobbing and wailing and clinging to Sylas as if to a branch in a whirlpool. And Sylas held him. It was all he could do. Held him and rocked him like a baby and murmured words of reassurance in his ear until he calmed.

So now they were to be held in The Hermitage, not in the relative comfort of the house in Lucranne. Deygan and Casian would visit less often. The king was having the room in which they would be held shelved from floor to ceiling to hold Sylas's books. All the books on changer lore and healing would be sent there from Banunis Castle's library—a whole wagon-load, if not more—so that Sylas could continue his studies in the hope of finding a way to reverse Jaevan's decay. Deygan had kept his promise about that.

Sylas too would keep to his vow. If it took to the end of his days, he would study. He would find what had condemned his friend to a life of silence, and he would reverse it, whatever the cost.

And on the island, the Lady, deprived of the changers to channel away her energy, stored up trouble. Soon the island would realise how much of a debt they had owed to their changer folk. The changers and the volcano—a magical symbiosis of giving and receiving energy—a relationship which had just been catastrophically sundered.

Deep in the Lady, the aiea gathered.

GLOSSARY: CROWCHANGER

aiea - the energy emitted by the mountain, Eurna (known by the Chesammos as the Lady), and which is used by the changers.

aiea-bar - the lower order energy, used by the changers and their kye to effect the transformation from human to bird form.

aiea-dera - the higher order energy, used by changer talents when accessing their abilities, and inaccessible to those with no talent.

ashini - Chesammos. Roughly translates as "you understand?" or "OK?"

blood elder - plant used by the changers to suppress changing. The root is stronger, and used to delay a youngster coming to the change. The leaf, which gives off a red sap that gives the plant its name, is used for the marks used to prevent changing in those who have already started the change.

caigani - Chesammos. A form of smallclothes made of a light cloth and knotted at the hip.

caiona - Chesammos. A headscarf wound around the head and across the face to protect from ash and fumes in the desert.

Cellondora - one of the desert Chesammos villages. Centre of the Chesammos rebellion.

cheen - a large, flat hooved animal, used to pull wagons across the desert.

Chesammos - the original inhabitants of Chandris. A peaceful people, they are characterised by their golden skins and dark hair, which is often curly or wavy.

esteia - a desert plant. It produces nut-like seeds, which are deadly poison.

Irenthi - the ruling people of Chandris, who invaded the island centuries ago and have ruled there since. Characterised by their blond hair and fair skin, they usually have blue eyes, but occasionally green.

Irmos - any of the race of people who are of mixed Irenthi-Chesammos blood.

kaba - a plant which produces a sap highly toxic to Chesammos and Irmos, but to which the Irenthi are largely immune, although it will make them very sick.

krastos - the curved blade used by linandra diggers to prise linandra stones from the walls of volcanic vents. It has a blunted edge, but a two-pronged tip for gouging the stones free.

kye - the bird spirits which occupy the world known as the Outlands, and which guide the changers in the use of their power.

Lady, the - the term used by the Chesammos for the mountain Eurna, which they revere as the source of life on the island.

linandra - a pale green crystalline rock, formed in volcanic vents in the ash desert. It is used by the Chesammos to denote a marriageable adult, and also by the changers in their pipes. It is very valuable, and one of the main exports from Chandris.

maisaiea-yelai - Chesammos. "If the Lady wills it" or "The Lady grant that it be so" are the closest translations.

medelerinn - a desert plant, used (in a tisane) as a mild analgesic.

Namopaia - one of the desert Chesammos villages, and home to Sylas and his family.

Omena - a legendary figure to the Chesammos, Omena Stormweaver prevented the first threatened eruption of Eurna after the changers came to the island. Her name is used as a mild oath, in the form "Omena's wings".

swanflower - a fleshy desert plant with a tap root long enough to reach water, even in the desert. Used by the Chesammos as famine food, emergency water supply, a salve for wounds, and when brewed, as an alcoholic drink.

tokai - a thorny bush, the spikes from which are used as rough needles by the Chesammos, and by the changers to mark the skin of young changers who are suppressing the change.

zacorro - a highly potent alcoholic drink, brewed by the Chesammos and drunk at their major feasts.